ROMANCE

SAVING GRACE

G·K
Hall
&Cº

Also published in Large Print from
G.K. Hall by Julie Garwood:

Rebellious Desire
Honor's Splendour
Guardian Angel
The Bride

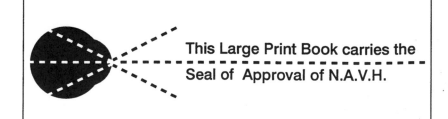

This Large Print Book carries the
Seal of Approval of N.A.V.H.

SAVING GRACE

JULIE GARWOOD

G.K. Hall & Co.
Thorndike, Maine

G.K. Hall Large Print Romance Collection edition.

Published in 1993 by arrangement with Pocket Books, a division of Simon & Schuster Inc.

The text of this Large Print edition is unabridged.
Other aspects of the book may vary from the original edition.

Set in 16 pt. News Plantin by Lynn M. Hathaway.

Printed in the United States on acid-free, high opacity paper. ∞

Library of Congress Cataloging in Publication Data

Garwood, Julie.
    Saving grace / Julie Garwood.
    p.   cm.
    ISBN 0-8161-5890-8 (alk. paper : lg. print).
    ISBN 0-8161-5891-6 (alk. paper : lg. print : pbk.)
    1. Great Britain — History — John, 1199-1216 — Fiction.
2. Large type books.   I. Title.
[PS3557.A8427S3   1993b]
813'.54—dc20   93-32414

In loving memory,
Mary Felicita Kennedy Murphy,
my saving grace

Prologue

Barnslay Monastery, England, 1200

Holy Bishop Hallwick, will you explain to us the hierarchy in heaven and on earth? Who is the most esteemed in God's eyes?" The student asked.

"Don't the apostles stand first in God's good graces?" the second student inquired.

"Nay," replied the wise bishop. "The archangel Gabriel, protector of women and children, our champion of the innocents, stands first above all others."

"Who next then?" the first student asked.

"All the other angels, of course," the bishop answered. "Next stand the apostles, with Peter first among the twelve, and then follow the prophets and miracle workers and those good teachers of God's word on earth. Last in heaven stand all the other saints."

"But who is the most important here on earth, Bishop Hallwick? Who is most blessed in God's eyes here?"

"Man," came the immediate reply. "And the

highest and most important among men is our holy pope."

The two students nodded acceptance of that dictate. Thomas, the elder of the two young men, leaned forward on his perch atop the stone wall outside the sanctuary. His brow was wrinkled with concentration. "Next in God's love stand the cardinals and then the other ordained men of God," he interjected.

"That is so," the bishop agreed, pleased with his student's guess.

"But who stands next in importance?" the second student asked.

"Why the rulers of kingdoms here on earth," the bishop explained. He sat down in the center of the wooden bench, spread his ornately decorated black robes, and then added, "Those leaders who fatten the church's treasury are more loved by God, of course, than those who hoard gold for their own pleasure."

Three more young men walked over to listen to their holy leader's lecture. They settled themselves in a half circle at the bishop's feet.

"Do married and then unmarried men stand next?" Thomas asked.

"Aye," the bishop replied. "And they are of the same position as the merchants and the sheriffs but just above the serfs chained to the land."

"Who next, Bishop?" the second student asked.

"The animals, starting with the most loyal, man's dog," the bishop answered, "and ending with the dull-witted oxen. There, I believe I have given you the full hierarchy to repeat to your students once you have taken your vows and are ordained men of God."

Thomas shook his head. "You've forgotten women, Bishop Hallwick. Where do they stand in God's love?"

The bishop rubbed his brow while he considered the question. "I have not forgotten women," he finally said. "They are last in God's love."

"Below dull-witted oxen?" the second student asked.

"Aye, below oxen."

The three young men seated on the ground immediately nodded their agreement.

"Bishop?" Thomas asked.

"What is it, my son?"

"Have you given us God's hierarchy or the church's?"

The bishop was appalled by the question. It smelled blasphemous to him. "They are the same, are they not?"

A great number of men who lived in the early centuries did believe that God's views were always accurately interpreted by the church.

Some women knew better. This is a story about one of them.

Chapter

1

England, 1206

The news was going to destroy her.

Kelmet, her faithful steward and senior in charge since Baron Raulf Williamson's hasty departure from England on the king's personal business, was given the responsibility of telling his mistress the god-awful news. The servant didn't put off the dreaded task, for he guessed Lady Johanna would wish to question the two messengers before they returned to London, if his mistress could speak to anyone after she'd heard about her beloved husband.

Aye, he needed to tell the gentle lady as soon as possible. Kelmet understood his duty well enough, and though he believed he was anxious to get it done, his feet still dragged as though mired in knee-deep mud as he made his way to the newly built chapel where Lady Johanna was in afternoon prayers.

Father Peter MacKechnie, a visiting cleric from the Maclaurin holding in the Highlands, was making his way up the steep incline from the lower bailey when Kelmet happened to spot him. The steward let out a quick sigh of relief before shouting a summons to the dour-faced priest.

"I've need of your services, MacKechnie," Kelmet bellowed over the rising wind.

The priest nodded, then scowled. He still hadn't forgiven the steward for his insulting behavior of two days past.

"Are you wanting me to hear your confession?" the priest shouted back, a hint of mockery in his thick brogue.

"Nay, Father."

MacKechnie shook his head. "You've got yourself a black soul, Kelmet."

The steward made no response to the barb but patiently waited until the dark-haired Scot had gained his side. He could see the amusement in the priest's eyes and knew then he was jesting with him.

"There is another matter more important than my confession," Kelmet began. "I've just received word . . ."

The priest wouldn't let him finish his explanation. "Today's Good Friday," he interrupted. "Nothing could be more important than that. You won't be getting communion from me come Easter morning unless you confess your sins today and beg God's forgiveness. You might begin with the distasteful sin of rudeness, Kelmet. Aye, that would be a proper start."

Kelmet held his patience. "I gave you my apology, Father, but I see that you still haven't forgiven me."

" 'Tis the truth I haven't."

The steward frowned. "As I explained yesterday and the day before, I would not allow you entrance into the keep because I was given specific orders by Baron Raulf not to let anyone inside while he was away. I was told even to deny Lady Johanna's brother, Nicholas, entry should he come calling. Father, try to understand. I'm the third steward here in less than one year's time, and I try only to hold onto my position longer than all the others."

MacKechnie snorted. He wasn't quite through baiting the steward. "If Lady Johanna hadn't intervened, I'd still be camped outside the walls, wouldn't I now?"

Kelmet nodded. "Aye, you would," he admitted. "Unless you gave up your vigil and returned home."

"I won't be going anywhere until I've spoken to Baron Raulf and set him straight about the havoc his vassal is causing on Maclaurin land. Plain murder of innocents is going on, Kelmet, but I'm praying your baron doesn't have any idea what an evil, power-hungry man Marshall has turned out to be. I've heard it said Baron Raulf's an honorable man. I hope that praise be true, for he must right this atrocity with all possible haste. Why, even now some of the Maclaurin soldiers are turning to the bastard MacBain for assistance. Once they've given him their pledge of loyalty and named him laird, all hell's going to break free. MacBain will go to war against Marshall and every

13

other Englishman preying on Maclaurin land. The Highland warrior is no stranger to fury or vengeance, and I'd wager my soul even Baron Raulf's hide will be in jeopardy once MacBain sees for himself the rape of the Maclaurin land by the infidels your baron placed in charge."

Kelmet, although not personally involved in the plight of the Scots, was still caught up in the story. There was also the fact that the priest was inadvertently aiding him in putting off his dreaded task. A few more minutes surely wouldn't hurt, Kelmet thought to himself.

"Are you suggesting this MacBain warrior would come to England?"

"I'm not suggesting," the priest countered. "I'm stating fact. Your baron won't have the slightest inkling he's here either until he feels MacBain's blade at his throat. It will be too late then, of course."

The steward shook his head. "Baron Raulf's soldiers would kill him before he even reached the drawbridge."

"They'd never get the chance," MacKechnie announced, his voice firm with conviction.

"You make this warrior sound invincible."

"I'm thinking he could be. 'Tis the truth I've never met another like him. I won't chill you with the tales I've heard about the MacBain. Suffice it to say you don't want his wrath pouring down on this keep."

"None of it matters now, Father," Kelmet whispered, his tone weary.

14

"Oh, it matters all right," the priest snapped. "I'm going to wait to see your baron for as long as need be. The matter is too grave for impatience to take hold."

Father MacKechnie paused to gather his control. He knew the Maclaurin issue was of no concern to the steward, yet once he started to explain, the anger he'd been carefully guarding inside spilled out and he wasn't able to keep the fury out of his voice. He forced himself to speak in a much calmer voice when he changed the topic.

"You're still a sinner, Kelmet, with the soul of an old dog, but you're an honest man trying to do your duty. God will remember that when you stand before Him on Judgment Day. If you're not wanting me to hear your confession now, then what service do you require?"

"I need your assistance with Lady Johanna, Father. Word has just arrived from King John."

"Yes?" MacKechnie prodded when the steward didn't immediately continue his explanation.

"Baron Raulf is dead."

"Good Lord above, you cannot mean it."

"It's true, Father."

MacKechnie gave a harsh gasp, then hastily made the sign of the cross. He bowed his head, pressed his hands together, and whispered a prayer for the baron's soul.

The wind sent the hem of the priest's black cassock slapping against his legs, but MacKechnie was too intent on his prayers to pay any attention. Kelmet turned his gaze to the sky. The clouds

15

were black, swollen, and being nudged overhead by an insistent, howling wind. The sound of the storm's advance was eerie, ominous . . . fitting.

The priest finished his prayer, made another sign of the cross, and then turned his attention to the steward again. "Why didn't you tell me right away? Why did you let me go on and on? You should have interrupted me. Praise God, what will happen to the Maclaurins now?"

Kelmet shook his head. "I don't have any answers for you, Father, regarding the baron's holding in the Highlands."

"You should have told me right off," the priest said again, still staggered by the black news.

"A few more minutes makes no difference," Kelmet replied. "And perhaps I was putting off this task by keeping you in conversation. It is my duty to inform Lady Johanna, you see, and I would greatly appreciate your help. She's so young, so innocent of treachery. Her heart is going to be broken."

MacKechnie nodded. "I've known your mistress for only two short days, but I've already seen she has a gentle nature and a pure heart. I'm not certain I can be of much help though. Your mistress seems to be very frightened of me."

"She fears most priests, Father. She has sound reason."

"And what would that reason be?"

"Her confessor is Bishop Hallwick."

Father MacKechnie frowned. "You needn't say another word," he muttered with disgust. "Hallwick's wicked reputation is well known, even in the Highlands. No wonder the lass is fearful. It's a wonder she came to my aid and insisted you let me in, Kelmet. That took courage, I'm realizing now. The poor lass," he added with a sigh. "She doesn't deserve the pain of losing her beloved husband at such a tender age. How long has she been married to the baron?"

"She's been his wife for over three years. Lady Johanna was little more than a child when she was wed. Father, please come with me to the chapel."

"Certainly."

The two men walked side by side. Kelmet's voice was halting when he next spoke. "I know I won't have the proper words. I'm not certain . . . how to say . . ."

"Be direct," the priest advised. "She'll appreciate that. Don't make her guess by giving her hints. Perhaps it would do us well to fetch a woman to help comfort your mistress. Lady Johanna will surely need another woman's compassion as well as our own."

"I don't know who I would ask," Kelmet admitted. "Just the day before Baron Raulf left, he replaced the entire household staff yet again. My lady barely knows the servants' names. There have been so many of them. My mistress keeps to herself these days," he added. "She's very kind, Father, but distant from her staff, and she has learned to hold her own council. 'Tis the truth she has no confidantes we could bring along with us now."

"How long has Baron Raulf been away?"

"Near to six months now."

"Yet in all that while, Lady Johanna hasn't come to depend upon anyone?"

"Nay, Father. She confides in no one, not even her steward," Kelmet said, referring to himself. "The baron told us he would only be away for a week or two, and we've been living with the expectation of his arrival home each and every day."

"How did he die?"

"He lost his footing and fell from a cliff." The steward shook his head. "I'm certain there's more to the explanation than I've been told, for Baron Raulf wasn't an awkward man. Perhaps the king will tell lady Johanna more."

"A freak accident then," the priest decided. "God's will be done," he added almost as an afterthought.

"It might have been the devil's work," Kelmet muttered.

MacKechnie didn't remark on that possibility. "Lady Johanna will surely marry again," he announced with a nod. "She'll inherit a sizable amount, won't she?"

"She'll gain a third of her husband's holdings. I've heard they're vast," Kelmet explained.

"Might one of those holdings be the Maclaurin land your King John stole away from Scotland's king and gave to Baron Raulf?"

"Perhaps," Kelmet allowed.

MacKechnie filed that information away for future use. "With your lady's golden-colored hair and handsome blue eyes, I would imagine every unattached baron in England will want to marry her. She's very beautiful, and though it's probably sinful of me to admit, I'll tell you I was quite affected by the sight of her. Her appearance could easily bewitch a man, even without the estate she'll have to offer."

They reached the narrow steps leading up to the chapel doors when the priest finished his remarks.

"She is beautiful," the steward agreed. "I've seen grown men openly gawk at her. Barons will certainly want her," he added, "but not in marriage."

"What nonsense is this?"

"She's barren," Kelmet said.

The priest's eyes widened. "Dear God," he whispered. He lowered his head, made the sign of the cross, and said a prayer for the dear lady's burden.

Lady Johanna was also in prayer. She stood behind the altar and said a prayer for guidance. She was determined to do the right thing. She held a parchment scroll in her hands, and when she finished her plea to God, she wrapped the scroll in linen cloths she had already spread on top of the marble surface.

She once again considered destroying the damning evidence against her king. Then she shook her head. Someday, someone might find the scroll, and if only one man learned the truth about the evil king who once ruled England, then perhaps a thread of justice might be served.

Johanna placed the scroll between the two marble slabs below the altar top. She made certain it was hidden from view and protected from damage. Then she said another quick prayer, genuflected, and walked down the aisle. She opened the door to go outside.

The conversation between Father MacKechnie and Kelmet immediately stopped.

The sight of Lady Johanna still affected the priest, and he acknowledged the truth without feeling a qualm of guilt. MacKechnie didn't consider himself caught by the sin of lust because he noticed the shimmer in her hair or stared a bit longer than necessary at her lovely face. In his mind, Johanna was simply one of God's creatures, a magnificent example, to be sure, of the Lord's ability to create perfection.

She was Saxon through and through with her high cheekbones and fair coloring. She was a little shorter in stature than others, for she was of only medium height, but she appeared taller to the priest because of the queenly way she held herself.

Aye, her appearance pleased the priest, and he was certain she pleased her God as well, as she truly possessed a kind and gentle heart.

MacKechnie was a compassionate man. He ached over the cruel blow the dear lady had already been given. A barren woman served no purpose in this kingdom. Her very reason for existing had been snatched away. The burden she carried, knowing of her own inferiority, was surely the reason he'd never seen her smile.

And now they were about to give her another cruel blow. "Might we have a word with you, m'lady?" Kelmet asked.

The steward's tone of voice must have alerted her that something was amiss. A guarded look came into her eyes, and her hands became fists at her sides. She nodded and slowly turned to go back inside.

The two men followed. Lady Johanna turned to face them when she'd reached the center of the aisle between the rows of wooden pews. The altar was directly behind her. Four candles provided the only light inside the chapel. The flames flickered inside their round glass globes spaced a hand's length apart on top of the long marble altar top.

Lady Johanna straightened her shoulders, folded her hands together, and kept her gaze firmly on the steward. She seemed to be bracing herself for foul news. Her voice was whisper soft, devoid of all emotion. "Has my husband returned home?"

"Nay, m'lady," Kelmet answered. He glanced over at the priest, received his encouraging nod, and then blurted out, "Two messengers have just arrived from London. They bring terrible news. Your husband is dead."

A full minute of silence followed the announcement. Kelmet began to clasp and unclasp his hands while he waited for the news to take root. His mistress didn't show any outward reaction, and he began to think she hadn't understood what he'd just said.

"It's true, m'lady. Baron Raulf is dead," he repeated in a hoarse whisper.

And still he saw no response. The priest and the steward shared a worried look, then looked back at Lady Johanna.

Tears suddenly gathered in her eyes. Father MacKechnie almost let out a sigh of relief. She understood the news.

He waited for her denial next, for in all his considerable years of consoling the bereaved, he'd seen most people use denial in order to cheat the truth a little longer.

Her own denial was swift and violent. "No!" she screamed. She shook her head so forcefully her long braid caught over her shoulder. "I will not listen to this lie. I will not."

"Kelmet has spoken the truth," Father Mac-Kechnie insisted, his voice low and soothing.

She shook her head at him. "This must be trickery. He cannot be dead. Kelmet, you must hunt down the truth. Who would tell you such a lie?"

The priest took a quick step forward to put his arm around the distressed woman. The anguish in her voice made him want to weep himself.

She wouldn't allow comfort. She backed up a space, gripped her hands together, and demanded, "Is this a cruel trick?"

"Nay, m'lady," Kelmet replied. "The news came from King John himself. There was a witness. The baron is dead."

22

"God rest his soul," the priest intoned.

Lady Johanna burst into tears. Both men hurried forward. She warded them off by backing up again. They stopped, uncertain now what to do. They watched as the broken-hearted woman turned away. She stumbled to her knees, crossed her arms over her stomach, and doubled over as though she'd just received a hard blow to her middle.

Her sobs were soul-wrenching. The men let her vent her desolation for long minutes, and when she was finally able to regain a little of her control and her sobs had lessened, the priest placed his hand on her shoulder and whispered words meant to comfort her.

She didn't brush his hand away. MacKechnie watched as she slowly regained her dignity. She took a deep calming breath, mopped her face with the linen square he handed her, and then allowed him to assist her to her feet.

She kept her head bowed when she addressed the men. "I would like to be alone now. I must . . . pray."

She didn't wait for their agreement but turned and walked to the first pew. She knelt down on the leather-padded kneeler and made the sign of the cross, signaling the beginning of her petitions.

The priest went outside first. Kelmet followed. He was just pulling the door closed behind him when his mistress called out to him.

"Swear it, Kelmet. Swear on your father's grave my husband is truly dead."

"I swear it, m'lady."

The steward waited another minute or two to see if there was anything his mistress wanted from him and then pulled the door completely shut.

Johanna stared at the altar for a long, long while. Her mind was a riot of thoughts and emotions.

She was too stunned to think reasonable thoughts.

"I must pray," she whispered. "My husband is dead. I must pray."

She closed her eyes, folded her hands together, and finally began her prayer. It was a simple, direct litany that came from her heart.

"Thank you, God. Thank you, God. Thank you, God."

Chapter

2

The Highlands of Scotland, 1207

The baron obviously had a death wish. The laird was going to accommodate him.

The MacBain had heard through the intricate gossip vine four days before that Baron Nicholas Sanders was making his way up the last steep, winter-covered hills to the Maclaurin holding. The Englishman wasn't a stranger and had in fact fought by the MacBain's side during a fierce battle against the English infidels who'd taken root on Maclaurin land. Once the invigorating fight was finished, MacBain had become laird over both his own followers and the Maclaurin clan; and as their new leader, he made the decision to allow Nicholas to stay on long enough to recover from his rather substantial injuries. MacBain believed he'd been very accommodating then, damned gracious too, but for good reason. As grating as it was to acknowledge, Baron Nicholas had actually saved MacBain's life during the battle. The laird was a proud man. It was difficult for him to say thank you, actually impossible, and so, in appreciation for saving the laird from an English sword aimed for his back, MacBain didn't let Nicholas bleed to death. Since they didn't have anyone experienced in the ways of healing, MacBain personally cleaned and wrapped the baron's injuries. His generosity hadn't stopped there, although in his mind he'd repaid the debt sufficiently. When Nicholas was strong enough to travel, the MacBain had let him have his magnificent horse back and gave him one of his own plaids to wear so he would have safe passage on his return to England. No other clan would dare touch a MacBain, so the plaid was actually better protection than chain mail.

Aye, he'd been hospitable all right, and now the baron was determined to take advantage of his good nature.

Damn it all, he really was going to have to kill the man.

There was only one bright thought that kept his mood from going completely sour. He would keep Nicholas's horse this time.

"Feed a wolf once, MacBain, and he's bound to come sniffing around here again for more food."

The laird's first-in-command, a thick-shouldered, blond warrior named Calum, made that remark with a forced sneer in his voice. The sparkle in his eyes indicated he was actually amused by the baron's arrival.

"Are you going to kill him?"

MacBain thought about the question a long minute before answering. "Probably." His voice had been deliberately blasé.

Calum laughed. "Baron Nicholas is a courageous man to come back here."

"Not courageous," MacBain corrected. "Foolish."

"He's coming up the last hill wearing your plaid as pretty as you please, MacBain."

Keith, the eldest of the Maclaurin warriors, shouted the announcement as he came strutting through the doorway.

"Do you want me to bring him inside?" Calum asked.

"Inside?" Keith snorted. "We're more out than in, Calum. The roof's gone from fire, and only three of the four walls are standing proud now. I'd say we're already outside."

"The English did this," Calum reminded his laird. "Nicholas . . ."

"He came here to rid the Maclaurin land of the infidels," MacBain reminded his soldier. "Nicholas had no part in the destruction."

"He's still English."

"I haven't forgotten." He pulled away from the mantel he'd been leaning against, muttered an expletive when a slat of wood crashed to the floor, and then walked outside. Both Calum and Keith fell into step behind him. They took their positions on either side of their leader at the bottom of the steps.

The MacBain towered over his soldiers. He was a giant of a man, fierce in appearance and temperament with dark black-brown hair and gray-colored eyes. He looked mean. Even his stance was belligerent. His legs were braced apart, his arms were folded across his massive chest, and a scowl was firmly in place.

Baron Nicholas spotted the laird as soon as his mount crested the hill. MacBain looked furious all right. Nicholas reminded himself that that was a usual condition. Still, the scowl was black enough to give the baron second thoughts. "I must be daft," he muttered to himself. He took a deep breath, then let out a shrill whistle of greeting. He added a smile for good measure and raised one fist in the air as a greeting.

The MacBain wasn't impressed with the baron's manners. He waited until Nicholas had reached the center of the barren courtyard before raising his hand in an unspoken signal to stop.

"I thought I'd been damned specific, Baron. I told you not to come back here."

"Aye, you did tell me not to come back," Nicholas agreed. "I remember."

"Do you also remember I told you I'd have to kill you if you ever set foot on my land again?"

Nicholas nodded. "I've a strong memory for details, MacBain. I remember that threat."

"Is this not open defiance then?"

"You could conclude it is," Nicholas answered with a negligent shrug.

The smile on the baron's face confused the hell out of MacBain. Did Nicholas think they were playing some sort of game? Was he that simple-minded?

MacBain let out a long sigh. "Take off my plaid, Nicholas."

"Why?"

"I don't want to get your blood on it."

His voice shook with fury. Nicholas hoped to God it was all bluster. He believed he was equal in muscle and strength to the laird, and he was certainly every inch as tall. Still he didn't want to fight the man. If he killed the laird, his plan would fail; and if the laird killed him, he'd never know what the hell the plan was until it was too late. Besides, the MacBain was much quicker in battle. He didn't fight fair either, a trait, Nicholas decided, he found impressive.

"Aye, it is your plaid," he shouted to the barbarian. "But the land, MacBain, well now, that belongs to my sister."

MacBain's scowl intensified. He didn't like hearing the truth. Taking a step forward, he pulled his sword from its sheath at his side.

"Hell," Nicholas muttered as he swung his leg over his stallion and dismounted. "Nothing's ever easy with you, is it, MacBain?"

He didn't expect an answer and didn't get one. He removed the plaid he'd worn draped like a banner across one shoulder and tossed it on the saddle of his horse, then reached for his own sword. One of the Maclaurin warriors rushed forward to lead the horse away. Nicholas paid him little attention and tried as well to ignore the crowd gathering in a circle around the courtyard. His mind was fully focused on his adversary.

"It was your brother-in-law who destroyed this holding and half the Maclaurin clan," MacBain roared. "And I have suffered your presence long enough."

The two giants matched glares. Nicholas shook his head. "Keep your facts straight, MacBain. It was my sister's husband, Baron Raulf, who placed the infidel, Marshall, and his sorry men in charge of this holding; but when Raulf died and my sister was freed from his control, she sent me here to rid the land of the traitorous vassals. She owns this holding, MacBain. Your King William the Lion forgot to barter it back from Richard when that good man was king of England and in such desperate need of coins for his crusades, but John never forgot what was passed down to him. He gave his land to his faithful servant Raulf, and now that he's dead, Johanna inherits. It's her land all right, like it or not."

Dredging up past offenses made both warriors furious. They advanced upon each other like raging bulls; the clash of their mighty swords drew blue sparks and ear-piercing sounds as steel slapped steel. The noise echoed down the hills, drowning out the crowd's grunts of approval.

Neither warrior said another word for at least twenty minutes. The fight consumed every ounce of their strength and their concentration. MacBain was the aggressor in this battle, Nicholas, the defender, as he blocked each deadly blow.

Both the MacBain warriors and the Maclaurin soldiers were thoroughly satisfied with the show.

Several muttered approval over the Englishman's quick moves, for in their minds Nicholas had already shown his superior skill by staying alive for so long.

MacBain suddenly twisted back and used his foot to trip the baron. Nicholas fell backward, rolled, and was back on his feet as quick as a cat before the laird could take advantage of the opportunity.

"You're being damned inhospitable," Nicholas panted.

MacBain smiled. He could have ended the battle when Nicholas had fallen backward, but he finally acknowledged to himself that his heart just wasn't in the fight.

"My curiosity is keeping you alive, Nicholas," MacBain announced, his breathing labored. His brow was covered with sweat even as he swung his sword in a wide, downward arch.

Nicholas arched his own sword upward, meeting the powerful blow. "We're going to be related, MacBain, like that or not."

It took a few seconds for the statement to penetrate. The laird didn't let up on his attack when he asked, "How can that be, Baron?"

"I'm going to become your brother-in-law."

MacBain didn't try to hide his astonishment over the baron's outrageous and surely demented announcement. He took a step back and slowly lowered his sword.

"Have you gone completely daft, Nicholas?"

The baron laughed. He tossed his weapon aside.

"You look as though you just swallowed your sword, MacBain."

After giving his observation, he lunged headfirst into the laird's chest. It felt as though he'd just rammed a stone wall. The ploy hurt like hell, but it proved effective. MacBain let out a low grunt. The two warriors went flying backward. MacBain let go of his sword. Nicholas ended up sprawled on top of the laird. He was too exhausted to move, and in too much pain to want to. MacBain shoved him aside, made it to his knees, and was about to reach for his sword again when he suddenly changed his inclination. He slowly turned to look at Nicholas.

"Marry an Englishwoman?"

He sounded horrified. He was out of breath, too. The last observation pleased Nicholas considerably; and just as soon as he was able to draw a deep breath again he would boast over the fact that he had worn the laird out.

MacBain stood up, then hauled Nicholas to his feet. He shoved him backward so he wouldn't think the action had been an act of kindness, then folded his arms across his chest and demanded an explanation.

"And who is it you believe I would marry?"

"My sister."

"You're mad."

Nicholas shook his head. "If you don't marry her, King John will give her to Baron Williams. He's a mean son of a bitch," he added in a gratingly cheerful voice. "God help you then,

MacBain. If Williams marries her, the men he'll send will make Marshall seem as good and just as the day is long."

The laird didn't show any outward reaction to that bit of news. Nicholas rubbed the side of his head in an attempt to ease the sting before continuing on. "You'll probably kill whoever he sends here," he remarked.

"Damned right I will," MacBain snapped.

"But Williams will only retaliate by sending more . . . and more . . . and more. Can you afford to risk constant war with England? How many more Maclaurins will die before it's settled? Look around you, MacBain. Marshall and his men damned near destroyed every building. The Maclaurins turned to you for help and made you their laird. They're depending on you. If you marry Johanna, the land will legally become yours. King John will leave you alone."

"Your king approves of this union?"

"He does." Nicholas's voice was emphatic.

"Why?"

Nicholas shrugged. "I'm not certain. He wants Johanna out of England, that much I know. He made that remark several times. He seemed eager for the marriage and agreed to give you the Maclaurin land the day you wed. I'll receive title to her holding in England."

"Why?" MacBain demanded again.

Nicholas sighed. "I believe my sister understands why John wants her settled so far away — he calls this place the ends of the earth — but

Johanna won't tell me what his reasons might be."

"So you would also profit from this marriage."

"I don't want the holding in England," he said. "It will only mean more taxes each year, and I already have enough to do rebuilding my own estates."

"Then why did you ask for your sister's . . ."

Nicholas didn't let him finish. "John understands greed," he interrupted. "If he thought I was only protecting my sister from Baron Williams, he might have declined my suggestion to marry her to you. He did insist upon a large fine, of course, but I've already paid it."

"You're contradicting yourself, Baron. If John wanted Johanna away from England, why would he consider marrying her to Baron Williams?"

"Because Williams is extremely loyal to John. Williams is his lapdog. He would keep my sister under control." Nicholas shook his head then. In a low whisper he said, "My sister was privy to some damning information, and John doesn't want his past sins coming back to haunt him. Oh, she could never give testimony in court against any man, not even her king, for she is a woman and, therefore, would not be listened to by any official. Still, there are barons ready to rebel against the king. Johanna could possibly ignite their fervor if she told whatever it is she knows. It's a puzzle, MacBain, but the more I reflect upon it, the more convinced I become that my king is actually afraid of what Johanna knows."

"If what you guess is true, I'm surprised he

34

hasn't had her killed. Your king is capable of such a foul deed."

Nicholas knew he would never gain MacBain's cooperation unless he was completely honest with him. He nodded once again. "He is capable of murder. I was with Johanna when she received the summons to go to London. I saw her reaction. I believe she thought she was going to her execution."

"Yet she's still alive."

"The king keeps her under close guard. She has private quarters and isn't allowed guests. She's living each day in fear. I want her away from England. Marrying you is my answer."

The laird was pleased by the baron's veracity. He motioned for him to walk with him and started toward the ruins he now called home. Nicholas fell into step beside him.

MacBain's voice was low when he remarked, "So it was you who came up with this clever plan."

"Yes," Nicholas replied. "And just in the breath of time. John was set to marry her to Williams six months ago, but she was able to resist."

"How?"

Nicholas grinned. "She demanded an annulment first."

MacBain's surprise was evident. "Why would she ask for an annulment? Her husband's dead."

"It was a clever stalling tactic," Nicholas explained. "There was a witness to her husband's death, but the body wasn't recovered. My sister told the king she wouldn't marry anyone as long as there was a shred of hope Raulf was still alive. He didn't die in England, you see. He was in a city built on the water, acting as John's envoy when the accident took place. The king wasn't going to be denied, of course, but because he's having so much difficulty with the church these days, he decided to go through proper channels. Johanna just received the papers. The annulment has been granted."

"Who was this witness to her husband's death?"

"Why do you ask?"

"Just curious," MacBain answered. "Do you know?"

"Yes," Nicholas answered. "Williams was the witness."

Gabriel stored that bit of information away in the back of his mind. "Why do you prefer me to the English baron?"

"Williams is a monster, and I cannot abide the thought of my sister being under his control. You were the lesser of two evils. I know you'll treat her well . . . if she'll have you."

"What nonsense is this? It isn't her decision to make."

"I'm afraid it is," Nicholas said. "Johanna must meet you first and then decide. It was the best I could do. In truth, she wouldn't marry anyone if she could continue to come up with the coins the king demands to stay unmarried. That is what she believes anyway. I know better. The king will marry her off one way or another."

"Your king is a greedy man," MacBain said. "Or is this special punishment designed to gain your sister's cooperation?"

"The tax?" Nicholas asked.

MacBain nodded. "No," Nicholas said. "John can force widows of his tenants in chief to remarry. If they're determined to remain free or to choose their own husbands, well, then they have to pay him a sizable fine each year."

"You mentioned you already paid the fine. You're assuming then that Johanna will find me acceptable?"

Nicholas nodded. "My sister doesn't know I paid the fine, and I would appreciate it if you didn't mention it when you meet her."

MacBain clasped his hands behind his back and went inside. Nicholas followed.

"I must consider this proposal of yours," the laird announced. "The thought of marrying an Englishwoman is hard to stomach, and when you add the fact that she is also your sister, it's almost unthinkable."

Nicholas knew he was being insulted. He didn't mind. The MacBain had proven his character during the battle against Marshall and his cohorts.

The laird might be a little rough around the edges, but he was also a courageous and honorable man.

"There's something else you should consider before you decide," Nicholas said.

"What is it?"

"Johanna's barren."

37

MacBain nodded to let Nicholas know he'd heard him but didn't comment on the news for several minutes.

Then he shrugged. "I already have a son."

"Do you mean Alex?"

"Yes."

"I was told at least three men could be his father."

"That is true," MacBain countered. "His mother was a camp follower. She couldn't name the man who fathered Alex. She believed it might be me. She died birthing the boy. I claim him as mine."

"Do any of the other men also claim him?"

"No."

"Johanna can't give you children. Will the fact that Alex is illegitimate matter in future?"

"It will not matter," MacBain announced, his voice hard and unbending. "I'm also illegitimate."

Nicholas laughed. "Do you mean that, when I called you bastard in the heat of battle against Marshall, I wasn't being insulting but truthful?"

MacBain nodded. "I've killed others for calling me that name, Nicholas. Count yourself fortunate."

"You'll be the fortunate one if Johanna decides to marry you."

MacBain shook his head. "I want what rightfully belongs to me. If getting the land means marrying the shrew, I'll do it."

"Why would you believe she's a shrew?" Nicholas asked, puzzled by MacBain's conclusion.

"You've given me sufficient clues to her character," MacBain answered. "She's obviously a stubborn woman because she refused to confide in her brother when asked what information she has against her own king. She needs a man who will control her — those were your words to me, Nicholas, so don't look so surprised — and last, she happens to be barren. She sounds appealing, doesn't she?"

"Aye, she is appealing."

MacBain scoffed. "I don't relish my future as her husband, but you are correct, I will treat her kindly. I imagine we'll find a way to stay out of each other's paths."

The laird poured wine into two silver goblets and handed one to Nicholas. Each raised his drink in a salute and then downed the contents. Nicholas understood proper etiquette in the Highlands. He promptly belched. MacBain nodded approval.

"I suppose this means you'll be coming back here whenever the mood strikes you?"

Nicholas laughed. MacBain sounded damned forlorn over the possibility.

"I'll need several plaids to take back with me," he said then. "You wouldn't want anything to happen to your bride, would you?"

"I'll give you more than a few, Nicholas," MacBain countered. "I want at least thirty men riding escort. Each will wear my colors for protection. You'll dismiss them when you reach Rush Creek. Only you and your sister will be allowed on our land. Is that understood?"

"I was jesting about the plaids, laird. I can take care of my sister."

"You'll do as I order," MacBain commanded.

Nicholas gave in. The laird changed the topic then. "How long was Johanna married?"

"A little over three years. Johanna would like to remain unmarried," Nicholas said. "But my sister's feelings are of no concern to John. He's kept her under lock and key in London. I've only been allowed a short visitation, and John was present all the while. As I told you earlier, my sister's a loose end he wants taken care of, MacBain."

MacBain frowned. Nicholas suddenly smiled. "How does it rub knowing you're the answer to King John's prayer?"

The laird wasn't amused. "I get the land," he remarked. "That is all that matters."

Nicholas's attention was turned when MacBain's giant wolfhound came loping through the entrance. The beast was a fierce-looking thing with a brindle-colored coat and dark eyes. Nicholas thought it weighed almost as much as he did. The hound spotted Nicholas when he rounded the corner and bounded down the steps. He let out a low, menacing growl that made Nicholas's hair stand on end.

MacBain snapped a command in Gaelic. His monstrous pet immediately went to his side.

"A word of advice, MacBain. Hide that ugly gargoyle when I bring Johanna here. She'll take one look at the two of you and turn right around and go back to England."

MacBain laughed. "Mark my words, Nicholas. I won't be denied. She will have me."

Chapter

3

I won't have him, Nicholas. You must be out of your mind if you think I would even consider becoming his wife."

"Appearances are deceiving, Johanna," her brother countered. "Wait until we're closer. You'll surely notice the kindness in his eyes. MacBain will treat you well."

She shook her head. Her hands were shaking so violently she almost dropped the reins to her mount. She tightened her hold on the leather straps and tried not to gape at the huge warrior . . . and the monstrous-looking animal leaning against his side.

They were nearing the courtyard of the desolate holding. The laird stood on the step leading up to the dilapidated keep. He didn't look particularly pleased by the sight of her.

She was sickened by the sight of him. She took a deep breath in an attempt to calm herself, then whispered, "What color are his eyes, Nicholas?" Her brother didn't know.

"You saw kindness in his eyes, yet you didn't notice the color?"

She had him there and they both knew it. "Men don't notice such insignificant things," he defended.

"You told me he was a gentle man with a soft voice and a quick smile. He isn't smiling now, is he, Nicholas?"

"Now, Johanna . . ."

"You lied to me."

"I did not lie to you," he argued. "MacBain saved my life not once but twice during the battle against Marshall and his men, and he refuses to even acknowledge it. He's a proud man but honorable. You must trust me on this. I wouldn't suggest you marry him unless I was convinced it would be a sound union."

Johanna didn't answer him. Panic was taking hold. Her gaze kept going back and forth between the huge warrior and the ugly beast.

Nicholas thought she was getting ready to faint. His mind raced for some clever thing to say to help her calm down.

"MacBain's the one on the left, Johanna."

She wasn't amused by his jest. "He's a very big man, isn't he?"

Her brother reached over to pat her hand. "He's no bigger than I am," he replied.

She pushed his hand away. She didn't want his comfort. She didn't want him to feel her trembling with cowardly fear either.

"Most wives would wish to have strong husbands to defend them. MacBain's size should be a comfort to you and a mark in his favor."

She shook her head. " 'Tis a mark against him," she announced.

She continued to stare at the laird. He seemed to be growing right before her eyes. The closer she got, the larger he became.

"He's handsome."

She blurted out her opinion in a voice that sounded like an accusation.

"If you think so," Nicholas decided to agree.

" 'Tis another mark against him. I don't want to be married to a handsome man."

"You aren't making sense."

"I don't have to make sense. I've decided. I won't have him. Take me home, Nicholas. Now."

Nicholas jerked on the reins to stop her mount, then forced her to look at him. The fear he saw in her eyes made his heart ache. Only he knew the purgatory she'd endured while married to Raulf, and although she wouldn't speak of it, he knew what her real terror was now. His voice was low and fervent when he said, "Listen to me, Johanna. MacBain will never hurt you."

She wasn't certain if she believed him or not. "I would never allow him to hurt me."

The vehemence in her reply made him smile with approval. Raulf hadn't been able to beat the spirit out of her. Nicholas counted that as a blessing.

"Think of all the reasons why you should marry him," he said. "You'll be away from King John and his cohorts, and they won't come here after you. You'll be safe here."

"There is that consideration."

"MacBain hates England and our king."

She nibbled on her lower lip. "That is another sound point in his favor," she admitted.

"This place, as bleak as it now looks, will one day be a paradise, and you'll have helped to rebuild it. You're needed here."

"Yes, I would help to rebuild," she said. "And I do long for warm weather. 'Tis the truth I only agreed to come here because you convinced me the land is much closer to the sun. I don't know why I hadn't realized that before. I must admit not having to wear a heavy cloak more than one month out of the year does have a wonderful appeal. You did say it was odd the weather was so chilly for this time of year."

Good God, he'd forgotten that little lie. Johanna hated the cold and knew absolutely nothing about the Highlands. He'd deliberately deceived her in his attempt to get her safely out of England and now felt guilty as hell. He'd corrupted a man of the cloth, too, for he'd begged Father MacKechnie to go along with the fabrication.

The priest had his own motives for wanting Johanna to marry the MacBain laird and had held his silence each time Johanna mentioned the appeal of such a warm, sunny climate. He had, however, glared at Nicholas whenever the topic came up.

Nicholas let out a sigh. He guessed that when

Johanna was knee deep in snow, she'd realize he'd lied to her. Hopefully by then her opinion of MacBain would have softened.

"Will he leave me alone, Nicholas?"

"Yes."

"You didn't tell him anything about my years with Raulf?"

"No, of course not. I wouldn't break my word to you."

She nodded. "And he knows, for certain, I cannot give him children?"

They'd been over that issue at least a dozen times on the journey up the hills. Nicholas didn't know what more he could say to reassure her. "He knows, Johanna."

"Why didn't it matter to him?"

"He wanted the land. He's laird now and has to put his clan above his own concerns. Marrying you was simply a way he could achieve his goal."

It was a cold, honest answer. Johanna nodded. "I'll meet him," she finally agreed. "But I won't promise you I'll marry him, so you can quit your smile right now, Nicholas."

MacBain had grown weary of waiting for his bride to come to him. He started down the steps just as she nudged her mount forward. He still hadn't gotten a proper look at her, as she was completely covered by a black cape and hood. Her smallness, however, surprised him. He'd expected a much larger woman given Nicholas's size.

Her appearance wasn't important to him. The marriage was a practical arrangement, nothing more. He assumed, however, that because she was Nicholas's sister, she would have the same dark coloring and auburn-colored hair.

He was mistaken. Nicholas dismounted first. He tossed the reins to one of the soldiers and went over to Johanna's side to assist her to the ground.

She was a little bit of a thing. The top of her head only reached her brother's shoulders. Nicholas had his hands on her arms and was smiling down at her. It was obvious he cared a great deal about his sister. MacBain thought his brotherly devotion a little overdone.

While Johanna untied the cord holding her cloak together, the soldiers began to line up behind their leader. The Maclaurin men clumped themselves together behind their laird and to the left of the wide steps while the MacBain warriors lined up behind their leader and on the right side. The six steps were filled with curious men in a matter of seconds. They all wanted to see the laird's bride.

MacBain heard the low grunts of obvious approval a scant second after Johanna removed her cloak and handed it to her brother. MacBain didn't think he made a sound, but he wasn't certain. The sight of her took his breath away.

Nicholas hadn't said a word about her appearance, and MacBain hadn't been interested enough to ask. He now looked at the baron and saw the laughter in his eyes. *He knows I'm rattled,* he thought to himself. MacBain masked his astonishment and turned his full attention back to the beautiful woman walking toward him.

Lord, she was a bonny lass. Her waist-length blond curls swayed with each step she took. The woman didn't seem to have any flaws. There was a light sprinkle of freckles across the bridge of her nose. He liked that. Her eyes were a vivid shade of blue, her complexion was pure, and her mouth, dear God, her mouth could drive a saint to lustful thoughts. He liked that, too.

Some of the Maclaurin soldiers weren't as disciplined in their reactions as the MacBain was. The two men standing directly behind their laird let out long, low whistles of appreciation. MacBain took exception to their rude behavior, however. He half-turned, lifted each man by his neck, and sent them both flying like cabers over the side of the steps. The other soldiers had to duck to get out of the way.

Johanna came to a quick stop, looked at the soldiers sprawled out on the ground, then looked back at their leader. The laird didn't even seem winded.

"A gentle man?" she whispered to Nicholas. "That was a lie, wasn't it?"

"Give him a chance, Johanna. You owe him and me that much."

She gave her brother a disgruntled look before turning back to the laird.

MacBain took a step forward. His wolfhound came with him and once again leaned against his master's side.

Johanna started praying for enough courage to keep walking. When she was just a foot or two away from the warrior, she stopped and then

47

executed a perfect curtsy.

Her knees were shaking so hard that she was pleased she didn't fall over on her face.

She heard a loud snort and several grunts while her head was bowed. She didn't know if the noises were sounds of approval or censure.

The laird was wearing his plaid. He had extremely muscular legs. She tried not to stare at them.

"Good day, Laird MacBain."

Her voice trembled. She was afraid of him. MacBain wasn't surprised. The sight of him had sent more than one young woman running back to the safety of her father. He'd never considered trying to change their reactions because he hadn't particularly cared.

He was caring now, however. He would never get the woman to marry him if he didn't do something to ease her fear. She kept giving worried glances down at his dog. MacBain assumed the hound also frightened her.

Nicholas wasn't being much help. He just stood there grinning like a simpleton.

MacBain demanded his assistance by glaring at him. He decided he shouldn't have done that when Johanna took a quick step back.

"Does she speak Gaelic?"

MacBain addressed his question to Nicholas. Johanna answered. "I have been studying your language."

She didn't speak in Gaelic when she answered. Her hands were folded together in front of her.

The knuckles were white from her hard grip.

Mundane conversation might put her at ease, MacBain decided. "And how long have you been studying our language?"

Her mind went blank. It was his fault, of course. His stare was so intense, unsettling, too, and she couldn't seem to form a thought. Dear God, she couldn't even remember what they were talking about.

He patiently asked her again. "Almost four weeks," she blurted out.

He didn't laugh. One of the soldiers snorted with amusement, but MacBain's glare stopped him.

Nicholas was frowning down at his sister, wondering why she hadn't told the laird the truth. It had been closer to four months since Father MacKechnie began instructing her. He caught the look of panic in his sister's eyes when she glanced up at him and he understood then. Johanna was simply too nervous to think straight.

MacBain decided he didn't want an audience during this important meeting.

"Nicholas, wait here. Your sister and I are going inside to talk."

After giving his command, MacBain moved forward to take hold of Johanna's arm. The hound came with him. She instinctively backed up, realized what she was doing and how that cowardly retreat must have looked to the laird, and quickly moved forward again.

The huge beast growled at her. MacBain

snapped an order in Gaelic. The hound immediately quit the low, menacing sound.

Johanna was looking ready to faint again. Nicholas knew she needed a bit of time to get her courage back. He took a step forward. "Why didn't you allow my men and Father MacKechnie past Rush Creek?" he asked.

"Your sister and I must come to terms before the priest is allowed here. Your men won't ever be allowed on our land, Nicholas. Have you forgotten my terms? We went over the details when you were last here."

Nicholas agreed with a nod. He couldn't think of anything further to ask.

"Father MacKechnie was very upset over your command to wait below," Johanna said.

MacBain didn't appear to be overly concerned about alienating a man of God. He shrugged. Her eyes widened in reaction. During the three years of her marriage to Raulf, she'd learned to fear priests; the ones she had known were powerful and unforgiving men. Yet MacKechnie wasn't like the others. He was a kind-hearted man who had risked his life to come to England so that he could plead for the Maclaurins.

She wouldn't have him insulted now. "Father MacKechnie is weary from the long journey, m'lord, and would surely appreciate food and drink. Please show him your hospitality."

MacBain nodded. He turned to Calum. "See to it," he commanded.

He thought his agreement over her request

50

would ease her fears about him. He had just proven he could be an accommodating man, after all. Yet she still appeared ready to bolt. Damn but she was a timid thing. His pet wasn't helping matters much. She kept worriedly glancing down at the dog, and every time she stared at him, the hound growled at her.

MacBain considered grabbing hold of her, tossing her over his shoulder, and carrying her inside, then changed his mind. The thought amused him, but he didn't smile. He held his patience, put his hand out to her, and simply waited to see what she would do.

From the look in his eyes, she knew he had guessed she was afraid of him and that he was finding her timidity amusing, too. She forced herself to take a deep breath, then put her hand in his.

He was huge everywhere. His hand was at least twice the size of her own, and he certainly must have felt her trembling. He was a laird, however, and she assumed he would never have attained that position of power without gaining a few gentlemanly manners along the way, and she therefore assumed he wouldn't mention her shameful condition.

"Why are you shaking?"

She tried to pull her hand away. He wouldn't let go. He had her now, and he wasn't about to let her get away.

Before Johanna could come up with a suitable explanation to his question, he turned and pulled

51

her along up the steps and through the doorway.

"Because of your unusual weather," she blurted out.

"Our what?" He looked confused.

"Never mind, Laird."

"Explain what you meant," he commanded.

She sighed. "Nicholas explained that the weather here is warm all year around . . . I thought he'd told you about his . . ." She started to say lie, then changed her mind. The laird might not understand how amused she'd been over her brother's outrageous fabrication about the Highlands.

"His what?" MacBain asked, curious over her sudden blush.

"He said it was unusual to have such cold winds here," she said.

MacBain almost burst into laughter. He caught himself in time. The weather was actually unusually warm for this time of year.

He didn't even smile. The lass had already shown she had tender feelings, and he didn't suppose laughing at her naïveté would soften her attitude toward him.

"And you believe everything your brother tells you?" he asked.

"Yes, of course," she answered so that he would know she was thoroughly loyal to her brother.

"I see."

"The cold is the reason I am trembling," she said for lack of a better lie to tell.

"No, it isn't."

"It isn't?"

52

"You're afraid of me."

He waited for her to lie to him again. She surprised him with the truth. "Yes," she announced. "I'm afraid of you. I'm afraid of your hound, too."

"Your answers please me."

He finally let go of her. She was so surprised by his remark she forgot to let go of his hand.

"It pleases you to know I fear you?"

He smiled. "I already knew you feared me, Johanna. I'm pleased because you admitted it. You could have lied."

"You would have known I was lying."

"Yes."

He sounded terribly arrogant, but she wasn't offended — she expected arrogance in a man as big and ferocious looking as this warrior. She realized she was holding onto him then and immediately let go. Then she turned to look around the entrance. To the right was a wide staircase with an ornately carved wooden railing. A hallway led behind the staircase, and on the left of the entryway was the great hall. It was in ruins. Johanna stood on the top step and stared at the devastation. The walls were charred from fire, and the roof above the hall, what little there was left of it, hung down in a long strip to rest against the blackened sides. The smell of old smoke still lingered in the air.

Johanna went down the steps and crossed the room. She was so disheartened by the sight of the destruction, she felt like weeping.

MacBain watched the change in her expression

as she looked around the room.

"My husband's men did this, didn't they?"

"Yes."

She turned to look at him. The sadness in her eyes actually pleased him. She was a woman with a conscience.

"A terrible injustice was done here."

"That is true," he agreed. "But you weren't responsible."

"I could have tried to plead with my husband . . ."

"I doubt he would have listened to you," MacBain announced. "Tell me something, Johanna. Did he know his vassal was causing such havoc here, or was he ignorant?"

"He knew what Marshall was capable of," she replied.

MacBain nodded. He clasped his hands behind his back and continued to stare at her. "You tried to right the injustice," he remarked. "You sent your brother here after Marshall."

"My husband's vassal had become a demigod. He didn't wish to hear the news that Raulf was dead and he was no longer needed here."

"He was never needed here." MacBain's voice had taken on a hard edge.

She nodded agreement. "No, he was never needed here."

He let out a sigh. "Marshall had found power. Very few men can give that up."

"Could you?"

He was surprised by her question. He started

to answer yes, of course he could, but he was new to his position as laird and honestly didn't know if he could step down or not.

"I've yet to be tested," he admitted. "I would hope, if it was for the good of the clan, I could do whatever was asked of me, but I cannot say for certain until I'm faced with such a challenge."

His honesty impressed her, and she smiled. "Nicholas was angry with you because Marshall had slipped away and you wouldn't let him go after him. He said the two of you argued, then you struck him into a sound sleep. When he next opened his eyes, Marshall was in a heap at his feet."

MacBain smiled. Nicholas had certainly softened the bloody tale.

"You're going to marry me, Johanna."

He sounded emphatic. He wasn't smiling now. Johanna braced herself against his anger and then slowly shook her head.

"Explain the reason behind your hesitation," he commanded.

She shook her head at him again. MacBain wasn't used to being contradicted, but he tried not to let his impatience show. He knew he wasn't very skilled in conversation with women. He certainly didn't know how to woo the fairer sex, and he knew he was making a muck out of this discussion.

Why in God's name had Johanna been given the choice in the first place? Nicholas simply should have told her she was going to get married, and that would have been the end of it. This discussion shouldn't even be taking place. Damn it all, they should be in the middle of their wedding ceremony, exchanging their vows.

"I don't like timid women."

Johanna's shoulders straightened. "I'm not timid," she announced. "I've learned to be cautious, m'lord, but I have never, ever been timid."

"I see." He didn't believe her.

"I don't like big men, even handsome ones."

"You think me handsome?"

How had he managed to turn her words into a compliment? He seemed surprised, too, as though he really wasn't aware of his own appeal. "You misunderstand, sir," she told him. "Being handsome is a mark against you." She ignored his incredulous expression and repeated, "And I especially dislike big men."

She knew she sounded ridiculous. She didn't care. She wasn't about to back down now. She looked him right in the eye while she folded her arms across her middle and frowned up at him. Her neck was already getting a crick in it from looking up.

"What think you of my opinion, m'lord?"

The challenge was there in her stance and her tone of voice. She was bravely standing up to him now. He had the sudden urge to laugh again.

He sighed instead. "They're daft opinions," he told her, being as blunt as possible.

"Perhaps," she agreed. "But it doesn't change how I feel."

MacBain decided he had wasted enough time on the discussion. It was high time she understood what was going to happen.

"It's a fact you aren't leaving here. You're staying with me, Johanna. We're going to be married tomorrow. That isn't an opinion by the way. It's fact."

"You would marry me against my will?"

"I would."

Hell, she looked terrified again. That reaction didn't sit well with him. He tried to use reason once again to gain her cooperation. He wasn't an ogre after all. He could be reasonable.

"Have you changed your mind in the past few minutes and now want to go back to England? Nicholas told me leaving England appealed to you."

"No, I haven't changed my mind, but . . ."

"Can you afford to pay the fine your king demands to stay unwed?"

"No."

"Is it Baron Williams? Nicholas mentioned to me that the Englishman wanted to marry you." He didn't give her time to answer. "It doesn't matter. I won't let you leave. No other man is going to have you."

"I don't prefer Baron Williams."

"I take it from the disgust in your voice this baron is also a handsome giant?"

"He's handsome only if you find pigs attractive, m'lord, and he's a small man in size with an even smaller mind. He is completely unacceptable to me."

"I see," MacBain drawled out. "So you dislike both large and small men. Have I got that right?"

"You're making fun of me."

"No, I'm making fun of your daft statements. Nicholas is just as big as I am," he reminded her.

"Yes, but my brother would never hurt me."

The truth was out. She'd blurted out the words before she could stop herself. MacBain raised one eyebrow in reaction to the telling statement.

Johanna turned her gaze to the floor but not before he saw her blush.

"Please try to understand, Laird. If a pup bit me, I would have a fair chance of surviving, but if a wolf bit me, I don't believe I would have any chance at all."

She was trying so damned hard to be brave and failing miserably. Her terror was real and, Mac-Bain speculated, learned from past experiences.

Long minutes passed in silence. MacBain stared at her. She stared at the floor.

"Did your husband . . ."

"I will not talk about him."

He had his answer. He took a step toward her. She didn't back away. He put his hands on her shoulders and commanded her to look up at him. She took her time obeying.

His voice was a low, gruff whisper when he spoke. "Johanna?"

"Yes, m'lord?"

"I don't bite."

Chapter

4

They were married the following afternoon. MacBain agreed to wait that long so Father MacKechnie could prepare for the ceremony.

It was the only issue he was willing to bend on, however. Johanna wanted to return to the campsite and stay the night in her own tent near her brother, the priest, and her loyal men. Laird MacBain wouldn't hear of it. He ordered her to sleep in one of the newly built cottages along the hill, a tiny one-room affair with a single window and a stone hearth.

Johanna didn't see the laird again until the ceremony, nor did she see her brother until he came to collect her. MacBain had posted two guards outside her door. She was afraid to ask if the soldiers were there to keep outsiders from entering or to keep her from leaving.

She didn't get much sleep. Her mind raced from one worry to another. What if MacBain turned out to be like Raulf? Dear God, could she survive purgatory again? The possibility that she could be marrying another monster made her weep with self-pity. She was immediately ashamed of herself. Was she really such a coward after all? Had Raulf been right to ridicule her?

No, no, she was a strong woman. She could handle anything that came her way. She would not give into the fear or allow herself to have such low thoughts about herself. She had value, damn it . . . didn't she?

Johanna had believed her confidence in herself had returned after Raulf's death. For the first time in over three years, she lived without fear. Her days were filled with blissful peace. Even after King John had dragged her to his court, he left her alone in her own private chambers. No one bothered her. There was a garden directly outside her door. She spent most of her days there.

The peaceful interlude was over, however, and she was now being forced into another marriage. She was bound to disappoint the laird. And what would he do then? Would he try to make her feel ignorant and unworthy? By God, she wouldn't let that happen. Raulf's attacks had been so cleverly disguised, and she'd been so young and childishly naive, she hadn't realized until it was almost too late exactly what he was doing. It was a slow, insidious attack upon her character, relentless too, and it went on and on and on until she felt as though he'd sucked the very light out of her.

She tried to fight back then. And that was when the beatings began.

Johanna forced herself to block the memories.

She fell asleep praying for a miracle.

Nicholas came to get her during the nooning hour. He took one look at her pale face and shook his head.

"Have you so little faith in your brother's judgment? I have told you MacBain's an honorable man," he reminded her. "You have no reason to fear him."

She placed her hand on her brother's arm and walked by his side. "I do have faith in your judgment," she whispered.

Her voice lacked conviction, but he wasn't insulted. He understood her fear. The memory of seeing her battered face when he'd stopped to pay a visit, and Raulf hadn't had time to hide her away, instantly filled him with rage yet again.

"Please don't frown, Nicholas. I'm conquering my fear. It will be all right."

Nicholas smiled. He couldn't believe his sister was actually trying to comfort him now.

"Aye, your marriage will be all right," he said. "Do you know, if you would just look around you, you'd catch a glimpse of your future husband's character. Where did you sleep last night?"

"You know very well where I slept."

"It's a brand-new cottage, isn't it?"

He didn't give her time to answer. "I can see three others from here, all looking freshly built. The wood hasn't weathered yet."

"What is it you're trying to tell me?"

"A selfish man would consider his own comforts first, wouldn't he?"

"Yes."

"Do you see a new keep?"

"No."

"Calum is MacBain's first-in-command over the MacBain warriors, Johanna, and he told me the cottages are for the elderly in the clan. They come first, for they are most in need of warm fires and roofs over their heads at night. MacBain puts himself last. Think about that, Johanna. I found out there are two bedchambers on the east side above the stairs in the keep proper. Neither was disturbed by fire. Yet MacBain hasn't spent a single night there. He sleeps outside with the other soldiers. Doesn't that tell you something about the man's character?"

Her smile was all the answer he required.

The color came back into her face. Nicholas nodded with satisfaction.

They had almost reached the edge of the courtyard when they stopped to watch the crowd of men and women working to prepare for the ceremony. Since the chapel had been gutted by fire, the wedding would take place in the courtyard. A makeshift altar consisting of a wide, flat wooden board was propped on top of two empty ale barrels. A woman spread a white linen cloth over the board. Father MacKechnie waited until the covering was in place, then put a beautiful golden chalice and plate in the center. Two more women were kneeling on the ground in front of the barrels, arranging bouquets of flowers in front of the wood.

Johanna started walking forward again. Nicholas took hold of her hand to stop her.

"There is something more you need to know," he began.

"Yes?"

"Do you see the child sitting on the top step?"

She turned to look. A little boy, surely no more than four or five summers, sat all alone on the top step. His elbows rested on his knees, and his head was propped up by his hands. He was watching the preparations. He looked terribly unhappy.

"I see him," Johanna said. "He looks forlorn, doesn't he, Nicholas?"

Her brother smiled. "Aye, he does," he agreed.

"Who is he?"

"MacBain's son."

She almost toppled over. "His what?"

"Lower your voice, Johanna. I don't want anyone to overhear this conversation. The boy belongs to MacBain. There's speculation he might not be his son, of course, but MacBain has made it clear he accepts him."

She was too astonished to speak.

"His name's Alex," Nicholas remarked for lack of anything better to say. "I can tell I've given you a bit of a shock, Johanna."

"Why didn't you tell me sooner?" She didn't give him time to answer. "How long was MacBain married?"

"He wasn't."

"I don't understand . . ."

"Yes, you do. Alex is illegitimate."

"Oh."

She didn't know what to think about that. "The

boy's mother died during childbirth," Nicholas added. "You might as well know it all, sister. The woman was a camp follower. There are at least three other men who could claim the boy."

Her heart went out to the little one. She turned to look at him again. He was an adorable child with dark curly hair. From the distance separating them, she couldn't see the color of his eyes. She wagered they were gray, like his father's.

"Johanna, it's important for you to know MacBain acknowledges the boy as his son."

She turned to her brother. "I heard you both the first and the second time you mentioned that fact."

"And?"

She smiled. "And what, Nicholas?"

"Will you accept him?"

"Oh, Nicholas, how can you ask me such a thing? Of course I will accept him. How could I not?"

Nicholas let out a sigh. His sister didn't understand the ways of their harsh world. "It's a bone of contention among the Maclaurins," he explained. "MacBain's father was the Laird Maclaurin. He went to his deathbed without ever acknowledging his son."

"Then the man I'm marrying is also illegitimate?"

"Yes."

"Yet the Maclaurins made him their laird?"

Nicholas nodded. "It's complicated," he admitted. "They needed his strength. He does carry his father's blood, and they've conveniently forgotten

64

he was born a bastard. The boy, however . . ."

He didn't say another word. He would leave the conclusions to her. Johanna shook her head. "Do you suppose the little one's upset about the wedding?"

"It would appear he's upset about something."

Father MacKechnie drew their attention by waving to them. Nicholas took hold of Johanna's elbow and started forward. She couldn't take her gaze away from the child. Lord, he looked pitiful and lost.

"They're ready," Nicholas announced. "Here comes MacBain."

The laird walked across the courtyard and took his place in front of the altar. His hands were at his sides. The priest moved to stand next to him. He again motioned Johanna forward.

"I can't do this, not without . . ."

"It's going to be all right."

"You don't understand," she whispered, smiling. "Wait here, Nicholas. I'll be right back."

The priest waved to Johanna. She waved back, smiling. Then she turned around and walked away.

"Johanna, for the love of God . . ."

Nicholas was muttering to the air. He watched as his sister made her way around the crowd. When she headed for the steps, he finally understood what her errand was.

Nicholas turned his gaze to MacBain. His expression revealed nothing of his thoughts.

The priest craned his neck to watch Johanna,

then turned to MacBain and nudged him with his elbow.

Johanna slowed her pace when she neared the steps, for she didn't want the little one to run away before she got to him.

The news that MacBain had a son had filled her with joy and relief. Finally she had her answer to the question that plagued her. MacBain obviously didn't care she was barren because he already had an heir, illegitimate or not.

The guilt she'd been carrying dropped away like a heavy cloak from her shoulders.

MacBain couldn't contain his frown. Damn, he hadn't wanted her to find out about the boy until they were married and she couldn't change her mind. Women were peculiar in their attitudes, he knew, and he was certain he was never going to understand exactly how their minds worked. They seemed to take exception to such odd things. Most, he'd heard, didn't accept mistresses, and some of the wives of the other warriors he knew didn't acknowledge bastards. MacBain had every intention of forcing Johanna to acknowledge his son, but he'd hoped to get her settled in first.

Alex spotted her coming his way and immediately buried his face in his hands. He had skinny knees. They were caked with dirt. When he peeked up to look at her, she saw his eyes. They weren't gray like his father's, but blue.

Johanna paused on the bottom step and spoke to the child. MacBain started to go after his bride, then changed his mind. He folded his arms across his chest and simply waited to see what would happen. He wasn't the only one watching. Silence filled the courtyard as every MacBain and every Maclaurin turned to look.

"Does the boy understand English?" Father MacKechnie asked.

"Some," MacBain answered. "She told me you were instructing her in Gaelic. Has she learned enough to converse a bit with Alex?"

The priest shrugged. "Probably," he allowed.

Johanna talked to the child for several minutes. Then she reached out her hand to him. Alex jumped to his feet, tripped down the stairs, and put his hand in hers. She leaned down, brushed the hair out of his eyes, adjusted his plaid from drooping over his shoulders, and then pulled him along by her side.

"He understands that," MacKechnie whispered.

"What does he understand?" Calum asked.

The priest smiled. "Acceptance."

MacBain nodded. Johanna reached Nicholas's side and took hold of his arm again. "I'm ready now," she announced. "Alex, go and stand beside your father," she instructed. "It is my duty to come to the two of you."

The little boy nodded. He ran down the length of the path and took his place on his father's left. MacBain glanced down at his son. His expression was contained, and Johanna couldn't tell if he was pleased or annoyed. His gaze stayed on her, but once she started to walk toward him, he unfolded his arms and reached down to touch the top of his son's head.

Nicholas gave her away in marriage. She didn't resist when he placed her hand in MacBain's. He was damned proud of his sister. He knew she was nervous, but she didn't try to cling to his side. She was positioned between the two warriors, with her future husband on her right and her brother on her left. Johanna stood straight, held her head high, and looked straight ahead.

She was dressed in a white ankle-length chainse and matching knee-length bliaut. The square neckline of her wedding attire was embroidered with pale pink and green threads fashioned into the design of dainty rosebuds.

She smelled like roses, too. The scent was faint, yet vastly appealing to MacBain. Father MacKechnie took a small bouquet of flowers from the corner of the altar and handed it to her before hurrying around to the other side to begin the mass.

MacBain kept his gaze on his bride. She was an utterly feminine creature, and God's truth, he didn't know what he was going to do with her. His main worry was that she wouldn't be strong enough to survive such a harsh life. He forced the concern aside. It had become his duty to make certain she survived. He would protect her from danger, and if she needed to be pampered, then by God he would see she was pampered. He didn't have the faintest idea how, but he was an intelligent man. He would find out. He wouldn't let her dirty her hands either or do any backbreaking work, and he would demand she rest each and every day. Taking care of her was the very least he could do in appreciation for the land she'd given him, and surely that was the only reason he was worrying about her comforts now.

The wind blew a strand of hair in her face. She let go of his hand to brush the strand of hair back over her shoulder. It was a dainty, feminine action. The curly mass of gold seemed to float down her back. Her hand shook so hard that the nosegay she held against her waist was rapidly dropping petals.

When she didn't take hold of his hand again, he was so bothered that he grabbed her hand and hauled her up close to his side. Nicholas saw the possessive action and smiled.

The ceremony was going along quite nicely until Father MacKechnie asked her to promise to love, honor, and obey her husband. She considered his request a long minute. Then she shook her head and turned to the groom.

She motioned for him to lean down and stretched up on tiptoe so that she could whisper in his ear.

"I will try to love you, m'lord, and I'll certainly honor you because you'll be my husband, but I don't believe I'll obey you much. I've found that total submissiveness doesn't agree with me."

She was wringing the petals off the stems of her flowers while she explained her position. She couldn't look him in the eye either but stared at his chin while she waited for his reaction.

MacBain was too astonished by what she'd just said to him to notice how worried she was. He had to force himself not to laugh.

"Are you jesting with me?"

He hadn't whispered his question. Since he wasn't overly concerned about their audience overhearing their discussion, she wasn't going to be concerned either. Her voice was every bit as forceful as his had been when she gave him her answer.

"Jest with you during the middle of our wedding vows? I think not, m'lord. I'm very serious. Those are my conditions. Do you accept them?"

He did laugh then. He simply couldn't help himself. Her burst of courage was short-lived. She felt embarrassed and humiliated, but the issue was too important to let pass.

There was only one course of action left. She straightened her shoulders, jerked her hand away from his, and shoved the bouquet of flowers at him. Then she made a curtsy to the priest, turned around, and walked away.

The message was clear. Still, there were a few Maclaurin soldiers who were slow to catch on.

"Is the lass leaving?" Keith, the commander over the Maclaurin soldiers, whispered his question in a voice loud enough for everyone to hear.

"She's getting away, MacBain," another called out.

"It appears she is leaving," Father MacKechnie interjected. "Did I say something to displease her?"

70

Nicholas started to go after his sister. MacBain grabbed him by his arm and shook his head at him. He shoved the bouquet at the baron, muttered something under his breath, and then went after his bride.

She'd almost made it to the edge of the clearing before MacBain caught up with her. He grabbed her by her shoulders and turned her around. She wouldn't look up at him. He forced her chin up with his hand.

She braced herself for his anger. He would surely lash out at her. She was a strong woman, she reminded herself. She would withstand his wrath.

"Will you try to obey?"

He sounded exasperated. She was so astonished by his attitude she smiled. She wasn't such a weakling after all, she thought to herself. She had just stood up to the laird and forced him to negotiate. She wasn't certain she'd won much, but she definitely hadn't lost anything.

"Yes, I will try," she promised. "Upon occasion," she hastily added.

He rolled his eyes heavenward. He'd allowed quite enough time on the topic, he decided. He grabbed hold of her hand and dragged her back to the altar. She had to run to keep up with him.

Nicholas quit frowning when he spotted his sister's smile. He was highly curious to find out what the argument had been about, of course, but he thought he'd have to wait until the wedding ceremony was over before he could find out what happened.

71

He didn't have to wait after all. Johanna accepted the bouquet from her brother and turned back to the priest.

"Please forgive the interruption, Father," she whispered.

The priest nodded. He again asked her to love, honor, and obey her husband. He added the word *please* this time.

"I will love, honor, and try to obey my husband upon occasion," she answered.

Nicholas started laughing. He now understood what the argument had been about. The Maclaurins and the MacBains let out a collective gasp. They were horrified.

Their laird scanned his audience and glared them into silence. Then he turned his scowl on his bride. "Obedience and submissiveness aren't necessarily the same thing," he snapped.

"I was taught that they were," she defended.

"You were taught wrong."

His frown was frightening enough to start her fretting again. Dear God, she really couldn't go through with this. She didn't have the strength.

She shoved the bouquet of flowers at MacBain again and turned to leave. The laird slammed the flowers into Nicholas's outstretched hand and grabbed hold of Johanna before she could get away.

"Oh, no, you don't," he muttered. "We aren't going through this again."

To prove he meant what he'd just said, he threw his arm around her shoulders and anchored her into his side. "We're going to get this done before nightfall, Johanna."

She felt like a fool. The priest was staring at her with a look on his face that suggested he thought she'd lost her mind. She took a breath, accepted her flowers from her brother again, and then said, "Pray forgive me for interrupting you again, Father. Please continue."

The priest mopped his brow with his linen square, then turned his attention to the groom. Johanna barely paid attention to the priest's lecture on the merits of being a good husband. She was too busy trying to get past her embarrassment. She decided she was sick of worrying. Her decision was made, and that was that. She said a quick prayer and made up her mind to put her fears in God's hands. Let Him do the worrying.

It was a sound plan, she decided. Still, she wished He would give her a sign that everything really would turn out all right. That notion made her smile. She was being terribly fanciful. She was a woman, and, therefore, last in God's love, or so she'd been told over and over again by Bishop Hallwick. God certainly didn't have time to listen to her paltry concerns, and she was probably committing a sin of vanity just by hoping for any kind of sign.

She let out a little sigh. MacBain heard the sound and turned to look down at her. She smiled weakly up at him.

It was MacBain's turn to answer the priest's questions. He started with his name and title.

He was called Gabriel.

God had given her a sign. Johanna's eyes widened, and she thought her mouth might have dropped open.

She was quick to regain control of her emotions. Her thoughts weren't controlled, though. They raced with questions. Had his mother deliberately named him after the highest of angels, the most esteemed in God's love? Johanna remembered her religion lessons well about the archangel. He was known as the protector of women and children. She remembered the wonderful stories passed down through the generations from mother to child about the most magnificent of all the angels. Her own mother had told her Gabriel would always watch out for her. He was her own special archangel and was to be called upon for aid in the dead of night when nightmares came creeping into her dreams. The archangel was the champion of the innocents and the avenger of evil.

She shook her head. She was being overly romantic, that was all. There wasn't anything symbolic about her husband's name. His mother had probably been in a fanciful mood when he was born. There was also the possibility he was named after a relative, too.

She couldn't convince herself. Lack of sleep made her easy prey for such foolish thoughts, she supposed. Still, she had prayed for a miracle last night, and just minutes before she'd wished for a sign of some sort to let her know everything was going to be all right.

Johanna had seen a drawing a holy man had made in charcoal of Gabriel. She still remembered every detail of the rendering. The archangel had been depicted as a giant warrior with a gleaming sword in his hand. He had wings.

The man standing beside her didn't have wings, but he was certainly a giant warrior with his sword at his side.

And his name was Gabriel. Had God answered her prayer after all?

Chapter
5

His mama should have named him Lucifer. Johanna came to that conclusion by the end of the day. Barbarian or Savage would have been suitable alternative names, she thought to herself. Her husband had the devil inside him with his arrogant, high-handed orders. The man was also completely devoid of all civilized manners.

Didn't he know it wasn't polite to fight on his wedding day?

Oh, Gabriel started out pleasant enough. As soon as Father MacKechnie gave the final blessing and the mass was over, her new husband turned her to face him. He was handed a beautiful multicolored plaid. It matched the one he was wearing. He draped the long, narrow cloth over her right shoulder. A second plaid made with different tones was draped over her left shoulder. The first, her husband explained, was the MacBain plaid; the second, the Maclaurin. He waited until she nodded understanding, then pulled her into his arms and kissed the breath right out of her.

She had expected only a quick peck. She got ravaged. MacBain's mouth was hard and hot. The heat the passionate kiss sparked made her cheeks turn pink. She considered pulling away, then gave up the idea. The kiss became so consuming, she didn't have the strength or the inclination.

The laughter in the background finally caught Gabriel's attention. He abruptly ended the kiss, nodded with satisfaction when he saw the bemused expression on his bride's face, and then turned his attention to the priest.

She wasn't as quick to recover. She sagged into her husband's side.

Father MacKechnie hurried around the side of the altar to give his congratulations. "Well now, that was a fine wedding ceremony," he announced.

Alex wiggled his way between his father and Johanna. She felt him tugging on her skirts and smiled at the child.

The priest drew her attention again with a snort of laughter. "For a minute there, I didn't believe we'd get it done."

Both her husband and the priest looked at Johanna. She smiled back. "I never doubted," she remarked. "Once I make up my mind to do something, I get it done."

Neither man looked as though he believed the boast. The priest pulled Alex away from Johanna's skirts and moved him to stand on his father's left. "Shall we begin the receiving line?" he suggested. "The clan will want to come forward to offer their good wishes."

Gabriel continued to stare at his bride. He acted as though he wanted to tell her something but couldn't get the words out.

"Did you wish to say something to me, Gabriel?"

"Don't call me that. I dislike the name."

"But it's a fine name."

He grunted. She tried not to take exception to that rather barbaric sound. "You should be proud to have such a grand name."

He grunted again. She gave up. "What should I call you?" she asked him, trying to be accommodating.

"Laird," he suggested.

He didn't look like he was jesting with her. She wasn't about to agree with his suggestion. It was ridiculous for a husband and wife to use such formal names. She decided to use diplomacy to gain his cooperation, for she didn't believe defiance would work now.

"But when we're alone?" she asked. "May I call you Gabriel then?"

"No."

"Then what . . ."

"If you must address me, call me . . . call me MacBain. Aye, that name will do."

"If I must address you? Have you any idea how arrogant you sound?"

He shrugged. "No, but it's good of you to say I'm arrogant."

"No, it isn't."

He was through discussing the topic. "You were right to include the boy."

Because he'd sounded so gruff and because she was still reacting to the ludicrous suggestion that she call him MacBain, it took a full minute for her to realize he was actually thanking her.

She wasn't certain how to respond. She nodded, then said, "He should have had a proper bath before the ceremony."

MacBain tried not to smile. He really shouldn't let her get away with such open rebukes, but God's truth, he was so pleased to see she had some spirit inside her, he didn't chastise her.

"Next time I'll see that he does."

It didn't take any time at all for his barb to hit. The implication that he would marry again wasn't lost on her.

"You like having the last word, don't you, Laird?"

"Aye, I do," he admitted with a grin.

Alex, his father noticed, was staring up at Johanna with a look of rapture on his face. The priest had moved him to the side for the receiving line, but the boy had already squeezed himself next to Johanna again.

His bride had won over the boy in a matter of minutes. MacBain found himself wondering how long it would take him to win her affections. It was a foolish thought. Why did he care how she felt about him? The marriage had secured him the land, and that was all that mattered.

The soldiers from both clans came forward, one

by one, to introduce themselves to Johanna and to give their laird their congratulations. The women came forward next. One young red-haired lady who introduced herself as Leila from the Maclaurin clan handed Johanna a beautiful bouquet of purple and white flowers. She thanked the woman for her gift and thought to add the flowers to the nosegay she'd been gripping in her other hand. When she saw the mess she'd made of the flowers Father MacKechnie had given her, she burst into laughter. The flowers were gone. Had she been holding a bouquet of stems throughout the ceremony?

Alex was fidgety by the time the introductions were finished. The women hurried back and forth across the courtyard with trays of food to put out on the tables the men were assembling. Gabriel was deep in conversation with two Maclaurin soldiers.

Johanna turned to Calum and Keith. "There are six horses in the meadow below," she began.

"One's to be my very own," Alex blurted out.

MacBain heard his son's comment and turned back to look at Johanna. His smile was devilish. "So that is how you won him over," he remarked.

She ignored her husband and kept her attention on the soldiers. "They are my wedding gift to my husband . . . and Alex," she hastily included. "Will you please send someone to fetch them?"

The soldiers bowed and went to see the task completed. Alex tugged on the hem of Johanna's bliaut to get her attention.

"Did Papa give you a gift?"

His father answered his question. "Nay, I didn't, Alex."

She contradicted him. "Yes, he did, Alex."

"What did he give you?" the little boy asked.

MacBain was also curious to hear what she had to say. She was smiling at Alex.

"He gave me a son."

MacBain was taken aback by her declaration. His son wasn't certain what she'd meant.

"But I'm his son," he declared. He pointed at his chest so she would be sure to understand.

"Yes," Johanna answered.

The boy smiled. "Is a son better than six horses?"

"Of course."

"Better than even a hundred?"

"Yes."

Alex was convinced of his importance. His chest puffed up with pride.

"How old are you?" Johanna asked.

He opened his mouth to answer, then closed it again. From the puzzled look on his face, she assumed he didn't know. She turned to her husband to get her answer. He shrugged. He obviously didn't know either.

She was appalled. "You don't know your son's age?"

"He's young," MacBain answered.

Alex immediately nodded agreement over his father's announcement. "I'm young," he repeated. "Papa, could I go look at the horses?"

Gabriel nodded. His son let go of Johanna's bliaut and went chasing after Calum and Keith.

Father MacKechnie had witnessed the scene between the child and Johanna. "The lad's taken with her, isn't he?" he remarked to the laird as he watched Alex run across the yard.

"She bribed him," MacBain drawled out.

"Yes, I did," Johanna agreed.

"Men aren't so easily won over," her husband remarked.

"I'm not interested in winning any man over, Laird. Please excuse me. I would like to talk to my brother."

It was a wonderful dismissal, yet completely ruined when Gabriel grabbed hold of her hand and pulled her back.

Nicholas had to come to her. He was surrounded by women, of course, because of his handsome looks and his gift for charm, and Johanna had to wait several minutes before her brother noticed her motioning to him and disengaged himself from his admirers.

Nicholas addressed MacBain first. "I'll be sending men here in a month or two to help with the rebuilding."

MacBain shook his head. "You will not send any soldiers here. We'll kill them the minute they set foot on our land."

"You're a stubborn man, MacBain."

"How much was the fine you paid to your king?"

"What fine?" Johanna asked.

Both Nicholas and Gabriel ignored her question. Her brother gave MacBain the sum. Gabriel announced he would reimburse the baron for the expense.

Johanna finally caught on. She turned to her brother. "Do you mean to say our king made you pay a fine? Why, Nicholas?"

"Because we chose your husband, Johanna. He agreed . . . for a price."

"If I'd agreed to marry his choice?" she prodded.

"Williams?" Nicholas asked.

She nodded.

"Then there wouldn't have been a fine, of course."

"You lied to me. You told me you didn't have enough coins to loan me to pay the tax to John so I could remain free for one more year's time."

Nicholas let out a sigh. "I did lie," he admitted. "You were putting off the inevitable, and I was concerned about your safety. Damn it all, you were held prisoner in London. I couldn't be certain you'd be safe for long, and there was also the worry John might give the Maclaurin land to someone else."

She knew he was right. She knew he loved her, too, and was thinking only about her safety. "I forgive you your deception, Nicholas."

"Go home, Baron. Don't come back. You've done your duty. Johanna is my responsibility now."

Johanna was stunned by her husband's rudeness. "Now?" she blurted out. "You want him to go home now?"

"Now," her husband repeated.

"My brother . . ."

"He isn't your brother."

She was so outraged by his behavior, she felt like screaming. Her husband wasn't paying her any attention now. His gaze was directed on Nicholas.

"I should have known," he said. "You don't look like brother and sister, and when Johanna gave the priest her full name, I realized you weren't related. Your feelings for her —"

Nicholas wouldn't let MacBain continue. "You're very astute," he interrupted. "Johanna doesn't have any inkling, Laird. Leave it be."

"Laird . . ."

"Leave us, Johanna. This discussion doesn't concern you."

His tone of voice didn't suggest she argue. She started wringing the petals off the fresh bouquet while she looked at the grim expression on each man's face.

She didn't have to make up her mind to leave or stay. Father MacKechnie had heard enough to know a fight was brewing. He took hold of Johanna's arm, feigned enthusiasm, and said, "You'll be hurting the women's feelings if you don't taste their special dishes. Come along now. They'll fret until they get a wee bit of praise from their new mistress. Do you remember how to say thank you in Gaelic?"

The priest half-dragged, half-nudged her away from the two men. Johanna kept looking back over her shoulder to see what was happening. Nicholas looked furious. So did MacBain. Her husband, she noticed, was doing most of the talking. Nicholas happened to glance her way, noticed she was watching him, and then said something to MacBain. Her husband nodded. The two men turned and disappeared down the slope.

She didn't see either one of them again until the sun was fading from the sky. She let out a loud sigh of relief when she spotted her husband and her brother coming back up the hill. Streaks of orange from the sun's descent filled the sky behind them. Their silhouettes, made black by the distance and the sun's trickery, made them appear mystical. They seemed to rise out of the earth like mighty, invincible godlike warriors. They moved with such easy grace.

They were the fittest warriors she'd ever seen. The archangel Gabriel was surely smiling down at the pair. They were, after all, surely fashioned in his image.

Johanna smiled over her fanciful thoughts. Then she got a good look at their faces. She let out a horrified gasp. Nicholas had a bloody nose. His right eye was swollen shut. MacBain didn't appear to be in any better condition. Blood poured down from a cut high on his forehead. There was another cut seeping blood at the corner of his mouth.

She didn't know who to yell at first. She in-stinctively thought to run to Nicholas and give him holy hell while she measured the extent of his injuries, but by the time she'd lifted the hem of her skirts and started running, she realized she should probably go to Gabriel first. He was her husband now, and he should come first in her thoughts. There was also the fact that, if she was able to soothe his temper, he might be more willing to listen to reason and allow her brother to stay a few more days.

"You've been fighting."

She shouted the accusation when she reached her husband. He didn't believe he needed to agree. It was damned obvious they'd been fighting, and he didn't particularly care for the anger in her voice.

Johanna pulled the linen square she kept tucked in the sleeve of her gown and stretched up on tiptoe to pat the blood away from the cut so she could see how deep the injury was. She gently brushed his hair back, out of her way.

He jerked his head back. He wasn't used to anyone fretting over him, and he didn't know how to react.

"Do stand still, m'lord," she ordered. "I'm not going to hurt you."

MacBain stood still and allowed her to fuss over him. Damn, but she pleased him, though not because she was acting concerned about him now. Nay, it was the fact that she'd come to him first.

"Have you resolved whatever was bothering you?" she asked.

"I have," MacBain answered. He sounded surly.

She looked over at her brother. "And you, Nicholas?"

"Yes." His tone was every bit as irritated as her husband's.

She turned back to her husband. "Why did you deliberately provoke Nicholas? He is my brother, you know," she added with a nod. "My parents took him in when he was just eight years old. He was there when I was born and has been called brother by me from the moment I could speak. You owe him an apology, husband."

MacBain ignored her suggestion and grabbed hold of her wrist so she would stop poking at his cut, then turned to Nicholas.

"Say your good-byes now," he ordered. "You won't see her again."

"No!" Johanna cried out. She pulled away from her husband and ran to her brother. She threw herself into his arms.

"You didn't tell me the truth about him," she whispered. "He isn't a gentle man. He's hard and cruel. I can't bear the thought of never seeing you again. I love you. You protected me when no one else would. You believed in me. Nicholas, please take me home with you. I don't wish to stay here."

"Hush, Johanna. It's going to be all right. MacBain has good reason for wanting me and my men to stay away from here. Learn to trust him."

Nicholas held MacBain's gaze while he gave his sister his instructions.

"Why doesn't he want you to come back?"

Nicholas shook his head. His silence told her he wasn't going to explain. "What message would you like me to give Mother? I'll see her next month."

"I'm going home with you."

Her brother's smile was filled with tenderness. "You're married now. This is your home. You have to stay with your husband, Johanna."

She wouldn't let go of him. Nicholas leaned down, kissed her forehead, and then pulled her hands away from him. He gently nudged her toward her husband.

"Treat her well, MacBain, or by all that's holy, I'll come back here and kill you."

"That would be your right," MacBain answered. He walked past Johanna to slap his hand against Nicholas's. "You and I have come to an understanding. My word is my bond, Baron."

"As my word is my bond, Laird."

The two men nodded. Johanna stood there with tears streaming down her face as she watched her brother walk away. His mount had already been made ready for him. Nicholas gained his stallion's back, then rode down the hill and out of sight. He never looked back.

Johanna turned around and found that her husband had also left. She was suddenly alone. She stood at the edge of the clearing feeling as bleak and desolate as her surroundings. She didn't move until the sun had disappeared from the sky. The bone-chilling wind finally gained her attention. She shivered with the cold and rubbed her arms as she slowly made her way back to the courtyard. There wasn't a Scot in sight, or so she thought, until she reached the center of the clearing. She saw her husband then. He was leaning against the door to the keep, watching her.

Johanna wiped the tears away from her face, straightened her appearance, and hurried forward. She climbed the steps with only one intention. Childish though it probably was, she was determined to tell him how much she disliked him.

She never got the chance. MacBain waited until she was close enough, then pulled her into his arms. He held her tight against his chest, dropped his chin to rest on the top of her head, and hugged her.

The man was actually trying to comfort her. His actions thoroughly confused her. He had been the one, after all, to cause her this upset. Yet now he was trying to soothe her.

Damn it all, it was working. She knew she was overly exhausted from the long, difficult day, and surely that was the reason she didn't try to pull away from him. He was wonderfully warm; she told herself she needed his heat to chase away the cold. She was still going to give him hell, but she'd wait until she was warm first.

Gabriel held her for several minutes while he patiently waited for her to regain her composure.

She finally pulled away from him. "Your rudeness toward my brother made me most unhappy, m'lord."

She hoped for an apology. She realized after a minute of waiting, she wasn't going to get one.

"I would like to go to bed now," she announced. "I'm very sleepy. Would you please show me the way back to my cottage? I'm not certain where it is in the darkness."

"The cottage you slept in last night belongs to one of the MacBains. You won't sleep there again."

"Then where do I sleep?"

"Inside," he answered. "There are two chambers above the stairs. The Maclaurins were able to stop the fire before it reached the steps."

He pulled the door wide and motioned for her to go inside. She didn't move.

"May I ask you something, m'lord?"

She waited for his nod, then said, "Someday will you explain why you sent my brother away and ordered him never to return?"

"In time you'll understand," he answered. "But if you don't, I'll be happy to explain."

"Thank you."

"I can be accommodating, Johanna."

She didn't snort because it wouldn't have been ladylike. The look in her eyes told him she didn't believe him.

"I released your brother from a burden, wife."

"And I was his burden?"

Gabriel shook his head. "No, you weren't his burden," he answered. "Go inside now."

She decided to obey his command. The woman who had handed her the fresh bouquet of flowers after the wedding ceremony was standing at the foot of the stairs.

"Johanna, this is . . ."

She didn't let her husband finish. "Leila," she said. "Thank you again for the beautiful flowers. It was most thoughtful of you."

"You're very welcome, m'lady," the woman replied. She had a soft, musical voice and a pleasing smile. Her hair was as red as fire and every bit as mesmerizing. Johanna guessed her age to be near her own.

"Was it difficult for you to leave your family and friends to come here?" Leila asked.

"There were no friends close by," Johanna answered.

"What about your staff? Our laird surely would have granted you permission to bring your lady's maid."

Johanna didn't know how to answer the question. She barely knew her staff. Raulf had changed the household every other month. At first she believed he was just overly demanding. Later she caught on. He wanted to keep her isolated, without anyone to confide in. She was to depend only upon him. After his death, she'd been forced to London and hadn't formed any attachments while a prisoner in King John's court.

"I would not have allowed any other Englishwoman here," MacBain said when Johanna hesitated in giving her answer.

"They were content to stay in England," Johanna interjected.

Leila nodded, then turned and started up the steps. Johanna followed her.

"Do you think you'll be happy here?" she asked over her shoulder.

"Oh, yes," Johanna answered, praying she was right. "I'll be safe here."

MacBain frowned. Johanna had no idea how much that comment said about her past. He stood at the bottom of the steps, watching his bride.

Leila wasn't as astute as her laird. "But I asked you if you'd be happy," she said with a bit of laughter in her voice. "Of course you'll be safe here. Our laird will protect you."

She could take care of herself, Johanna thought. She didn't tell Leila that, however, for she didn't want the woman to think she wasn't grateful to have the laird's protection. She turned around to look at her husband.

"Good night, m'lord."

"Good night, Johanna."

Johanna followed Leila up the rest of the steps. The landing was partially blocked by a stack of wooden crates on the left so no one would pitch over into the great hall or the hallway below. A narrow corridor was on the opposite side. There were candles perched inside bronzed holders braced against the wall to light the way. Leila started telling Johanna about the keep and begged her to ask questions that came to mind. Another woman named Megan waited inside the first chamber with a bath ready for Johanna. She had dark brown hair and hazel eyes and also wore the

Maclaurin plaid. Her smile was just as inviting as Leila's.

Their easy acceptance of Johanna helped her relax. The bath felt wonderful. She told them how thoughtful they were to think she would enjoy the luxury.

"Our laird ordered the bath for you," Megan explained. "Since a MacBain gave up his bed for you last night, it was the Maclaurins' turn to do something for you."

"It was only fair," Leila added.

Before Johanna could ask what she meant by that remark, Megan turned the topic. She wanted to talk about the wedding. "You looked so beautiful, m'lady. Did you do the embroidery work on your dress? It was quite lovely."

"Of course she didn't do the work herself," Leila said. "Her maid . . ."

"But I did do the sewing," Johanna interjected.

The conversation continued all during her bath. Johanna finally bid the ladies good night and went down the hall to the second chamber.

The room was warm inside and very appealing. There was a hearth against the outside wall, a huge bed draped with the MacBain plaid along the opposite wall, and a window overlooking the meadow below. A thick fur covering on the window blocked the night winds, and that protection, added to the fire blazing away in the hearth, made the room most inviting.

The bed all but swallowed her up. She imagined four people could sleep under the covers together side by side without touching each other. Her feet were cold, but that was the only discomfort she felt. She considered getting out of her bed in search of a pair of woolen stockings, then decided the task would require too much effort. She probably should have taken the time to braid her hair, she thought with a loud yawn. It was going to be full of tangles in the morning. She decided she was too tired to care. She closed her eyes, said her prayers, and went to sleep.

The door opened just as she was drifting off. Her mind didn't register what was happening until she felt the side of the bed sag. She slowly opened her eyes. It was all right, she told herself. It was Gabriel and not an intruder sitting on the side of the bed.

He was taking his boots off. She tried not to be alarmed. "What are you doing, m'lord?"

Her voice was a groggy whisper. He looked over his shoulder to answer her. "I'm getting ready for bed."

She closed her eyes again. He thought she'd gone back to sleep. MacBain sat there staring down at her for several minutes. She rested on her side, facing him. Her hair, as golden as a sunset, was spread over her shoulders like a coverlet. She looked exquisite to him. Innocent and fragile as well. She was much younger than he'd supposed she would be, and after he and Nicholas had resolved their differences and the baron had wisely decided to obey his commands, he'd asked him exactly how old his sister was. Nicholas couldn't remember the date of her birth, but he'd said she'd been little more than a child when her parents received the order from King John to marry her to his favored baron.

Johanna suddenly bolted upright in the bed. "Here? You think to sleep here, m'lord?"

She'd choked on the question. He nodded, wondering why she looked so panic-stricken.

Her mouth dropped open. She was too stunned to speak. Gabriel stood up, untied the piece of leather holding his plaid in place, then tossed the strip of leather on the nearby chair. His plaid dropped to the floor.

He was stark naked. She squeezed her eyes shut. "Gabriel . . ." His name came out in a low whisper.

She'd closed her eyes, but not before she'd gotten a thorough look at his backside. It was enough to make her feel fainthearted. The man was bronzed from the sun from neck to ankles, and how in heaven's name was that possible? Did he walk around without a stitch on during the sunlight hours?

She wasn't about to ask him. She felt the covers being pulled back, then felt the sag of the bed again as he stretched out beside her. He started to reach for her.

She bounded to her knees and turned around to face him. He was on his back and hadn't bothered to cover himself. She grabbed hold of the blanket and fairly tossed it over his middle. She could feel her face burning with embarrassment.

"You've been tricked, m'lord. Aye, you have!" she blurted out in a near shout.

Gabriel didn't know what in God's name had come over her. She looked terrified. Her eyes filled with tears, and he wouldn't have been surprised if she'd burst into sobs.

"How was I tricked?" He'd deliberately kept his voice calm and low. He stacked his hands behind his head and acted as though he had all the time in the world to wait for her answer.

His casual attitude helped to calm her. She took a deep breath, then said, "My brother didn't tell you. He said he had explained . . . Oh, God, I'm so sorry. I should have made certain you knew. When I found out you already had a son, I thought you knew about me and that it didn't matter. You had an heir. You . . ."

Gabriel reached up and put his hand over her mouth. Tears were streaming down her face. He kept his voice soothing when he said, "Your brother's an honorable man."

She nodded. He removed his hand from her mouth, then gently tugged her down next to him. "Yes, Nicholas is an honorable man," she whispered.

The side of her face rested on his shoulder. He could feel her tears as they dropped on his skin.

"Nicholas wouldn't trick me."

"I didn't think he would." She sounded bewildered.

A long minute passed while he waited for her to tell him what was bothering her.

"Perhaps he forgot to tell you . . . or thought he had."

"What did he forget to tell me?"

"I cannot have children."

He waited for her to continue. "And?" he asked when she didn't say another word.

She'd been holding her breath, waiting for his reaction. She thought he'd be furious. He didn't appear to be, however. He was casually stroking her arm. An angry man wouldn't caress. He would strike.

Johanna decided he didn't understand. "I'm barren," she whispered. "I thought Nicholas told you. If you want the marriage annulled, I'm sure that Father MacKechnie will see to the petition."

"Nicholas did tell me, Johanna."

She bolted up in the bed again. "He told you?" She looked thoroughly confused. "Then why are you here?"

"I'm here because I'm your husband and this is our wedding night. It's a usual occurrence to share the bed."

"Do you mean you wish to sleep here tonight?"

"Damned right I mean to," he answered.

She looked incredulous now. "And every other night," he announced.

"Why?"

"Because I'm your husband," he explained.

He pulled her down next to him again, rolled to his side, and leaned over her. He gently brushed the hair away from the side of her face.

His touch was gentle and soothing. "Are you

here just to sleep, m'lord?"

"No."

"Then you wish to . . ."

"Yes," he said, irritated by how horrified she looked now.

"Why?"

She really didn't understand. His own observation soothed his pride, but he couldn't control his exasperation with her. "Johanna, weren't you married for three years?"

She was trying not to stare into his eyes. It was a difficult task. They really were quite beautiful. The color was the purest of gray. He had nice high cheekbones, too, and a straight nose. He really was a handsome devil, and even though she tried not to care, her heartbeat reacted to his nearness. It was racing now. His scent was appealing, too. He smelled clean, male. His hair was damp. Gabriel had had a bath before coming to bed.

She shouldn't have thought that was nice. She did, though. She really should get hold of her undisciplined thoughts. What he looked like or how he smelled shouldn't matter.

"Are you going to answer me before daylight?"

She remembered his question. "I was married three years."

"Then how can you ask me if I want to sleep with you?"

His confusion didn't make any sense to her. "For what purpose? I can't have your children."

"You've mentioned that," he snapped. "There's

98

another reason I want to bed you."

"What other reason?" she asked suspiciously.

"There's pleasure in the marriage act. Have you never experienced it before?"

"I don't know about pleasure, m'lord, but I'm most familiar with disappointment."

"Do you think I'll be disappointed, or do you believe you will be?"

"Both of us will be disappointed," she said. "Then you'll become angry. It's really for the better if you leave me alone."

He wasn't about to agree to that suggestion. She acted as though she had everything all figured out. He didn't need to ask where she'd gotten her opinions. It was apparent to him she'd been sorely mistreated by her first husband. She was so damned innocent and vulnerable. MacBain thought it a pity Raulf was dead. He would have liked to kill him.

He couldn't change the past for her, however. All he could do was concentrate on the present and their future together. He leaned down and kissed her brow. He was pleased to see she didn't flinch or try to turn away.

"Tonight is the first time for you —"

He was going to explain that it would be their first time together and that it would be a new beginning for both of them, but Johanna interrupted. "I'm not a virgin, m'lord. Raulf came to my bed many times during our first year as man and wife."

That statement caught his curiosity. He leaned

back to look at her. "And after the first year?"

"He went to other women. He was most disappointed in me. Aren't there any women you could go to?"

She sounded enthusiastic over the possibility. He didn't know if he should be insulted or amused. Most wives didn't wish to share their husbands. Johanna looked eager enough to run outside and recruit a mistress for him. Hell, she'd probably give up her side of the bed, too.

"I don't want any other women."

"Why not?"

She had the gall to look disgruntled. He was having difficulty believing this bizarre conversation. He grinned and shook his head. "I want you," he insisted.

She let out a sigh. "I suppose it's your right."

"Yes, it is."

He pulled the covers away. She jerked them back in place. "Just one moment please," she said. "I would like to ask you an important question before you begin."

He frowned over her request. She turned her gaze to his chin so he wouldn't see how frightened she was becoming as she waited for his agreement or his denial.

"What is your question?"

"I would like to know what will happen when you're disappointed." She dared a quick look up into his eyes, then hastily added, "I would like to prepare myself."

"I won't be disappointed."

100

She didn't look as though she believed him. "But when you are?" she persisted.

He held onto his patience. "Then I will have no one to blame but myself."

She stared at him a long minute before letting go of her death grip on the covers. While he watched, she folded her hands together on top of her stomach and closed her eyes. The look of resignation on her face made him shake his head in frustration.

It was inevitable, he supposed. Gabriel was going to get his way, and she was intelligent enough to know it.

She wasn't in a complete panic. She remembered the pain involved in the mating act; and although she certainly wasn't looking forward to the god-awful discomfort, it wouldn't be unbearable. It wouldn't kill her. She had gotten through the ordeal before, she reminded herself; she could get through it again. She would survive.

"All right, m'lord. I'm ready."

Lord, she was an exasperating woman. "Nay, Johanna," he countered in a low, gruff whisper.

He reached for the ribbon holding her gown in place and pulled the string free. "You aren't ready yet, but you will be. 'Tis my duty to make you want me, and I won't take you until you do."

She didn't show any outward reaction to his promise. God's truth, she looked as though she'd just been placed inside a wooden box. The only thing missing was a flower clutched between her rigid fingers, MacBain decided. Then he'd know for certain she was dead and about to be put in the ground.

He decided he was going to have to change his approach. His bride was alarmingly pale and as tense as the string on his bow right now. She was on guard against him. That fact didn't bother him overly much, for he understood her reasons, even if she didn't. He was going to have to wait until she had calmed down just a little. Then he would begin his gentle attack. His strategy wasn't complex. He was simply going to overwhelm her. Hopefully she wouldn't realize what was happening to her until it was too late. Her shields would be down; and once passion ignited, there wouldn't be much room in her mind for fear.

He'd already learned his bride was a gentle lady. The expression on her face when she'd been talking to his son before the wedding told him she was a compassionate, caring woman. He didn't know if she had a passionate nature, however, but he was determined to find out before either one of them left the bed.

MacBain leaned down, kissed her brow, and then rolled onto his back and closed his eyes.

Long minutes passed before she realized he was actually going to sleep. She turned to stare at him. Why had she been given this reprieve?

"Have I already disappointed you, m'lord?"

"No."

She continued to watch him, waiting for further explanation. He didn't say another word to appease her curiosity.

Not understanding his motives made her worry all the more. "What would you like me to do?" she asked.

"Take your shift off."

"And then?"

"Go to sleep. I won't touch you tonight."

His eyes were closed, and he, therefore, didn't see the change in her expression. He heard her sigh though, speculated it was due to relief, and couldn't help but become a little irritated with the woman. Hell, it was going to be a long, long night before he found satisfaction.

She couldn't make any sense out of his order. If he was going to leave her alone, why did he care if she wore a nightgown or not? Perhaps the command was just his way of saving face, she thought to herself. She wasn't about to argue with him, not now, not after she'd been given this wonderful gift.

Since his eyes were closed, she didn't have to concern herself with modesty. She got out of the bed, took her gown off, folded it neatly, then walked around to the other side of the bed to put the garment on the chair next to it. His plaid was on the floor. She picked it up, folded it, and put it on top of her nightgown.

The air inside the chamber had become frigid, and the floorboards were freezing cold against her bare feet. She hurried to get back under the covers before her toes turned to ice.

His heat drew her close to his side, but she was careful not to touch him. She turned on her side, giving him her back, and ever so slowly edged closer and closer to him.

It took her a long time to relax. She was afraid to trust him, yet afraid not to because he was now her husband and deserved her trust, until he'd proven he wasn't worthy, of course. Nicholas trusted him. Her brother was the most honorable man she'd ever known, save for her father. Nicholas was also an excellent judge of character. He wouldn't have suggested she marry the laird if he didn't believe Gabriel was a good, decent man. There was also the telling fact that her husband hadn't forced himself on her. Why, he was actually being very accommodating.

The heat from his body radiated against her back. It felt wonderful. She moved just a little bit closer until the backs of her thighs touched the tops of his. She was sound asleep minutes later.

Gabriel decided he was going to get a high place in heaven no matter how mortal his past sins were and all because of the consideration he'd shown his bride tonight. Anticipation made his forehead break out in a cold sweat. Rolling in hot coals wouldn't have been as painful as this wait, he decided. He believed he could endure any amount of physical pain, but lying next to her with lustful thoughts raging through his mind now made this night one hell of a challenge. She wasn't helping matters much. She kept pressing her backside up against his groin. It was the sweetest torture he'd ever experienced and he had to clench his jaw tight against the provocation.

The fire burned down to embers in the hearth and it was well after midnight before he decided he'd waited long enough. He put his arm around Johanna's waist and leaned down to nuzzle the side of her neck. She awakened with a start. She went completely rigid, but only for a minute or two, and then she put her hand on top of his where it rested just below her breasts. She tried to push his hand away. He wouldn't move. She was groggy from sleep, and the wet kisses he placed on her neck were actually making her shiver with heat, not cold. It felt too good to worry about. Just to make certain he didn't think he was going to be allowed any more liberties, however, she laced her fingers through his to keep his hand from moving.

He knew what her plan was. He wasn't deterred. He teased her earlobe with his teeth, then with his tongue while he gently disengaged his hand from her hold and slowly began to caress the undersides of her full breasts with his knuckles.

The sensations coursing through her body were extremely pleasant, surprising, too. Odd, but his touch made her restless for just a little more. His breath was sweet and warm against her skin. She instinctively tried to get away from him and yet tried to get closer at the same time. Her body was contradicting her mind. Until she felt the hard evidence of his arousal. A tremor of panic took hold. She turned to him. She was going to demand he keep his word. He had promised he wouldn't touch her tonight. Surely he hadn't forgotten.

"You promised you wouldn't touch me to-night."

He kissed the frown away from her brow. "I remember."

"Then . . ."

He kissed the bridge of her nose. Johanna suddenly found herself surrounded by his heat. He'd pinned her to the bed with his body and covered her from head to feet. His hard thighs rested between hers. His arousal was pressed intimately against the soft curls shielding the core of her femininity. The feel of his hard body against hers made her gasp with fear and pleasure.

"Gabriel . . ."

He threaded his fingers through her hair and cupped the sides of her face. He leaned down until he was just inches away from her. His gaze was settled on her mouth.

"It's past midnight, Johanna. I kept my word to you."

He didn't give her time to protest or panic. He silenced her with a kiss. His mouth was hard and hot as it settled on top of hers. His tongue swept inside to rid her of any argument she might have wanted to make.

Gabriel wanted her to forget her fears before her mind became ruled by them. No matter how much he wanted her, he knew he would never force himself on her. If Johanna couldn't get past her apprehensions tonight, then he would wait and try again tomorrow . . . and tomorrow . . . and tomorrow. In time she would surely learn to trust him and then hopefully rid herself of her own inhibitions.

The kiss wasn't tender, but ravenous and carnal. She wasn't resisting him and was, in fact, kissing him just as thoroughly. A low groan of pleasure sounded in the back of his throat when her tongue timidly brushed against his.

The sexy sound of approval made her a little bolder. She was so overwhelmed by her own reaction to the arousing loveplay, she could barely think. She rubbed her feet against his legs in a restless motion and tried to remember to breathe.

She tasted as good as he'd fantasized she would. His mouth slanted over hers again and again, and he didn't let up his assault against her defenses for a long while. He made love to her mouth with his tongue, slowly penetrating and then receding, forcing her to respond with his deliberate teasing.

He meant to overwhelm her, and overwhelmed she was. Within minutes she was trembling with desire. When his hands moved to her breasts and his thumbs brushed across her sensitive nipples, she let out a low moan of pleasure. She couldn't stop herself from arching up against his hands, deliberately trying to get a little more of his sweet torment.

He had to make her put her arms around him. Her hands were fists at her sides until he dragged his mouth away from hers and told her what he wanted her to do.

And still she didn't cooperate. He lifted his head

to look at her. He smiled with pure male satisfaction then. Johanna looked dazed by what was happening to her. There was passion in her eyes. He lowered his head again. He gave her another open-mouthed, tongue-dueling kiss just to let her know how pleased he was with her and then took hold of her hands and put them around his neck.

"Hold onto me," he commanded in a rough whisper. "Pull me close."

She had the grip of a warrior. Gabriel slowly kissed a path to her chest. He palmed her breasts with his hands, then leaned down to take one nipple into his mouth. Her nails raked his shoulders in reaction. He grunted with raw pleasure.

Gabriel had been in complete control of the loveplay; but when his hand slid down her flat, smooth, silky belly and moved lower to touch her intimately, and he began to caress the very heat of her, he lost his own composure. The folds hidden beneath her soft curls were slick, wet, and incredibly hot. His thumb rubbed across the sensitive nub of flesh as his fingers slowly penetrated her.

She cried out in fear now, for the intensity of the pleasure he forced on her was new, too frightening for her to understand or control. She tried to push his hand away, even as her body contradicted that action to move restlessly against him.

Dear God, she didn't know her own mind. "Gabriel, what is happening to me?"

Her nails dug into his shoulder blades and her

head rolled to the side as he continued his love-making. He shifted his position so he could soothe her with another kiss.

"It's all right," he whispered in a voice that sounded out of breath. "You like how this feels, don't you?"

He didn't give her time to answer him. His mouth took possession of hers again. His tongue moved inside just as his fingers plunged deep inside her tight sheath.

She came undone. Passion such as she'd never known before ignited in the pit of her stomach and spread like wildfire through her body. She clung to her husband, whimpering now, demanding with her slow, erotic movements to end the overwhelming bliss.

And still he held back. The pressure building inside him was almost unbearable. All he wanted to think about was sinking into her beckoning heat. He fought against the raging desire and continued to make love to her with his mouth and his fingers. When she suddenly tightened around him, he knew she was about to find her own release. He immediately shifted positions again so that his arousal was pressed against the opening of her sheath. He braced himself on his elbows, held her jaw with his hand, and demanded that she look at him.

"Say my name, Johanna."

His voice sounded harsh and angry. The intensity in his expression indicated his restraint.

"Gabriel," she whispered.

He kissed her quick and hard. He dragged his mouth away, looked down into her eyes, and demanded, "Now and forever. Say the words, wife. Say them now."

Every nerve in her body was screaming for release. He gripped her shoulders while he waited for her pledge.

"Now and forever, Gabriel."

His head dropped to her shoulder. With one powerful surge, he imbedded himself fully inside her. He was surrounded by liquid heat. Dear God, she was tight and so damned hot he could barely stand the sweet agony.

He couldn't stay still inside her, giving her body time to adjust to his invasion, and in the back of his mind was the worry he might be hurting her, yet he was powerless against the all-consuming demand of his own body now. His thrusts weren't measured but hard and urgent. She raised her knees to take him deeper inside. She surrounded him, squeezed him. He groaned with pure animal pleasure. It was exquisite agony. She became wild in his arms. She clung to her husband and met his demand by arching up against him. Her thighs tightened around him, and her whimpers, soft and incredibly sexy, drove him wild. He had never experienced such passion before. She held nothing back. Her complete surrender to him quickened his own. He didn't want it to be over. He slowly withdrew until he'd almost become separate from her, then sank back again.

Gabriel was mindless now to everything but

110

giving her fulfillment and finding his own. His breathing was harsh and choppy, and when he felt the tremors of her climax and heard her call his name with a mixture of wonder and fear, he couldn't hold back any longer. He poured his seed into her with a loud, lusty groan.

Johanna's body seemed to splinter apart with her orgasm. She thought she'd died. Never in her wildest imaginings could she have thought such bliss was possible. It was the most shattering and wondrous of experiences.

She had actually allowed herself the freedom to give herself completely to Gabriel, and dear Lord, her reward had been most astonishing. Her husband had held her close and kept her safe during the raging storm, and the sheer beauty of their lovemaking made tears come to her eyes.

She was too exhausted to weep. He had certainly drained her of her strength. He collapsed on top of her. She thought that she might have taken all of his strength, too. Yet his weight didn't crush her. She realized then his arms were still braced at her sides. As physically spent as he appeared to be, he still sought to protect her.

The scent of their lovemaking filled the air around them. Their heartbeats pounded frantic beats.

Gabriel was the first to recover. His immediate concern was for his wife. God, had he hurt her?

"Johanna?" He forced his strength back into his arms and lifted himself up so that he could look at her. The concern in his expression was evident. "Did I . . ."

Her laughter stopped his question. There was such joy in the sound, he couldn't help but smile in reaction.

"Aye, you did," she whispered.

The woman was a puzzlement to him. "How can you laugh and cry at the same time?"

"I'm not crying."

He brushed his fingertips across one cheekbone to wipe the wetness away. "Aye, you are crying. Did I hurt you?"

She slowly shook her head. "I didn't know it could be like this between a man and a woman. It was very beautiful."

Those words made him nod with arrogant satisfaction. "You're a passionate woman, Johanna."

"I never knew I was . . . not until tonight. Gabriel, it was most enjoyable. You made me . . ."

She couldn't come up with the right word to describe how she'd felt. He was happy to supply it for her. "Burn?"

She nodded. "I didn't realize some husbands liked to kiss and caress before mating," she said.

He leaned down, kissed her mouth, and then rolled onto his back, away from her. "It's called preparation, wife."

"It's nice," she whispered with a sigh. Raulf's idea of preparation was to pull the covers back. Johanna immediately blocked the memory. She didn't want to mar the beauty of what had just happened with ugly pictures from the past.

She didn't want Gabriel to go to sleep. God's truth, she wanted him to make love to her again.

She couldn't believe her own boldness and had to shake her head over her own surprisingly wanton behavior.

Johanna pulled the covers up and closed her eyes. An unsettling thought began to nag her. Now that they had mated, shouldn't one of them leave? Raulf had always come to her bed, and, after he'd finished with her, immediately left. Since Gabriel was acting as though he was going to sleep, she decided it was her duty to leave him.

She wanted to stay, but the thought of being ordered to leave would sting her pride. It was better not to give him the chance to order her to go, she supposed. Johanna battled with the worry for several minutes.

Gabriel was having disconcerting thoughts of his own. His cunning plan to overwhelm his bride while her defenses were down had been turned around on him. Hell, she'd overwhelmed him. He'd never lost his discipline so thoroughly with any other woman, never, ever felt this vulnerable, and he began to wonder what she would do if she knew she had such power over him. He scowled just thinking about it.

Johanna moved to the side of the bed. She reached for her robe before she stood up. She kept her back to her husband while she put the garment on. Her shoes, she remembered, were near the door.

And still she hesitated to leave. She couldn't understand her own mind. She felt miserable now and lonely, and she couldn't imagine why she wanted to weep. Their lovemaking had been wonderful, yet now she was filled with new uncertainty. Nay, she didn't understand this change in her, but she imagined she would have the rest of the dark hours to think about it. She doubted she would get any sleep, and by morning light she would have worked herself up into a state of exhaustion.

Gabriel looked as though he'd already gone to sleep. She tried to be as quiet as possible as she made her way to the door. She was just reaching for the latch when he stopped her.

"Where do you think you're going?

She turned to look at him. "To the other chamber, m'lord. I assumed that was where you wanted me to sleep."

"Come back here, Johanna."

She slowly walked back to his side of the bed. "I didn't mean to wake you."

"I wasn't asleep."

He reached for the belt of her robe. His voice sounded only mildly curious when he asked, "Why do you want to sleep alone?"

"I don't want to," she blurted out.

He used the sleeves of her robe to pull the garment off. She was shivering with the cold. That observation amused him. He thought it was damned hot in the chamber. He pulled the cover back then and simply waited for her to get into bed again.

She didn't hesitate. She climbed over her husband. Gabriel put his arms around her and pulled her close. The side of her face rested on his shoulder. He pulled the covers up, let out a loud yawn, and then said, "You will sleep in this bed with me every night. Do you understand, Johanna?"

She bumped his chin when she nodded. "Is it usual in the Highlands for husbands and wives to sleep together?"

He gave her a roundabout answer. "It's going to be usual for you and me."

"Yes, m'lord."

Her whispered agreement, given so quickly, pleased him. He tightened his hold on his bride and closed his eyes.

"Gabriel?"

He grunted his reply.

"Are you pleased you married me?"

She was sorry she'd asked the question the minute the words were out of her mouth. Now he would know how vulnerable she was feeling and how horribly insecure she really was.

"The land belongs to me now. That pleases me."

He was a brutally honest man. She thought she should probably admire that trait. She didn't though, not tonight. She decided she wanted him to lie to her and to tell her he was happy to have her for his wife. God, she was becoming daft. She didn't want to be married to a man who would blatantly lie to her. No, of course she didn't.

She knew she wasn't making any sense. Surely exhaustion was the reason she was having such foolish, unimportant thoughts. What did she care if he wanted her or not? She had gained exactly what she had set out to gain when she married him. She was free from King John's tentacles. Yes, she was free . . . and safe.

She had gotten exactly what she'd bargained for, and so had he. The land now belonged to him.

"You're too soft. I should have preferred a strong, tough-skinned woman."

She was almost asleep when she heard his comment. Since she didn't know what to say in reply, she kept silent.

Another minute passed before he spoke again. "You're too tender for life here. I doubt you'll survive a full year. I probably should have preferred a more robust, unemotional woman. Aye, you won't last a full year here."

He didn't sound particularly disturbed by that possibility. She tried not to take exception. She wasn't going to try to talk him out of his opinions either. Arguing that she was indeed a very strong woman with every bit as much endurance as any of the Highland women would have been useless. Gabriel had already formed his opinions and only time together would prove to him she wasn't a summer flower. She really did have stamina. She had already proven to herself she was a survivor. In time she would prove it to him.

"You're a timid lass. I probably should prefer a woman who was more forceful."

It took a supreme act of will to keep silent. She had asked him one simple question. A quick yes or no would have been sufficient answer. He seemed to be taking delight in listing her faults though. She could hear the laughter in his voice. Her husband, she was learning, was a bit rude.

"You have daft opinions. I should probably prefer a wife who always agreed with me."

She started drumming her fingers in irritation on his chest. He put his hand on top of hers to stop the telling action.

Johanna let out a loud yawn. It was a deliberate hint for him to let her go to sleep. A thoughtful husband would have ceased his litany of insults immediately.

Gabriel wasn't particularly thoughtful. "The least little thing frightens you," he remarked, remembering the expression on her face when she had first seen his wolfhound. "I should probably prefer a woman my hound would be afraid of," he added.

The heat radiating from his body made her drowsy. She draped one of her legs over his thighs and scooted closer.

"You're too thin by half," Gabriel said then. "The first northern wind will blow you over. I should probably prefer a big, strapping woman."

She was too sleepy to debate with her husband. Outrage took too much concentration. Johanna fell asleep listening to her husband as he continued to list her countless flaws.

"You're terribly naive, wife," he said when he remembered she had told him the year-round warm climate appealed to her. She had believed her brother's outrageous lie.

"Aye, you're naive all right," he said again.

Long minutes passed before Gabriel decided to finally answer her question.

"Johanna?"

She didn't answer him. He leaned down, kissed the top of her head, and then whispered, " 'Tis the truth, I am pleased I married you."

Chapter

6

Johanna awakened to the sound of pounding. A crash followed. She thought the roof had caved in. She bolted up in the bed just as the door opened. Gabriel walked inside. She grabbed hold of the covers and pulled them up to cover her chest.

She knew she looked a sight. Her hair hung down over her face, obstructing her view. She clutched the covers with one hand and brushed her hair back over her shoulders with her other hand.

"Good morning, Laird MacBain."

He found her attempt at modesty amusing, considering the fact that he'd stroked every inch of her body during the night. She was blushing, too.

"After last night, I don't believe you need to be embarrassed with me, Johanna."

She nodded. "I will try not to be embarrassed," she promised.

Gabriel walked over to the foot of the bed. He clasped his hands behind his back and frowned at her.

She smiled back.

"It isn't morning," he announced, "but after-noon."

Her eyes widened in surprise. "I was exhausted," she blurted out in defense of having slept half the day away. "I'm usually awake at dawn, m'lord, but the journey here was very tiring. What is that pounding noise I'm hearing?" She added the question in an attempt to turn the topic away from her laziness.

"The men are working on the new roof above the great hall."

He noticed the dark circles under her eyes. Her skin was pale. He was sorry he'd awakened her. Then the hammering started again, and he realized that noise would have shaken her awake anyway. Gabriel decided he shouldn't have allowed the work on the roof to begin today. His bride needed rest, not distraction.

"Was there something you wanted, m'lord?"

"I wanted to give you your instructions."

She smiled again, an indication, she hoped, of her willingness to take on whatever duties he wanted to give her.

"Today you will wear the MacBain plaid. Tomorrow you will switch to the Maclaurin colors."

"I will?"

"You will."

"Why?"

"You're mistress here over both clans and must try not to slight either faction. It would be an insult if you wore my colors two days in a row. Do you understand?"

He believed he'd been very specific. "Nay," she replied. "I don't understand. Aren't you laird over both clans?"

"I am."

"So you are, therefore, considered everyone's leader?"

"That is so."

He sounded terribly arrogant. He looked arrogant, too. His presence was . . . commanding. He fairly towered over the bed. And yet he'd been so incredibly gentle last night. The memory of their lovemaking made her sigh.

"Now do you understand me?" he asked, perplexed by the wide-eyed stare she was giving him.

She shook her head, trying to clear her thoughts. "No, I still don't understand," she confessed. "If you're . . ."

"It isn't your place to understand," he announced.

She hid her exasperation. He seemed to want her agreement. He wasn't going to get it. She simply continued to stare at him and wait for his next outrageous remark.

"There is one more instruction I would give you," Gabriel said. "I don't want you to concern yourself with work of any kind. I want you to rest."

She was certain she hadn't heard him correctly. "Rest?"

"Yes."

"In heaven's name why?"

He frowned over her incredulous expression. It

was apparent to him why she should rest. Still, if she needed to hear his reason, he would give it.

"It's going to take you time to recover."

"Recover from what?"

"From your journey here."

"But I've already recovered, m'lord. I slept the morning away. I'm fully rested now."

He turned to leave. "Gabriel?" she called out to stop him.

"I asked you not to call me by that name."

"Last night you demanded I say your name," she reminded him.

"When?"

She immediately started blushing. "When we were . . . kissing."

He remembered. "That was different," he told her.

"What was? Kissing me or demanding I say your name?"

He didn't answer her.

"Gabriel is a fine name."

"I am through discussing this," he announced. She didn't know what to make of his behavior. She decided to put the matter of his name aside for the moment. He was reaching for the door latch and she wanted to ask him something before he left. "May I go hunting this afternoon?"

"I've just explained I want you to rest. Don't make me repeat myself."

"But you aren't making any sense at all, m'lord."

He turned around and walked back to the side

of the bed. He looked irritated, but only mildly so.

He didn't intimidate her. The realization popped into her mind all at once. She smiled in reaction. She didn't understand why she felt that way, but she did. She was actually speaking her mind, too, and that was a pleasant first in a long, long while. It felt . . . liberating.

"I've already explained I've recovered from my journey here," she reminded him.

He clasped her jaw in his hand and tilted her head back so she would have to look into his eyes. He almost smiled when he saw how disgruntled she looked.

"There is another reason I want you to rest," he announced.

She gently nudged his hand away. She was getting a crick in her neck looking up at him. "And what might your reason be, m'lord?"

"You're weak."

She shook her head. "You mentioned that opinion last night, husband. It wasn't true then and it isn't true now."

"You are weak, Johanna," he repeated, ignoring her protest. "It's going to take you time to build up your strength. I'm aware of your limitations, even if you aren't."

He didn't give her time to argue over his decision. He leaned down, kissed her, and then left the chamber.

As soon as the door closed behind him, she threw off the covers and got out of bed.

How could her husband form such unbending opinions about her character so quickly? He couldn't possibly know her limitations. He hadn't known her long enough. It was unreasonable for him to draw any conclusions about her.

Johanna continued to think about her husband while she washed and dressed. Father MacKechnie had explained what she would be expected to wear underneath the plaid. She put on the Highland dress, a white long-sleeved underblouse and skirt, then donned the MacBain plaid. She fashioned perfect pleats around her waist, tossed one end of the long strip of material over her right shoulder so the plaid would cover her heart, and secured the garment with a narrow brown leather belt.

She thought about unpacking her bow and arrows and ignoring her husband's command altogether, then changed her mind. Open defiance probably wouldn't sit well with Gabriel. She had already learned he was a proud man, and she didn't believe she could achieve anything by challenging his decision.

Still, there was always more than one way into a castle. Her mother used to whisper that reminder to Johanna when she argued with her father. Johanna's mother was a wise woman. She was loyal to her husband, of course, but over the years she had learned how to get around his stubborn moods. Johanna had learned from her mother's example. The dear woman was full of clever sayings she'd passed down to her daughter. She never tried to manipulate her husband, she explained, for manipulating would be dishonorable, and the end, after all, didn't always justify the means. She was very clever, though, and usually found a way to placate everyone in her household.

Unbeknownst to her mother, Johanna's father frequently took her aside when she was bickering with her mother as well. He too had advice to give regarding the delicate methods he employed to get along with his wife when she was in one of her stubborn moods. Johanna's mother's suggestions made far more sense than her father's recommendations. She learned something more important from her father, however. He loved his wife and would do anything in his power to make her happy. He just didn't want his wife to know it. The two of them played a game of sorts where both were the victors. Johanna thought their marriage a bit strange, but they had been very happy together, and she thought that was all that mattered.

Johanna only wanted to live a quiet, peaceful life. In order to achieve her goal, she would simply make certain she stayed out of her husband's way. She wouldn't interfere in his affairs, and she would definitely try to get along with him. In return, she expected him to try to get along with her and stay out of her way. After her years with Raulf, Johanna believed with all her heart that being left alone would make her happy.

She turned her attention to straightening up the chamber. She made the bed, swept the floor, unpacked her clothes and put them away in the chest, and then tucked her three satchels under the bed. She was in a hurry to get outside, for it had turned out to be a glorious day. When she tied the fur covering back from the window, sunlight flooded the chamber. The scent of the Highlands filled the air. The view was breathtaking. The meadow below was as green as emeralds. The hills beyond were thick with giant pine and oak trees. Splashes of color dotted the landscape; red, pink, and purple wildflowers clustered together along a winding path that seemed to lead all the way to heaven.

After eating a small meal, Johanna decided to take little Alex with her on a walk across the meadow and up the path beyond. She would gather a skirt full of flowers to put on the mantel.

Finding the little boy turned out to be quite a challenge. She went downstairs and stood at the entrance to the great hall, waiting for one of the soldiers to notice her. There were four men tearing at the far wall and another three high up on the roof, working on the slats.

Everyone seemed to notice her at once. The pounding stopped. Since they were all staring at her, she made a curtsy in greeting before asking if they knew where Alex might be.

No one answered her. She was feeling extremely selfconscious. She repeated her question but kept her gaze centered on the soldier standing in front of the hearth. He smiled, scratched his beard, and then shrugged at her.

Finally Gabriel's first-in-command explained. "They don't understand you, m'lady."

She turned to the soldier and smiled. "They speak only Gaelic, m'lord?"

"Aye," he answered. "They speak only Gaelic. Please, you needn't call me your lord. I'm only a soldier here. Calum will do."

"As you wish, Calum."

"You're a bonny lass, wearing our plaid."

He seemed embarrassed giving her that compliment. "Thank you," she answered, wondering what the word *bonny* meant.

She turned back to the men watching her and asked them her question in Gaelic. She frowned with concentration. The language was difficult, tongue twisting in fact when she was so nervous inside, but when she'd finished her question, only one of the older men openly winced. The others smiled.

Still no one answered her. They all turned to stare at the hem of her gown. She looked down to see if something was amiss. Then she turned to Calum, hoping for an explanation. His eyes, she noticed, sparkled with amusement.

"You asked them if they'd seen your feet, m'lady."

"I meant to ask if they'd seen Gabriel's son," she explained.

Calum gave her the proper word to use. She again turned and repeated her question.

The men shook their heads. She thanked them for their attention and turned to leave. Calum hurried ahead of her to open the door.

"I must work on my accent," she announced.

"I could tell from that one gentleman's expression I was making a muck of it."

Aye, she was making a muck of it, Calum thought to himself. He wasn't about to agree, however, because he didn't want to injure her feelings.

"The men appreciate the fact that you're trying, m'lady."

"It's the burr, Calum," Johanna decided. "I haven't quite captured it yet. It's a very challenging language," she added. "You could be a help if you would."

"How?" he asked.

"From this moment on, speak only Gaelic when you address me. I believe I'll catch on much quicker if your language is all I hear."

"Certainly," Calum agreed in Gaelic.

"Excuse me?"

"I said certainly, m'lady," Calum explained.

She smiled. "Have you seen Alex?"

He shook his head. "He might be down at the stables," he said. He spoke in Gaelic and pointed in the direction of the stables in an attempt to help her guess what he'd just said.

Because she was concentrating on interpreting what he was saying to her, she barely paid any attention to what was going on in the courtyard. There were soldiers everywhere, but she didn't notice what they were doing.

She finally figured out what Calum had said, blurted out her thank you, and went running across the yard.

She suddenly found herself in the middle of a

sparring exercise. Calum grabbed her by her shoulders and pulled her back just in the nick of time. A lance nearly sliced her down the middle.

One of the Maclaurin soldiers let out a loud expletive. Gabriel had been watching the sparring from the opposite side of the yard. He saw his wife's near miss and immediately shouted a halt to the training session.

Johanna was horrified by her own behavior. Such inattention was shameful. She picked up the lance the soldier had dropped and handed it to the man. His face was flaming red. She didn't know if he was embarrassed or furious.

"Pray forgive me, sir. I wasn't watching where I was going."

The dark-haired soldier gave her a quick nod. Calum still had his hands on her shoulders. He gently tugged her back.

She turned to thank him for his quickness in coming to her aid. She spotted her husband coming her way. Her smile faltered when she took in the look on his face.

The soldiers were all staring at her. The MacBain warriors were smiling. The Maclaurins were frowning.

That mixed reaction confused her. Then Gabriel was standing in front of her, blocking her view. His attention was centered on Calum. He didn't say a word, just frowned at the soldier. Johanna realized Calum still had hold of her. The minute the soldier released his grip, his laird turned his attention and his scowl on her.

Her heart started pounding with her fear. She desperately tried to hold onto her composure. She wasn't about to let him know how frightened she was.

She decided not to give him time to berate her. "I was very inattentive, m'lord, sinfully so. I could have been killed."

He shook his head. "You could not have been killed. You insult Calum by suggesting he would have allowed you injury."

She wasn't going to argue with her husband. "I meant no insult," she said. She turned to Calum. "Please accept my apology. I wished to soften my husband's anger with me by being the first to acknowledge my foolishness."

"Do you have a problem with your sight?" Gabriel asked.

"No," she answered.

"Then why in God's name didn't you see my men were fighting with weapons?"

She mistook his exasperation for anger. "I have explained, m'lord. I wasn't paying attention."

Her husband didn't show any reaction to her explanation. He simply continued to stare at her. He was waiting for his temper to calm. Seeing his wife come so close to death had frightened the hell out of him. It was going to take him a long while to get over it.

A full minute passed in silence. Johanna thought her husband was considering her penance.

"I apologize for interrupting your important work," she said. "If you wish to strike me, please do so now. The wait is becoming unbearable."

Calum couldn't believe what he'd just heard. "M'lady . . ."

He was stopped from saying more when Gabriel raised his hand for silence.

The second his hand moved, she backed up. It was a protective action learned from past lessons. She realized what she was doing and immediately moved forward again.

Her husband had best understand she wasn't going to let the past repeat itself. "I would warn you, m'lord. I cannot stop you from striking me, but the minute you do I'll leave this holding."

"Surely you cannot believe our laird would . . ."

"Stay out of this, Calum."

Gabriel gave his command in a hard voice. He was furious over the insult his wife had just given him, but damn it all, the fear was real. He had to remind himself that she didn't know him well and, therefore, had only jumped to the wrong conclusions.

He took hold of Johanna's hand, started up the steps, then heard the pounding and immediately changed directions. He wanted privacy for this important discussion.

She tripped over the step when her husband turned, righted herself, and hurried to keep up. Calum shook his head as he watched his laird drag his mistress behind him. It wasn't Lady Johanna's awkwardness that caused him to frown but the paleness that had come over her complexion. Did she believe her laird was going to take her someplace private so he could beat her without an audience?

Keith, the red-haired leader of the Maclaurin soldiers, walked over to stand next to Calum. "What has you frowning?" he asked.

"Lady Johanna," Calum answered. "Someone has filled her head with dark tales about our laird. I believe she's afraid of him."

Keith snorted. "Some of the women are already saying she's afraid of her own shadow. They've given her a nickname," he added. "After just one look at her, they're calling her Courageous. 'Tis a pity, their mockery, for they're judging her without giving her a fair chance."

Calum was furious. In calling her Courageous, they, of course, meant just the opposite — they believed her to be a coward. "MacBain better not hear of this," he warned. "Who started this blasphemy?"

Keith wasn't about to give him the name. The woman was a Maclaurin. "Who it was isn't important," he argued. "The name caught on. The way Lady Johanna trembled at the sight of the laird's hound started some of the women smirking, and the frightened look in her eyes each time MacBain spoke to her made them conclude she was . . ."

Calum interrupted him. "She's timid, perhaps, but certainly not a coward. You'd best put the fear of God in your women, Keith. They think they're so damned clever with their game. If I hear the name from any Maclaurin, I'll retaliate."

132

Keith nodded. "It's easier for you to accept her," he said. "But the Maclaurins aren't so forgiving. Remember, it was her first husband who destroyed all we'd worked so hard to build. It's going to take time for them to forget."

Calum shook his head. "A Highlander never forgets. You know that as well as I."

"Then to forgive," Keith suggested.

"She had nothing to do with the atrocity done here. She doesn't require anyone's forgiveness. Remind the women of that important truth."

Keith nodded agreement. He didn't believe his reminder would make much difference, however. The women were set against her, and he couldn't imagine what he could say to change their opinions.

Both warriors kept their gazes on their laird and his bride and watched until they disappeared down the hill.

Gabriel and Johanna were quite alone now, but he still didn't stop. He continued walking until they reached the meadow. He wanted to rid himself of his anger before he talked to her.

He finally stopped. Then he turned to look at her. She wouldn't look at him. She tried to tug her hand away from his, but he wouldn't let go of her.

"You've given me a grave insult by suggesting I would harm you."

Her eyes widened in surprise. He sounded furious enough to kill someone. Yet he felt injured that she thought he would strike her.

"Have you nothing to say to me, wife?"

"I interrupted your training session."

"Yes, you did!"

"I almost caused a soldier to harm me."

"Yes!"

"And you appeared to be very angry."

"I was angry!"

"Gabriel? Why are you shouting?"

He let out a sigh. "I like to shout."

"I see."

"I had thought that in time you would learn to trust me. I have changed my mind. You will trust me," he commanded. "Starting now, this minute."

He made it sound so simple. "I do not know if that is possible, m'lord. Trust must be earned."

"Then decide now that I've earned it," he ordered. "Tell me you trust me, and mean it, damn it."

He knew he was asking the impossible. He sighed again. "No man is allowed to beat his wife here. Only a coward would mistreat a woman, Johanna. None of my men are cowards. You have nothing to fear from me or anyone else here. I will forgive you your insult because you didn't understand. I will not be as tolerant in future. You would do well to remember that."

She stared into his eyes. "But if I do insult you in future? What would you do?"

He didn't have the faintest idea, but he wasn't about to admit it. "It will not happen again."

Johanna nodded. She started to turn around to go back to the courtyard, then changed her mind.

134

Her husband deserved an apology. "Sometimes I react before I have had time to think it through. Do you understand, m'lord? It seems to be instinctive. I really will try to trust you, and I thank you for your patience."

He could tell from the way she was wringing her hands together that her confession was difficult for her. Her head was bowed and her voice sounded with bewilderment when she added, "I don't understand why I expect the worst. I never would have married you if I'd believed you would mistreat me, yet there seems to be a tiny part of me that has difficulty believing."

"You please me, Johanna."

"I do?"

He smiled over the surprise in her voice. "You do," he repeated. "I know the confession was difficult for you. Where did you think you were going when you tried to run through a lance?" He added the question in an effort to change the subject. His wife looked like she might start weeping at any moment and he wanted to help her calm her emotions.

"To find Alex. I thought we could take a walk to look over the holding."

"I ordered you to rest."

"I was going to take a restful walk. Gabriel, there's a man crawling on all fours behind you."

She whispered the news and moved closer to her husband. He didn't turn around to look. He didn't need to. "That's Auggie," he explained.

Johanna moved to stand next to her husband

so she could get a closer look at the man. "What is he doing?"

"Digging holes."

"Why?"

"He uses his staff to hit stones into the holes. It's a game he enjoys."

"Is he daft?" she whispered, lest the old man overhear her.

"He won't harm you. Leave him be. He has earned his leisure."

Her husband took hold of her hand and started back up the hill. Johanna kept glancing back over her shoulder to get a better look at the man crawling his way across the meadow. "He's a MacBain," she blurted out. "He's wearing your plaid."

"Our plaid," her husband corrected. "Auggie's one of us," he added. "Johanna, Alex isn't here. He was taken back to his mother's brother's family early this morning."

"How long will he be away?"

"Until the wall is finished. When the holding is secure, Alex will come home."

"And how long will that be?" she asked. "A son needs his father, Gabriel."

"I'm aware of my duties, wife. You needn't instruct me."

"But I may give my opinion," she countered. He shrugged.

"Have you begun work on your wall?" she asked.

"It's half done."

"Then how long before . . ."

136

"A few more months," he answered. "I don't want you walking in the hills without a proper escort," he added with a frown. "It's too dangerous."

"Is it too dangerous for all the women or just for me?"

He kept silent. She had her answer then. She held her exasperation. "Explain these dangers to me."

"No."

"Why not?"

"I haven't the time. Simply obey my commands and we'll get along quite well."

"Of course we'll get along if I obey your every command," she muttered. "Honestly, Gabriel, I don't believe . . ."

"The horses are sound."

His interruption turned her concentration. "What did you say?"

"The six horses you gave me are sound."

She let out a sigh. "We're through discussing obedience, aren't we?"

"Aye, we are."

She laughed.

He grinned. "You should do that more often."

"Do what?"

"Laugh."

They'd reached the edge of the courtyard. Gabriel's manner underwent a radical change. His expression hardened. She thought the serious look was for the benefit of his audience. Every soldier was watching.

"Gabriel?"

"Yes?" He sounded impatient.

"May I offer an opinion now?"

"What is it?"

"It's daft to use the courtyard for your training session as well as dangerous."

He shook his head at her. "It wasn't dangerous until this morning. I want you to promise me something."

"Yes?"

"Don't ever threaten to leave me."

The intensity in his demand surprised her. "I promise," she answered.

Gabriel nodded, then started to walk away. "I won't ever let you go. You do understand that, don't you?"

He didn't expect an answer. Johanna stood there for several minutes watching as her husband rejoined the training session. Gabriel was proving to be a complex man. Nicholas had told her the laird would marry her to secure the land. Yet Gabriel acted as though perhaps she were important to him, too.

She found herself hoping her guess was true. They would get along much better if he liked her.

She noticed Gabriel talking to Calum. The soldier glanced her way, nodded, and then started walking toward her. She didn't wait to find out what order her husband had given his first-in-command. She turned around and ran down the hill to the meadow. The MacBain soldier named Auggie intrigued her. She wanted to find out what game

138

it was that required digging holes in the ground.

The elderly man had a stock of white hair. He stood up when she called out to him. Deep lines around his mouth and eyes made her guess him to be at least fifty years old, perhaps even older. He had beautiful white teeth, handsome brown eyes, and a warm, inviting smile.

Until she spoke to him. Johanna made a quick curtsy, then introduced herself in Gaelic.

He squeezed his eyes shut and grimaced as though in acute pain. "You're slaughtering our beautiful language, girl," he announced.

He spoke so fast, his words tripped together, and his brogue was as thick as her mama's stew. Johanna didn't understand a word he'd said. Auggie was forced to repeat his insult three times before she gained the meaning.

"Please tell me, sir, which words I'm mispronouncing."

"You're doing a fair job ruining all of them."

"I would like to learn this language," she persisted, ignoring his comical expression of horror over her accent.

"It would take too much discipline for an Englishwoman to become fluent," he said. "You would have to concentrate. I don't believe you English have that ability."

Johanna couldn't understand much of what he said. Auggie dramatically slapped his forehead. "By all that's holy, you're taking the fun out of my insults, girl. You aren't understanding a word I'm saying."

He cleared his throat and spoke again, though this time in French. His command of the language was impressive, and his accent, impeccable. Johanna was impressed. Auggie was an educated man.

"I can see I've surprised you. Did you judge me simpleminded?"

She started to shake her head, then stopped herself. "You were crawling about on your knees, digging holes. I did jump to the conclusion you were a bit . . ."

"Crazed?"

She nodded. "I apologize, sir. When did you learn to speak . . ."

He interrupted her. " 'Twas years and years ago," he explained. "Now what was it you wanted, interrupting me in the middle of my game?"

"I was wondering what your game was," she said. "Why do you dig holes?"

"Because no one will dig them for me."

He snorted with laughter after giving her his jest.

"But your reason?" she persisted.

"The game I play requires holes to catch my stones if my aim is true. I use my staff as my club and round pebbles I strike forward. Would you like to have a try, lass? The game's in my blood. Perhaps you'll catch the fever, too."

Auggie took her arm and pulled her along to where he'd left his staff. He showed her how he wanted her to hold onto the wooden pole, and when she'd braced her shoulders and her legs just the way he believed she should, he stepped back to give her further instruction.

"Give it a good whack now. Aim for the hole straight ahead."

She felt ridiculous. Auggie really was a little daft. But he was also a gentle man, and her interest in what he was doing seemed to please him. She wasn't about to hurt his feelings.

She hit the round stone. It rolled to the edge of the hole, teetered, and then dropped in.

She immediately wanted to try again. Auggie beamed with pleasure. "You've caught the fever," he announced with a nod.

"What is this game called?" she asked as she knelt to retrieve her pebble. She retraced her steps to her original position, tried to remember the correct stance, and then waited for Auggie to answer.

"The game doesn't have a name, but it dates back to olden days. Once you've mastered my short holes, lass, I'll take you along to the ridge with me, and you can try for distance. You'll have to do your part, though, and find your own stones. The rounder the better, of course."

Johanna missed on her second try. Auggie told her she wasn't paying attention. She had to try again, of course. She was so intent on pleasing him and hitting the hole, she didn't even realize they were now speaking Gaelic.

She spent a large part of the afternoon with Auggie. Calum had obviously been given the duty of watching out for her. He appeared at the top of the hill every now and then to make certain she was still there. And staying out of mischief, she supposed. After a few hours Auggie called a halt to the game and motioned her over to the opposite side of the meadow where he'd left his supplies. He took hold of her arm and let out a grunt when he lowered himself to the ground. Then he motioned her to sit beside him. He handed her a leather pouch.

"You're about to have a treat, lass," he announced. "It's *uisgebreatha.*"

"Breath of life," she translated.

"Nay, water of life, girl. I've got my own brewing kettle, fashioned it myself after the one I studied at the MacKay holding. Our laird let me bring it along when we came to the Maclaurins. We're all castouts, you know, every one of us. I was a Maclead before I pledged myself to the MacBain."

Johanna was intrigued. "Cast out? I don't understand what you mean, sir."

"All of us were tossed out of our own clans for one reason or another. Your husband's fate was decided the day he was born a bastard. When he'd grown into manhood, he gathered us together and trained the younger ones to become fine warriors. Each of us has a talent, of course. You'll be tasting mine if you'll quit your lingering. I'm wanting a wee taste myself."

It would have been rude to decline the invitation. Johanna lifted the pouch, flipped the cork off, and took a sip of the liquid.

She thought she'd swallowed liquid fire. She let out a gasp, then started coughing. Auggie delighted in her reaction. He slapped his knee first, then pounded her between her shoulder blades to get her breathing properly again.

"It's got a fair bite to it, doesn't it?"

She could only nod agreement. "Get on home now, lass," he ordered. "Laird MacBain will be wondering where you are."

Johanna stood up, then put her hand down to assist Auggie. "Thank you for a lovely afternoon, Auggie."

The old man smiled. "You've taken on my burr, lass. That pleases me. You're a clever one, aren't you now? You must have a spot of Highland blood running in your veins."

She knew he was teasing her. She bowed and turned to leave. "Would you be wanting to go to the ridge tomorrow, Auggie?" she called over her shoulder.

"I might," he called back.

"Will you take me with you if you do?"

Johanna couldn't quit smiling. The day had turned out to be quite wonderful. Granted, she'd started out by pricking her husband's temper, but that little incident hadn't been horrible, and the rest of the afternoon had been lovely. She'd learned something important about her husband, too. He could control his temper. Anger didn't control him.

That was a revelation. Johanna pondered the significance on her way back up the hill. Calum was waiting for her. He bowed his head in greeting, then walked by her side back to the keep.

"I noticed you were playing Auggie's game," the soldier remarked.

"It was most amusing," Johanna replied. "Do you know, Calum, I believe Auggie's one of the most interesting men I've ever known, save for my father, of course."

Calum smiled over her enthusiasm. "Auggie reminds me of my father, too. He tells the same kind of spicy tales about times past, and he laces his truths with legends like my father always did." Thinking to compliment her, Calum added, "Auggie would be pleased to be compared to your father."

She laughed. "He'd be insulted," she guessed. "My father was English, Calum. Auggie wouldn't get past that fact." She changed the subject then. "You have more important duties, I'm certain, than keeping your eye on me. Will my husband expect you to follow me around every day?"

"There is no duty more important than protecting my mistress, m'lady," the soldier answered. "Tomorrow, however, Keith will be assigned the duty of watching out for you."

"Keith is the first-in-command over the Maclaurin soldiers, isn't he?"

"That is so. He answers only to our laird."

"And you are first-in-command over the MacBain soldiers."

"Yes."

"Why?"

"Why what, m'lady?"

"Why isn't there just one commander over both

the MacBain and the Maclaurin soldiers?"

"Perhaps you might ask your husband that question," Calum suggested. "He has sound reasons for allowing the Maclaurins their own leader."

"Yes, I will ask him," she said. "I'm interested in learning all I can about the land and the people here. Where is my husband?"

"Hunting," Calum answered. "He should be back any time now. Do you realize, m'lady, we've been speaking Gaelic? Your grasp of our language is quite impressive given the fact you've only had a few short weeks of instruction before you came here."

She shook her head. "Nay, Calum, it was closer to four months of intense study under Father MacKechnie's supervision. I was a little nervous when I first met your laird, though I doubt you noticed for I'm very good at hiding my reactions. When he asked me how long I'd been studying Gaelic, I was a bit nervous and the answer flew out of my mind. I can tell from your occasional grimace I still haven't mastered the burr."

Odd, but as soon as Calum made the mention that she was speaking Gaelic, she started tripping over her words and mispronouncing something fierce.

They'd just crossed the courtyard when Calum spotted his laird.

"Here's your husband now, m'lady."

Johanna turned to greet Gabriel. She hurried to straighten her appearance. She brushed a strand of hair back over her shoulder, pinched her cheeks

145

for color, and adjusted the folds in her plaid. She noticed the condition of her hands then. They were caked with dirt from spending the afternoon digging with Auggie. Since there wasn't time to wash now, she hid them behind her back.

The ground fairly trembled as the band of warriors rode their mounts up the last slope. Gabriel led the soldiers. He was riding one of the horses she'd given him as a wedding gift. The mare he'd chosen was the most temperamental of the lot. She was also the prettiest in Johanna's estimation. Her coat was as white as fresh snow with nary a mark on her. She was much bigger than the other horses, thicker in muscle as well, and certainly carried Gabriel's weight easily.

"He's riding my favorite horse," Johanna told Calum.

"She's a beauty."

"She knows it, too," Johanna said. "Rachel's terribly vain. She likes to prance. It's her way of showing off."

"She's showing off because she's proud to carry our important laird," Calum announced.

She thought he was jesting with her. She burst into laughter, then noticed Calum wasn't even chuckling. She realized he was serious.

Calum didn't know what she'd found amusing. He turned to ask her, saw the smudges of dirt she'd brushed on her cheeks, and smiled in reaction.

Gabriel's hound came running toward his master from around the corner of the keep. The huge beast frightened the mare. Rachel tried to rear up and bolt at the same time. Gabriel forced her under control and dismounted. One of the soldiers led the horse away.

The hound rushed forward. With one leap, he planted his front paws on Gabriel's shoulders. The dog was almost as tall as his master now and just as ferocious looking. Johanna's knees went weak watching the two of them. Thankfully the dog held great affection for his master. He was diligently trying to lick Gabriel's face. Her husband turned away before his pet could bathe him. He gave him a sound slap of affection. Dust flew from the hound's thick gray coat. Gabriel finally pushed the dog down and turned to his wife.

He motioned her forward. She wondered if he expected her to plant her hands on his shoulders and kiss him in greeting. The thought amused her. She took a step forward, then came to a quick stop when the animal started growling at her.

Gabriel was going to have to come to her. She kept the hound in her sights, wary now, as her husband walked forward. The dog, she noticed, attached himself to Gabriel's side and came with him.

Gabriel was amused by her timidity. The dog obviously intimidated her. He couldn't imagine why. He heard the low growling. So did his wife. She backed up a step. Gabriel ordered his hound to quit his show of bluster.

Some of the Maclaurin soldiers were still seated atop their mounts, watching their laird and his wife. A few grinned when they saw her fear of the dog. Others shook their heads.

"Did your hunt go well, m'lord?" Johanna asked.

"It did."

"Was there enough grain to be taken?" Calum asked.

"More than enough," Gabriel answered.

"You went hunting for grain?" Johanna asked, trying to understand.

"And a few other necessary items," her husband explained. "There's dirt on your face, wife. What have you been doing?"

She tried to wipe the dirt away. Gabriel grabbed hold of her hands and looked at them.

"I was helping Auggie dig holes."

"I do not want my wife to dirty her hands."

He sounded as though he was giving her an important commandment. Her husband appeared to be more than just a little irritated with her.

"But I have just explained . . ."

"My wife does not do common tasks."

She was exasperated. "Have you more than one, m'lord?"

"More than one what?"

"Wife."

"Of course not."

"Then it would appear that your wife does indeed get her hands dirty," she said. "I'm sorry if that displeases you, though I really can't imagine why it does. I can tell you I'm certain to get them dirty again."

She'd tried to use logic to soothe him, but he wasn't in the mood to be reasonable. He shook his head and scowled at her. "You will not," he commanded. "You're mistress here, Johanna. You will not lower yourself to such tasks."

She didn't know if she should laugh or frown. She settled on a sigh instead. The man had the oddest notions.

He seemed to want some sort of answer. She decided to try to placate him. "As you wish, m'lord," she whispered, determined not to let her sudden irritation show.

She was trying to be submissive, Gabriel decided. He thought it was probably killing her. She had a murderous look in her eyes, but she held onto her serene smile, and her voice sounded humble.

Johanna turned to Calum. She ignored the grin on his face. "Where do the women wash?"

"There's a well behind the keep, m'lady, but most bathe in Rush Creek."

Calum was going to escort her. Gabriel took over the task. He grabbed hold of her hand and pulled her along.

"In future, water will be carried to you," he said.

"In future, I would appreciate it if you didn't treat me like a child."

He couldn't believe the anger he heard in her voice. Johanna wasn't quite so timid after all.

"I would also appreciate it if you didn't berate me in front of your soldiers."

He nodded. His quick agreement eased her irritation.

Her husband had a long-legged stride. They rounded the corner and started down the slope. Huts lined the hill, and more were clustered in a wide circle at the base. The well was in the center. Several of the Maclaurin women were standing in line with their buckets, waiting their turn to fetch fresh water. Several called out greetings to their laird. He nodded and continued on.

The wall was just beyond the line of huts. Johanna wanted to stop to look at it. Gabriel wouldn't let her. They passed through the opening of the mammoth structure and continued on.

Johanna had to run to keep up with her husband. By the time they reached the second slope, she was out of breath. "Do slow down, Gabriel. My legs aren't as long as yours."

He immediately slowed his pace. He didn't let go of her hand, however. She didn't try to pull away. She heard the women's laughter in the background and wondered what they found amusing.

Rush Creek was a wide, deep stream. It ran the length of the mountain, her husband explained, from the top to a pool at the bottom where their land bordered with the Gillevrey territory. Trees lined the sides of the waterway, and wildflowers were so abundant they seemed to be growing out of the water as well as along the banks. The area was breathtakingly beautiful.

Johanna knelt on the bank, leaned forward, and washed her hands. The water was clear enough for her to see the bottom. Gabriel knelt beside her, cupped a handful of the frigid water, and poured it over the back of his neck. Her husband's pet appeared out of the woods, moved to her side, growled once, and then began to drink from the creek.

Johanna wet her linen cloth and washed her face. Gabriel leaned back to watch her. Her every movement was graceful. She was a mystery to him, and he assumed his curiosity and his fascination were both due to the fact that he'd never spent any significant amount of time with any woman.

Johanna wasn't paying any attention to her husband. She spotted what appeared to be a perfectly round stone at the bottom of the stream, decided Auggie could use it for his game, and reached down to get it.

The creek was much deeper than she'd judged it to be. She would have gone in headfirst if her husband hadn't grabbed hold of her and hauled her back.

"It's usual to take your clothes off before you bathe," he said dryly.

She laughed. "I lost my balance. I was trying to get a stone that caught my eye. Will you fetch it for me?"

He leaned forward to look. "There are at least a hundred stones, wife. Which do you fancy?"

She pointed. "The perfectly round one," she replied.

Gabriel reached down, lifted the stone, and handed it to her. She smiled in appreciation. "Auggie will like this one," she announced.

Johanna moved further back on the grassy slope, tucked her feet under her plaid and dropped the stone into her lap. A light breeze brushed through the trees. The scent of pine and early heather filled the air. The area was secluded and peaceful.

"Scotland is very beautiful," she said.

He shook his head. "Not Scotland," he corrected. "The Highlands are beautiful."

Gabriel didn't seem inclined to hurry back to his duties. He leaned his back against the trunk of a pine tree, crossed one ankle over the other, and adjusted the sword at his side so it wouldn't be scratched. His dog moved to his other side and stretched out next to him.

Johanna stared at her husband for several minutes before speaking again. The man had the ability to mesmerize her. She thought the reaction was due to the fact that there was so much of him. He was certainly as tall as Nicholas but far more muscular. At least she thought he was.

"Tell me what you're thinking."

Her husband's command jarred her. "I've never seen Nicholas without a tunic on. That's what I was thinking. I believe you're more muscular than my brother, but since I haven't seen him . . . They were foolish thoughts, husband."

"Aye, they are foolish thoughts."

She didn't take exception to his agreement. His slow grin told her he was teasing. Gabriel looked very content with his eyes closed and the soft smile on his face. He really was a dashing man.

Johanna noticed his pet nudge Gabriel's hand and was immediately rewarded with a quick pat.

Her husband wasn't such a worry to her any longer. Not only could he control his temper, but he also had a gentle streak in his nature. The way his hound responded to him told her that much about his character.

Gabriel caught her staring at him. She blushed with embarrassment and turned her gaze to her lap. She didn't want to leave just yet. She was enjoying this peaceful interlude with her husband. She decided to draw him into further conversation before he could suggest they go back.

"Aren't Scotland and the Highlands the same, m'lord?"

"They are and they aren't," he answered. "We don't consider ourselves Scots as you English are so inclined to call us. We're either Highlanders or Lowlanders."

"From the tone of your voice when you said Lowlanders, I assume you don't particularly like those people."

"Nay, I don't like them."

"Why?"

"They've forgotten who they are," he explained. "They've become English."

"I'm English." She blurted out the reminder before she could stop herself.

She sounded worried. He smiled. "I'm aware of that fact."

"Yes, of course you are," she agreed. "Perhaps, in time, you'll forget."

" 'Tis highly doubtful."

She didn't know if he was jesting with her or not. She decided to turn the topic to a less sensitive one.

"Auggie isn't daft."

"No, he isn't. The Maclaurins believe that nonsense, not the MacBains."

"He's actually very clever, husband. The game he made up is most amusing. You must try it sometime. It requires skill."

He nodded agreement just to placate her. He found her defense of the old man admirable. "Auggie didn't invent the game. It's been around for long years. In the old days, stones were used, but the men also carved balls out of wooden blocks. Some even fashioned leather balls and filled them with wet feathers."

Johanna stored the information away for future use. Perhaps she could make a few of the leather balls for Auggie.

"He says I've caught the fever."

"God help us," Gabriel drawled out. "Auggie plays the game all day, every day, rain or shine."

"Why were you irritated over a little speck of dirt on my face and hands?"

"I've already explained my position. You're my wife now. You must behave accordingly. There's rivalry between the MacBains and the Maclaurins; and until the clans become accustomed to living together in peace, I must show only strength, not vulnerability."

"Do I make you vulnerable?"

"Aye, you do."

"Why? I want to understand," she told him. "Was it the dirt or was it the fact that I was spending the afternoon with Auggie?"

"I don't want you down on your knees, Johanna. You must act with proper decorum at all times. My wife will not do common work."

"You've already mentioned that opinion."

"It isn't an opinion," he countered. "It's a command."

She tried not to let him see how disgruntled she was becoming. " 'Tis the truth I'm surprised you concern yourself with appearances. You don't seem the sort to care what other people think."

"I don't give a damn about other people's opinions," he countered, irritated by her conclusion. "I do care about keeping you safe."

"What does my safety have to do with my behavior?"

Gabriel didn't answer her.

"You should have married a Maclaurin. That would have solved your problem uniting the clans, wouldn't it?"

"I should have," he agreed. "But I didn't. I married you. We'll both have to make the best of it, Johanna."

He sounded resigned. He was still in an agreeable mood and she decided to change the topic again with a question that surely wouldn't prick his temper.

"Why doesn't your wolfhound like me?"

"He knows you're afraid of him."

She didn't argue over that truth. "What is he called?"

"Dumfries."

The dog's ears picked up when his master spoke his name. Johanna smiled in reaction. "It's a peculiar name," she remarked. "How did you come by it?"

"I found the dog near the Dumfries' holding. He was caught in mire. I pulled him out," he added. "He's been with me ever since."

Johanna moved closer to Gabriel's side. She slowly reached over to pat the animal. The dog watched her out of the corner of his eye; when she was about to touch him, he let out a menacing unearthly sound. She quickly pulled her hand back. Gabriel took hold of her arm and forced her to touch the hound. The dog kept up the horrid noise but didn't try to bite her hand off.

"Did I hurt you last night?"

The switch in topics made her blink. She bowed her head so he wouldn't see her quick blush, then whispered, "You didn't hurt me. You asked me after we . . ."

Gabriel nudged her chin up with his hand. The look in her eyes made him smile. He found her embarrassment amusing.

The look in his eyes made her heartbeat race. She thought he might want to kiss her. She found herself hoping he would.

"Will you want to make love to me again, m'lord?"

"Will you want me to?" he asked.

She stared into his eyes a long minute before giving him her answer. She wasn't going to try to be coy or clever. She'd only make a muck of it, she decided, because she'd never learned the fine art of flirting like the other young ladies had while they lived the high, courtly life in London.

"Yes," she whispered, grimacing inside over the shiver in her voice. "I would like you to make love to me again. It wasn't half bad, m'lord."

Gabriel laughed over her jest. Her blush, he noticed, was now as red as fire. Her embarrassment hadn't stopped her from telling him the truth, however. He pulled away from the tree trunk and bent down to kiss her. His mouth brushed over hers in a tender caress. She sighed into his mouth and put her hands on his shoulders.

It was all the encouragement he needed. Before he realized his intent, he lifted her onto his lap, wrapped his arms around her waist, and kissed her again. His mouth covered hers and his tongue swept inside to taste, stroke, and drive her wild. She went weak in his arms. She clung to him and kissed him just as thoroughly. Johanna was a little stunned by how quickly her entire body responded to her husband. Her heartbeat became frantic; her arms and legs began to tingle, and she kept forgetting to breathe.

Gabriel was shaken by his own reaction to his wife. She wasn't able to hold a part of herself back. She trusted him to keep her safe, he believed, or she wouldn't have allowed herself to be so uninhibited. Her passionate response ignited his own, and God help him, he couldn't seem to gather enough control to hold back either.

Hell, he'd take her here and now if he didn't put a stop to the sweet torment. He abruptly pulled back. He shouldn't have looked into her eyes. They were cloudy with passion. Damn, he had to kiss her again.

They were both shaken when he finally called a halt to the lovemaking. His breathing was labored. So was hers.

"You make me forget myself, m'lord."

He took that as a compliment. He lifted her off his lap, then stood up. Johanna was still rattled. Her face was flushed, and her hands trembled when she smoothed the hair back into her braid. He watched her try to right her appearance with vast amusement.

Women flustered easily, he decided. This one quicker than most.

"My hair's a sight," she stammered out when she caught his smile. "I've a mind to cut it . . . with your permission, of course."

"What you do with your hair is no concern to me. You don't need my permission. I have more important matters to think about."

He softened his rebuke with a quick kiss. Then he bent down, picked up the stone she wanted to give to Auggie, and handed it to her. He had to put the pebble in her hand. Aye, she was flustered all right, and damn, that fact pleased him.

He winked at his wife and turned to walk back up the hill.

Johanna straightened the pleats of her plaid and then hurried to catch up with him.

She couldn't quit smiling. He knew his kisses had made mush out of her mind, she decided, because the look on his face was one of pure male satisfaction. She didn't mind his arrogance though.

Everything was going to be all right. Johanna did a lot of sighing on the way back up the hill. Yes, she thought to herself, she had made the right decision when she'd agreed to marry Gabriel.

Johanna was in such high spirits she barely minded Dumfries's bluster of growls each time she moved closer to Gabriel's side. Even the mighty beast wasn't going to ruin her good mood.

She brushed her hand against her husband's. He didn't take the hint. She nudged him again, and still he didn't catch on. She gave up trying to be subtle and took hold of his hand.

He acted as though she wasn't even there. His gaze was directed on the top of the hill, and she assumed his mind was already turned to thoughts of duties ahead. She didn't mind his inattention; and when they reached the cluster of workmen's huts, she pulled her hand away. She didn't think he would want to show affection in front of the clan. Gabriel surprised her by grabbing hold of her hand again. He gave her fingers a gentle squeeze, then increased his stride until she was once again running to keep up.

Lord, she was happy. Aye, she'd done the right thing. She'd married a good-hearted man.

Chapter
7

'Twas the truth she was married to a gargoyle.

Johanna came to this depressing conclusion after living with her husband for three long months. Gabriel was downright mean-hearted. He was outrageously stubborn, horribly set in his ways, and completely unreasonable with his orders. Those were his better qualities. He treated her like an invalid. She wasn't allowed to lift a finger, was waited on hand and foot, and was always followed around by one of his men. She put up with the nonsense for a good two months before her irritation got the better of her. She did protest then, but to no avail. Gabriel wouldn't listen. His ideas about marriage were most bizarre. He wanted her protected under lock and key, and God's truth, whenever she went outside for a breath of fresh air, he tried to chase her back inside.

Dinners were insufferable. She was expected to maintain her dignity throughout the meal, while chaos ruled around her. None of the men she dined with had any manners. They were loud, rude, and made horrid, disgusting noises.

And those were their better qualities. Johanna didn't criticize the soldiers. She felt it would be better if she continued to maintain her separation from the clan whenever possible. In her mind, uninvolvement meant peace, and that was the one goal she longed to gain.

Since Gabriel still wouldn't let her go hunting, she spent most of the daylight hours alone. Her husband believed she was too fragile for the strenuous exercise of lifting a bow and arrow, she supposed, and how in God's name did one debate that ludicrous opinion? To keep her skill from becoming rusty, she fashioned a target on a tree trunk at the base of the hill and practiced there with her bow and arrows. She really was quite good with the weapon and was proud to boast she'd actually bested Nicholas a time or two in target games.

No one bothered her while she was at her task. The women ignored her most of the time. The Maclaurins were openly hostile. Several young women followed the example set by their unspoken leader, a tall, robust woman with ruddy cheeks and white-blond hair named Glynis. She did a lot of unladylike snorting whenever Johanna walked past. Johanna didn't believe Glynis was an evil woman, though. She just didn't have any use for her mistress. If her guess was true, Johanna decided she couldn't fault the woman. While Glynis was working from early morning until nightfall in the fields beyond the line of trees with the other women, tending the fertile fields and nurturing their crops, Johanna was leisurely strolling around the holding, giving the appearance, she was sure, of a lazy queen of the manor.

No, Johanna didn't blame the women for resenting her. Gabriel was in part responsible for their opinion of her because he wouldn't allow her to interact with any of them, but Johanna was honest enough with herself to acknowledge she'd allowed the separation and hadn't done anything to change the women's opinions of her. She hadn't tried to be friendly with any of them, following old habits without taking the time to question her own motives.

She hadn't had any close friends in England because her husband wouldn't have allowed it. Everything was different in the Highlands, she reminded herself. The clan wasn't going to vanish or move away.

After three months of solitude, she had to admit that, though her life was peaceful, it was also lonely and boring. She wanted to fit in. Just as important, she wanted to help rebuild what her first husband had destroyed. Gabriel was too busy with the reorganization to worry about her problems. She wasn't about to complain to her husband anyway. The problem was hers to solve.

Once Johanna named the dilemma, she set about solving it. She no longer wanted to separate herself from the clan and tried to join in whenever possible. She was shy by nature, almost painfully so, but she still forced herself to call a greeting whenever she spotted one of the women hurrying by. The MacBains always responded with a smile or a kind word; most of the Maclaurins pretended they hadn't heard her. There were some exceptions, of course. Leila and Megan, the two Maclaurin women who'd assisted with her bath on her wedding night, seemed to like her, but the others refused her every offer of friendship.

She was confused by their attitude. She didn't know what she could do to change their minds about her. On Tuesday, when Keith was assigned the duty of looking out for her, she put the question to him.

"I would like your opinion, Keith, on a matter worrying me. I can't seem to find a way to gain acceptance from the Maclaurin women. Do you have a suggestion to offer?"

Keith scratched his jaw while he listened to her. He could tell she was upset by his clan's behavior toward her, yet hesitated to explain the reason because he knew he would hurt her feelings. After several days spent protecting her, his own attitude had softened. She was still somewhat timid, but she certainly wasn't a coward as some of the Maclaurin women believed.

Johanna noticed his hesitation. She thought he didn't want to talk about the problem because they were within hearing distance of some of his clansmen.

"Will you walk with me up the hill?"

"Certainly, m'lady."

Neither one said another word until they were

well away from the courtyard. Keith finally broke the silence. "The Highlanders have long memories, Lady Johanna. If a warrior goes to his death without avenging some slight, he still dies in peace because he knows that someday his son or grandson will right the wrong. The feuds are never forgotten, the sins never forgiven."

She didn't have the faintest idea what he was talking about. He looked terribly earnest though. "And not forgetting is important, Keith?"

"Aye, m'lady."

He acted as though he'd finished his explanation. She shook her head in frustration. "I still don't understand what it is you're trying to tell me. Please try again."

"Very well," the soldier responded. "The Maclaurins haven't forgotten what your first husband's men did here."

"And they blame me, is that it?"

"Some of them do blame you," he admitted. "You needn't worry about retaliation," he hastily added. "Revenge is a man's game. The Highlanders leave the women and children alone. There is also the fact that your husband would kill anyone who dared to touch you."

"I'm not concerned about my safety," she replied. "I can take care of myself. I can't fight memories though. I can't change what happened here. You needn't look so bleak, Keith. I believe I've won a few of the women over. I heard one of them call me courageous. She wouldn't have given me that high praise if she disliked me."

"The praise isn't praise at all," Keith announced, anger lacing his brogue. "I cannot allow you to believe it is."

"Now what are you trying to tell me?" she asked in frustration.

Getting a straight answer out of the Maclaurin soldier was proving to be a difficult task. Johanna held onto her patience while she waited for him to sort out in his mind whatever was worrying him.

Keith let out a loud sigh. "They call Auggie clever."

She nodded. "Auggie is very clever," she agreed.

He shook his head. "They believe he's daft."

"Then why in heaven's name do they call him clever?"

"Because he isn't."

The expression on her face told him she still hadn't caught on. "They call your husband merciful."

"Their laird would be pleased to hear such praise."

"Nay, m'lady, he would not be pleased."

And still she didn't understand. Keith believed it would be a cruel disservice to let her remain ignorant. "Your husband would be furious if he thought the Maclaurins truly believed he was a merciful man. The women, you see, gave the name that least fits. It's a foolish game they play. They actually believe their laird is ruthless. 'Tis the reason they admire him," he added with a nod. "A leader doesn't wish to be known as merciful or kind-hearted. He would see it as a weakness."

She slowly straightened her spine. She was starting to grasp the meaning behind the women's game.

"And so, if what you say is true, then they consider Auggie to be . . ."

"Dull-witted."

She finally understood. Keith saw the tears gather in her eyes before she turned away from him. "Then I'm not courageous in their minds. I'm a coward. Now I understand. Thank you for taking the time to explain, Keith. I know it was difficult for you."

"M'lady, please give me the name of the woman you heard call you . . ."

"I will not," she said as she shook her head. She couldn't look at the soldier. She felt embarrassed . . . and ashamed. "Will you excuse me please? I believe I'll go back inside now."

She didn't wait to gain his permission but turned and hurried down the hill. She suddenly stopped and turned back to the soldier. "I would appreciate it if you wouldn't mention this conversation to my husband. He doesn't need to be concerned about such unimportant matters as foolish games some women play."

"I will not mention it," Keith agreed. He was a little relieved she didn't want him to repeat the conversation to his laird, for he knew there would be hell to pay if the MacBain found out about the insult. The fact that the cruel behavior came from the Maclaurin women infuriated the soldier.

As their leader, he felt the heavy burden of conflicting duties. He had pledged his loyalty to the MacBain, of course, and would give his life to keep his laird safe. That pledge spilled over to his wife. He would do whatever was demanded of him to protect Lady Johanna from harm.

Yet, he was also leader over his own clan members and, as such, felt that the Maclaurin problems should be solved by Maclaurins, not the MacBains. Telling his laird about the women's cruelty toward Lady Johanna made him feel traitorous. Keith knew it was Glynis and her cohorts causing all the mischief. He decided to take the time to have a firm talk with the women. He would order them to show their mistress the respect her position dictated.

Johanna went up to her bedroom and stayed there the rest of the afternoon. She alternated between anger and self-pity. She was certainly suffering from hurt feelings because of the women's cruelty, but that wasn't the true reason she wept. Nay, what really bothered Johanna was the possibility they were right. Was she really a coward?

She didn't have any answers. She wanted to hide in her chamber, but she forced herself to go down to dinner. Gabriel would be home from his hunt, and Keith would be there as well, and she didn't want either one of them to guess she was having any difficulties.

The hall was crowded with soldiers. Most were already seated at the two long tables adjacent to each other on the right side of the room. The scent of new wood and fresh pine-scented rushes on the floor mingled with the hearty aromas of the food being carried into the hall on giant trenchers made from two-day-old black bread.

No one stood when she entered the hall. That oversight bothered her. She didn't believe the men were being deliberately rude, however. Several waved when they spotted her. The soldiers simply didn't realize they were supposed to stand when a lady walked into the room.

She wondered what would make these two groups of proud, good men really feel like one clan. They worked so hard to keep separate. When one of the Maclaurin soldiers told a jest, only the other Maclaurin soldiers laughed. None of the MacBains even smiled.

They sat at separate tables, too. Gabriel was seated at the head of one table, and every other stool, except for the one on his right reserved for her, was taken up with a MacBain soldier. The Maclaurins all sat together at the other table.

Tonight, Gabriel barely acknowledged her. He held a parchment scroll in his hands and was frowning while he read the message it contained.

Johanna didn't interrupt her husband. His men weren't as thoughtful.

"What does the Gillevrey want?" Calum asked his laird.

"M'lady, he's laird of the clan south of us," Keith explained in a shout from the other table. "The message came from him," he added. He turned his attention to his laird then. "What does the old man want?"

Gabriel finished reading the message and then rolled the scroll back. "The message is for Johanna."

Her eyes widened in surprise. "For me?" she asked as she reached for the scroll.

"You can read?" Gabriel asked.

"I can," she answered. "I insisted upon learning."

"Why?" her husband asked.

She shrugged. "Because it was forbidden," she whispered. She didn't tell him that Raulf had taunted her over and over again, saying she was too ignorant to learn anything of value and that she had felt compelled to prove him wrong. It had been a silent defiance on her part, for Raulf never knew she had conquered the difficult task of reading and writing. Her teacher had been too frightened of Raulf to tell him.

Gabriel wouldn't let Johanna have the scroll. His frown was fierce when he asked, "Do you know a baron by the name of Randolph Goode?"

Her hand froze in midair. In the space of a heartbeat, the color left her face. She felt faint and took a quick breath to try to calm herself.

"Johanna?" he prodded when she didn't immediately answer him.

"I know him."

"The message comes from Goode," Gabriel said. "Gillevrey won't let him cross his border unless I give permission for him to come here. Who is

169

this man and what does he want?"

Johanna could barely hide her agitation. She wanted more than anything to get up and run but refused to give in to the cowardly urge.

"I don't wish to speak to him."

Gabriel leaned back in his chair. He could see her fear and feel her panic. Her reaction to the news didn't sit well with him. Didn't she realize she was safe? Damn it all, he wasn't about to let anything happen to her.

He let out a sigh. She obviously didn't know, he realized. In time she would learn that he and his men would protect her from harm. She'd learn to trust him, too, and then messages from England wouldn't make her fearful at all.

Gabriel knew he was being arrogant. He didn't care. Right now he wanted most of all to soothe his wife. He didn't like seeing her frightened. He had one other motive as well. He wanted to get to the truth.

"Has this baron offended you in some way?"

"No."

"Who is he, Johanna?"

"I won't speak to him," she said again. Her voice shook with emotion.

"I want to know . . ."

He stopped his question when she shook her head at him. He reached over and captured her chin with his hand to force her to stop denying him.

"Listen to me," he commanded. "You don't have to see him or speak to him."

He gave her his promise in a low, fervent voice.

She looked wary now, and uncertain. "Do you mean it? You won't let him come here?"

"I mean it."

She visibly relaxed. "Thank you."

Gabriel let go of her and leaned back in his chair again. "Now answer my question," he ordered again. "Who in thunder is Baron Goode?"

Every soldier in the hall was silent now, watching and listening. It was obvious to all of them their mistress was frightened. They were curious to find out why.

"Baron Goode is a powerful man in England," she whispered. "Some say he's as powerful as King John."

Gabriel waited for her to continue. Long minutes passed before he realized she wasn't going to tell him more.

"Is he a favored baron with the king?" he asked.

"No," Johanna answered. "He hates John. There are many other barons who share Goode's opinion of their overlord. They've joined together, and some say Goode is their leader."

"You speak of insurrection, Johanna."

She shook her head and turned her gaze to her lap. "It's a quiet rebellion, m'lord. England is in turmoil now, and there are many barons who believe Arthur should have been named king. He was John's nephew. His father, Geoffrey, was John's older brother. He died a few months before the birth of his son."

Calum had tried to follow the explanation. He

frowned in confusion now. "M'lady, do you mean to tell us that when King Richard died, Geoffrey should have become king?"

"Geoffrey was older than John," she replied. "He was next in line, for Richard didn't have sons, you see. But Geoffrey had already died. Some believe his son should have been the rightful heir. They even rallied behind Arthur and his cause."

"So the barons fight over the question of the crown?"

Gabriel made the statement. Johanna nodded. "The barons prod their king whenever they're given the opportunity. John's made many enemies over the last several years. Nicholas believes one day there will be a full rebellion. Goode and the others are looking for a sound reason to rid the land of John now. They don't want to wait. John has proven to be a terrible king," she added in a whisper. "He has no conscience, not even toward the members of his own family. Do you know he turned against his own father and joined with France's king during the trouble? Henry died of a broken heart, for he had always believed that of all his children, John was most loyal to him."

"How did you learn all this?" Calum asked.

"From my brother, Nicholas."

"You still haven't explained why Goode would want to speak to you," Gabriel reminded her.

"Perhaps he thinks I could aid his cause to unseat John. Even if I could, I wouldn't. It would serve no purpose now. I will not involve my family in the struggle. Nicholas and my mother would both be made to suffer if I were to tell . . ."

"Tell what?" her husband asked.

She wouldn't answer him.

Calum nudged her with his elbow to gain her attention. "Does Arthur want the crown?" he asked.

"He did," she answered. "But I'm only a woman, Calum. I don't concern myself with England's political games. I can't imagine why Baron Goode would want to talk to me. I don't know anything that would aid his cause to unseat John."

She was lying. Gabriel didn't have any doubt about that fact. She was obviously terrified, too.

"Goode wants to ask you some questions," he remarked.

"About what?" Calum asked when his mistress remained silent.

Gabriel kept his gaze on his wife when he gave his answer. "Arthur," he said. "He's now convinced the king's nephew was indeed murdered."

Johanna started to stand up. Gabriel caught hold of her hand and forced her to stay where she was. He could feel her trembling.

"I will not talk to Goode," she cried out. "Arthur disappeared over four years ago. I don't understand the baron's renewed interest in the whereabouts of the king's nephew. I have nothing to say to him."

She had already told him more than she intended. When she'd spoken of Arthur, she used revealing words, such as *was* and *wanted*.

Johanna already knew the king's nephew was dead. Gabriel thought she might also know how Arthur had died and who had done the foul deed. He considered all the ramifications if his guess proved true, then shook his head. "England is a world away from us," he announced. "I will not allow any barons to come here. I never break my word, Johanna. You will not speak to any of them."

She nodded. Calum started to ask another question, but his laird's glare stopped him.

"We are finished discussing this matter," he commanded. "Give me your report on the progress of the wall, Calum."

Johanna was too upset to listen to the conversation. Her stomach was queasy, and she could barely swallow a bite of cheese. There was boar for the offering and leftover salted salmon, but she knew she'd gag if she tried to eat anything more.

She stared at the food, wondering how long she would have to sit there before she could be excused from the table.

"You should eat something," Gabriel told her.

"I'm not hungry," she replied. "I'm not used to eating such large meals close to bedtime, m'lord," she explained as her excuse. "In England, dinner was usually served between ten and noon, and a lighter fare was offered later in the day. It's going to take time to get accustomed to the change. Will you excuse me now? I would like to go upstairs."

Gabriel nodded permission. Since Calum was

staring at her, she bid him good night, then got up and walked toward the entrance. She spotted Dumfries lounging on the left of the steps and immediately altered her path to make a wide half circle around the beast. She kept her gaze on the hound until she had gotten past him, then hurried on.

She took her time getting ready for bed. Going through such simple, uncomplicated rituals made her feel calmer and more in control of her fear. She forced herself to concentrate on each little task. She added two logs to the fire in the hearth, washed, and then sat down to brush her hair. She hated the chore. It seemed to take forever to get all the tangles out. Her scalp ached from the weight of the heavy mass, and by the time she was finished, she was too tired to braid it.

Johanna had run out of chores, and so she tried to think about other mundane things, for she believed that if she could block her fear, it would eventually go away.

"Gabriel's right," she whispered. "England is a world away from here."

I'm safe, she thought to herself, *and Nicholas and Mama will continue to be safe in England as long as I remain silent.*

Johanna put her brush down and made the sign of the cross. She prayed for courage first and divine guidance next, and last of all she said a prayer for the man who should have been king. She prayed for Arthur.

Gabriel came into the room just as she was finishing her petitions. He found his wife sitting on the side of the bed staring at the flames in the fireplace. He bolted the door, pulled off his boots, and then walked over to the opposite side of the bed. She stood up and turned around to face him.

She looked so damned sad to him.

"Nicholas told me King John is afraid of you."

She turned her gaze to the floor.

"Where did he get that notion?"

"Johanna?"

She looked up at him. "Yes?"

"Eventually you will tell me what you know. I won't demand. I'll wait. When you're ready to confide in me, you will."

"Tell you what, m'lord?"

He let out a sigh. "You'll tell me what's scaring the hell out of you."

She thought about protesting, then changed her mind. She didn't want to lie to Gabriel.

"We are married now," she said. "And it isn't just your duty to protect me, Gabriel. It is also my duty to keep you safe whenever I can."

He didn't know what she meant by the outrageous remark. Keep him safe? Hell, she had it all backward in her mind. He was supposed to protect her and watch his own back. He would make certain he stayed alive long years so he could take care of her and Alex.

"Wives do not protect their husbands," he decided aloud.

"This wife does," she countered.

He was about to argue with her, but she turned

his attention. She didn't say a word. She simply untied the belt to her robe and took the garment off. She wasn't wearing anything underneath.

His breath caught in the back of his throat. Dear God, she was beautiful. The firelight behind her cast a golden glow to her skin. There wasn't a single flaw to mar her appeal. Her breasts were full, her waist was narrow, and her legs were long.

Gabriel didn't remember taking his clothes off. He held her stare for long, silent minutes, until his heart was slamming inside his chest and his breathing was harsh with his arousal.

Johanna fought her embarrassment. She knew she was blushing because she could feel the heat in her face.

They both reached for the covers at the same time. Then they reached for each other. Johanna was still on her knees when Gabriel pulled her into his arms. He rolled her onto her back, covered her with his body, and kissed her.

She wrapped her arms around his neck and held him close. She was desperate for his touch. She wanted him tonight. She needed his comfort and his acceptance.

He needed satisfaction. His hands roughly caressed her shoulders, her back, her thighs. The feel of her silky skin inflamed him.

Johanna didn't need to be coaxed into responding. She couldn't stop stroking him. His body was so hard, his skin so wonderfully hot, and the way he made love to her with his mouth and hands aroused her to a fevered state in bare minutes.

It wasn't possible to be inhibited with Gabriel. He was a demanding lover, rough and gentle at the same time. He stroked the fires inside her with his intimate caresses, and when his fingers penetrated her and his thumb rubbed against the most sensitive nub hidden beneath her sleak folds, she became wild.

He took her hand and put it on his hard arousal. She squeezed him; he growled low in his throat. He whispered erotic praise and instructions of how he wanted her to caress him.

Gabriel couldn't stand the sweet agony for very long. He roughly pulled her hands away from him, lifted her thighs, and thrust deep inside her. She cried out with pleasure. Her nails raked his shoulders, and she arched up against him to take more of him inside. He almost spilled his seed then and there. It took every ounce of discipline he possessed to hold back. His hand moved down between their joined bodies, and he stroked her with his fingers until she found her fulfillment. Then he allowed his own.

His orgasm consumed him. He groaned with raw pleasure as he poured his hot seed into her. She kept calling his name, and he called God's.

Gabriel collapsed on top of his wife with a loud, satisfied grunt. He stayed inside her, unwilling to let go of the bliss he'd just experienced.

Johanna didn't want to let go of her husband just yet. She felt cherished when she was being held by him. She felt safe too . . . and almost loved.

His weight soon became crushing. She finally had to ask him to move so she could draw a proper breath.

He didn't know if he had enough strength. That thought amused him. He rolled to his side, taking her with him, then pulled the covers up and closed his eyes.

"Gabriel?"

He didn't answer her. She poked him in the chest to gain his attention. He grunted in response.

"You were right. I am weak."

She waited to hear his agreement. He said nothing. "A northern wind could probably blow me over," she said, repeating the words he'd spoken on their first night as man and wife.

He remained silent. "I might even be a little timid."

Several minutes passed before she spoke again. "But the other things, they aren't true. I won't let them be true."

She closed her eyes and said her prayers. Gabriel thought she'd fallen asleep. He was about to do the same. Then her voice, whisper-soft, yet filled with conviction, reached him.

"I'm not a coward."

Chapter

8

"Who dared to call you a coward?"

Johanna was jarred out of a sound sleep by her husband's booming voice. She opened her eyes and looked at him. Gabriel was standing at the side of the bed, glaring down at her. He was fully dressed and looked furious.

He needed to be appeased, she decided with a yawn. She sat up in bed and shook her head at him. "No one called me a coward," she told him in a sleepy voice.

"Then why did you say . . ."

"I thought you needed to know," she explained. "And I needed to say the words."

He lost the edge of his anger. She tossed the covers back and started to get out of bed. Gabriel stopped her by pulling the covers up and ordering her to go back to sleep.

"You will rest today," he commanded.

"I have rested long enough, m'lord. It's time for me to begin my duties as your wife."

"Rest."

Lord, he was stubborn. The set of his jaw told her it would be pointless to argue with him. She didn't have any intention of lounging in bed all day, but she wasn't going to debate the issue with her husband.

He turned to leave. She stopped him with her question. "What are your plans for this fine day?"

"I'm going hunting for more supplies."

"Like grain?" she asked. She got out of bed and reached for her robe.

"Like grain," Gabriel agreed.

Johanna put her robe on and tied the belt at her waist. He watched her lift her hair from underneath the collar. The action was feminine and graceful.

"How does one hunt for crops?"

"We steal them."

She let out a loud gasp. "But that's a sin," she blurted out.

Gabriel was vastly amused by the look of horror on his wife's face. Stealing seemed to upset her. He couldn't imagine why.

"If Father MacKechnie gets wind of this, he'll have your hide."

"MacKechnie's not back yet. By then all my sins will have been committed."

"You cannot be serious."

"I'm most serious, Johanna."

"Gabriel, you aren't just committing the sin of theft," she instructed. "You're also committing the sin of contemplation."

She looked like she expected some sort of an-

181

swer. He shrugged. She shook her head at him.

"It isn't your place to censure me, wife."

He expected an apology. He got a contradiction instead. "Oh, yes, it is my place to censure you, m'lord, when the topic is your soul. It is my place to instruct you, sir, for I am your wife, and I, therefore, must worry about your soul."

"That's ridiculous," he countered.

She gasped again. He almost laughed but stopped himself in time. "You think it ridiculous that I worry about you?"

"Do you?"

"Yes, of course."

"Then you are beginning to have affection for me?"

"I didn't say that, m'lord. You turn my words on me. I worry about your soul."

"I do not need your worry or your lectures."

"A wife is allowed to give her opinions, is she not?"

"Yes," he agreed. "When asked for her opinions, of course."

She ignored his qualification. "It is my opinion that you should barter for what you need."

He couldn't control his exasperation. "We don't have anything of value to trade," he told her. "Besides, if the other clans can't protect what they own, they deserve to have their supplies taken. It's our way, wife. You'll get used to it."

He was finished discussing the topic. She wasn't. "Such justification . . ."

"Rest," Gabriel ordered as he pulled the door closed behind him.

She was married to a stubborn man. Johanna decided not to bring up the topic of stealing again. Gabriel was right. It wasn't her place to instruct him or any of the other clansmen. If they all wanted to spend their eternities in hell, so be it. What did she care?

Johanna spent the morning practicing with her bow and arrows and spent the afternoon playing Auggie's senseless, yet vastly enjoyable, game.

Auggie had become her only real friend. He spoke only Gaelic to her, and she found the more relaxed she was, the less difficult the language became. The older man was patient and understanding with her and answered every question she put to him.

She told him how upsetting she found Gabriel's thievery. Auggie wasn't sympathetic and, in fact, championed his laird's cunning.

They were standing on the ridge, striking long shots while they discussed her worry. Most of the stones shattered from the force of the blow.

"The English destroyed our reserves. Our laird will make certain the clan doesn't go hungry this winter," he announced. "How can you call that a sin, lass?"

"He's stealing," she countered.

Auggie shook his head. "God will understand."

"There's more than one way into a castle, Auggie. Gabriel should find another way to feed the clan."

The old man positioned his staff against the round stone, braced his legs apart, and gave a swing. He squinted against the sunlight to see how far he'd hit the stone, nodded with satisfaction, and turned back to his mistress.

"My stone traveled thrice the distance of an arrow. Beat that one, little worrier. See if you can't put your stone right next to mine."

Johanna turned her attention to the game. She surprised a whoop of laughter out of Auggie when she matched his distance. Her stone came to rest just inches away from his.

"You've a knack for the game, lass," Auggie praised. "We'd best go back now. I've kept you from your duties longer than I had a right."

"I don't have duties," she blurted out. She tucked her staff under her arm and turned to her friend. "I've tried to take over the running of the household, but no one listens to me. The MacBains are more polite though. They smile while I instruct them, then go about their business without paying any heed to what I've said. The Maclaurin servants are far more rude, embarrassingly so. They completely ignore me."

"What does our laird have to say about this behavior?"

"I haven't told him. I'm not going to either, Auggie. This is my dilemma to solve, not his."

Auggie took hold of Johanna's arm and started down the steep hill. "You've been here how long now?"

"Almost twelve weeks."

"You were content for a time, weren't you now?"

She nodded. "I was content."

"Why?"

She was surprised by his question. She shrugged. "Coming here made me . . . free. And safe," she hastily added.

"You were like a dove with a broken wing," Auggie said. He patted her hand before continuing. "And as timid as I've ever seen."

"I'm not timid now," she countered. "At least not when I'm with you."

"I've seen the changes in you. The others haven't. In time I imagine they will notice you've got a bit of gumption."

She didn't know if she'd just been given a setdown or praise. "But the stealing, Auggie. What should I do about my husband?"

"Leave it be for now," he suggested. " 'Tis the truth I can't get riled up about a little thieving. My laird promised to bring me barley, and I'm anxious to have it, sin or not. It's for the making of my brew," he added with a nod. "The English drank all of my reserves, lass." He snorted with laughter, leaned closer to her side, and whispered, "They didn't get to the barrels of liquid gold though."

"What are barrels of liquid gold?"

"Do you remember the break in the pines beyond the ridge?"

"Yes."

"There's a cave directly behind," he announced.

185

"It's full of oak barrels."

"But what's inside the barrels?"

"The water of life," he answered. "Brew as old as ten, even fifteen, years now. It should be tasting like gold I'll wager. One of these days I'll take you there to have a look for yourself. The only reason it's stayed untouched is because the English didn't know it was there for the taking."

"Does my husband know about the cave?"

Auggie thought about the question a long while before answering. "I don't recall telling him," he admitted. "And I'm the only one who remembers when the old Maclaurin chieftains stored the barrels there. They weren't telling, of course, but I followed them one afternoon without their knowing. I can be quiet when I set my mind to the task," he added with a nod.

"When did you last go inside the cave?"

"A few years back," Auggie told her. "Do you notice, Johanna, that when you wear the MacBain plaid you play a fair game, but when you're wearing the Maclaurin colors, you can't hit a thing?" He was talking nonsense, of course. He liked to tease her. She thought it was just his way of showing affection.

As soon as they reached the courtyard, Auggie took off down the hill. She spotted Keith, bowed to him, and then hurried past. She'd felt uncomfortable around the Maclaurin soldier ever since he'd explained the real meaning behind the nickname the Maclaurin women had given her.

She also wanted to wash her hands before her

186

husband came home and noticed how dirty they were. He could be very unreasonable about her appearance; but since he demanded little enough from her, she tried to please him whenever possible.

Johanna was just starting up the steps to her home when a shout sounded behind her. She turned and saw soldiers running toward her. Several had their swords drawn.

She didn't know what all the fuss was about. "Get inside, m'lady. Pull the door closed behind you." Keith shouted his instruction. Johanna wasn't going to argue with the soldier or question him now. She assumed they were under attack by intruders and hurried to do as she was ordered.

Then she heard the low, menacing growl. She turned around again. She spotted her husband's pet slowly making his way across the courtyard. She cried out at the sight of the beast. Dumfries was covered with blood. From the distance she could see his left hindquarter had been ripped to shreds.

The hound was trying to come home to die. Johanna's eyes filled with tears as she watched Dumfries struggle.

The soldiers made a wide circle around the dog. "Go inside, Lady Johanna." Keith bellowed his order. She suddenly understood what they meant to do. They were going to kill the wolfhound to put him out of his misery. The way they warily moved toward the hound told her they believed he might turn on one of them.

Johanna wasn't about to let any more harm come to the dog. One soldier started to move forward with his sword raised to strike.

"Leave him alone."

The fury in her shout gained every soldier's attention. They turned to look at her, their surprise most evident in their gaping expressions.

A few of the Maclaurin soldiers actually backed away from the dog. The MacBain warriors didn't move from their positions, however.

Keith rushed up the steps. He grabbed hold of Johanna's arm. "You needn't witness this," he announced. "Please go inside."

She jerked her arm away from the soldier's hold. "Dumfries wants to come inside. He sleeps by the fire. That's where he's going. Hold the doors open, Keith. Do it now."

She shouted the last of her command before turning back to the other soldiers. She didn't believe Dumfries would allow any of the men to assist him. She knew the dog must be in terrible pain, for his gait faltered again and again as he slowly made his way over to the steps.

"M'lady, at least get out of his range."

"Tell the men to let him come inside."

"But m'lady . . ."

"Do as I've ordered," she commanded. "If anyone touches Dumfries, he'll answer to me."

The tone of her voice told Keith it was pointless to argue with her. He gave the command, then grabbed his mistress's arm again and tried to drag her back through the entrance.

"The doors, Keith. Keep them open."

Johanna didn't take her gaze off the dog when she gave the order. Leila and Megan, the two Maclaurin women assigned the duty of cleaning the great hall and the chambers above, came running to the doorway.

"Dear God," Megan whispered. "What happened to him?"

"Get back, m'lady," Leila cried out. "Poor Dumfries. He can't make it up the steps. They'll have to kill him . . ."

"No one's touching him," Johanna snapped. "Megan, fetch my needle and threads. Leila, there's a satchel under my bed filled with jars of herbs and medicines. Get it for me."

Dumfries collapsed on the third step. He let out a whimper and tried to stand up again. He alternated between yelps and growls now. Johanna couldn't stand the sight of his agony a moment longer. She'd hoped to approach the hound inside by the fire while he was at rest but knew he wouldn't make it inside without her.

She pulled away from Keith and ran to help. The dog let out a loud growl when she approached him. She slowed her pace, put her hand out, and began to whisper words meant to soothe the beast.

Keith once again tried to drag her back. The hound let out an even louder growl when the soldier touched her.

She ordered Keith back. She looked up and saw that two MacBain soldiers had their arrows notched to their bows. They were protecting her

189

whether she wished it or not. If the hound tried to snap at her, their arrows would kill him before real damage was done.

Johanna's compassion for the wounded animal warred with her fear. Aye, she was terrified; and when she slowly bent down to put her arms around the beast, she couldn't control her own whimpers.

The hound didn't let up his growling, but he allowed her assistance.

Johanna didn't realize her own strength. The dog leaned into her side. She almost toppled over from the weight, righted herself, and once again wrapped her arms around him. She held him behind his front legs. Bent as she was to her task, the side of her face was pressed against his neck. She kept up a steady stream of encouraging words and half-dragged the dog up the rest of the steps. It was backbreaking work, but when they'd cleared the last step, the dog found new strength and pulled away from her. He growled again and went in through the opening.

Dumfries paused at the top of the steps leading down into the great hall. Johanna again came to his assistance and half-carried him down the stairs.

Men putting the finishing touches on the mantel with their brushes quickly moved out of the way as Dumfries walked toward them. The dog circled the area in front of the hearth twice, then began to whimper. He was obviously in too much pain now to lie down.

Megan came running with the supplies Johanna had requested. Her mistress sent her back with the order to get the blanket off the bed.

"I'll get a fresh one from the chest, m'lady," Megan called out.

"No," Johanna said. "Take the one from my bed, Megan. Dumfries will be comforted by my husband's scent."

A few minutes later Megan tossed the blanket to her mistress. Johanna knelt down on the floor and made a bed for the dog. When she was finished, she patted the cover and ordered the dog down.

Dumfries circled once again, then collapsed on his side.

"You've gotten the beast inside, m'lady," Keith whispered from behind her. "That was quite an accomplishment."

She shook her head. "That was easy," she answered. "What comes next is a little more challenging. I'm going to sew him up. 'Tis the truth I dread the duty. Dumfries isn't going to understand."

She patted the side of Dumfries's neck again before leaning forward on her knees to look at the deep gash in his left flank.

"You can't be serious, m'lady. The hound will kill you if you touch his injury."

"I sincerely hope not," Johanna replied.

"But you're afraid of him." The soldier blurted out the reminder.

"Yes," she agreed, "I am afraid. It doesn't change anything though, does it? Dumfries still has an injury and I still have to sew him up. Leila?

191

Have you found the jars of medicines?"

"Aye, m'lady."

Johanna turned and spotted Leila and Megan standing side by side on the top step. Megan held up the needle and ball of white thread, and Leila clutched her mistress's gray satchel in her arms.

"Bring them to me, please, and put them on the blanket."

Leila and Megan didn't move from the top of the steps. They started toward her when she motioned to them but stopped suddenly. Dumfries was at it again, growling low in his throat. The sound he made was very like what Johanna imagined a demon let loose from hell would make. It was quite chilling.

The women were afraid to come any closer. The realization astonished Johanna. She thought she was the only one who found the hound intimidating. She took sympathy on the women and went over to collect her supplies from them.

"Do be careful, m'lady," Leila whispered.

Johanna nodded. She was ready to begin her work a few minutes later. Keith wasn't about to let her take the chance of being bitten by the hound while she worked on him. He knelt down behind Dumfries and positioned himself so that he could easily grab hold of the dog's neck and pin him down if he tried to harm his mistress.

The dog amazed both Johanna and the soldier. He never made a sound all the while she prodded at him. Johanna made enough noise for the two of them. She whispered apologies and moaned every time she touched the injury with the linen square she'd soaked in the cleaning salve. She knew the medicine burned, and so she blew on each spot after she'd applied the thick liquid.

Into the chaos came Gabriel. Johanna had just threaded the needle when she heard her husband's voice behind her.

"What the hell happened?"

Johanna let out a little sigh of relief. She turned on her knees to look up at her husband. Lord, she had never been so relieved to see him. She watched as he walked across the hall to stand over her. His big hands were settled on his hips. His gaze was directed on his hound.

Keith immediately stood up. The other soldiers who'd followed him into the great hall moved back to give Keith room.

"I'd wager Dumfries met up with a wolf or two," Keith speculated.

"Think he found our pet?" Calum asked the question. He walked over to stand next to Keith.

Johanna went back to her task. She tied the knot in her thread, then put the needle down and reached for the second jar of medicine.

"You have another pet, m'lord?" she asked while she gently dabbed the yellow ointment on the cut. She used another linen square to smooth the healing salve along the jagged edges.

"The Maclaurins call one particular wolf Pet. Your hand's shaking."

"I can see it is."

"Why?"

"Your dog terrifies me."

Johanna finished dabbing the medicine on the injury. The salve would protect the cut from infection. It also had a side benefit of numbing the area. Dumfries would barely feel the sting of her needle.

"Yet she's tending him, Laird."

"I can see she is, Keith," Gabriel replied.

"The difficult part's over," Johanna said. "Dumfries shouldn't feel the rest of my prodding. Besides . . ."

"Besides what?"

She whispered her explanation, but Gabriel couldn't make out the words. He knelt down beside his wife. He placed his hand on the dog's neck. Dumfries immediately tried to lick his fingers.

"What did you just say?" he asked his wife while he stroked his hound.

"I said, you're here now," she whispered. She glanced over, saw his arrogant expression, and immediately added, "Dumfries will be comforted. He has great affection for you, m'lord. I imagine he knows you'll keep him safe."

"You know it too, Johanna."

She knew he expected her agreement. She decided his arrogance would get completely out of hand if she admitted she did feel safe when he was near, and so she remained silent.

It didn't take her any time at all to sew the injury closed. Gabriel helped her wrap wide cotton strips around and around the dog. He tied the ends together.

"He won't leave this alone for long," her husband predicted.

She nodded. She was suddenly overwhelmed with fatigue. Fear had drained her of her strength she supposed.

She collected her supplies and stood up. A crowd of curious men and women stood behind her. Johanna spotted Glynis in the group and immediately turned her gaze away.

"She carried your dog inside, MacBain. Aye, she did."

As Keith told a somewhat exaggerated version, Johanna continued through the crowd. She hurried up the steps and down the hall to her chamber. She put her supplies away, washed her hands again, and then took off her shoes so she could stretch out on the bed. She planned to rest for just a few minutes and then return to the hall for dinner.

She fell asleep a few minutes later. Gabriel came up to the room twice during the evening to look in on her. He finally came to bed around midnight after making certain Dumfries was resting comfortably.

Johanna barely moved while her husband took off her clothes. She opened her eyes once, frowned up at him, and then promptly fell asleep again. Gabriel took a fresh blanket from the chest and covered his wife before he stripped out of his own clothes and got into bed beside her.

He didn't have to reach for her. The minute he was settled, she rolled over into his embrace.

He pulled her closer. She tucked her head under his chin.

Gabriel recounted in his mind the story Keith had related to him. He tried to picture his wife wrapping her arms around Dumfries and dragging the hound up the steps.

The courage his wife had shown pleased him. Still, he didn't want her to take such chances in future. Dumfries had been in pain, and a wounded animal, no matter how loyal, wasn't to be trusted.

Tomorrow he would order her never to take such risks again. Gabriel fell asleep worrying about his delicate little bride.

Chapter

9

Gabriel knew, before he'd even opened his eyes the following morning, that his wife wasn't in bed with him.

Hell, it was just a little past dawn, and he as laird and husband should have been the first to leave the bed. His irritation softened, however, with the thought that she was probably downstairs waiting for him in the great hall. She had looked worried about Dumfries the night before, he remembered, and she was no doubt still fretting over the animal.

The Maclaurin plaid was draped over a chair. Johanna had gotten her days mixed up, for she had obviously dressed in the MacBain colors two days in a row. The Maclaurins were sure to kick up a fuss, and damn it all, he didn't have time for such puny, inconsequential matters.

Both Keith and Calum were already waiting for him in the hall. They bowed to their laird when he appeared at the entrance.

"Where's my wife?"

Calum and Keith exchanged a worried look, then Calum stepped forward to answer. "We thought she was above the stairs with you, MacBain."

"She isn't."

"Then where is she?" Calum asked.

Gabriel glared at the soldier. " 'Twas the question I just put to you," he snapped.

Dumfries lifted his head at the sound of his master's voice. His tail thumped against the rushes. Gabriel went over to the hound, bent down on one knee, and pounded the side of the dog's neck.

"Do I have to carry you outside, Dumfries?"

"Lady Johanna has already taken your pet outside, Laird."

Leila called out the news from the entrance. She hurried down the steps, smiled at Calum and Keith, and then turned to her laird. "She gave him food and water, too. She declared your pet's feeling much better today."

"How would she know so soon he's better?" Keith asked.

Leila smiled. "I asked her the very same question, and she told me his growl is a little stronger today. That was how she knew he had improved."

"Where is she?" Gabriel demanded.

"She went riding," Leila answered. "She declared it was too fine a day to stay inside."

"My wife went riding alone?"

Gabriel didn't wait for an answer. He muttered a dark blasphemy as he left the hall. Keith and Calum started after him.

"I take full responsibility should anything happen to our mistress," Keith announced. "I should have gotten here sooner. Today's my day to protect her," he added as explanation. "Damn but I wish she'd stay where she's put."

"But she was wearing the MacBain plaid," Leila called out.

"She shouldn't be," Keith said.

"But she is, sir."

Calum scratched his jaw. "She's gotten her days mixed up," he decided aloud. He winked at Leila when he passed her, then increased his stride to catch up with Keith.

Gabriel controlled his worry by getting angry. He'd been most specific with his wife during the past several weeks. She was to rest, damn it. Riding out alone in the hills infested with wolves wasn't his idea of a rest. Did he have to keep her under lock and key? By God, he'd ask her that question just as soon as he found her.

Sean, the stable master, spotted his laird coming his way and immediately prepared his stallion for the day's hunt. He was just leading the black beauty out when Gabriel reached him. He snapped the reins out of Sean's hands, grunted a response to the stable master's greeting, and gained his stallion's back in one fluid motion. The horse was in a full gallop by the time he'd crossed the meadow.

Auggie heard the pounding of hooves and lifted his head. He was down on his knees measuring the distance from one hole he'd just dug to the next. He hurried to stand up and bowed when his laird stopped his mount a scant foot away.

"Good day to you, Laird MacBain."

"Good day to you, Auggie," Gabriel responded. He scanned the meadow, then turned his gaze back to the old warrior. "Have you seen my wife?"

"I'm seeing her now, MacBain."

Auggie motioned with his hand. Gabriel turned in his saddle and looked up. He spotted Johanna immediately. She was on the north ridge, seated atop her mount.

"What the hell is she doing?" he muttered to himself.

"Contemplating her circumstances," Auggie answered.

"What in God's name does that mean?"

"I wouldn't be knowing, MacBain. I'm just repeating her words to me. She's been up there over an hour. I'd wager she's worked it all out in her mind by now."

Gabriel nodded. He goaded his mount into a full run. "It's a fine day to ride," Auggie shouted.

"It's a finer day to stay inside," Gabriel muttered in reply.

Johanna was just about to ride back down to the meadow when she noticed her husband coming up the ridge. She waved in greeting, then folded her hands together on top of the reins and waited for him to come to her.

She was more than ready to take him on, she decided. She took a deep breath in anticipation. It was time for her to put her new plan into action. She was a little nervous, but that was to be expected. She wasn't used to taking charge. That wasn't going to stop her though. By God, she was responsible for her destiny, she thought to herself. She needed to explain that fact to her husband.

Johanna had awakened a full hour before dawn and had spent the time thinking about all the changes she wanted to make. Most involved her own behavior, but there were also a few changes she planned to help her husband make.

Gabriel's pet had actually started her thinking. Johanna had learned something very revealing when she'd taken care of the dog's injury. First came the observation that his growl was all bluster, a sign of affection really. Second came the realization she didn't need to fear the beast. A firm pat and a kind word had won her Dumfries's loyalty. This morning, when she'd fed the wolfhound, he'd growled with affection while he licked her hand.

Not unlike his master.

Her husband's scowls no longer worried her. Johanna had to remind herself of that fact when he reached her side.

"You were ordered to rest," he snapped, his voice hard with anger.

She ignored his hostile greeting. "Good morning, husband. Did you sleep well?"

Gabriel was so close to her, his right leg pressed against her left thigh. Johanna couldn't suffer his frown long and turned her gaze to her lap. She didn't want his glare to bother her concentration. She had quite a bit to say to her husband, and it was important she remembered every one of her thoughts.

He noticed his wife had her bow and arrows in a leather carrier strapped to her back. Bringing the weapon along showed good sense, he decided, providing she was accurate in the event of an attack. Practicing with a target pinned to a tree was one thing, but the real proof in her ability would be shown on a moving target . . . such as a hungry wolf or an angered, charging boar. Those thoughts led to the reminder of the dangers lurking in the hills beyond. His scowl immediately intensified.

"You blatantly disregarded my instructions, Johanna. You are not allowed . . ."

She leaned to the side of her saddle, reached up, and gently stroked the side of his neck with her fingertips. The caress had been butterfly light, and over before he even had time to react, but it still managed to break his concentration.

Her touch stunned him. Johanna sat back, folded her hands together, and smiled up at him.

He had to shake his head to clear his thoughts. Then he started over again.

"You have no idea of the dangers . . ."

She did it again. Damned if she didn't deliberately break his concentration by stroking the side of his neck. He grabbed hold of her hand before she could pull away.

"What the hell are you doing?"

"Patting you."

He started to say something, then changed his mind. He stared at her a long minute, trying to understand what had come over her.

"Why?" he finally demanded, his expression wary.

"I wanted to show you affection, m'lord. Does my touch displease you?"

"No," he growled.

He grabbed hold of her chin with his hand and leaned down. His mouth covered hers in a long, hard kiss.

She melted against his side, put her arms around his neck, and clung to him as the kiss deepened.

Johanna didn't know how it happened; but when her husband finally pulled back, she was seated on his lap.

He held her close. She collapsed against his chest, let out a little sigh, and smiled with satisfaction.

She wanted to laugh. Dear God, it really worked. She had just proven a most important theory. Gabriel and his hound were actually very much alike. Her husband liked to bluster as much as his pet did.

"It is permitted for a wife to show her husband affection."

He was giving her his approval, she supposed. And Lord, did he sound arrogant. She leaned away from him so she could look up at him.

"Is it permitted for a husband to take his wife riding?"

"Of course. A husband can do anything he wishes to do."

So can a wife, she thought to herself. "Why are

you always so serious, m'lord? 'Tis the truth you don't smile enough to suit me."

"I'm a warrior, Johanna."

From the look on his face she assumed he believed he'd given her a full and logical explanation.

He lifted her back on her mount. "You rarely smile," he remarked. "Why is that?"

"I'm a warrior's wife, m'lord."

She smiled after giving him her tart answer. He couldn't help but grin.

"You're very handsome when you smile, m'lord."

"But you dislike handsome men, remember?"

"I remember. I was trying to compliment you, sir."

"Why?"

She didn't answer him. "What were you doing up here all by yourself?"

She answered his question with one of her own. "Could you spare an hour and ride with me? I'm on a hunt to find a cave Auggie told me about. There's a treasure inside."

"And what is this treasure?"

She shook her head. "You'll have to help me find the cave first. Then I'll tell you what's inside. I know how busy you are, but surely one hour won't matter, will it?"

He frowned while he considered her request. He did have important duties set aside for today and they should come first, of course. Riding for sheer pleasure didn't make any sense at all to him. It wasn't . . . productive.

Yet the idea of spending a few minutes, and

that was surely all he could spare, with his beautiful wife did appeal to him.

"You may lead the way, Johanna. I'll follow."

"Thank you, m'lord."

She looked overwhelmed with gratitude. His gentle little wife derived such joy from little pleasures. Gabriel suddenly felt like an ogre because he had taken time to consider her request.

Johanna wasn't about to give him time to change his mind. She wanted to get him away from his holding . . . and his responsibilities so that she could have a long talk in private with him. She grabbed the reins and goaded her mount into a full run down the hill.

She was a skilled rider. The realization surprised him. She seemed too delicate for any outdoor skills.

Gabriel was content to stay behind her until they reached the forest. Then he took over the lead.

They criss-crossed back and forth while they looked for the entrance to the cave. After an hour's search, Johanna was ready to give up. "Next time we must ask Auggie to ride with us. He'll point the way."

They broke through the trees and stopped in a narrow clearing next to the stream overlooking the valley.

"Are you ready to go back?" Gabriel asked.

"I wanted to talk to you first, m'lord, and if I weren't so hungry, I would beg you to stay here the rest of the day. It's so lovely. Do you notice how green and lush your valley is?" Her eyes sparkled with mischief when she added, "And to think you have such a mild climate all year long. I count myself fortunate each and every day. Aye, I do."

Gabriel found her enthusiasm refreshing. He'd never seen her in such a lighthearted mood before. It warmed his heart. God's truth, he was reluctant to leave, too.

"I can take care of satisfying your hunger, wife."

She turned to look at him. "Will you hunt for food?"

"Nay, I carry everything we'll need."

Gabriel dismounted, then assisted her to the ground. "You're too thin, Johanna. You barely weigh two stones."

She ignored his criticism. "Where is this food you boast of, husband? Will it appear like manna from the sky, do you suppose?"

He shook his head. She watched as he lifted the flap of his saddle and removed a flat metal plate. Behind the saddle was a bag tied with a string.

He motioned her to walk over to the clearing. He tied the reins of both their mounts to one of the branches before he joined her.

"Take off your plaid, Johanna. We'll use it for a blanket. Spread it on the ground near the pines."

"It probably isn't decent."

The sassy tone of her voice told him she didn't mind if she was decent or not. Her lighthearted mood puzzled him and made him determined to find out what had caused this change. Johanna was usually very reserved.

A few minutes later, she was seated on her plaid

watching Gabriel prepare their food. He'd started a fire with peat and twigs, then placed the metal plate in the center of the flames. He then sprinkled oatmeal from the pouch into one cupped hand, added water he'd gathered from the stream, and quickly formed a thick oat cake. He dropped the mixture on the plate, and while it cooked, he made another.

The oatmeal cake tasted like baked sticks mixed with dust to Johanna, but because her husband had taken the time and trouble to prepare the food, she didn't let him know how horrid it tasted.

Gabriel thought the expression on her face while she nibbled on the oatmeal was comical. She made several trips to the stream for drinks of water to wash the food down, and she could only eat half the cake before she declared she was quite full.

"It was thoughtful of you to bring the food along," she remarked.

"Every warrior always carries his food on his back, Johanna." He sat down beside her, leaned back against the tree trunk, and added, "We take everything we need for a hunt or a war. Highlanders are self-sufficient. We don't have need for bread or wine or carts loaded down with pots and caldrons like the pampered English soldiers. Our plaids are our tents or our blankets, and what other food we want, we take from the land."

"Or steal from the other clans?"

"Yes."

"It's wrong to take without permission."

"It's our way," he explained once again.

"Do the other clans steal from you?"

"We don't have anything they would want."

"Do they all steal from each other?"

"Of course."

"It's most barbaric," she decided aloud. "Don't any of the lairds ever barter for what they need?"

"Some do," Gabriel answered. "Twice a year council meetings are held near the Moray Firth. Clans not feuding attend. I've heard there's a fair amount of bartering done then."

"You've heard? Then you've never attended any of these meetings?"

"No."

She waited for turther explanation. He remained silent. "Haven't you been invited?"

She sounded incensed over the possible insult. "Every laird is invited, wife."

"Then why in heaven's name haven't you attended?"

"I haven't had the time or the inclination. Besides, as I've already explained to you several times now, we don't have anything to barter."

"But if you did?" she asked. "Would you attend the council meeting?"

He shrugged his answer.

She let out a sigh. "What does Father Mac-Kechnie have to say about stealing?"

His wife seemed obsessed with her worry about the priest's opinion. "He doesn't criticize us if that's what you're thinking. He knows it would be pointless to argue. Survival comes before paltry concerns such as venial sins."

She was quite astonished by her husband's

attitude. Damned envious, too. It would be nice not to worry about sinning all the time.

"Father MacKechnie is an unusual priest."

"Why do you say that?"

"He's very kind. That makes him unusual."

Gabriel frowned over her comment. "What are the priests in England like?"

"Cruel." She blurted out her belief and immediately felt guilty because she'd lumped all the men of God in with the few mean-hearted ones she'd known. "Some are probably kind-hearted," she added with a nod. "I'm certain some are very good men who don't believe women come last in God's love."

"Women are what?"

"Last in God's love," she explained. She straightened up but kept her head bowed. "You might as well know I'm not in good standing with the church, Gabriel."

She acted as though she was giving him a dark confession. "And why is that, Johanna?"

"I'm a rebel," she whispered.

He smiled. She thought he might think she was jesting. "I am a rebel," she said again. "I don't believe everything the church teaches."

"Such as?" he asked.

"I don't believe God loves women less than he loves oxen."

Gabriel had never heard of anything so preposterous. "Who told you . . ."

She interrupted him. "Bishop Hallwick liked to list God's hierarchy as a reminder to me of my insignificance. He said that unless I learned true humility and submissiveness, I would never sleep with the angels."

"This bishop was your confessor?"

"For a time," she answered. "Because of Raulf's important position, the bishop was his advisor and his confessor. He dictated many penances."

Gabriel could all but taste her fear. He leaned forward and put his hand on her shoulder. She flinched in reaction.

"Explain these penances," he commanded.

She shook her head. She was sorry she'd brought up the topic. "When will Alex come home?"

He knew she was deliberately changing the subject. He decided to let her have her way. His wife was full of strange worries; and from the way she was gripping her hands together now, he assumed Bishop Hallwick was at the top of her list of concerns.

"Alex will come home when the wall is finished," he answered. "You asked me the very same question yesterday. Did you forget my answer?"

"I'll probably ask you again tomorrow."

"Why?"

"A son should live with his father. Is he content to wait? Is he happy with his mother's family? Do you trust the people looking out for his welfare? A child as young as Alex needs his father's attention," she ended.

She was actually insulting him by asking such questions. Did she believe he would leave his son in the hands of infidels?

Gabriel didn't believe she was trying to be insolent. The worried look on her face showed how concerned she was about the boy.

"Alex would tell me if he was unhappy or unfairly treated."

She shook her head vehemently. "Nay, he might not tell you. He might be suffering in silence."

"And why would he suffer in silence?"

"Because he would be ashamed, of course. He'd believe he'd done something wrong to merit such cruel treatment. Bring him home, Gabriel. He belongs with us."

Gabriel hauled her onto his lap and nudged her chin up. He stared down at her a long minute, trying to understand what was going on inside her mind.

"I'll bring him home for a visitation."

"When?"

"Next week," he promised. "I'll ask him then if he's unhappy or mistreated."

His hand moved to cover her mouth so she wouldn't interrupt him. "And," he added in a firmer voice when she dared to shake her head, "he'll tell me the truth. Now I would like for you to answer a question for me, Johanna."

He pulled his hand away, waited for her nod, and then asked, "How long did you suffer in silence?"

"You misunderstand," she said. "I had a wonderful childhood. My parents were gentle, loving people. Father died three years ago. I still miss him something fierce."

"And your mother?"

"She's all alone now. Do you know, I never would have agreed to come here if it weren't for Nicholas's promise to look out for her. He's a devoted son."

"You probably saw your parents often while you were married to the baron, but the distance from this holding to your mother's home is simply too great to allow more than one visitation a year, wife."

"You would let me go to my mother?"

She looked astonished. "I would take you," he answered. "But only once a year. You can't expect to see your family as often as you did when you were married to the Englishman."

"But I never saw my mother or father then."

It was his turn to look astonished. "Didn't your husband allow visitations?"

She shook her head. "I didn't want to see them . . . not then. Shouldn't we go back now? It's getting late, and I've kept you from your important duties long enough."

He frowned with irritation. Johanna wasn't making any sense at all to him. She'd looked elated when he told her she could return to her mother's home once a year, yet contradicted herself with the mention that she'd chosen not to see her relatives during the years she'd been married to the baron.

Gabriel didn't like half answers. He was going to demand she give him a full explanation now.

"Johanna," he began, his voice a low growl. "You contradict yourself. I don't like puzzles . . ."

She unfolded her hands from her lap and reached up to stroke the side of his neck. Her action caught him by surprise, but he refused to be distracted. He took hold of her hand so she wouldn't interrupt him again and continued, "As I said, I don't like . . ."

She patted the opposite side of his neck with her other hand. Gabriel was distracted. He let out a sigh over his own lack of discipline, grabbed her other hand, pulled her close, and kissed her.

He thought only to taste her, but her enthusiastic response made him hungry for more. He became more demanding. His mouth slanted over hers, and his tongue warred with hers in mock loveplay.

She wanted more. She pulled her hands away from his grasp and wrapped them around his neck. Her fingers threaded through his hair, and she moved restlessly against him, trying to get closer.

Her sweet response to his touch made him want to forget himself. It took extreme strength of will to pull back. He closed his eyes so he wouldn't be tempted by her sexy mouth and let out a loud growl of frustration.

"Now is not the time, wife." His voice was hard.

"No, of course not." Her voice was whisper soft.

"The dangers here . . ."

"Yes, the dangers . . ."

"I have duties."

"You must think me shameless to try to pull you away from your important responsibilities."

"Aye, you are," he agreed with a grin.

The man was driving her to distraction. His hand

was caressing the side of her thigh as he listed all the reasons why they should immediately return to the holding.

She was having difficulty paying attention to what he was saying to her. Little things kept getting in the way. His clean male scent for one. Gabriel smelled like the outdoors. It was most appealing.

So was his voice. It was deep and vibrant. She wasn't intimidated by the gruffness in his tone. 'Twas the truth she found it arousing.

"Gabriel?"

His hand moved up higher on her thigh. "What is it?"

"I wanted to talk to you about important decisions I'd made."

"You may tell me later, Johanna."

She nodded. "Are there wolves here?" she asked.

"Sometimes," he replied.

"You don't seem concerned."

"The horses will give us sufficient warning. Your skin feels like silk."

She leaned back just a little so she could kiss his chin. His hand moved to the junction of her thighs. She instinctively parted them. He cupped her softness and began to stroke her while his kiss turned wet and hot.

Disrobing was awkward and frustrating as well because it took so long, and the ties holding her skirts together knotted when she tugged on them. Gabriel took over the task. He was just as inept, but stronger. He tore the satin slip apart.

Gabriel suddenly became impatient. He couldn't wait any longer. He forced her to straddle his hips, lifted her up, and then made himself stop.

"Take me inside," he commanded, his voice a hoarse whisper. He wanted to shout *now* but said instead, "When you're ready, wife."

She gripped her husband's shoulders with her hands and slowly lowered herself on top of him. They stared into each other's eyes until Gabriel was fully imbedded inside her.

The pleasure was almost unbearable. She squeezed her eyes shut and let out a little whimper. When she moved forward to kiss him, she felt a hot rush of ecstasy. She deliberately moved again.

God, her slow, teasing motions drove him wild. He grabbed hold of her hips and showed her what he wanted her to do. Their lovemaking became frantic. Both lost control. Gabriel found fulfillment before she did but helped her gain her own when he slipped his hand down between their joined bodies and stroked her. She tightened all around him and buried her face in the crook of his neck. She whispered his name with a sob as her orgasm consumed her.

Gabriel held her close for several minutes, then nudged her chin up and kissed her hard. His tongue mated with hers in a lazy fashion. And then he pulled away.

He didn't give her much time to recover. He kissed her once again and told her to get dressed. The day, he declared, was wasting away.

She tried not to be hurt by his attitude. She

wanted to linger but knew his duties still waited for him.

They washed in the stream, dressed, and walked side by side to their mounts.

"You will not go out alone again, Johanna. I forbid it."

She didn't agree or disagree with that instruction. He gave her a hard look before lifting her onto her horse. Johanna adjusted the strap of her carrier on her shoulders, slipped the bow over her arm, and then took the reins from his hands.

"When we return to the holding, you will rest."

"Why?"

"Because I have told you to," he countered.

She wasn't in the mood to argue with him. She wasn't about to let him leave in such a brittle mood either. "Gabriel?"

"Yes?"

"Did you enjoy our time together?"

"Why do you ask me such a question? It should be obvious to you I enjoyed touching you."

After giving her that backhanded bit of praise, he walked over to his mount and gained the saddle.

"It isn't obvious," she blurted out.

"It should be," he countered.

She wanted compliments, he supposed. His mind immediately went blank. He wasn't any good at small talk or wooing. Still, the forlorn look on her face told him she was in need of more praise. He didn't want their interlude to end with her looking dejected.

"You made me forget my duties."

There, that statement of fact would surely convince her how tempting she was to him.

It sounded like an accusation to her. "I apologize, Gabriel. It won't happen again."

"I was giving you a compliment, you daft woman."

Her eyes widened in surprise. "You were?"

Apparently she didn't believe him. "Of course it was a compliment. A laird doesn't often forget his duties. Such ill discipline would cause havoc, and so, you see, I was indeed giving you a compliment."

"Most compliments aren't given in a roar, m'lord. That may have been the reason I didn't understand."

He grunted. She didn't know what that rude sound was supposed to mean. The discussion was over, however. Gabriel slapped her horse's left flank to get her moving.

He didn't speak to her again until they reached the stables. Then he reminded her he wanted her to rest.

"Why must I rest? I'm not decrepit, m'lord."

"I don't wish you to become ill."

The set of his jaw told her it was pointless to argue with him. She was too irritated to let the topic go, however. "You're being unreasonable. I don't wish to stay in bed all day. I wouldn't be able to sleep at night."

Gabriel lifted her to the ground, then took hold of her hand and dragged her back toward the keep. "I would allow you to sit by the fire in the hall.

You may even sew if you're so inclined."

The picture he painted in his mind appealed to him. He smiled just thinking about Johanna doing such feminine things.

She was glaring up at him. He was so surprised by her reaction to his suggestion, he laughed.

"You have very specific ideas about how I should spend my days, m'lord. I wonder where you came up with them. Did your mother often sit by the fire and sew?"

"No."

"Then how did she fill her days?"

"With backbreaking work. She died when I was very young."

The look on his face and his tone of voice told her he didn't want her to pursue the topic. He was obviously sensitive about his childhood. The simple comment had told her quite a bit about how his mind worked, however. Backbreaking work had killed his mother . . . and wasn't that the reason Gabriel wanted her to rest her days away?

She knew she shouldn't question him further, but curiosity overrode caution. "Did you love your mother?"

He didn't answer her. She tried a different question. "Who raised you after she died?"

"No one and everyone."

"I don't understand."

He'd increased his stride as though trying to run away from her inquisition. He stopped suddenly and turned to her.

218

"You don't need to understand. Go inside, Johanna."

Her husband could be very rude when he wanted to be. He dismissed her from his thoughts without a single glance back to see if she was going to obey his orders.

Johanna stood on the steps for several minutes thinking about her husband. She wanted to understand him. She was his wife now, and it was therefore important that she know what made him happy and what pricked his temper. Once she'd established those facts, she would know how to respond.

"What has you frowning so, m'lady?"

Johanna jumped a foot, then turned to smile at Keith. "You startled me," she admitted, stating the obvious.

"I didn't mean to," the Maclaurin warrior replied. "I noticed you looked upset, and I wondered if I could do something to improve your mood."

"I was just thinking about your laird," she answered. "He's a complicated man."

"Aye, he is," Keith agreed.

"I would like to understand how his mind works."

"Why?"

She lifted her shoulders in a shrug. "Direct questions don't work," she remarked. "Still, there's more than one way into a castle."

Keith misunderstood. "Aye, there are two entrances, three if you count the pathway through the cellar."

"I wasn't referring to this holding," she explained. "I meant that there is always more than one way to get what you want. Do you see?"

"But there are still just two entrances to the keep, m'lady," Keith stubbornly insisted.

She let out a sigh. "Never mind, Keith."

The soldier turned the topic. "Will you go walking with Auggie this afternoon?"

"Perhaps," she replied. She hurried up the steps to go inside. Keith rushed ahead of her to pull the doors open.

"Today's Thursday, m'lady."

He'd blurted out the reminder. She smiled. "Yes, it is," she agreed. "Please excuse me. I want to check on Dumfries," she added when the soldier stayed by her side. She assumed he wanted to know what her plans were. She really needed to find a way to convince Gabriel she didn't need an escort. Both Keith and Calum were driving her daft following her around. She'd had to resort to sneakery in order to go riding this morning, but she knew she wouldn't be able to pull that trick again. They were on to her now. Besides, using deceit to get what she wanted wasn't very honorable. Johanna removed her carrier from her back and put the pouch with her bow and arrows in the corner by the steps.

"Then you knew it was Thursday all the while?" Keith asked.

"I hadn't thought about it, sir. Is it important?"

He nodded. "You should be wearing the Maclaurin colors today."

"I should. But yesterday . . ."

"You wore the MacBain plaid, m'lady. I specifically remember."

She could tell the soldier found her error distressing. "It's important I remember, isn't it?"

"Yes."

"Why?"

"You wouldn't want to insult either clan, would you?"

"No, of course not. I'll try to remember in future, and I do thank you for pointing out my mistake. I shall go upstairs immediately and change."

"But the day's half done, m'lady. You might as well keep the MacBain plaid on. You could wear the Maclaurin colors tomorrow and the day after. That would right the insult."

"She should wear the MacBain colors every other day, Keith. It's unacceptable for MacBain's wife to wear your colors two days in a row."

Calum made that announcement from the doorway. Johanna started to agree with his suggestion, but Keith's expression changed her mind. Since he looked more irritated than Calum, she decided to agree with him.

Neither soldier was particularly interested in her opinion or agreement however.

"Calum, I believe Keith is correct when he . . ."

"She will not wear your clan's colors two days in a row."

"She will," Keith countered with a glare. "She wants to get along, Calum. You would do well to follow her example."

"That's a change of heart, isn't it? You said not an hour ago you wished she'd stay where she was put."

"I meant no insult. It would make my task easier if she would let me know where she . . ."

"Since when is looking after one woman, a tiny one at that, a difficult task? And while I'm thinking about it, since when do you decide where she stays? I believe, since she's a MacBain now, it's my duty to put her where . . ."

"No one's going to put me anywhere."

The soldiers ignored her protest. They were fully involved in their heated argument. She'd started out with the thought to placate the men. Now she wanted to throttle both of them.

Johanna reminded herself that she had vowed to get along with everyone in the clan, even mule-headed commanders. Since they were ignoring her, she slowly backed away. They didn't notice. She turned then and hurried down the steps and went over to the hearth where Dumfries was resting.

"The Highlanders have peculiar notions about everything, Dumfries," she whispered. She knelt down and patted the dog. "Why would grown men care what their women wore? I can see you don't have any answers. Quit your growling. I'm going to look under your bandages to make certain you're healing properly. I won't hurt you. I promise."

The injury was healing nicely. Dumfries was thumping his tail by the time she'd finished re-adjusting his bandage and giving him a bit of praise.

Keith and Calum had taken their argument outside. Johanna went upstairs, changed into the Maclaurin plaid, and then returned to the great hall to help with the preparations for dinner. Fortunately Leila and Megan were assigned the duty today. The other women wouldn't listen to her. Janice, a pretty woman with reddish blond hair, was the worst offender. She would turn her back on Johanna in the middle of her request and walk away. Kathleen was another Maclaurin with a negative attitude toward her mistress. Johanna wasn't certain how she was going to change the women's behavior, but she was determined to try.

Leila and Megan were exceptions to the Maclaurins' united rule of ignoring her. They seemed eager to assist her. Their acceptance of her as their mistress made her like them all the more.

"What is it you wish done, m'lady?" Leila asked.

"I would like you to fetch a skirt full of wildflowers for the tables," Johanna said. "Megan, you and I will put linens on the tables and put the trenchers out."

"The hall's looking fit, isn't it?" Megan remarked.

Johanna agreed. It smelled clean, too. The scent of pine mingled with the fresh outdoors aroma of the rushes on the floor. The hall was large enough to hold at least fifty warriors. It was sparsely furnished, though. She was just noticing that fact when two soldiers came down the stairs carrying two tall-backed chairs.

"Where do you think you'll be putting those?" Megan demanded.

"By the hearth," one of the men replied. "We're following our laird's directions."

Megan frowned. She flipped the white linen cloth over the table and bent to smooth the material. "I wonder why . . ."

Johanna interrupted. She took hold of the other end of the cloth and pulled it down to the opposite end of the long table. "He wants me to sew by the fire," she explained. She let out a sigh then. The soldiers carried the chairs across the room. Dumfries started growling. The men were both young, and both were obviously a little intimidated by the hound's bluster. They altered their directions to make a wider path around the dog.

Johanna was sympathetic to their fear. She considered telling them Dumfries wouldn't hurt them, then changed her mind. The soldiers would be embarrassed if she let them know she was aware of their discomfort. She pretended to be too busy adjusting the cloth to notice.

The chairs were placed at an angle in front of the fireplace. The men bowed to their mistress after she'd thanked them and hurried out of the hall.

The chairs had plump seat and back cushions. One chair, she noticed, was covered with the MacBain plaid; the other, the Maclaurin.

"Good heavens, do you suppose I'll have to alternate chairs the way I do the plaids?"

"I beg your pardon, m'lady?" Megan paused

in her task of putting the stack of bread trenchers on the table. "I didn't quite make out what you were saying."

"I was just muttering to myself," Johanna explained. She took half the stack from Megan and went to set the other table.

"Wasn't it thoughtful of our laird to think about your comforts? As busy as he is, he still thought to have chairs carried in for you."

"Yes," Johanna hurriedly agreed, lest Megan think she wasn't appreciative of her husband's consideration. "I believe I'll work on my tapestry tonight. That should please my husband."

"You're a good wife to want to please him."

"Nay, Megan, I'm not a very good wife."

"But of course you are," Megan countered.

Gabriel walked inside in time to hear the Maclaurin woman's remark. He paused at the top step, waiting for his wife to turn around and notice him. She was busy placing trenchers on the table in front of each stool.

"A good wife is a submissive wife."

"Is being submissive a bad thing?" Megan asked.

"It doesn't seem to agree with me," Johanna replied, trying to make light of the painful topic.

"You seem very submissive to me," Megan announced. "I haven't noticed you ever disagreeing with anyone, m'lady, especially your husband."

Johanna nodded. "I have tried to do his bidding because he has proven to be considerate of my feelings. It will please him to have me sit by the fire and work on my sewing, and since I do enjoy the task, I will accommodate."

"That's good of you, wife."

Gabriel drawled out his opinion. Johanna turned around to look at her husband. She blushed with embarrassment. She felt as though she'd just been caught doing something sinful.

"I wasn't being disrespectful, m'lord."

"I didn't believe you were."

She stared at him a long minute trying to guess what he was thinking. His expression was contained, and she couldn't tell if he was angry or amused with her.

She was a fair sight to him with her face all flushed pink with her embarrassment. She looked worried. For that reason he didn't smile. It occurred to him that his wife had come a long way since they were married. In just a little under three months, she'd conquered her fear of him. She no longer trembled at the sight of him. She was still too damned timid to suit him, but he hoped, with time and patience, she'd outgrow that flaw.

"Was there something you wanted, husband?"

He nodded. "We don't have a healer here, Johanna. Since you've proven handy with a needle and thread, I want you to sew up Calum. He got his arm sliced through by an inexperienced soldier he was trying to train."

Johanna was already hurrying toward the steps to fetch her supplies. "I would be happy to help. I'll just collect the things I'll need and come right back down. Poor Calum. He must be in terrible pain."

Her prediction proved false. When Johanna returned to the great hall, Calum was waiting for her. He was seated on one of the stools and was being bathed in attention by the women surrounding him.

Leila, Johanna noticed, was most upset by Calum's condition.

She stood on the opposite side of the table pretending to be arranging the flowers she'd collected. Her eyes were misty, and she kept glancing over to look at the soldier. Calum was ignoring her.

The Maclaurin woman obviously held affection for the MacBain soldier. She was trying hard not to let her feelings show. Johanna wondered if it was because Calum hadn't shown any interest in her or if Leila hid her true feelings because she was a Maclaurin and Calum was a MacBain. One thing was certain. Leila was miserable. Johanna knew it wasn't her place to interfere; but Leila was such a dear woman, she really wanted to try to help.

Suddenly, another Maclaurin woman came rushing past Johanna. "I'll be happy to sew you up, Calum," Glynis called out. The woman who'd given Johanna the nickname Courageous was smiling at the soldier. "It won't matter to me that you're a MacBain. I'll do a fair job all the same."

Johanna stiffened her spine and hurried across the room. "Please move aside," she ordered. "I'll take care of Calum. Leila? Bring me a stool."

Gabriel came back into the hall, saw the crowd, and immediately dismissed them.

Johanna studied the injury. It was a long, narrow cut that started at Calum's left shoulder and ended just above his elbow. It was deep enough to require threads to hold it together so it would heal.

"Does it pain you, Calum?" she asked, her voice filled with sympathy.

"Nay, m'lady, not at all."

She didn't believe him. She put her supplies on the table and sat down on the stool next to the soldier. "Then why are you grimacing, sir?"

"I have displeased my laird," Calum explained in a low whisper. "The paltry cut is proof to him I wasn't paying attention."

After giving her his explanation, he glanced back over his shoulder to frown at Leila. She immediately lowered her gaze. Johanna wondered if the soldier held the Maclaurin woman responsible for his inattention.

Calum didn't even flinch while she worked on his injury. It took her a long time to clean the cut, but stitching it up didn't take much time at all. Leila assisted her by tearing long strips of white cotton material to use as a bandage.

"There," Johanna declared when she was finished. "You're as good as new, Calum. Don't get the bandage wet, and please don't put any strain on my threads by lifting anything heavy. I'll change the bandage every morning," she added with a nod.

"He can take care of that chore."

Gabriel walked over to the hearth. He knelt down on one knee to greet his pet.

"I would prefer to change the bandages, m'lord," Johanna called out. She moved back so Calum could stand up, then walked around to the other side of the table. Leila had left the flowers in a clutter on the tabletop. Johanna was going to put them in the porcelain vase of water before they started wilting.

"Don't contradict my orders, wife."

Gabriel stood up and turned to his soldier. His voice was filled with anger when he ordered him to leave the hall. "Get back to your duties, Calum. You've wasted enough time. Leila, stay put. I want to have a word with you before you leave."

The harshness in her husband's voice astonished Johanna. He was obviously furious with the soldier, and some of his anger was spilling over to Leila. The Maclaurin woman looked stricken. Johanna's heart went out to the woman. She wanted to defend her. She decided she would have to find out what Leila had done to displease her laird first.

"I've just instructed Calum not to lift anything heavy, m'lord."

"He's going to be working on the wall."

"Do you mean carrying rock?" She sounded horrified.

"I do." He sounded mean.

"He can't."

"He will."

She picked up a flower and stuffed it into the vase. She wasn't paying any attention to what she was doing. She was fully occupied glaring at her husband.

She wasn't being fair, she decided. Her husband just didn't realize how severe Calum's injury was. "The cut was quite deep, m'lord. He shouldn't be doing any work at all."

"I don't care if he lost his arm, wife. He will work."

"He'll tear my stitches."

"He can use one hand or kick the stones for all I care. Leila?"

"Yes, Laird MacBain?"

"You will not distract my soldiers when they're at work. Do you understand me?"

Tears filled her eyes. "Yes, Laird MacBain. I understand. It won't happen again."

"See that it doesn't. You may leave now."

Leila made a quick curtsy and turned to leave. "Do you wish me to return tomorrow to help your mistress?"

Johanna was about to say yes. Gabriel beat her with his answer. "It isn't necessary. One of the MacBain women will take over your chores."

Leila went running out of the hall. Johanna was infuriated with her husband. She rammed another flower into the vase and shook her head at him.

"You've crushed her feelings, m'lord."

"Her feelings won't get her killed," he snapped.

"What is that supposed to mean?"

"Come, Dumfries. It's time to go outside."

Johanna shoved the rest of the flowers into the vase and then hurried over to block her husband's

230

exit. She stopped just a foot away from him.

Her hands were settled on her hips and her head was tilted all the way back so she could look him in the eye.

His wife wasn't acting timid now. God's truth, there was fire in her eyes. Gabriel was so pleased by the gumption his wife was showing, he felt like grinning.

He scowled instead. "Are you questioning my motives?"

"I believe I am, m'lord."

"It isn't permitted."

She changed her approach. "Giving my opinion is permitted," she reminded him. "And it's my opinion you embarrassed Leila with your criticism."

"She'll survive," he snapped.

It was difficult but she didn't back away from his glare. "A good wife would probably let the matter drop," she whispered.

"Aye, she would."

She let out a sigh. "I don't suppose I'm a very good wife then, Gabriel. I still want to know what Leila did to make you angry."

"She damned near got my soldier killed."

"She did?"

"Aye, she did."

"But surely not on purpose," she defended.

He leaned down until his face was just inches away from hers. "Calum is at fault. He seems to have caught your affliction, wife. He wasn't paying attention to what he was doing."

She straightened her spine. "Are you referring to that little incident I was involved in, husband, when I accidentally walked into the middle of your training session?"

"I was."

"It's rude of you to bring that up," she announced.

He didn't look like he cared if he was being rude or not. "Staying alive is more important than hurt feelings," he muttered.

"That is true," she conceded.

Dumfries interrupted with a loud bark. Gabriel turned, called to his pet, and left the room without sparing his wife a backward glance.

Johanna thought about the conversation the rest of the afternoon. She knew she probably shouldn't have interfered in her husband's decisions regarding his clanspeople. She hadn't been able to stop herself, though. In the few months she'd been married, she'd grown quite fond of both Calum and Leila.

In truth, she was surprised by her own behavior. In the past she'd learned not to form any attachments because involvement led to caring, and then her first husband would have yet another weapon to use against her. Her affection for her staff put them in jeopardy.

Chelsea had been Johanna's first lesson. She was the cook's assistant, just about Johanna's own age, and a very sweet-tempered girl. Raulf knew Johanna enjoyed helping in the kitchens. She mentioned to him how she liked being around Chelsea

232

because the girl had such a quick wit and found pleasure in everything she did.

Chelsea broke an egg one morning. Cook reported the loss to Raulf. He broke Chelsea's leg that afternoon. Bishop Hallwick had advised the punishment for such a grievous offense was adequate penance.

Things were as different as night and day here, however. She could have friends here and not worry about their safety.

Father MacKechnie joined them for dinner. He looked weary from his journey to and from the Lowlands but was full of news he wanted to share about the latest happenings in England.

The soldiers were all talking at once, and it was difficult to hear what the priest had to say.

"Pope Innocent is surely going to excommunicate King John," Father MacKechnie reported in a near shout so he'd be heard. "The country will soon be put under an interdict."

"What has he done to warrant such harsh treatment?" Johanna asked.

"John was determined to put his own man in the position as archbishop of Canterbury. Our pope wouldn't have his interference. He announced his choice, an outsider to England, I understand; and John, furious over the selection, gave the order not to allow the man into England."

One of the Maclaurin soldiers made a quick jest the other soldiers found vastly amusing. Johanna had to wait until the howling coming from the second table had calmed before speaking again.

"What will happen if the country is placed under an interdict?"

"The subjects will suffer, of course. Most of the priests will have to flee from England. No masses will be said, no confessions heard, no marriages performed. The only sacraments Pope Innocent will allow will be baptisms for the innocent newborns and extreme unction for the dying, providing the family can find a priest to administer the sacrament in time. It's a sorry state of affairs, Lady Johanna, but the king doesn't seem too upset by such dire circumstances."

"He'll probably rob from the churches as a method of getting even." Gabriel made that speculation. Johanna agreed.

Father MacKechnie was appalled by the possibility. "He'll burn in hell if he does," he muttered.

"His soul's already lost, Father."

"You cannot know for certain, lass."

Johanna lowered her gaze. "No, I cannot know for certain."

Father MacKechnie changed the subject. "Prince Arthur's dead," he announced. "Some think he died at Eastertime four years ago."

Father MacKechnie paused. "There's talk the prince was murdered."

Gabriel was watching Johanna now. He noticed her complexion had turned as pale as milk.

"He probably was murdered," Calum said.

"Yes, but the question plaguing the barons is . . ."

"Who killed him," Calum supplied.

"Exactly," the priest agreed.

"What is the current speculation?" Gabriel asked.

"Most of the barons believe King John had Arthur killed. He's denying any knowledge of his nephew's fate, of course."

"The king is the only one with a strong motive," Calum said.

"Perhaps," Father MacKechnie agreed.

"A toast to a fair day's work."

The shout came from Keith. The Maclaurin soldiers all stood with their goblets in their hands. The MacBain soldiers followed. They met between the two tables, struck their goblets against each other's, and then downed what was left of the dark ale. Most of the drink had spilled to the floor.

Johanna excused herself from the table. She went upstairs to collect her bag with her half-completed tapestry, needle, and threads and then returned to the hall. She sat down in one of the chairs and began to work.

She had just pulled the first stitch through the burlap when she was asked to move.

"You're sitting in the MacBain chair, m'lady," Keith advised. He stood in front of Johanna with his hands clasped behind his back. Three other Maclaurin soldiers stood behind their commander. They blocked her light, and every one of them looked terribly concerned over what they obviously considered to be a serious slight.

She let out a sigh. "It matters where I sit, doesn't it, Keith?"

"Aye, m'lady. You're wearing the Maclaurin colors tonight."

"You should be sitting on the Maclaurin cushion."

The three soldiers flanking their leader immediately nodded.

She didn't know if she wanted to laugh at the disgruntled looking soldiers or shout at them. A hush descended over the group as they waited to see what she would do.

"Let her sit where she wants to sit," a MacBain soldier shouted.

Johanna found the entire situation ludicrous. She peeked around the soldiers to look at her husband, hoping for a bit of guidance. Gabriel was watching her, but he didn't show any outward reaction to what was going on. He was leaving the decision to her, she supposed.

She decided to placate the Maclaurins. It was still Thursday, after all. "Thank you for your instruction, Keith, and for being so patient with me."

She tried to sound sincere. She couldn't quite keep the amusement out of her voice though. The men moved back when she stood up. One even bent down to move her bag of threads for her.

Johanna walked to the other side of the hearth and sat down in the Maclaurin chair. She adjusted her skirts, tucked in a loose pleat, and then picked up her tapestry again and went back to work.

Her head was bent to her task. She pretended

intense concentration, for the Maclaurins were still watching her. When she heard several grunts that she assumed were rude noises of approval, she had to bite her lower lip so she wouldn't start laughing.

Father MacKechnie stayed by Gabriel's side throughout the rest of the evening. He was catching his laird up on all the latest happenings with the other clans. Johanna found the discussion fascinating. The topic was feuding, and it seemed to her that every clan in the Highlands was currently involved in some sort of an argument. The reasons the priest gave for the warring were even more astonishing to her. Why, the slightest breach or insult set tempers boiling. Sneezing seemed to be enough of a reason to go into battle.

"The Highlanders like to fight, don't they, Father?" Johanna didn't look up from her tapestry when she called out her question.

Father MacKechnie waited until the Maclaurin soldiers had filed out of the hall before answering her. Johanna was pleased to see the men leave. They were so loud and rambunctious, and it was difficult to discuss anything without shouting every word.

It was blissfully quiet once the men had taken their leave. None of them had bothered to bow to their mistress. She tried not to take offense, for at least they had given her husband that bit of respect.

She repeated her question to the priest. "Aye, they do like to fight," Father MacKechnie agreed.

"Why is that, do you suppose?"

"It's considered honorable," the priest explained.

Johanna missed a stitch, frowned, and set about righting the damage. She kept her gaze on her task when she asked her husband if he agreed with the priest.

"Aye, it is honorable," Gabriel said.

She found their opinions daft. "Banging heads together is considered honorable? I can't imagine why, m'lord."

Gabriel smiled. Johanna's choice of words, added to her exasperated tone of voice, amused him.

"Fighting lets the Highlanders show off those qualities they most admire, lass," the priest explained. "Courage, loyalty to their leader, and endurance."

"No warrior wishes to die in his bed," Gabriel interjected.

"They consider it a sin," the priest advised.

She dropped her needle and looked up at the men. She was certain they were jesting with her. They both looked sincere, however. She still wasn't convinced. "Which sin would that be?" she asked, her suspicion apparent.

"Sloth," Gabriel told her.

She almost snorted. She caught herself in time. "You must think me naive to believe that tall tale," she scoffed.

"Aye, you are naive, Johanna, but we aren't jesting with you. We do consider it a sin to die in our beds."

She shook her head so he'd know she wasn't believing any of his nonsense, then went back to sewing. The priest continued with his news. Gabriel was having difficulty paying attention. His gaze kept returning to his wife.

She enchanted him. Contentment such as he'd never known before swelled inside his chest. When he was very young and foolish and all alone, he would fall asleep each night thinking about his future. He made up dreams about the family he would have. His wife and his children would belong only to him, and they would, of course, live in his castle. Gabriel often pictured his wife sitting by the fire doing some feminine task . . . such as sewing.

The images he'd conjured up in his mind as a little boy kept the harsh reality of his stark life from overwhelming him. The fantasies helped him survive.

Yes, he'd been terribly young and tender back then. Time and training had toughened him, however, and he'd outgrown the need for such foolish dreams. He no longer felt the need to belong. He'd learned to depend solely upon himself. Dreams were for the weak. Aye, he thought to himself, he was strong now and his dreams were all but forgotten.

Until now. The memories came flooding back as he stared at his wife.

Reality was a hell of a lot better than fantasies, Gabriel decided. He'd never imagined having a wife as beautiful as Johanna. He hadn't known what contentment was or how he would feel or how fierce his need would become to protect her.

Johanna happened to look up and caught her husband staring at her. His expression puzzled her. He seemed to be staring through her as though he was lost in some important thought. Aye, he must be thinking about something troublesome, she guessed, because his frown had become ferocious.

"I could use a spot of *uisgebreatha*," Father MacKechnie announced. "Then I'll be looking for my bed. Lord, I'm weary tonight."

Johanna immediately got up to serve the priest. A jug filled with Highland brew was kept on the chest against the wall behind Gabriel. She carried the jug over to the table and filled the priest's goblet.

She turned to serve her husband next. Gabriel declined the drink with a shake of his head.

Father MacKechnie took a long swallow and promptly grimaced. "I'd wager this hasn't aged more than a week at most," he complained. "It tastes like sour swill."

Gabriel smiled. "You'll have to complain to Auggie. The drink came from his kettles."

Johanna's curiosity was captured by the priest's remark about aging. "Is it important how long the drink waits?"

"It ages, lass," the priest corrected. "It doesn't wait. And yes, it's important. The longer, the better, some experts say."

"How long?" she wanted to know.

"Why, as long as ten or twelve years in the oak barrels," Father MacKechnie speculated. "It takes a patient man to wait that long for a taste, of course."

"Is the drink more valuable then?"

Johanna put the jug down on the table. She stood next to her husband's side while she waited for the priest to finish his drink and answer her.

She put her hand on Gabriel's shoulder. Her gaze was intent upon the priest, and Gabriel doubted she was even aware she was touching him. The unconscious show of affection pleased him considerably, for it was proof to him that she'd completely conquered her fear of him. And that, he decided, was an important first step. He was out to gain her trust. Oh, he remembered demanding she give him her trust, but he'd realized right after giving her that high-handed order that trust would have to be earned. Gabriel believed he was a patient man. He would wait. In time she would realize her good fortune and value his protection. She would learn to trust him, and with that trust came loyalty.

A man couldn't ask for anything more from his wife.

The priest pulled him away from his thoughts when he said, "The drink is very valuable once it's been allowed to age. Men would kill for pure *uisgebreatha*. The Highlanders, you see, take their drinking seriously. 'Tis the reason they call it the water of life, lass."

"Would they barter for goods if aged brew was offered in trade?"

"Johanna, why does this topic interest you?" Gabriel asked.

She shrugged. She didn't want to tell him about the barrels of liquid gold Auggie had mentioned to her. She would have to gain permission from her friend first. She also wanted to see for herself that the barrels were still inside the cave. Besides, it would be a nice surprise for Gabriel; and if the value was as high as Johanna guessed, her husband would have something to barter with for supplies.

"Father, would you honor us by taking over the vacant chamber upstairs tonight?" Johanna asked.

The priest turned his gaze to his laird. He waited for him to extend his invitation.

"It's a comfortable bed, Father," Gabriel remarked.

Father MacKechnie smiled. "I'll be happy to take it," he said. "It's most hospitable of you to open your home to me."

Father MacKechnie stood up, bowed to his laird, and then went to collect his things. Johanna walked back over to her chair, gathered her tapestry and needle and put them back inside her bag. Gabriel waited for her near the entrance.

"You may leave your sewing on the chair, wife. No one will bother it."

Dumfries came back into the hall, passed Johanna on her way to the stairs, and growled at her. She patted the hound before continuing on.

Gabriel followed Johanna up the stairs. She seemed preoccupied with her thoughts while she prepared for bed. He added a log to the fire, then stood up, leaned against the mantel, and watched her.

"What are you thinking about?"

"This and that."

"That isn't a proper answer, Johanna."

"I was thinking about my life here."

"You've made the transition without much difficulty," he remarked. "You should be happy."

Johanna tied the belt to her robe and turned to her husband. "I haven't made any transition, Gabriel. 'Tis the truth I've been living in limbo. I've been caught between two worlds," she added with a nod.

Her husband sat down on the side of the bed and pulled his boots off.

"I meant to talk to you about this topic earlier today," she said. "But there didn't seem to be enough time."

"Exactly what is it you're trying to tell me?"

"You and all the others have been treating me like a visitor, Gabriel. Worse, I've been acting like one."

"Johanna, you aren't making any sense. I don't take strangers to my bed. You're my wife, not a visitor."

She turned her gaze to the fire. She was thoroughly disgusted with herself. "Do you know what I've realized? In my bid to protect myself, I've become completely self-consumed. I'll have to go to confession tomorrow and beg God's forgiveness."

"You have no need to worry about protecting yourself. It's my duty to take care of you."

She smiled in spite of her irritation. Gabriel sounded insulted. "No, it is my duty to take care of myself."

He didn't like hearing her opinion. His scowl was as hot as the fire. "Do you deliberately try to rile me by suggesting I can't take care of you?"

She hurried to soothe him. "Of course not," she answered. "I'm pleased to have your protection."

"You contradict yourself, woman."

"I'm not trying to confuse you, Gabriel. I'm just trying to sort things out in my mind. When someone's hungry and there isn't any food, well then that someone is consumed day and night with the worry of finding something to eat. Isn't that true, husband?"

Gabriel shrugged. "I would imagine so."

"For a long time I've been consumed with fear. I lived with it for so long, it seemed to take control of me, but now that I'm safe, I've had time to think about other matters. Do you understand?"

He didn't understand. He didn't like seeing her frown either. "I've told you, you please me. You needn't be worried."

She was exasperated. Since she was turned away from her husband, she felt it safe to smile. "Gabriel, as surprising as this may be for you to hear, I'm not overly concerned about pleasing you."

He was surprised all right as well as irritated. "You're my wife," he reminded her. "It is therefore your duty to want to please me."

Johanna let out a sigh. She knew her husband didn't understand what she was trying to explain. She couldn't fault him. She barely understood herself.

"I meant no insult, m'lord."

She sounded sincere. Gabriel was appeased. He came up behind her and wrapped his arms around her waist. Then he leaned down to kiss the side of her neck.

"Come to bed now. I want you, Johanna."

"I want you, too, Gabriel."

She turned around and smiled at her husband. He lifted her into his arms and carried her to bed.

They made slow, sweet love to each other, and when they each had found their fulfillment, they held each other close.

"You do please me, woman." His voice was gruff with affection.

"Remember your praise, m'lord, for I'm certain there will be times in future when I don't please you."

"Is this a worry or a prophecy?"

She leaned up on her elbow and gently stroked the side of his neck. "Nay, I give you only the truth."

She turned his attention with her question about his intentions for tomorrow. He wasn't accustomed to discussing his plans with anyone, but he was in the mood to make her happy and so he went into detail about the hunt he planned and the items he and his men planned to steal.

She vowed not to lecture him. She couldn't keep

silent more than a few minutes, though, and hurled herself into a speech about the merits of probity. She mentioned the wrath of God on Judgment Day. Gabriel wasn't impressed with her speech about fire and brimstone. He yawned in the middle of it.

"Husband, it's my duty to help you lead a good, honest life."

"Why?"

"So you'll get to heaven, of course."

He laughed. She gave up. She fell asleep worrying about her husband's soul.

Chapter
10

The first thing Johanna noticed when she came downstairs the following morning was her tapestry. The half-completed wall hanging had been ripped to shreds. Her bag wasn't intact either. The culprit was busy chewing on one of the burlap straps. He'd already devoured the other one.

Dumfries knew he'd gotten into mischief. He tried to crawl under one of the chairs when she shouted his name and started toward him. The chair went crashing to the ground; Dumfries started howling, and Megan came running from the buttery.

The dog sounded like a demon let out of hell. The frightening sound he made was loud enough to shake the rafters. The noise terrified Megan. Even though the hound wasn't paying her any attention, she was still extremely cautious when she bent to pick up the tapestry.

Keith and Calum both heard the commotion and came running inside. They came to a dead stop on the top step. Gabriel was right behind them.

He shoved the soldiers out of the way and started down the steps.

Johanna was involved in a tug of war with Dumfries. The dog was winning. She was trying to get her bag out of his mouth. She was concerned the hound would choke on the strap he was trying to swallow.

"Good God, Megan, what have you done to your lady's tapestry?" Keith demanded when he finally figured out what she was holding in her hands. He scowled at the Maclaurin woman and shook his head.

Johanna didn't take her attention away from the hound when she called out to Keith. "Sir, you do honestly believe Megan ate the thing?"

Calum started laughing. Johanna lost her footing and went flying backward. Gabriel caught her. He lifted her out of his way and turned to his pet. Johanna ran around her husband to stand in front of the hound.

"Gabriel, don't you dare strike your dog."

She shouted her command so she'd be heard over Calum's laughter. Gabriel looked like he wanted to shout at her.

"I have no intention of striking him. Get out of my way, woman, and quit wringing your hands. I'm not going to hurt him. Dumfries, quit that damned howling."

Johanna didn't move. Gabriel lifted her out of his way, then knelt down on one knee and forced the dog's mouth open so he could pull the strap free. Dumfries didn't want to let go. He yelped in protest before he gave in.

Gabriel wouldn't let her comfort the dog. He stood up, grabbed her by the shoulders, and demanded she kiss him good-bye.

"In front of your men?" she whispered.

He nodded. She started to blush. His mouth captured hers in a long, lingering kiss. She sighed then. She was a bit rattled when he pulled away.

"You look tired, wife. You should rest."

Gabriel made the remark on his way to the doors. She chased after him.

"You cannot be serious, m'lord."

"I'm always serious, m'lady."

"But I only just got out of bed. Surely you don't expect me to take a nap now."

"I do expect you to rest," he called over his shoulder. "And change your plaid, Johanna. You're wearing the wrong one."

"It's Friday, m'lady." Calum added the reminder.

She let out a loud, unladylike sigh. Megan waited until the men had left, then hurried over to her mistress. "Do go inside and sit down, Lady Johanna. You don't want to overdo."

Johanna felt like screaming. She resisted the urge. "For the love of . . . Megan, do I look ill to you?"

The Maclaurin woman studied her closely before shaking her head. " 'Tis the truth you look fit to me."

"Are you going to sit down and rest?" Johanna asked.

"I've got work to do," Megan answered. "I don't have time to sit."

"Neither do I," Johanna muttered. "It's high time I took an interest in the running of this household. I've been entirely too self-consumed. All that's going to change, however. Starting now."

Megan had never seen her mistress sound so commanding. "But, m'lady, your husband has ordered you to rest."

Johanna shook her head. She rattled off the list of chores she wanted to complete by nightfall, gave Megan permission to enlist the help of two more servants, and then announced she was going to speak to Cook about dinner.

"Please fetch my bow and arrows from my chamber," Johanna requested. She started toward the back of the keep. "If Cook's in an accommodating mood, we'll have rabbit stew for dinner. I'm certain I can cajole Auggie into doing a spot of hunting with me. I'll be back before the nooning hour, Megan."

"You can't go hunting, m'lady. Your husband forbade you to leave."

"No, he didn't," Johanna countered. "He merely suggested I rest. He never once mentioned hunting, now did he?"

"But he meant . . ."

"Don't try to second-guess your laird. And quit your worrying. I promise I'll be back before I'm missed."

Megan shook her head. "You won't get ten paces outside before you're spotted by Keith . . . or is it Calum responsible for looking out for you today?"

"I'm praying each believes the other has that duty."

She hurried out the back door, turned left, and crossed the courtyard to the building housing the kitchen. She introduced herself to Cook and added an apology for taking so long to make her acquaintance. Cook's name was Hilda. She was an older woman with streaks of gray in her red hair. She wore the MacBain plaid. She seemed appreciative of Johanna's interest in her duties and took her on a tour of the pantry.

"If I'm lucky on my hunt and snare some rabbits, would you be willing to prepare them for our dinner tonight?"

Hilda nodded. "I make a fine rabbit stew," Hilda boasted. "But I'll need at least ten, unless they're plump. Then nine will do."

"Wish me good hunting then," Johanna called out. She hurried back to the great hall, took her bow and arrows from Megan, and then left by the back door again.

She took the long way around to the stables. Sean didn't want to saddle her horse for her. She coaxed him into the duty with a smile and a promise not to leave the meadow. She implied she had Gabriel's permission. It wasn't an outright lie, just a little fabrication, but she still felt guilty.

She had another mare made ready for Auggie. It was presumptuous on her part to assume he would agree to ride with her, she supposed, but she didn't want to waste any time. If Auggie did go with her, she didn't want to have to go back to the stables. Keith or Calum would surely try to stop her then.

Auggie was lining up his shot in the center of the meadow when Johanna interrupted him.

"I'm not in the mood to go hunting for rabbits," he announced.

"I was hoping you'd be more agreeable," Johanna countered. "And while we were looking for our rabbits, I thought you might be inclined to show me exactly where the cave is hidden. I couldn't find it yesterday."

Auggie shook his head. "I'll ride as far as the ridge with you, girl, and point the direction once again, but that's as much time as I'm willing to take away from my game."

Auggie climbed up on the horse, took the reins from Johanna, and led the way.

"I'd like your permission to tell my husband about the barrels of liquid gold," she said.

"It weren't a secret I was keeping, lass."

"Would you be willing to share the brew with your laird? He could use it to barter for supplies."

"The drink belongs to my laird. I owe my life to MacBain, but you wouldn't be knowing about that. Most of the MacBains pledged their loyalty for good reason. He gave them their pride back. I won't be denying him anything, least of all Highland brew. Why, I'd even quit my game if he asked me to," he added with a dramatic nod.

Auggie stopped at the top of the ridge and pointed to the line of trees angling down the north side. He told Johanna to start counting the trees, starting at the base of the hill with the crooked pine and working her way back up. She reached the number twelve when he stopped her.

"That's the break you're looking for, between those trees," he instructed. "You were taking the wider path higher up when you went looking, weren't you, lass?"

"I was," she replied. "Will you please reconsider and come along with me?"

Auggie declined her invitation a second time. "Let the younger soldiers trail you, Johanna. And don't be telling the Maclaurins about the liquid gold. Let our laird decide what he wants to do with the treasure."

"But the Maclaurins are part of our clan now, Auggie," she argued.

The old MacBain warrior snorted. "They keep their noses up in the air around us," he said. "Think they're so high and mighty, they do. None of them were cast out, you see."

"I don't see," Johanna countered. "I was told they begged my husband to give them aid against the English and . . ."

"That's true," Auggie interrupted. "His father was the Laird Maclaurin. 'Course he never acknowledged his bastard son, not even when death was waiting on his last breath. The Maclaurins have conveniently forgotten MacBain's a bastard. They know he's got Maclaurin blood in him, I suppose. Still, they don't have any use for the rest of us."

Johanna shook her head. "I'll wager the MacBain soldiers fought by their leader's side during the battle to save the Maclaurins."

"You'd win a fair amount then, for it's true, we did fight with our laird."

"Have the Maclaurins forgotten that fact?"

She was getting riled over the Maclaurins' attitude and trying not to let it show. Auggie smiled. "You're outraged for the MacBains, aren't you, girl? You're making yourself one of us."

The sparkle in Auggie's handsome eyes made her smile. His praise and his opinion of her were both important. In the short time she'd known him, she'd come to value his friendship . . . and his guidance. Auggie took the time to listen to her. 'Twas the truth no one else did. He never told her to rest either, she thought to herself.

"Now what has you scowling?"

She shook her head. "I was just considering my circumstances," she remarked.

"Again? You'll give yourself a pounding headache thinking about your circumstances all the time. Good hunting, Johanna," he added with a nod. He turned his mount and headed back to his meadow.

Johanna rode in the opposite direction. She'd almost reached the path Auggie had shown her when a white-haired rabbit came racing into the clearing. She tucked the reins under her left knee, reached for an arrow, secured it in her bow and took aim. The rabbit went down just as another came loping across her path.

Something must have spooked the animals into leaving their hiding places, for in less than twenty minutes, she'd collected eight plump ones and one rather scrawny one. She stopped at the stream, washed her arrows, and put them back in her pouch. The rabbits were tied by a string to the back of her saddle.

Three Maclaurin soldiers caught up with her just as she was heading back for home. They were young warriors and probably still in training, she supposed, because none of them had any scars on his face or arms. Two of the men had blond hair. The third soldier was dark haired with clear green eyes.

"Our laird will be unhappy to know you're riding alone, m'lady," said one of the fair-haired soldiers. Johanna pretended she hadn't heard him. She untied the string from her saddle and handed the rabbits to the soldier.

"Will you please take these back to Cook? She'll be waiting for them."

"Certainly, m'lady."

"What is your name, sir?"

"Niall," the soldier answered. He motioned to the other blond young man and said, "He's called Lindsay. Michael's behind me."

"It's a pleasure to meet all of you," Johanna announced. "Do excuse me now. I'm intent on following this trail."

"Why?" Michael asked.

"I'm looking for something," Johanna said, deliberately giving the soldier only a half answer. "I won't be gone long."

"Does our laird know what you're about?" Michael asked her the question.

"I don't remember if I mentioned my plan or not," she blatantly lied.

Niall turned to his companions. "Stay with our mistress while I take her bounty back to the keep."

Johanna was happy for their escort. She turned her attention back to her task and led the way through the forest. The trail narrowed and then became broken bits with bushes barring her way. Sunlight filtered through the limbs of branches arched above her like a lush canopy. The young soldiers smiled over her whispered praise of the beauty surrounding her.

"We aren't in church, m'lady," Michael shouted. "There isn't any need to lower your voice."

"Exactly what is it you're looking for?" Lindsay asked.

"A cave," Johanna answered.

The path split into two directions. Johanna turned her mount to the left, then ordered the soldiers to take the other direction. Neither soldier would leave her side, however.

"Then please mark this spot so that when we backtrack, we'll remember which direction we haven't taken yet."

She untied the ribbon holding her braid together and handed it to Michael. The soldier was in the process of securing the blue strip to one of the low-hanging branches when Johanna's mare started misbehaving. Rachel's ears flattened, and she let out a loud snort as she pranced to the side of the path. Johanna tightened her hold on her reins and ordered the mare to behave.

"Something's frightening her," she remarked. She glanced back over her shoulder to see what might have startled her mare. Then Michael's horse caught Rachel's frenzy and reared up.

"We'd best get back to the clearing," Lindsay suggested. He was diligently struggling to keep his own horse under control.

Johanna was in agreement with the suggestion. She nudged Rachel with her knees and tried to get the mare to turn.

Rachel suddenly bolted. Johanna only had enough time to duck her head when her horse broke through the bushes. The mare wouldn't be calmed. Johanna had her hands full trying to control the animal and block the branches at the same time.

She couldn't imagine what had caused the sudden tantrum. One of the soldiers shouted to her. She couldn't make out the words, however. Rachel veered to the left and continued on, in a full gallop now. She heard another shout, turned to look back over her shoulder but couldn't see the soldiers. She turned around again and put her hand in front of her face to block yet another branch. She wasn't able to push the obstacle aside. Johanna was literally plucked from her saddle. She went flying to the side and ended up underneath a leafy bush. The breath was knocked out of her. She let out a low groan and sat up. Part of the bush sprang away from her leg and slapped her in the face. She muttered an unladylike expletive and stood up. She tried to rub the sting out of her backside.

She kept expecting Lindsay and Michael to come to her assistance. Her mare was nowhere in sight. The forest was quiet now, eerily so, and she assumed the soldiers had taken a different turn. They were probably still chasing after her horse. She would have to wait until they caught up with Rachel and realized their mistress was missing. Then they would surely backtrack to look for her.

Johanna collected her bow and arrows and went over to sit on a low boulder to wait for the soldiers. The musty scent of peat and fresh pine needles filled the air. Johanna waited a long while before deciding she was going to have to walk back to the clearing. She wasn't quite certain of the direction, for her horse had turned several times during her run.

"I'll probably walk in circles for the rest of the day," Johanna muttered.

Gabriel was going to be furious with her, too. She couldn't fault him, she supposed. It wasn't safe to go strolling through the forest, especially with wild animals roaming about.

She notched an arrow to her bow just as a precaution and started walking. A good fifteen minutes later, she thought she was back where she'd started. Then she changed her mind. The boulder in front of her was much larger than the one she'd sat on. She believed she was going in the right direction after all and started walking again.

She found the cave quite by accident. She had stopped in front of another large boulder blocking her path and was trying to decide if she would go to the left or the right. The opening was on her left and was as tall as she was. It was flanked on both sides by tall, narrow trees.

Johanna was so excited about her find, she forgot caution. She literally ran inside. The corridor was lit by sunlight filtering through the cracks in the ceiling. When she reached the end of the pathway, the cave opened into a room the size of the great hall at the keep. On her left were narrow shelves of rock protruding from the wall that resembled broken steps. On her right were the barrels. There were at least twenty of the round casks, perhaps more. The chieftains who'd stored them inside had placed them on their sides. The bottom ones rested on rock. The barrels formed a pyramid that reached the top of the cavern.

Time hadn't rotted the oak. It was actually quite dry inside the cavern.

Johanna was thrilled with the find. She wanted to run all the way back to the keep and demand that Gabriel come and see the treasure.

She'd have to wait until her husband returned from his day of hunting, she remembered. She let out a sigh then. "Call a dog a dog, Gabriel," she muttered to herself. He wasn't hunting. He was stealing. Aye, it was a day of thievery, she thought to herself, but certainly his last, for come hell or heaven she was going to make him learn the fine art of bartering.

Aye, she was going to save his sorry soul whether he wanted her to or not.

Johanna went back outside to wait for the soldiers to fetch her. She walked over to the boulder and climbed up on top. She leaned against the trunk of a giant tree, folded her arms across her middle, and waited.

The soldiers were certainly taking their time. A good hour passed before her impatience got the better of her. She guessed she was going to have to find her own way back home.

Johanna pulled away from the tree, adjusted her bow on her shoulder, and was just about to jump down from the boulder when she heard a snarling sound coming from the bushes directly in front of her. She froze. The noise intensified. The horrid sound reminded her of Dumfries, but she knew it wasn't Gabriel's pet. He was at the keep. It had to be a wolf making all the commotion.

Then she saw the eyes staring up at her. They were yellow. Johanna didn't scream. Dear God, she wanted to. She wanted to run, too, but she didn't dare.

Another rustling sound came from across the tiny clearing . . . another pair of murky yellow eyes staring at her. The snarling echoed around her now. She heard a movement behind her and knew then she was surrounded.

She didn't have any idea how many wolves were there, waiting to prey upon her. She didn't panic. There simply wasn't time for that frivolity.

She found out something amazing about herself, too. She could fly. God's truth, she was certain she flew up the branches of the tree. She certainly didn't remember climbing. She'd almost made it to safety, too, when one clever wolf caught hold of the hem of her plaid. He was in a frenzy to pull her back. His jaws were locked on the material, his head shaking back and forth with his determination. Johanna was draped over a branch, holding her hand over the top of her carrier so her arrows wouldn't spill to the ground and clutching the tree with her other hand. It was a precarious position. Her feet were only inches above the wolf's teeth.

She didn't dare look down. She wrapped her legs around the branch and tried to undo her belt so she wouldn't be trapped by the plaid. It took her long minutes and when she was finished, she let the material drop down to the wolves.

She was finally free. She kept climbing, whimpering now, and when she was finally high enough up to convince herself she was safe, she settled herself in the crook of a heavy branch and the tree's trunk.

She finally gathered enough courage to look down. Her heart felt as though it had just dropped to the pit of her stomach. Dear God, there were at least six of the beasts. They circled the tree, growling and snapping up at her and at each other, and there was one, perhaps their leader, who made Dumfries look like a pup. She shook her head, denying what she was seeing. Wolves didn't get that large. Did they?

They couldn't climb trees either . . . or could they? The giant wolf started butting his head against the tree trunk. She thought that was an extremely ignorant thing to do. Two of the other wolves were shredding her plaid. They seemed to be in a frenzy, too.

They didn't look like they had any intention of leaving her alone. Johanna worried over her circumstances a long while. When she finally accepted the fact that she was indeed safe, she started worrying about Michael and Lindsay. She didn't want them to ride into a pack of wolves, and she didn't know if the monsters would leave when they heard the horses coming. Aye, they were monsters all right, and they didn't look like they would run from anything or anyone.

Johanna's attention was turned when she caught a movement to her left. One wolf had climbed to the top of the rocked entrance of the cave. The animal looked as though he was getting ready to spring at her. Johanna didn't know if the wolf would make the distance or not. She wasn't going to wait to find out, however. She slipped her bow from her shoulder, pulled out an arrow, then shifted her position ever so slightly and took aim.

She caught the wolf in midflight. The arrow went through one eye. The animal crashed down to the ground and landed just a foot away from the others. They immediately turned on the dead animal.

In the next twenty minutes or so, Johanna killed three more. She'd heard that wolves were clever animals. These weren't. They were safe from her arrows as long as they stayed below her, for the branches obstructed her aim, but one after another climbed up on the rock and tried to leap into the tree to get her. They were slow to catch on, she decided, when the fourth wolf followed the same path the first three had taken.

Her fingers ached from holding her arrow against the string of her bow. She wanted to get the giant wolf in her sights. In her mind, he was surely the one who had injured Dumfries. She didn't know why she'd come to that conclusion. Perhaps it was the dried black blood on the animal's fangs when he bared his teeth at her. He seemed to be more demon than animal. His eyes never left her. He was such an evil-looking beast. Johanna shivered with disgust and fear.

"You're the one they call Pet, aren't you?"

She didn't expect an answer, of course. She began to wonder if her worrisome situation had made her mind snap. She was, after all, talking to demons now. She sighed over her own behavior.

Why wouldn't the wolf leave? And where in heaven's name were Michael and Lindsay? They surely hadn't forgotten her, had they?

Johanna didn't believe her day could get much worse.

She was wrong. She hadn't counted on the rain.

She'd been too busy to notice the sunlight had disappeared, and God only knew she didn't have time to look up at the sky and see rain clouds. She was so intent on protecting herself from the wolves, she didn't have time to think about anything else. It didn't matter, she supposed. Knowing ahead of time wouldn't have changed anything. She still got drenched.

Lightning crackled through the trees. A torrential downpour followed. The branches became slick, as though they'd been greased with lard instead of water. Johanna couldn't get her arm all the way around the trunk. She was afraid to adjust her position, fearing she'd slide down.

The monster still waited at the base of the tree. Johanna's hands were shaking from holding her bow and arrow. Her fingers cramped.

She heard her name being shouted. She whispered a prayer of thank you to her Maker before shouting back. Odd, but she thought she heard her husband's voice. That couldn't be possible, of course. He was hunting.

The pounding of horses coming her way finally encouraged the wolf to leave. Johanna was ready. As soon as the streak of lightning moved away from the tree, she dispatched her arrow. She missed her mark. She'd aimed for his middle, but the arrow caught him in the backside. The wolf let out a howl of distress and circled back toward her. Johanna hurried to put the beast out of his misery. She grabbed another arrow from her carrier, sighted it to her bow, and took aim again.

264

She had little liking for the kill. Even though he looked very like something the devil had let out of hell, the wolf was still one of God's creatures. He served a purpose more holy than her own, or so she'd been told, and though she didn't have a clue as to what the purpose was, she still felt guilty.

The MacBain soldiers came riding around the curve in the path just as Johanna's arrow sliced down through the air and killed the wolf. The animal was lifted back and up by the force of the arrow, then collapsed in a heap on the ground in front of the warriors' horses.

Johanna leaned back against the trunk and let go of her bow. She clenched and unclenched her hands in an effort to get the cramps out of her fingers. She suddenly felt nauseated. She took a deep breath and peeked around the branch to look at the soldiers below.

As soon as she regained a bit of strength, she was going to give the men hell for making her wait so long. Then, after they offered her their apologies, she was going to make them give her their pledge not to mention this shameful incident to their laird. By God, she'd nag that promise out of every one of them.

"Are you all right, m'lady?"

She couldn't see the soldiers' faces. She recognized Calum's voice though.

"Yes, Calum," she called back. "I'm quite all right."

"She doesn't sound all right," said Keith. In a

near shout, he added, "You killed our pet."

The Maclaurin soldier sounded stunned. Johanna felt an explanation was necessary. She didn't want any of the soldiers to think she had derived any sort of malicious satisfaction or pleasure from killing the beasts.

"It isn't how it looks," she shouted down.

"You didn't kill them?"

"They look like her arrows," Keith remarked.

"They wouldn't leave me alone, sir. I had to kill them. Please don't tell anyone, especially our laird. He's too busy to be bothered by such an insignificant incident."

"But m'lady . . ."

"Calum, don't argue with me. I'm not in the mood to be polite. I've had a trying morning. Just give me your word you'll keep my secret."

Johanna's skirt was caught on the branch. While she worked at tugging it free, she waited for the soldiers to give her their pledges. She wasn't going to get down from her perch until they did.

Gabriel would be furious. Just thinking about his reaction gave her goosebumps.

The men still hadn't given her their promise. "It's little enough to ask," she muttered to herself.

Calum started laughing. It didn't take her any time at all to understand why.

Gabriel already knew.

"Come down here. Now."

The fury in her husband's voice almost shook her out of the tree. Johanna grimaced. She leaned back against the crook in the tree, hoping to hide from her husband . . . and his wrath. She quickly realized what she was doing, muttered an unlady-like expletive under her breath, and then leaned forward. She pushed a limb out of her way and looked down. She wished she hadn't. She spotted Gabriel right away. He was looking up at her. His hands rested on the pommel of his saddle and he appeared to be only mildly irritated.

She knew better. Her husband hadn't been able to keep the anger out of his voice when he'd rudely bellowed his command.

His mount was between Keith's and Calum's. Johanna let go of the branch and leaned back against the trunk of the tree. She could feel her face heat up with embarrassment. Gabriel had obviously been there all the while she was demanding his soldiers keep her secret from him.

Some sort of explanation was probably due now, she supposed, and given enough time, she could surely come up with something plausible. Johanna decided she wasn't going to move until she did.

It was taking all of Gabriel's concentration to keep his anger under control. He turned his gaze to the ground and once again counted the number of dead wolves, just to make certain his eyes hadn't deceived him. Then he looked back up at her.

She hadn't moved to do his bidding. God's truth, she couldn't. The threat of the wolves wasn't over yet. There was still one down below, waiting to pounce on her.

"Johanna, get down here."

She didn't appreciate his surly tone of voice.

She would have told him so, too, but she didn't believe her opinion would matter much to him. She guessed she'd better try to accommodate him.

Unfortunately, her legs refused to accommodate her. She'd been gripping the branch with her thighs for so long, they seemed to turn to jelly when she tried to scoot down the trunk.

In the end, Gabriel had to come up and fetch her. He had to peel her hands away from the branch. She couldn't seem to let go.

He placed her arms around his neck, then pulled her up against him. His one arm was spanning her waist, his other was draped over the branch to keep the two of them from slipping.

He didn't move for a long minute. Johanna hadn't realized how cold she was until the heat from his body began to warm her. She was shaking now.

So was he, she noticed. Was he so furious with her, he was shaking with rage?

"Gabriel?"

The fear he heard in her voice was his undoing. "You will cease being afraid of me, damn it," he told her in a low, furious whisper. "God's truth, I would like to throttle some sense into you, woman, but I won't ever harm you."

His rebuke stung. She hadn't done anything to cause his displeasure . . . except perhaps ignoring his ridiculous order to rest. Aye, she thought to herself, she did disregard his suggestion.

"I have already ceased being afraid of you, damn it," she muttered against the side of his neck. She let out a sigh then. Gabriel was partial to honesty, and she supposed she'd only prick his anger further if she didn't give him the full truth now.

The man looked ready to throttle something all right. "I'm not afraid of you most of the time," she added in a rush. "Why are you so angry with me?"

He didn't answer her question. He couldn't. He was still in jeopardy of bellowing at her. He would wait until he had his temper under control before explaining she'd taken a good twenty years off his life by giving him such a scare.

Her husband tightened his hold on her. Her question had obviously upset him. She couldn't imagine why. She wasn't a mind reader, after all. She thought about mentioning that fact, then changed her mind. It wouldn't do her any good at all to incite his fury. She was his wife and therefore should try to soothe him.

She decided to change the topic. She'd start with praise, thinking to please him. "You were right, husband. The woods are infested with wolves."

It was the wrong thing to say to him. She came to that conclusion when his grip tightened and he let out a loud, shuddering breath.

"I'm getting you all wet, m'lord," she blurted out, trying to turn his attention away from her unfortunate mention of wolves.

"You're soaked through," he snapped. "You're going to catch a fever and be dead in a week."

"I will not," she announced. "I'll change into dry clothing and be as fit as ever. You're squeezing the breath out of me, husband. Do let up on your hold."

Gabriel ignored her request. He let out an expletive, then suddenly moved. She tightened her hold on his neck and closed her eyes. She'd let him worry about keeping the branches out of her face on the way down.

He wouldn't let her walk. He carried her over to his mount, lifted her up higher, and then dropped her onto the saddle. He wasn't overly gentle about the task.

She immediately tried to straighten her underskirts. The material was stuck to her skin. She knew she didn't look like a decent lady now, glanced down, and let out a gasp of dismay when she saw how her clothing was clinging to her breasts. She quickly threaded her fingers through her hair and pulled it forward to cover her chest.

Thankfully the soldiers weren't paying her any attention. Gabriel stood with his back to her and ordered the removal of the wolves. Calum and Keith jumped down from their mounts to tie ropes around the wolves' necks.

"Drag them back to the ridge and burn them," Gabriel commanded. He tossed the reins to Johanna's mare in Lindsay's direction and ordered him and the other soldiers to return to the keep.

He wanted a moment alone with his wife.

Calum gave her a sympathetic look before taking his leave. He obviously believed she was going to catch hell. So did Keith, if his dour expression was an indicator.

She held her head high, folded her hands together, and pretended to be composed.

Gabriel waited until his soldiers had left before turning back to her. He put his hand on her thigh to get her to look at him.

"Have you nothing to say to me, wife?"

She nodded. He waited. "Well?" he finally demanded.

"I wish you would get over your anger."

"That isn't what I want to hear."

She put her hand on top of his. "You expect an apology, don't you? Very well, then. I'm sorry I ignored your suggestion to rest."

"Suggestion?"

"You needn't bellow at me, husband. It's rude."

"Rude?"

She didn't understand why he needed to repeat what she'd just said. He didn't understand why she wasn't hysterical over her encounter with the wolves. Didn't she understand what could have happened? Dear God, he couldn't quit thinking about it. She could have been torn apart by the wild beasts.

"Johanna, I want you to promise me you'll never again leave the keep without a proper escort."

His voice sounded hoarse. She thought it might be due to the fact that he was trying to keep himself from shouting at her. If that deduction was true, then her husband was actually being considerate of her feelings.

"M'lord, I don't want to become a prisoner in your home," she explained. "I've already had to

271

resort to trickery just so I could do a spot of hunting. I should be able to come and go as I please."

"You should not."

"With an escort then?"

"Damn it, woman, that's just what I . . ."

"Suggested?"

"I didn't suggest. I demanded a promise from you."

She patted his hand. He wasn't in the mood to be soothed, however. He motioned to the ground beneath the tree where her shredded plaid lay. "Don't you realize you could have been torn apart as quickly and as easily as your plaid?"

The truth had been slow to dawn on her. Her eyes widened in surprise. He thought she was finally beginning to understand her jeopardy. He nodded. "Aye, you could have been killed, wife."

She smiled. It wasn't the reaction he'd hoped to gain. How could he ever teach her caution if she didn't understand the dangers all around her?

He scowled with frustration. "I have been trying to get used to having a wife, Johanna. You make the adjustment difficult. Why in God's name are you smiling?"

"I have only just realized, m'lord, that your anger is due to my near miss. I believed you were upset because I disregarded your suggestion to rest. Now I understand," she added with a nod. " 'Tis the truth you're beginning to care for me. Your heart has softened, hasn't it, husband?"

He wasn't about to let her jump to such foolish conclusions. He shook his head. "You're my wife and I will always protect you. That is my duty, Johanna. But I'm a warrior, first and always. You seem to have forgotten that important fact."

She didn't know what in heaven's name he was talking about. "What does being a warrior have to do with your attitude toward me?"

"Matters of the heart do not concern me," he explained.

She straightened her shoulders. "They don't concern me either," she replied, lest he believe she'd been hurt by his opinion. "And I, too, thought only to get used to having you around."

He could tell from the look in her eyes he'd somehow injured her feelings. He reached up, cupped the back of her neck with his hand, and pulled her toward him. He kissed her long and hard. She put her arms around his neck and kissed him back. When he pulled away, she almost slumped off her mount. He put his hands on her waist to keep her from falling.

"Give me your promise before we leave."

"I promise."

Her immediate agreement improved his mood. It didn't last long. Damned if she didn't deliberately provoke his temper again.

"Exactly what did I just promise, m'lord?"

"You promised not to leave the keep without a proper escort!"

He really hadn't meant to shout, but Lord, she made him crazed. What had they been discussing for the past ten minutes?

Johanna trailed her fingers down the side of his

neck. His frown was intense, and she thought only to soothe him. She added a little praise to her caress of affection.

" 'Tis the truth you make me forget everything when you kiss me. That is the reason I forgot what I promised you, m'lord."

He couldn't fault her for admitting the truth. There were times when he was also affected by her kisses. Certainly not as often as his wife, of course, he qualified to himself.

Johanna swung her leg over the saddle and tried to get down. Gabriel tightened his hold on her waist to keep her from moving.

"I would like to show you something," she announced. "I had thought to wait until tomorrow, for I judged it would take you that long to forget about today's little incident, but I've changed my mind, Gabriel. I want to show you now. My surprise will surely improve your mood. Do let me down."

"I'm never going to forget about today's incident," he muttered. He kept up his scowl while he assisted her to the ground, then caught hold of her hand when she tried to walk away from him.

He reached up to retrieve her bow from the back of the saddle, then followed her into the cave. He had difficulty getting through the entrance. He had to squeeze his way through and keep his head tucked; but once he'd reached the cavern proper and saw the barrels, he quit his muttering over the inconveniences his wife forced on him.

Her enthusiasm over the find was more pleasing to him than the treasure itself.

"Now you will have something of value to barter," she announced. "And you'll have no need to steal again. What say you to that, m'lord?"

"Ah, Johanna, you take the joy out of my hunts," he replied.

She didn't like hearing that. "It is my duty to save your soul, husband, and by God, I'm going to try, with or without your cooperation."

He laughed. The sound echoed throughout the cavern, bouncing from stone to stone.

Gabriel was able to maintain his cheerful mood until it dawned on him that his wife had gone inside alone to find the treasure.

"You could have walked into their lair!" he suddenly bellowed.

The swift change in his behavior caught her by surprise. She took a step back away from her husband. He immediately softened his tone. "What would you have done if wolves had followed you in here?"

She could tell he was struggling to control his temper. Gabriel really was a kind-hearted man. He knew she didn't like it when he shouted and was, therefore, trying to accommodate her.

From the look in his eyes, she guessed it was killing him.

She didn't dare smile. He'd think she wasn't taking the topic seriously.

"It is true, m'lord, I didn't consider that possibility. I was so excited when I found the cave,

I forgot to be cautious. Still," she added in a rush when he appeared ready to interrupt her, "I believe I would have been all right. Yes, I would have," she added with a nod. "Why, I probably would have flown up those barrels. 'Tis the truth I flew up the tree to get away from the horrid beasts. I almost didn't make it. One grabbed hold of the hem of my plaid and I . . ."

The expression on her husband's face told her she shouldn't have gone into such explicit detail. Gabriel was getting all riled up again.

She knew he was beginning to care about her all right. His heart was softening toward her whether he wanted to admit it or not. He wouldn't be this upset if he didn't care, would he?

Johanna was pleased with this proof of her husband's affections until she realized how much it mattered to her. Then she began to worry. Why did she care how he felt about her? Was she also softening in her feelings toward him? Good God, was she beginning to love the barbarian?

The possibility appalled her. She shook her head in denial. She wasn't about to allow herself to become so vulnerable.

Gabriel was relieved to see her frown. She'd gone pale, too. He nodded with satisfaction. The woman was finally understanding what could have happened to her.

"I was beginning to believe you were completely lacking in common sense," he muttered.

"I have plenty of common sense," she boasted in reply.

He wasn't going to argue with her. He dragged her back outside. While she waited, he blocked the entrance with stones so the animals couldn't get inside.

She rode on his lap back to the keep. The sun was shining again by the time they reached the ridge.

Johanna forced herself to put her worries aside. She could certainly control her own emotions, after all; and if she didn't wish to love Gabriel, then, by God, she wouldn't.

"You're as tense as the string on your bow, wife. I can understand why, of course. You've finally realized how close you came to death today. Lean back against me and close your eyes. You should rest."

She did as he suggested. She thought to have the last word on the topic, however. "Never once did I believe I was going to die, m'lord. I knew that eventually you or the other soldiers would find me. I was safe in the tree."

"You were still worried," he told her.

"Of course I was worried. There were wild wolves circling below me."

She was getting tense again. He squeezed her. "You were also worried because you believed you disappointed me," he remarked.

She rolled her eyes heavenward. Her husband certainly had an ego. "You think I believed I disappointed you?"

He frowned over the laughter he heard in her voice. "Yes, of course," he answered.

"Why?"

"Why what?"

"Why did I believe I disappointed you?"

He let out a long sigh. "You realized you caused me needless concern," he answered.

"So you admit you were worried about me?"

"Damn it, woman, I just said I was."

She smiled. Gabriel sounded surly again. She didn't turn around to look at his face, but she knew he was scowling. She patted his arm in an attempt to soothe him.

"I'm happy to know you were concerned about me, even if you thought it was a needless inconvenience."

"It was that, all right."

She ignored his rebuke. "Still, you should learn to have faith in me, m'lord. I can take care of myself."

"I'm not in the mood for one of your jests, Johanna."

"I wasn't jesting."

"Aye, you were."

She quit trying to argue with him. After thinking about the topic for several minutes, she decided she really couldn't fault her husband for believing she couldn't take care of herself. She'd acted like a coward when she'd first met him, and she'd been very timid ever since. No, she couldn't blame him for believing she needed watching over. In time, however, she hoped to change his mind. She didn't want her husband to continue to think she was a weakling.

"Johanna, I don't want you to mention the barrels in the cave to anyone."

"As you wish, husband. Do you know what you'll do with them?"

"We'll discuss it later, after supper," he promised.

She nodded. Then she turned the topic. "How did you find me? I thought you went hunting for the day."

"There was a change in plans," he explained. "The MacInnes laird and ten of his soldiers were spotted crossing our border."

"Are they coming to your home, do you suppose?"

"Yes."

"What do they want?"

"I'll find out when they get here," he answered.

"And when will that be?"

"Late this afternoon."

"Will they stay for dinner?"

"No."

"It would be rude not to invite them to eat with you."

He shrugged. She wasn't deterred by his lack of interest. As his wife, she felt it was her duty to instill some manners in her husband.

"I shall instruct the servants to prepare places at your tables for your guests," she announced.

She waited for him to argue with her and was pleasantly surprised when he remained silent.

Johanna turned her attention to planning the menu. A sudden thought occurred to her. She let out a gasp. "Good Lord, Gabriel, you didn't steal from the MacInnes clan, did you?"

"No," he answered, smiling over the outrage in her voice.

She relaxed against him again. "Then we don't have to worry they're coming here to fight."

"Fight with only ten soldiers? No, that isn't a concern," he drawled out.

The amusement in his voice made her smile. Her husband was feeling more cheerful now. Perhaps his good mood was due to the fact that he was going to have company.

She would make certain the evening went well. There wouldn't be enough rabbit stew to go around unless she went hunting for more. She discarded that idea. The rabbits would have to simmer for several hours or be too tough to eat, and there wasn't time for that, anyway. Johanna decided she would change her clothes, then go to Cook and discuss the problem. Hilda would know how to stretch the meal, and Johanna would, of course, offer to help with the preparations.

She wished she could get rid of the Maclaurin soldiers for the night. They were so terribly loud, disruptive, and horribly rude. Why, the way they tried to outbelch each other was downright disgusting.

Still, she didn't want to hurt their feelings. They were part of Gabriel's clan now and would, therefore, have to be included.

They reached the courtyard. Gabriel dismounted first, then turned to assist her. He held her longer than necessary. She smiled up at her husband while she waited for him to let go of her.

"Johanna, you will not get into further mischief. I want you to go inside and . . ."

"Let me guess, m'lord," she interrupted. "You want me to rest, don't you?"

He smiled. Lord, she was fetching when she was disgruntled. "Aye, I do want you to rest."

He leaned down, kissed her, and then turned to lead his mount back to the stables.

Johanna shook her head over her husband's ridiculous orders. How could she take the time to rest when they had company coming for dinner?

She hurried inside, propped her bow and carrier against the wall at the bottom of the steps, and then went up to her chamber. It didn't take her long to change into dry clothes. Her hair was still too wet to properly braid. She tied it with a ribbon behind her neck, then hurried downstairs again.

Megan was standing by the doors, peeking outside.

"What are you doing, Megan?"

"The MacInnes soldiers are here."

"So soon?" Johanna asked. She went over to stand beside Megan. "Shouldn't we open the doors and welcome them inside?"

Megan shook her head. She moved out of the way so her mistress could look outside, then whispered, "Something's wrong, m'lady. Look at the way they're all frowning. They've carried along an offering for our laird though. Do you see the burlap draped over the laird's lap?"

"Let me have a look." Father MacKechnie whispered his request from behind the two women.

Johanna bumped into the priest when she turned around. She begged his forgiveness over her clumsiness, then explained why she'd been caught peeking at their company.

"Their behavior is most contradictory," she said. "They're all scowling, but it's apparent they've carried along a gift for your laird. Perhaps their frowns are all for show."

"Nay, that can't be," Father MacKechnie replied. "The Highlanders aren't at all like the English, lass."

"What do you mean, Father? Men are men, regardless of how they dress."

The priest let the door close before answering her. "In my experiences with the English, I've noticed a peculiar trait. They always seem to have a hidden motive behind their actions."

"And the Highlanders?" she asked.

Father MacKechnie smiled. "We're a simple group, we are. What you see is what you have. Do you understand? We don't have time for secret motives."

"The MacInnes soldiers are frowning because they're angry about something," Megan interjected. "They aren't clever enough to use trickery."

The priest nodded agreement. "We have no use for subterfuge. Laird MacInnes looks as mad as a hornet someone just tried to swat. He's in a snit all right."

"Then we will have to do our best to soothe him. He is company, after all," she reasoned.

"Megan, please go and tell Cook we'll be having eleven more for supper. Be sure to offer our assistance with the preparations. I'll be along in just a minute."

Megan hurried to do her mistress's bidding. "Cook won't mind the inconvenience," she called over her shoulder as she started down the hallway to the back door. "She's a MacBain, after all. She knows better than to complain."

Johanna frowned over that puzzling remark. Why did it matter if Cook was a MacBain or a Maclaurin? Megan had already disappeared, and so Johanna decided she'd have to wait until later to ask her for a proper explanation.

The priest turned her attention then when he pulled the door open. She stood behind him. "Which one is the laird?" she asked in a whisper.

"The old man with the bulging eyes seated atop the speckled mount," Father MacKechnie answered. "You'd best stay here, lass, until your husband has decided if he's going to let them come inside or not. I'll go out and speak to them."

Johanna nodded agreement. She stayed behind the door but peeked out to watch the priest. Father MacKechnie went down the steps and shouted his greeting.

The MacInnes soldiers ignored the priest. Their expressions seemed to be set in stone. Johanna found their behavior sinful. None of the men bothered to dismount either. Didn't they realize how offending their conduct was?

Johanna turned her attention to their laird. Father MacKechnie had been right, she decided. The man did have bulging eyes. He was old, too, with wrinkled skin and thick eyebrows. His gaze was directed on Gabriel. Johanna spotted her husband walking across the clearing. He stopped when he was several feet away from the MacInnes soldiers.

The laird said something that clearly infuriated Gabriel. Her husband's expression turned dark, chilling. Johanna had never seen that look before. She shivered in reaction. Gabriel looked ready to do battle.

The MacBain warriors walked over to stand behind their laird. The Maclaurins joined them.

The MacInnes laird motioned to one of his men. The soldier quickly dismounted and strutted over to his leader's side. He looked like his laird, and Johanna thought he might be his son. She watched as he lifted the long burlap bag from his laird's lap. He adjusted the weight in his arms, turned, and walked around the front of the speckled mount. He stopped just a few feet away from Gabriel, lifted the sack, and threw it to the ground.

The bag tore open. Dust flew up in the air; and when it cleared, Johanna saw what the laird's gift was. A woman, so bloody and bruised her face was barely recognizable, spilled out and rolled onto her side. She was naked, and there wasn't a spot on her body left unmarked.

Johanna staggered back away from the door. She whimpered low in her throat. She thought she was going to throw up. She was so sickened by the sight of the broken woman, she wanted to weep

284

with shame . . . and scream with fury.

She didn't do either. She reached for her bow and arrows instead.

Chapter
11

Johanna's hands shook, and all she could think about was being accurate with her aim when she killed the bastards who had committed this foul act.

Gabriel was shaking with his own fury. His hand moved to the hilt of his sword. He couldn't believe a Highlander would disgrace himself so thoroughly with such cowardly behavior. Yet the proof was on the ground in front of him.

Laird MacInnes looked smug now. Gabriel decided he would kill him first.

"Are you responsible for beating this woman to death?"

He hadn't asked the question; he'd roared it.

The MacInnes leader frowned in reaction. "She ain't dead. She's breathing still."

"Are you responsible?" Gabriel demanded again.

"I am," the laird shouted back. "I surely am."

It sounded like a boast to Gabriel, who started to pull his sword free. Laird MacInnes noticed the action and suddenly realized his tenuous position.

He hurried to explain his reasons for beating the woman.

"Clare MacKay was placed in my household by her father," he shouted. "She was pledged to marry my eldest son, Robert." He paused to nod at the soldier standing next to his mount before continuing on. "I was going to unite our two clans and become a power to be reckoned with, but the bitch was soiled three months past, MacBain, and by one of your own. It be no use denying the truth, for your plaid was spotted by three of my men. Clare MacKay spent a full night with the man. At first she lied and claimed she stayed the night with her cousins. I was fool enough to believe her. Once she discovered she was carrying, she had the gall to boast about her sin. Isn't that the way of it, Robert?"

"Aye, it is," his son answered. "I won't marry a whore," he bellowed. "A MacBain ruined her, a MacBain can have her."

After rendering his judgment, he turned his gaze to the woman. He spit at the ground near her, then moved forward to stand over the unconscious woman with his hands on his hips and a leer on his face.

He drew his booted foot back, then started to bring it forward, intent on giving the woman a hard kick.

An arrow stopped him cold. Robert let out a screech of pain and staggered back. The arrow was imbedded in his thigh. His hands moved to his leg as he turned, shouting still, to see who had injured him.

287

Johanna stood on the top step in front of the keep. Her gaze was fully directed on the soldier. She nocked another arrow to the string of her bow and kept the man in her sights.

She waited for an excuse to kill him.

Everyone was watching her now. Gabriel had moved to intervene when Robert swung his leg back to kick the woman. The arrow struck the soldier before he could. He turned, saw the look on his wife's face, and immediately started toward her.

None of the others moved for a long minute. The Maclaurins were clearly stunned by what they'd just witnessed. The MacBains were just as surprised and certainly just as impressed.

The soldier she'd injured moved close to the woman. Johanna thought he was going to try to hurt her again.

She couldn't let that happen. "Try to kick her again, and by God, I'll put an arrow through your black heart."

The fury in her voice washed over the group of soldiers. Robert immediately backed away. The priest hurried forward and knelt down beside the woman. He made the sign of the cross and whispered a blessing.

"She's daft," Robert whispered.

Gabriel's followers heard his remark. Three of the MacBain soldiers started forward. Calum waved them back with a motion of his hand.

"Our laird will decide what's to be done," he ordered.

Keith stood beside Calum. He couldn't restrain himself. "She isn't daft," he bellowed. "But I'll be certain to let our laird know your opinion of his wife."

"My son wasn't being insulting," Laird MacInnes defended. "Just speaking the truth. Look at her eyes. She's gone crazed all right. And over what, I ask you? 'Tis just a whore on the ground."

Gabriel wasn't paying any attention to anyone but his wife now. He reached the steps but didn't touch her. He moved to stand next to her side.

Johanna ignored her husband. She slowly turned until she had Laird MacInnes in her sights.

She was pleased to notice his ugly face turn stark white. His thick lips pinched into a pucker of worry.

"Which one of you beat this woman?"

The laird didn't answer her. He turned his gaze to his left and then to his right. It was as though he was looking for a means of escape.

"You may not kill him."

Gabriel gave his command in a low whisper only she could hear. Johanna didn't show any outward reaction to his order.

He repeated his command. She shook her head. She kept the laird in her sights when she spoke to her husband.

"Do you believe the woman deserved this treatment? Do you think she's less important than dull-witted oxen?"

"You know better than to ask me such questions," he countered. "Give me your bow and arrow."

"No."

"Johanna . . ."

"Look what they did!" she cried out.

The agony in her voice made his heart ache. His wife was close to completely losing her composure. He couldn't allow that to happen.

"Do not let them see your distress," he ordered. "That would be a victory for them."

"Yes," she whispered. Her hands started shaking, and she let out a low whimper.

"The longer we stand here, the longer the lass goes without proper care. Give me your weapon."

She couldn't let go. "I can't let them hurt her anymore. I can't. Don't you see? I have to help her. I prayed for someone to help me. No one would. But I can help her. I have to . . ."

"I won't let them hurt her," he promised.

She shook her head again. Gabriel decided to take a different approach. It seemed as though an hour had passed since he'd joined her on the steps, yet he knew less than a few minutes had actually gone by. The length of time didn't matter to him. He didn't care how long it took for her to regain her control. The bastard MacInnes soldiers would have to wait. Gabriel could have taken the weapon away from her, of course. He didn't want to. He wanted her to give it to him.

"Very well then," he said. "I'll order my men to kill every one of them. Will that suit you?"

"Yes."

He couldn't mask his surprise. He let out a sigh, then turned to give the order. He wasn't one to bluff. If she wanted him to kill the infidels, then he would accommodate her. Hell, he'd been looking for an excuse anyway. Pleasing his wife would do well enough.

"Calum," he shouted.

"Aye, MacBain?"

"No," Johanna blurted out.

Gabriel turned to her. "No?"

Tears gathered in her eyes. "We can't kill them."

"Yes, we can."

She shook her head. "It would make us no better than they if we let our anger control our actions. Make them go away. They turn my stomach."

The strength was back in her voice. Gabriel nodded, satisfied. "Give me your bow and arrow first."

She slowly lowered her arms. What happened next so surprised her, she didn't even have time to react. Gabriel snatched her weapon out of her hands, half-turned, took aim, and dispatched the arrow with incredible speed and accuracy.

A howl of pain followed. The arrow found its target in the shoulder of the same MacInnes soldier she'd injured. Robert, the laird's son, had slipped his dagger from his belt and was just about to hurl the weapon when Gabriel spotted the movement. Neither Calum nor Keith had even had time to shout a warning.

Laird MacInnes went into a rage on his son's behalf. Gabriel's fury was far worse. He shoved

Johanna behind his back, tossed the bow to the ground, and reached for his sword.

"Get the hell off my land, MacInnes, or I'll kill you now."

The MacInnes soldiers didn't waste time leaving. Gabriel wouldn't let Johanna move until the courtyard was clear.

"Keith, send ten Maclaurin soldiers to follow them to our border," he ordered.

"As you wish, MacBain," Keith shouted back.

The minute her husband moved, Johanna skirted her way around him and ran down the steps. She crossed the clearing, untying her belt as she ran. She had her plaid off before she knelt down next to the battered woman and used the material to cover her. She placed her hand on the side of the woman's neck, felt the pulse beating there, and almost wept with relief.

Father MacKechnie put his hand on Johanna's shoulder. "We'd best get her inside," he whispered.

Calum bent down on one knee and leaned forward to lift the woman. Johanna screamed at the soldier. "Don't touch her!"

"She can't stay here, m'lady," Calum argued, trying to reason with his distraught mistress. "Let me carry her inside."

"Gabriel will carry her," Johanna decided. She took a deep breath in an attempt to calm herself. "I didn't mean to shout at you, Calum. Please forgive me. You shouldn't be lifting her anyway. You'll tear your stitches."

Calum nodded. He was surprised and pleased his mistress had offered him an apology.

"Is she dead?" Keith asked.

Johanna shook her head. Gabriel pulled her to her feet then and bent down to lift the MacKay woman into his arms.

"Be careful with her," Johanna whispered.

"Where do you want me to put her?" Gabriel asked. He stood up, cradling the sleeping woman in his arms.

"Give her my room," Father MacKechnie suggested. "I'll find another bed tonight."

"Do you think she'll live?" Calum asked as he followed his laird across the courtyard.

"How the hell do I know?" Gabriel asked.

"She'll survive," Johanna announced, praying she was right.

Calum ran ahead to open the doors. Johanna followed her husband through the entrance. Hilda was just coming down the hallway from the back door. She spotted her mistress and called out to her.

"Might I have a word with you about our menu for tonight's dinner guests?"

"We aren't having guests," Johanna said. "I would rather eat my supper with the devil or King John himself than suffer the MacInnes' company."

Hilda's eyes widened. Johanna started up the steps after her husband, then stopped. "I seem to be snapping at everyone, Hilda. Please forgive me. I'm not myself today."

She didn't wait for Hilda to accept her apology

but hurried on up the steps. A few minutes later, their guest was settled in bed. Gabriel stood by his wife's side while she checked for broken bones.

"She appears to be intact," Johanna whispered. "The blows to her head worry me. Look at the swelling above her temple, Gabriel. I don't know how severe the damage is. She might not ever wake up."

Johanna didn't realize she'd started crying until her husband ordered her to stop. "It won't do her any good if you fall apart. She needs your help, not your tears."

He was right, of course. Johanna mopped the wetness away from her cheeks with the backs of her hands. "Why did they cut her hair like that?"

She reached down and touched the side of the woman's head. Clare MacKay had thick, dark brown hair. It hung straight down but barely covered her ears. The MacInnes men hadn't used scissors. The edges were too jagged. They'd used a knife instead.

Humiliation, Johanna decided. Aye, that was their reason behind the foul deed.

"It's a miracle she's still breathing," Gabriel said. "Do what you can, Johanna. I'm going to let Father MacKechnie come inside now. He'll want to give her the last rites."

Johanna wanted to shout a denial. The sacrament of extreme unction was given only to those poor souls hovering at death's door. Reason told Johanna it was the logical thing to do. Yet the woman was breathing, damn it all, and Johanna didn't want to consider the possibility she wouldn't recover.

"Just as a precaution," Gabriel insisted to gain her cooperation.

"Yes," she whispered, "just as a precaution." She straightened up. "I'm going to make her more comfortable," she announced then. She crossed the room to fetch the pitcher of water and the bowl from the chest and carried them back to the bed. She was going to put them on the floor near her feet, but Gabriel thoughtfully moved the chest close to her. He started for the door as she hurried across the room again to collect a stack of linen cloths.

Gabriel reached for the latch, then suddenly stopped. He turned around to look at his wife. She wasn't paying him any attention now. She hurried back to the bed, sat down on the side, and dipped one of the cloths into the bowl of water she'd just poured.

"Answer a question for me," he ordered.

"Yes?"

"Were you ever beaten like this?"

Johanna didn't look up at her husband when she gave her answer. "No."

He hadn't realized he'd been holding his breath. He let it out after she gave him her reply.

Then she qualified her answer. "He rarely struck my face or my head. Once, though, he was less careful."

"And the rest of your body?"

"Clothing hid those bruises," she answered.

She didn't have any idea how her explanation affected him. Gabriel was shaken. It was a wonder to him she'd ever agreed to marry again. Hell, he'd demanded she trust him. He felt like a complete fool now. If he were in her position, he sure as certain wouldn't have trusted anyone ever again.

"She won't have scars," Johanna whispered. "Most of the blood on her face is from her nosebleed. It's a wonder they didn't break it. She's a pretty woman, isn't she, Gabriel?"

"Her face is too swollen to tell what she looks like," he answered.

"They shouldn't have cut her hair."

She seemed obsessed over that minor punishment. "Cutting her hair was the least of their offenses, Johanna. They shouldn't have beaten her. Dogs receive better treatment."

Johanna nodded. *And oxen,* she thought to herself.

"Gabriel?"

"Yes?"

"I'm glad I married you."

She was too embarrassed to look at her husband when she told him how she felt, and so she pretended great interest in wringing every drop of water out of her cloth.

He smiled. "I know you are, Johanna."

His arrogance was really getting out of hand. It warmed her heart, though. She shook her head, then went back to her task and began to clean the blood away from Clare MacKay's face. She whispered words of comfort while she worked. She doubted Clare could hear her, but it made Johanna feel better to tell her over and over again that she was safe now. She added the promise that no one would ever hurt her again.

Gabriel pulled the door open and found the hall-way crowded with women. They all wore the MacBain plaid.

Hilda stood in front of the group. "We would like to offer to help with the care of the woman," she said.

"Father MacKechnie must give her the last rites before you go inside," Gabriel ordered.

The priest was waiting at the back of the crowd. He heard his laird's announcement and immediately pushed his way through the women, begging their indulgence. He went inside the chamber, hurried to the foot of the bed where he'd left his satchel, and pulled out a long, narrow purple stole. He kissed each fringed end, whispered his prayers, and draped the material over his neck.

Gabriel pulled the door closed. He went down-stairs. Calum and Keith were waiting for him at the bottom of the steps.

They followed their laird into the great hall.

Gabriel spotted the plaid on the floor in front of the hearth. His dog was missing. "Where the hell is Dumfries?"

"Out prowling," Calum suggested.

"He took off early this morning," Keith added.

Gabriel shook his head. Johanna would pitch a fit if she noticed the dog was gone. She'd fret about his stitches.

He forced his mind back to more important matters. "Calum, call all the MacBain soldiers together," he commanded then. "I want each man to tell me he didn't touch Clare MacKay."

"And you will believe . . ."

Keith quit his question when his laird scowled at him. "None of my warriors will lie to me, Keith," Gabriel snapped.

"But if one admits he did in fact spend the night with the woman? What will you do then?"

"That isn't your concern, Keith. I want you to ride to Laird MacKay and tell him what took place here today."

"Do I tell him his daughter is dying or do I soften the truth?"

"Tell him she's been given the last rites."

"And do I tell him a MacBain . . ."

"Tell them exactly what Laird MacInnes charged," Gabriel commanded, his impatience evident. "Damn, I wish I'd killed the bastards when I had the chance."

"You'd have a war on your hands if you did, MacBain," Keith pointed out.

"War has already been declared," he snapped. "Think I will so easily forget the fact that the laird's son tried to kill my wife?"

He was shouting by the time he finished his question. The Maclaurin warrior shook his head. "Nay, Laird," he rushed out. "You will not forget, and I stand beside you on this issue."

"Damned right you do," Gabriel countered.

Calum took a step forward then. "The MacKays

might also wage war if they believe a MacBain did in fact compromise Clare MacKay."

"None of my men would act so dishonorably," Gabriel snapped.

Calum nodded agreement. Keith wasn't convinced. "MacInnes said your plaid was spotted," he reminded his laird.

"He was lying to us," Calum argued.

"Laird MacInnes also said Clare MacKay admitted she spent the night with a MacBain," Keith said.

"Then she's lying," Calum replied.

Gabriel turned his back on his soldiers. "I have given both of you your duties. See them completed."

The soldiers immediately left the hall. Gabriel stood by the hearth a long while.

He had one hell of a problem on his hands. He knew, without a doubt, that none of his men was responsible for disgracing Clare MacKay.

Yet the MacBain plaid had been spotted . . . three months ago.

"Hell," Gabriel muttered to himself. If Laird MacInnes was telling the truth, there could only be one answer, only one man responsible for the damnable mess.

Nicholas.

Chapter
12

Clare MacKay didn't wake up until the following morning. Johanna stayed with the woman most of the night until Gabriel came into the chamber and literally dragged her away. Hilda was happy to take over the watch for her mistress.

Johanna had only just returned to the room and settled herself in a chair by the side of Clare's bed when the woman opened her eyes and spoke to her.

"I heard you whispering to me."

Johanna was given quite a start. She jumped up and went over to Clare.

"You're awake," she whispered, her relief almost overwhelming.

Clare nodded. "How do you feel?" Johanna asked.

"I ache from my head to my toes."

Johanna nodded. "You have bruises from your head to your toes," she replied. "Does your throat hurt, too? You sound hoarse."

" 'Tis the truth I did a lot of screaming," Clare said. "May I have a drink of water?"

Johanna hurried to fetch the goblet. She helped Clare sit up. She tried to be as gentle as possible, but the woman still grimaced in pain. Her hand shook when she reached for the goblet.

"Was there a priest here? I thought I heard someone praying."

"Father MacKechnie gave you the last rites," Johanna explained. She put the goblet on the chest and sat down in her chair again. "We didn't know if you would survive or not. It was just a precaution," she added in a rush.

Clare smiled. She had beautiful white teeth and dark brown eyes. Her face was still terribly swollen, of course, and Johanna could tell from the way she tried not to move she was still in terrible pain.

"Who did this to you?"

Clare closed her eyes. She avoided answering the question by asking one of her own. "Last night . . . you said I was safe. I remember hearing you whisper those words to me. Were you telling the truth? Am I safe here?"

"Yes, of course you are."

"Where is here?"

Johanna hurried to introduce herself and then explained what had happened. She deliberately left out the mention about the arrow she'd put in Robert MacInnes's thigh and the arrow her husband put in his shoulder. By the time she was finished with her explanation, Clare was falling asleep again.

"We'll talk later," she promised. "Sleep now,

Clare. You may stay with us for as long as you wish. Hilda will bring you something to eat in just a little while. You'll . . ."

Johanna quit talking when she realized Clare MacKay was sound asleep. She tucked the covers around the woman, moved her chair back, and left the room.

Gabriel was reaching for his boots when Johanna walked into their chamber.

"Good morning, m'lord," she said in greeting. "Did you sleep well?"

He frowned in reaction. Johanna went over to the window and pulled the furs back. From the yellow cast in the sky, she guessed it was only a few minutes past dawn.

"You were told to stay in bed," he said. "Did you wait until I fell asleep and then leave again?"

"Yes."

His frown intensified. She decided to try to placate him. "I thought I would rest for a few minutes before going downstairs. I am weary."

"You look half dead."

"My appearance isn't important," she announced even as her hands flew to her hair and she tried to tuck the curls back into her braid.

"Come here, Johanna."

She walked across the room to stand in front of him. He reached down to untie the belt holding her plaid in place.

"You will stay where you're put," he announced.

She tried to slap his hands away. "I'm not a

302

piece of jewelry or a trinket only to be taken off a shelf when the mood strikes you, m'lord."

Gabriel caught hold of her chin and leaned down to kiss her. He thought only to get her to quit frowning, but her lips were so damned soft and appealing, he forgot his reason. He put his arms around his wife and hauled her up against him.

His kisses made her weak-kneed and dizzy. She put her arms around her husband's waist and held tight. She decided it was quite all right to allow him to rob her of her every thought. He was her husband, after all. Besides, when he was kissing her, he couldn't scowl . . . or lecture.

She didn't remember undressing or getting into bed. Gabriel must have carried her there. He'd taken his clothes off, too. He covered her with his body, captured the sides of her face with his hands, and gave her a searing kiss. His tongue moved inside her mouth to rub against hers.

She loved to touch him, to feel his hot skin under her fingertips, to caress the splay of hard muscle along his upper arms and shoulders. When she wrapped her arms around her husband, she felt as though she'd captured his strength and his power.

He was a wonder to her, a revelation. Gabriel was as strong as the fittest of warriors, and yet so incredibly gentle whenever he touched her.

She loved the fact that she could make him lose his control. She didn't have to guess that might be true either; Gabriel told her. She felt . . . free with him, and completely uninhibited as well, for her husband seemed to like whatever she wanted to do.

He made her lose her own control, of course. She wasn't one to scream her demands, but by the time he quit his teasing and moved to mate with her, she was wild to make him end this sweet torment.

She cried out when he entered her, and he immediately stopped. "God, Johanna, I didn't mean to . . ."

"Oh, God, I hope you did mean to," she whispered. Her nails dug into his shoulder blades. She wrapped her legs around his thighs and squeezed him tight inside her. "Gabriel, I don't wish you to stop now. I want you to move."

He thought he'd died and gone to heaven. He ignored her command and leaned up on his elbows to look into her eyes. He saw the passion there and almost lost all his control then. Dear Lord, she was beautiful . . . and so damned giving.

"You're a lustful wench." He was trying to tease her, but his voice sounded gruff. "I like that," he added with a groan when she moved so restlessly against him.

Gabriel had made her burn for him and now refused to give her fulfillment or take his own.

"Husband, this activity requires your participation," she cried out, her frustration beyond reason now.

"I thought I'd drive you daft first," he told her in a husky whisper.

It turned out to be an empty boast, for Gabriel

felt as though he was the one who lost his mind when she dragged him down for a long, passionate kiss and moved against him so provocatively. His discipline deserted him. His movements became forceful and demanding, though surely no more demanding than his wife's.

They found fulfillment together. Johanna held onto her husband as wave after wave of ecstasy washed over her. She felt safe in his strong arms, certainly sated, and almost loved. It was more than she'd ever had before or ever dreamed was possible.

She fell asleep sighing.

Gabriel thought he might have crushed her to death. She went completely limp in his arms. He rolled onto his side and whispered her name. She didn't answer him. She was breathing though. Had passion sent her into a dead faint? Gabriel smiled, for that possibility did appeal to him. He knew the true reason, of course. Johanna was exhausted. She'd spent most of the night watching over their new charge.

He leaned down, kissed her brow, and got out of bed. "You will rest," he whispered. He smiled then. The little woman was actually obeying him. Of course she hadn't heard his order; she was already sound asleep, but it still made him feel damned happy to give a command he knew would be obeyed.

Gabriel covered his wife, got dressed, and quietly left the chamber.

The day started out pleasant enough, but it

soured fast. Calum was waiting for his laird in the great hall with the announcement that another petition had arrived from Baron Goode requesting an audience with Lady Johanna. The messenger who delivered the request came from Laird Gillevrey again and waited by Calum's side to hear Gabriel's reply.

"Is the baron waiting at the border of your land?" he asked the soldier.

"Nay, Laird. He sent a representative. His goal is to convince Lady Johanna to meet with Baron Goode near England's border."

Gabriel shook his head. "My wife isn't going anywhere. She doesn't want to speak to Baron Goode. England is a part of her past now, and she looks only to her future here. Tell your laird I thank him for acting as mediary. I'm sorry he's been inconvenienced by the English. I'll find a way to repay him for his efforts in keeping the baron and his vassals away from my holding."

"What exactly do you wish me to tell the representative?" the soldier asked. "I'll memorize every word, Laird MacBain, and recount just as you've spoken."

"Tell him my wife will not speak to any barons and that it would be foolish indeed if they continue to pester her."

The messenger bowed and left the hall. Gabriel turned to Calum. "You will not mention this to my wife. She doesn't need to know the baron is again trying to get to her."

"As you wish, Laird."

Gabriel nodded. He tried to put the irritant of the English baron behind him, but his day still didn't improve. The Maclaurins weren't getting any of their duties done, and there were three accidents before noon. The soldiers were preoccupied; they acted as though they'd been given a grave insult and couldn't stand the thought of working side by side with the MacBain soldiers. It was apparent they blamed the MacBains for the mess they believed they were in.

Odd but the Maclaurins didn't like warring much. Gabriel found their attitude puzzling. He thought they might have lost their zest for battle after they lost almost all they owned when last under seige by the English. Still, Gabriel found their attitude a shameful trait. Highlanders should embrace war, not abhor it.

The merging of the two clans was taking longer than he'd anticipated. He had wanted to give each clansman time to adjust to all the changes, but he now realized he had been too damned accommodating. All that was going to stop. His followers would either put their differences aside or suffer his displeasure.

Work on the wall was going at a snail's pace. On a usual day, one MacBain soldier could do the work of three Maclaurins. Today didn't qualify as usual, however. The Maclaurins were muttering like old men. Their concentration certainly wasn't on their work, and nothing significant was getting done.

Gabriel's patience was at an end. He was about

to challenge a few of the blatant offenders when Calum chased him down with the report that yet another messenger had arrived.

Gabriel wasn't in the mood for another interruption. He much preferred the idea of bashing a few Maclaurin heads together. He didn't particularly care for the news he was given either. The news was sure to please his wife, however, he supposed.

He wanted Johanna to be happy. He wasn't certain why it mattered to him, but he was honest enough to admit her happiness was important.

Hell, he was getting soft. The messenger was shaking in his boots by the time Gabriel gave him permission to leave. He made him repeat the message he wanted taken back to England, for the man's attention was interrupted when Dumfries came running into the hall. The dog growled; the man bolted, and Gabriel found his first smile since early morning.

Johanna's reaction to the news wasn't what he expected. He was going to wait until dinner to tell her, but she came down the stairs just as the messenger was trying to run through the closed doors and wanted to know what the stranger wanted.

Dumfries was snapping at the man's heels. Johanna was appalled by the treatment their visitor was receiving. She pushed the dog out of the way, then opened the doors for the man. She bid him good day, but she didn't think he heard her. He was halfway across the courtyard, running like a madman, and Gabriel's laughter surely drowned out her words.

She shut the doors and walked over to the steps. Her husband stood by the hearth, grinning like a well-gifted man on Christmas morn. She shook her head at him.

"It isn't polite to frighten our guests, m'lord."

"He's English, Johanna," he explained. He believed he had just given her an adequate excuse for his conduct.

She looked worried. She hurried down the steps and walked over to her husband. "He was a messenger, wasn't he? Who did he bring news from? Was it King John? Or did Baron Goode send another request?"

She'd gone from worry to terror in less than a minute's time. Gabriel shook his head. "He didn't bring bad news, wife. The message came from your mother."

She grabbed hold of Gabriel's hand. "Is she ill?"

Gabriel hurried to soothe her. He hated seeing her frightened. "She isn't ill," he said. "At least I don't believe she is," he added. "She wouldn't be coming here if she was sick, would she?"

"Mama's coming here?"

She'd shouted the question. He was astonished. Johanna looked ready to swoon. Her reaction wasn't at all what he expected.

"This news does not please you?"

"I have to sit down."

She collapsed into one of the chairs. Gabriel walked over to stand in front of her. "Answer me, wife. If the news doesn't make you happy, I'll have Calum catch the messenger and tell him to deny the request."

She bounded to her feet. "You'll do no such thing. I want to see my mother."

"Then what in God's name is the matter with you? Why are you acting as though you've just received foul news?"

She wasn't paying any attention to her husband. Her mind raced from one thought to another. She was going to have to get her house organized. Aye, that duty came first. Dumfries would have to have a bath. Was there time to teach the hound some manners? Johanna wasn t about to let the dog growl at her mama.

Gabriel grabbed hold of his wife by her shoulders and demanded she answer him. She asked him to repeat his question.

"Why isn't this good news, wife?"

"It's wonderful news," she countered. She added a look that suggested she thought he'd lost his mind. "I haven't seen Mama in over four years, Gabriel. It will be a joyful reunion."

"Then why in God's name do you look so ill?"

She shrugged his hands away from her shoulders and started pacing in front of the hearth. "There's so much to do before she gets here," she explained. "Dumfries will need to be bathed. The keep must be cleaned from top to bottom. I won't have your pet growling at my mama, Gabriel. I'll have to teach him some manners. Oh God, manners." She whirled around to look at her husband. "The

310

Maclaurins don't have any."

She'd wailed out her last remark. Gabriel didn't know whether to laugh or frown over her rattled behavior.

He ended up smiling. She frowned in reaction. "I won't have my mama insulted," she snapped.

"No one's going to insult her, wife."

She snorted with disbelief. "I won't have her disappointed either. She trained me to be a good wife." She put her hands on her hips and waited. Her husband didn't have anything to say. "Well?" she demanded when he stubbornly remained silent.

He let out a sigh. "Well, what?"

"You're supposed to tell me I'm a good wife," she cried out, her frustration evident.

"All right," he soothed. "You're a good wife."

She shook her head. "No, I'm not," she admitted.

He rolled his eyes heavenward. He didn't know what she expected from him. He guessed she'd tell him when she got herself under control, and he patiently waited.

"I've been remiss in my duties. All that's in the past, however. I shall start teaching your men proper manners at dinner tonight."

"Now, Johanna," he began, a warning in his voice. "The men are . . ."

"Don't you interfere, Gabriel. You needn't worry. Your soldiers will listen to my instructions. Do you think you'll be home by dinner?" she asked.

He was confused by the question. He was home now, damn it all, and dinner would be served in just a few minutes. Still, she was rattled now, he reminded himself. Perhaps she didn't realize what time it was.

"I'm home now," he reminded her. "And dinner . . ."

She didn't let him finish. "You have to leave."

"What?"

"Go and get Alex, husband. I've been very patient with you," she added when he started frowning. "Your son should be home when Mama gets here. Alex will probably need a bath, too. I'll put him in the creek with Dumfries. God only knows what manners your son's been taught. Probably none." She paused to sigh. "Go and fetch him."

She tried to leave the hall after giving him that order. He caught hold of her and forced her to turn around to look at him.

"You do not give me commands, wife."

"I cannot believe you take this opportunity to become surly, husband. I don't have time to placate you today. I have important duties to see to," she added. "I want Alex home. Do you want to shame me in front of my mama?"

She seemed appalled by that possibility. Gabriel let out a loud sigh. He barely remembered his own mother and therefore couldn't imagine why Johanna would become so agitated over a visitation. It was obviously important that all go well, however.

And he did want his wife to be happy. He decided to tell her the true reason.

"Alex stays with his relatives until . . ."

"The wall's taking forever," she interrupted.

"There is another reason, wife."

"What is it?"

"I don't want him here until the Maclaurins and the MacBains have put their differences aside. I don't want Alex to suffer any . . . slights."

She'd been struggling to get away from his grasp until he gave her that explanation. Then she went completely still. Her expression was incredulous.

"Why would anyone slight Alex? He's your son, isn't he?"

"Probably."

"You claim him. You can't change your mind now. Alex believes you're his father, Gabriel —"

He put his hand over her mouth to get her to cease her instructions to him. His smile was filled with tenderness, for it occurred to him that his gentle wife had never once considered denying Alex's rightful place in their household. Hell, she was demanding fair treatment.

She deserved to understand his motives for keeping the boy away. Gabriel dragged her over to a chair. He sat down, then pulled her onto his lap.

She immediately turned timid. She wasn't used to sitting on her husband's lap. Anyone could walk in and see them together. She worried over that possibility for a moment or two, then pushed the concern aside. What did she care what others thought? Gabriel was her husband, after all. It was his right. Besides, she liked being held by him.

'Twas the truth she was beginning to like him more than she'd ever thought was possible.

"Quit daydreaming," Gabriel ordered when he saw the look on her face. She did look as though she was dreaming as she stared off into space. "I want to explain something to you."

"Yes, husband?"

She put her arm around his neck and began to stroke his skin. He told her to stop, but she ignored his command. He frowned in reaction.

"When the Maclaurins were in such desperate need of a leader to battle the English, they sent a contingent to me."

She nodded, frowning now for she couldn't imagine why Gabriel wanted to tell her what she already knew. She didn't interrupt him, however. He looked intense, and it would have been rude for her to interrupt him with the news that she already knew the reason why he was now laird. Nicholas had explained the situation to her, and Father MacKechnie had been happy to give her more details.

There was also the fact that this was the first time Gabriel was taking the time to share his concerns with her. Whether he realized it or not, he was making her feel involved in his life and important.

"Please continue," she requested.

"After the battle was finished and the English were no longer a threat, the Maclaurins were content to have me for their leader. Of course, they weren't given the option," he added with a nod. "They weren't as receptive to my followers."

"Didn't the MacBain soldiers fight with the Maclaurins against the English?"

"They did."

"Then why aren't the Maclaurins thankful now? Have they forgotten?"

Gabriel shook his head. "Not all of the MacBains could fight. Auggie is one example. He's too old for battle now. I thought, given time, the Maclaurins and the MacBains would learn to adjust, but now I realize that isn't going to happen. My patience is at an end, wife. The men will either get along and work together or suffer my displeasure."

He was growling just like Dumfries by the time he finished his explanation. She stroked the side of his neck. "What happens when you're displeased?"

He shrugged. "I usually kill someone."

She was certain he was jesting with her. She smiled. "I won't allow fights in my house, husband. You'll have to do your killing somewhere else."

He was too stunned by what she'd just said to take exception to her command. Johanna had just called the keep her house. It was a first, for until this moment, she'd always referred to everything as his. Gabriel hadn't realized how much her separation, deliberate or not, had bothered him.

"Is this your home?"

"Yes," she answered. "Isn't it?"

"Yes," he agreed. "Johanna, I want you to be happy here."

He sounded puzzled by his own admission. She couldn't help but become a little disgruntled over that notice.

"You sound surprised," she said. Lord, he had beautiful eyes. She thought she could be content to look at her husband all day long and not grow bored. He really was a handsome devil.

"I am surprised," he admitted.

He suddenly wanted to kiss her. Her mouth was so damned appealing to him. So were her eyes. They were the clearest color of blue he'd ever seen. Hell, he even liked the way she frowned at him. He had to shake his head over that foolish realization. Wives should never let their husbands see their displeasure . . . should they?

"Some husbands want their wives to be happy," Johanna decided aloud. "My father certainly wanted Mama to be happy."

"And what did your mother want?"

"To love my father," she answered.

"And what do you want?"

She shook her head. She wasn't about to tell him she wanted to love him. Such a declaration would make her vulnerable . . . wouldn't it?

"I know what you want," she blurted out in an attempt to take the attention away from her feelings. "You want me to sit by the fire and sew at night and rest my days away. That's what you want."

She'd become almost rigid in his arms. She

wasn't stroking his neck now either. She was pulling his hair. He reached up, took hold of her hand, and put it in her lap.

"Oh, I forgot one last thing," she blurted out. "You'd like me to stay where you put me, isn't that right?"

"Don't jest with me, wife. I'm not in the mood."

She wasn't jesting with him, but she didn't think it would be a good idea to tell him so. She didn't want to goad his temper. She wanted him to stay in a good mood so he would let her have her way.

"There's more than one way to skin a fish," she announced. He didn't know what the hell she was talking about. He didn't think she did either. For that reason he didn't ask her to explain. "I believed, given time, that we would get used to each other," he told her.

"You make us sound like the Maclaurins and the MacBains," she countered. "Are you getting used to me?"

"It's taking longer than I expected," he told her.

He was deliberately getting her riled. Johanna was trying not to let him see how upset she was becoming. The proof was in her eyes, however. They were now the color of blue fire. Aye, she was irritated all right.

"I haven't had much experience with marriage," he reminded her.

"I have," she blurted out.

He shook his head. "You weren't married. You were in bondage. There's a difference."

She couldn't fault his reasoning. She had been

in bondage. However, she didn't want to dwell on her past. "And just what does my first marriage have to do with the topic under discussion?"

"What exactly is the topic?"

"Alex," she stammered out. "I was explaining to you that there is always more than one way to skin a fish. Don't you understand?"

"How in God's name would I understand? No one skins fish here."

She thought he was being deliberately obtuse. He certainly didn't appreciate clever sayings. "I meant that there is always more than one way to attain a goal," she explained. "I won't have to use force to get the Maclaurins to behave. I'll use other methods."

She could tell he was finally considering the matter. She pressed her advantage. "You told me I should trust you. 'Tis the truth you ordered me to," she reminded him. "Now I will give you the same command. Trust me to take care of Alex. Please bring him home."

He couldn't deny her. "Very well," he agreed with a sigh. "I'll get him tomorrow, but he'll only come here for a short visitation. If all goes well, then he'll stay. Otherwise . . ."

"It will go well."

"I won't have him put in jeopardy."

"No, of course not."

She tried to get off his lap. He stopped her by grabbing hold of her.

"Johanna?"

"Yes?"

"Do you trust me?"

She stared into his eyes for a long minute. He believed she was thinking the question over before she gave her answer. The possibility chafed. They'd been married for over three months now, and that was surely time enough for her to learn to trust him.

"Your hesitation irritates me," he snapped.

She didn't seem particularly bothered by that fact. She touched the side of his face with her hand. "I can tell it does," she whispered. "Yes, Gabriel, I trust you."

She leaned forward and kissed him. The wonder in her voice, added to the show of affection, made him smile.

"Do you trust me?"

He almost laughed until he realized she was being serious. "A warrior doesn't trust anyone, Johanna, but his laird, of course."

"Husbands should trust wives, shouldn't they?"

He didn't know. "I don't believe it's necessary." He rubbed his jaw, then added, "Nay, it would be foolish."

"Gabriel?"

"Yes?"

"You make me want to tear my hair out."

"Begging your pardon, mistress," Hilda called out from the doorway. "May I have a moment of your time?"

Johanna jumped off her husband's lap. She was blushing by the time she turned to the cook and bid her enter the hall.

"Who's sitting with Clare?" she asked.

"Father MacKechnie's with her now," Hilda answered. "She wanted to speak to him."

Johanna nodded. Gabriel stood up. "Why didn't you tell me she was awake?"

He didn't give her time to answer but started for the steps. Johanna hurried after him. "I promised her she could stay here," she blurted out.

Her husband didn't answer her. She pushed Dumfries out of her way and chased her husband up the steps.

"What are you thinking to do?" she demanded.

"I'm just going to talk to her, Johanna. You needn't worry."

"She isn't up to a long conversation, husband, and Father MacKechnie might be hearing her confession now. You shouldn't interrupt."

The priest was just opening the door to come out when Gabriel reached the chamber. He nodded to Father MacKechnie as he passed him. Johanna was right behind her husband.

"You will wait here while I talk to her," Gabriel commanded.

"But she might be afraid of you, husband."

"Then she'll have to be afraid."

He shut the door in his wife's face. Johanna didn't have time to be outraged over his rudeness. She was too worried about Clare MacKay.

She put her ear to the door and tried to listen. Father MacKechnie shook his head and pulled her away.

"Let your husband have his privacy," he suggested. "You should know by now our laird would never hurt a woman."

"Oh, I do know that," Johanna rushed out. "Still, Clare MacKay wouldn't know, would she?"

The priest didn't have an answer for her. She turned the topic then. "Did you hear Clare's confession?"

"I did."

Johanna's shoulders slumped. Father MacKechnie thought that was an odd reaction. "Confession's a sacrament," he reminded his mistress. "She wanted absolution."

"At what price?" Johanna asked in a whisper.

"I'm not understanding your question, lass."

"The penance," she blurted out. "It was severe, wasn't it?"

"You know I cannot discuss the penance," he said.

"Bishop Hallwick liked to boast about his penances," Johanna blurted out.

The priest demanded several examples. The one that most repelled her she saved for last. "One leg for one egg," she said. "The bishop laughed after he suggested that punishment to my first husband to inflict upon a serving girl."

Father MacKechnie plied her with questions, and when she'd given him her answers, he shook his head.

"I'm ashamed to hear this," he admitted, "for I would like to believe all priests are good men doing God's important work here. Bishop Hallwick will have his day of reckoning when he stands before his Maker and tries to explain away his deliberate cruelty."

"But, Father, the church stands behind the bishop. He takes his penances from the good book. Why, even the length of the stick is given."

"What are you talking about? What stick?" the priest asked, thoroughly confused.

She didn't understand why he didn't know what she was talking about. "The church dictates how a husband and wife should behave," she told him. "A submissive wife is a good and holy wife. The church approves beating women and, in fact, recommends such punishment because women will try to rule their husbands if they're not kept submissive."

She paused to take a breath. Discussing the topic was upsetting to her, but she didn't want the priest to see her distress. He might ask her why she was distraught, and then she'd have to confess a dark and surely mortal sin.

"The church frowns on murder, of course. A husband shouldn't beat his wife to death. A stick is preferred over a fist. It should be wooden, not metal, and no more than this long."

She held her hands out to show him the measurement. "Where did you hear these rules?"

"Bishop Hallwick."

"Not everyone in the church believes . . ."

"But they're supposed to believe," she interrupted, her agitation apparent now. She was wringing her hands together and trying not to let the priest see how close she was to losing her composure.

"Why is that, lass?"

Why didn't he understand? He was a priest, after all, and should be most familiar with the rules governing women.

"Because women are last in God's love," she whispered.

Father MacKechnie kept his expression contained. He took hold of Johanna's arm and led her down the hallway. He didn't want his laird to come outside and see his wife in such a distressed state.

There was a bench against the wall adjacent to the steps. The priest sat down, then patted the spot next to him. She immediately sat down. Her head was bowed, and she pretended great interest in straightening the pleats of her plaid.

Father MacKechnie waited another minute or two for his mistress to regain her composure before he asked her to explain her last remark.

"How would you know women are last in God's love?"

"The hierachy," she answered. She repeated from memory what she'd been taught, her head bowed all the while. When she was finished, she still refused to look at the priest.

He leaned back against the wall. "Well, now," he began. "You've given me quite a list to mull over in my mind. Tell me this, Johanna. Do you truly believe dim-witted oxen . . ."

"It's dull-witted, Father," she interrupted.

He nodded. "All right then," he agreed. "Do you believe dull-witted oxen will have a higher place in heaven than women?"

Father MacKechnie was such a good man. She didn't want to disappoint him. She wasn't going to lie to the priest though, no matter what the consequences.

"No," she whispered. She glanced up to see how her denial affected the priest. He didn't look horrified. She took a breath and then blurted out, "I don't believe any of it. I'm a heretic, Father, and will surely burn in hell."

The priest shook his head. "I don't believe it either," he told her. "It's nonsense made up by frightened men."

She leaned back now. She was clearly astonished by Father MacKechnie's attitude. "But the church's teachings . . ."

"The teachings are interpreted by men, Johanna. Don't be forgetting that important fact."

He took hold of her hand. "You aren't a heretic," he announced. "And now I want you to listen to what I have to say. There is but one God, Johanna, but two ways of looking at Him. There's the English way and the Highlander's way."

"How are they different?"

"Some of the English pray to a vengeful God," Father MacKechnie explained. "The children are raised to fear Him. They are taught not to sin because of the terrible retaliation in the next life, you see. The Highlanders are different, though certainly no less loved by God. Do you know what the word *clan* means?"

"Children," she answered.

The priest nodded. "We teach our children to love God, not fear Him. He is compared to a kind, good-hearted father."

"And if a Highlander sins?"

"If he is repentant, he will be forgiven."

She thought about his explanation a long while before she spoke again. "Then I am not damned because I don't believe God loves women least of all?"

The priest smiled. "No, you are not damned," he agreed. "You have as much value as any man. To tell you the truth, lass, I don't believe God keeps a list or hierarchy."

She was so relieved to hear she wasn't alone in her opinions and that she wasn't a heretic because she refused to believe Bishop Hallwick's dictates, she wanted to weep. "I don't believe God wants women beaten into submission," she whispered. "Still, I don't understand why the church has so many cruel rules against women."

Father MacKechnie let out a sigh. "Frightened men came up with these rules."

"What would they be afraid of, Father?"

"Women, of course. Now don't go repeating this to anyone, Johanna, but there are actually some men of God who believe women are superior. They don't want them to get the upper hand. They believe, too, that women use their bodies to get what they want."

"Some women probably do," Johanna agreed. "But only some."

"Yes," the priest said. "Women are certainly

stronger. No one can dispute that fact."

"We aren't stronger," Johanna protested, smiling now for she was certain the priest was jesting with her.

"Yes, you are," Father MacKechnie countered. Her smile proved contagious, and he couldn't help but grin. "Think many men would have more than one child if they were the ones suffering through childbirth?"

Johanna laughed. The priest had painted an outrageous picture. "Women have been given a harsh lot in this life," Father MacKechnie continued. "Yet they survive and, in fact, find ways to flourish in such a restrictive setting. They certainly have to be more clever than men, lass, to get their voices heard."

The door opened to Clare MacKay's chamber, and Gabriel came out. He turned to pull the door closed behind him.

Both Johanna and Father MacKechnie stood up. "Thank you, Father," she whispered. "You've helped me sort out a difficult problem."

"From the look on your husband's face, I would wager he could use a little help sorting out his problem." He'd whispered his remark, then raised his voice when he turned to his laird. "Did your conference go well, Laird MacBain?"

The scowl on Gabriel's face should have been proof enough to the priest that the conference hadn't gone well. Johanna decided Father Mac-Kechnie was just trying to be diplomatic.

Gabriel shook his head. "She refuses to name

the man responsible," he said.

"Perhaps she didn't know his name," Johanna suggested, instinctively coming to Clare MacKay's defense.

"She told me she spent a full night with the soldier, Johanna. Do you honestly believe she didn't bother getting his name?"

"Gabriel, you needn't raise your voice to me."

After giving her husband a good frown, she tried to walk around him so she could go to Clare's room. Her husband grabbed hold of her arm.

"Let her rest," he commanded. "She fell asleep during my questions." He turned his attention to the priest and added, "If her face wasn't distorted from the beating, I would have each one of my men come up here and look at her. Perhaps seeing her would nudge their memory."

"Then you believe a MacBain . . ."

"No, I don't believe one of my own is responsible," Gabriel said. "My men are honorable."

"Did Clare say it was a MacBain?" Johanna asked.

He shook his head. "She wouldn't answer that question either," he said.

"MacBain, Keith's back from the MacKay holding!"

Calum shouted the announcement from the entryway. Gabriel nodded to the priest, let go of his wife's arm, and went downstairs. He fairly ripped the doors off their hinges and went outside. Calum hurried to keep up with his laird. The doors slammed shut behind the two warriors.

Johanna spent the next hour wrestling with Dumfries while she removed his stitches. He carried on like a baby; and when she was finally finished poking at him, she spent a long while soothing him. She was sitting on the floor. Dumfries obviously didn't realize how big he was, for he tried to climb onto her lap.

She was certain she smelled as horrid as the dog and decided it was high time Dumfries had a proper bath. Megan fetched her a rope. Johanna looped one end around the dog's neck, collected her container of rose-scented soap, and dragged the hound out the back door and down the hill.

She ran into Glynis at the water well. Johanna was already a bit out of sorts. The constant worry about Clare MacKay preyed on her mind, and Dumfries's shameful beliavior was draining her strength. Her arms ached from dragging him along. Johanna believed she would have been able to control her anger if she'd been in a better frame of mind.

Glynis was polite enough to call out a proper greeting to her mistress before asking about Clare MacKay. "You aren't thinking of letting that whore sleep under the same roof with our laird, are you?"

Johanna came to a dead stop. She slowly turned to look at the Maclaurin woman. "Clare MacKay isn't a whore!" she shouted at the woman. She was about to add a forceful thought or two about the rewards Glynis would receive in the next life if she showed compassion now but changed her mind. Glynis deserved a good kick in her backside.

Johanna resisted the impulse and decided to give her a kick in her arrogance instead.

"I didn't mean to raise my voice to you, Glynis, for it isn't your fault you were led to believe Clare MacKay was a whore. Still, given your nickname, I would think you above all others would reserve judgment until you had all the facts. The Maclaurins wouldn't have given you such a name if you weren't worthy, now would they?" she asked. She nodded to the other women lined up at the wall.

Glynis shook her head. She looked confused and wary. Johanna sweetened her smile. "We have only Laird MacInnes's word that Clare didn't act honorably, and we aren't about to believe anything that man tells us, are we now? Clare's a welcomed guest in my house. I expect her to be treated with dignity and respect. Do excuse me now. Dumfries and I are going to Rush Creek. Good day, Glynis."

Johanna tightened her hold on her rope and walked away. She started counting. She could hear the women whispering among themselves behind her. She doubted Glynis would be able to contain her curiosity for more than a minute or two.

She was wrong. The Maclaurin woman called out to her before Johanna had even reached the number ten.

"What nickname have you heard, m'lady?"

Johanna slowly turned around. "Why, Glynis, I thought you knew. They call you Pure."

Glynis let out a little gasp and she visibly blanched. Johanna should have felt guilty over her lie. She didn't, though. The Maclaurin woman thought she was so terribly clever with her back-handed insults. She didn't know Johanna understood the names were actually the opposite of what they really meant.

"Dumfries," she whispered, "we're going to let her simmer until tomorrow. By then Glynis will have realized how cruel her game is. Then I'll tell her I made up the name."

Guilt wouldn't allow Johanna to wait that long. By the time she'd bathed the dog, she was feeling miserable. She was certain that if she was struck by lightning at that very moment, she'd go straight to hell.

She decided to go to Glynis's cottage and confess her sin. She was drenched from head to shoes, thanks to Dumfries's misbehaving in the creek, and she was given several stares on her way back to the well.

"M'lady, what happened to you?"

Leila asked her the question. She backed away from the dog and kept her gaze on the hound while she waited for her mistress to answer her.

"I gave Dumfries a bath. He pushed me in the creek," Johanna explained. "Twice as a matter of fact. Where does Glynis live? I wish to have a word with her."

Leila pointed out the cottage. Johanna dragged the dog along by her side, muttering over his stubbornness. She reached the cottage, hesitated for only a minute while she pushed her hair out of her face, and then pounded on the door.

Glynis pulled the door open. Her eyes widened when she saw her mistress. Johanna noticed Glynis's eyes looked teary. Lord, had her cruel remark made her cry? Johanna's guilt intensified. She was a little surprised, too, for Glynis was such a big, strapping woman, almost manly in her build, she didn't think she was the sort to ever weep.

She spotted Glynis's husband sitting at the table then. She didn't want him to overhear what she was going to say.

"Could you spare me a moment of your time, Glynis? I would like to speak to you in private."

"Yes, of course," Glynis answered. She glanced over her shoulder, then turned back to her mistress. She had a worried expression now. Johanna guessed she didn't want her husband listening in either.

Introductions were made. Glynis's husband was a head shorter than his wife. He had red hair, freckles on his face and arms, and handsome white teeth. His smile seemed sincere.

Johanna was invited inside. She declined as graciously as possible, using her sorry condition as her excuse.

She asked Glynis to please step outside instead. When the Maclaurin woman had closed the door behind her, Johanna motioned her close.

Glynis started to walk forward, then stopped. Dumfries's low growl obviously intimidated her.

Johanna ordered the dog to quit his bluster before she gave her apology.

"I came here to tell you I made up the nickname. No one calls you Pure," she announced. "I did it out of spite, Glynis, and I'm sorry for my sin. I caused you needless worry, but in my defense I will tell you I was thinking to teach you a lesson. It stings to have the tables turned on you, doesn't it?"

Glynis didn't answer her question, but her face turned pale. Johanna nodded. "I know you're the one who came up with the name for me. I also know that when you call me Courageous, you're really meaning I'm a coward."

"That was before, m'lady," Glynis stammered out.

"Before what?"

"Before we knew you well and realized you weren't a coward at all."

Johanna wasn't going to be swayed by that bit of praise. She was certain Glynis was only trying to ease her way out of an awkward situation.

"I do not care for your foolish games," she announced with a nod. "Father MacKechnie boasted that the Highlanders never hide their feelings. They don't use subterfuge."

She had to take the time to explain what that word meant before continuing. "I find I admire that trait, Glynis. If you think I'm a coward, then have the courage to say it to my face. Don't make up silly games. They're hurtful . . . and very like something the English would do."

If Glynis nodded anymore vehemently, Johanna thought her neck would snap.

"Did you tell our laird?" she asked.

Johanna shook her head. "This matter doesn't concern him."

"I will stop giving nicknames, m'lady," Glynis said then.

"And I apologize if you were hurt by my cruelty."

"Were you hurt by mine?"

Glynis didn't answer for a long minute. Then she nodded. "I was," she whispered.

"Then we are even. Auggie isn't daft," she added. "He really is clever. If you spent any time at all with him, you'd realize that."

"Yes, m'lady."

"There," Johanna announced. "We've settled this problem. Good day to you, Glynis."

She made a curtsy and turned to leave. Glynis followed her to the edge of the path. "We only called you Courageous until you put Dumfries back together with your threads, m'lady. Then we changed your name."

Johanna was determined not to ask, but curiosity won out. "And what did you change my name to?"

She braced herself for the insult she knew was coming.

"Timid."

"Timid?"

"Aye, m'lady. We call you Timid."

Johanna was suddenly in a fit mood again. She smiled all the way home.

They called her Timid. It was a fair start.

Chapter
13

Johanna didn't see her husband until dinner. The men were already seated at the two tables when she walked down the steps into the great hall. No one stood up. Gabriel wasn't there yet. Both Father MacKechnie and Keith were also absent. The servants were busy putting oblong platters of meat on the table. The aroma of the mutton filled the air. A wave of nausea caught Johanna by surprise. She thought the soldiers' behavior was the reason she was suddenly feeling ill. They were grabbing handfuls of food before the trenchers were even placed in front of them. They weren't waiting for their laird to join them or for the priest to give the blessing before dinner.

Enough was enough. Mama would have heart failure if she witnessed such shameful behavior at her dinner table. Johanna wasn't about to be shamed in front of her dear mother. She'd die first. Or kill a couple of the Maclaurins, she thought to herself. They were the worse offenders, though the MacBain soldiers were certainly trying to keep up.

Megan noticed her mistress standing by the entrance. She called out to her, realized Johanna couldn't hear her over the noise the men were making, and walked across the hall to speak to her.

"Aren't you going to have your supper?" she asked.

"Yes, of course."

"M'lady, you don't look well. Are you feeling all right? You're as pale as flour, you are."

"I'm fine," Johanna lied. She took a deep breath in an attempt to get her queasy stomach under control. "Please fetch me a large bowl. Bring one that's cracked."

"Whatever for, m'lady?"

"I might have to break it."

Megan thought she'd misunderstood her mistress. She asked her to repeat her explanation. Johanna shook her head. "You'll understand soon enough," she promised.

Megan ran to the buttery, grabbed a heavy porcelain bowl from the shelf, and hurried back to her mistress.

"This one's chipped," she announced. "Will it do?"

Johanna nodded. "Stand back, Megan. Sparks are about to fly."

"They are?"

Johanna called out to the soldiers first. She knew they wouldn't hear her over all the racket, but she thought she should at least attempt ladylike conduct at first. She tried clapping her hands together next. Finally she whistled. Not one of the soldiers looked up.

She gave up trying to be diplomatic. She lifted the bowl and hurled it across the room. Megan let out a loud gasp. The bowl crashed into the stone hearth and splintered to the floor.

The effect was just as she'd hoped. Every man in the hall turned to look at her. They were silent, looking incredulous, and she couldn't have been more pleased.

"Now that I have your attention, I have several instructions to give you."

Several mouths dropped open. Calum started to stand up. She told him to stay where he was.

"You meant to throw the bowl?" Lindsay asked her that question.

"Yes," she answered. "Please listen to me," she explained. "This is my house and I would therefore appreciate it if you would follow my rules. First, and most important, none of you will eat until your laird has been seated and served. Do I make myself clear?"

Most of the soldiers nodded. A few of the Maclaurins looked irritated. She ignored their frowns. Calum, she noticed, was smiling. She ignored him, too.

"But what if our laird doesn't come in for supper?" Niall asked.

"Then you'll wait until your mistress has been seated and served before you eat," she answered.

There was a considerable amount of grumbling over her dictate. Johanna held onto her patience.

The men turned back to their trenchers.

"I'm not finished giving you my instructions," Johanna called out.

Her voice was drowned out by the clatter again.

"Megan, fetch me another bowl."

"But m'lady?"

"Please."

"As you wish."

Less than a minute passed before Megan handed her mistress a second bowl. Johanna immediately hurled it at the hearth. The loud crash turned everyone's attention again. Several of the Maclaurin soldiers were giving her surly looks now. She decided a threat or two would be appropriate retaliation.

"I won't throw the next bowl at the hearth," she announced. "I'll throw it at one of your heads if you don't pay attention to me."

"We're wanting to eat, m'lady," another soldier shouted.

"I'm wanting your attention first," she replied. "Listen carefully. When a lady enters the room, the men stand."

"You interrupted our supper to tell us that?" Lindsay shouted. He added a nervous laugh and nudged his neighbor's side with his elbow.

She put her hands on her hips and repeated her dictate. Then she waited. She was pleased to see every soldier finally stand up.

She smiled, satisfied. "You may sit down."

"You just told us to stand up," another Maclaurin muttered. Lord, they were dense. She tried

337

to hide her exasperation.

"You stand when a lady enters, and you sit when she gives you permission."

"What do we do when she comes in and then goes right back out again?"

"You stand, then sit."

"Seems a nuisance to me," another Maclaurin remarked.

"I'm going to teach you manners even if it kills you," she announced.

Calum started laughing, but her glare stopped him.

"Why?" Niall asked. "What do we need manners for?"

"To please me," she snapped. "There won't be anymore belching at my tables," she said.

"We can't belch?" Calum asked, looking astonished.

"No, you can't!" she said in a near shout. "You can't make any other rude noises either."

"But it's a compliment, m'lady," Niall explained. "If the food and drink are good, a belch is due praise."

"If you enjoy your food, you'll simply tell your host it was a fine meal," she instructed. "And while we're on the topic of food, I'll tell you I find it gravely offensive when I see one of you ripping food from your neighbor's trencher. That's going to stop right now."

"But m'lady —" Lindsay began.

She cut him off. "You aren't going to slam your goblets together when you give a toast," she announced. "The ale spills everywhere."

"We do it on purpose," Calum explained.

Her eyes widened over that admission. Niall hurried to tell her why. "When we toast, we make certain some of our ale spills into the other goblets. That way, if there's poison in one, everyone will die. Don't you see, m'lady? We do it to ensure no one will try trickery."

She couldn't believe what she was hearing. Were the Maclaurins and the MacBains that suspicious of each other?

The Maclaurins dared to turn their backs on her again. Johanna was infuriated by their rudeness. They were being deliberately loud now in their bid to drown out her voice.

"Megan?"

"I'm fetching it, m'lady."

Johanna lifted the pitcher in the air, turned toward the Maclaurin table, and was just about to throw the thing when it was snatched out of her hand. She turned around and found Gabriel standing right behind her. Keith and Father MacKechnie flanked his sides.

She didn't have any idea how long they'd been standing there, but the stunned look on Father MacKechnie's face indicated it had been long enough.

She could feel herself blushing. No wife wished to be caught screaming like a shrew or throwing things to get attention. Johanna wasn't about to let her embarrassment deter her, however. She'd started this and by God she was going to finish it.

"What in God's name are you doing, wife?"

His deep tone of voice, added to his frown, made her wince. She took a deep breath, then said, "Do stay out of this. I'm in the middle of giving my instructions to the men."

"No one seems to be paying you any attention, m'lady," Keith pointed out.

"Did you just tell me you want me to stay out . . ." Gabriel was too flabbergasted to continue.

She caught the gist of what he wanted to say. "Yes, I do want you to stay out of this," she agreed before turning her attention to Keith. "They will pay attention or suffer my displeasure," she promised.

"What happens when you're displeased?" the Maclaurin soldier asked.

She couldn't think of a suitable answer. Then she remembered what Gabriel had said he'd do when he was displeased.

"I'll probably kill someone," she boasted.

She was certain she'd impressed the Maclaurin soldier with that announcement. She added a nod so he wouldn't know she was bluffing and waited for his reaction.

It wasn't what she expected. "You're wearing the wrong plaid, m'lady. Today's Saturday."

She suddenly wanted to strangle Keith. A loud belch sounded behind her. She reacted as though she'd just been stabbed in the back. She let out a loud gasp, snatched the pitcher out of her husband's hand, and turned to the men.

Gabriel caught her before she could do any damage. He tossed the pitcher to Keith, then turned her around to face him.

"I asked you not to interfere," she whispered.

"Johanna . . ."

"Is this my home or isn't it?"

"It is."

"Thank you."

"Why are you thanking me?" he asked, wary now. She was up to something all right. The glint in her eyes told him so.

"You just agreed to help me," she explained.

"No, I didn't."

"You should."

"Why?"

"Because this is my home, isn't it?"

"Are we back to that?"

"Gabriel, I would like a free hand in the running of my household. Please?" she whispered.

He let out a sigh. Damn but it was impossible for him to deny her anything. He wasn't even certain what he was agreeing to, but he still nodded.

"How many more bowls and pitchers will you throw?"

"As many as it takes," she replied.

She turned around and hurried over to stand at the head of the Maclaurin table.

"Keith, if you'll take one end, and Father, if you would be so good as to lift the other end, I'll run ahead and hold the doors open. Gentlemen," she added, her gaze directed on the soldiers seated at the table now, "please help by carrying your stools. This shouldn't take us any time at all."

341

"What are you thinking to do?" Keith asked.

"Moving the table outside, of course."

"Why?"

"I want to make the Maclaurins happy," she explained. "They're part of my clan now and I believe they should be content."

"But we don't want to move outside," Lindsay blurted out. "Why would you think we would? I only just got the honor of eating with my laird. I want to stay here."

"No, you don't," Johanna countered. She smiled just to confuse the warrior.

"I don't?"

"You'll all be much more content outside because you won't have to follow any of the rules of my household then. 'Tis the truth you all eat like animals. You might as well eat with them. Dumfries will be happy for the company."

All of the Maclaurins looked at Keith. He looked at his laird, received his nod, and then cleared his throat. It was up to him to set his mistress straight.

"I don't believe you understand the situation here, m'lady. This keep has belonged to the Maclaurin clan for as long as anyone can remember."

"It belongs to me now."

"But, m'lady . . ." Keith began.

"What does she mean when she says our land belongs to her?" Niall asked.

Johanna folded her hands together. Gabriel walked over to stand next to her.

"I'll be happy to explain, but only once, so please

try to follow along," she said. "Your king bartered this land away. Is everyone here in agreement with that fact?"

She waited until the soldiers nodded. "King John gave the holding to me. Does everyone agree with that fact?"

"Yes, of course," Keith agreed. "But you see . . ."

She wouldn't let him finish. "Pray forgive me for interrupting you, but I'm anxious to finish this explanation."

She turned her attention back to the soldiers. "Now then — and do pay attention, please, for I hate repeating myself — when I married your laird, the land became his. Do you see how simple it is?"

Her gaze settled on Lindsay. He nodded to make her happy. She smiled. The room suddenly started to spin. She blinked, trying to bring everyone back into focus. She grabbed hold of the edge of the table to balance herself. A wave of nausea washed over her, then just as rapidly disappeared. It was the meat, she thought to herself. The awful smell was making her sick.

"You were saying, lass?" Father MacKechnie prodded, beaming with satisfaction over the gumption his mistress was showing in front of the men.

"What's got her so riled, I wonder?"

Johanna didn't know who asked that question. It came from the MacBain table. She turned her gaze to those men and answered.

"Megan said something the other day that took

me by surprise," she said. "I've mulled it over in my mind, and I still don't understand why she would make such a comment."

"What did I say?" Megan asked. She hurried over to stand on the opposite side of the Maclaurin table so she could face her mistress.

"You told me Cook would be happy to do anything I asked because she was a MacBain and knew better than to complain. I wondered what you meant, of course, but now I think I understand. You actually believe Hilda should be thankful she's allowed to live here. Isn't that right?"

Megan nodded. " 'Tis the truth she should be thankful." The Maclaurin soldiers all nodded in unison.

Johanna shook her head at them. "I believe you've all got it backward," she said. "The Maclaurins don't have any claim to this keep or this land, and that, gentlemen, is also fact. My husband happens to be a MacBain. Have you forgotten that?"

"His father was laird over the Maclaurins," Keith interjected.

"He's still a MacBain," she pointed out again. "He's been very accommodating. He's more patient than I am," she added with a nod. "Regardless, I believe the MacBains have graciously allowed all of you Maclaurins to stay on. I really hate to bring this prickly topic up now, but I've received important news, you see, and I really must get my household in order. It would sadden me to see you leave, but if the rules are too difficult

344

for you to follow, and if you can't get along with the MacBains, then I don't believe there's much choice."

"But the MacBains are the outsiders," Lindsay stammered out.

"Aye, they are," Keith agreed.

"They were," Johanna said. "They aren't now. Do you see?" No one did see. Johanna wondered if they were just being incredibly stubborn or just plain ignorant. She decided to try to make them understand one last time.

Gabriel wouldn't let her. He pulled her back and took a step forward.

"I'm laird here," he reminded the soldiers. "I decide who stays and who goes."

Keith immediately nodded agreement. "Are we allowed to speak freely?"

"You are," Gabriel replied.

"Every one of us has pledged our loyalty to you," he began. "But we aren't particularly loyal to your followers. We're weary of war and want to rebuild before we go into battle again. Yet one of the MacBains has instigated war with the MacInnes clan and now refuses to come forward and admit his transgression. Such behavior is cowardly."

Calum jumped to his feet. "You dare call us cowards?"

Dear God, what had she started? Johanna was feeling sick again. She was certainly sorry she'd said anything. Two of the Maclaurins stood up. A fight was brewing all right, and it was all her doing. Gabriel didn't seem inclined to put a stop to it either. He looked completely unaffected by the threatening atmosphere, almost bored in fact.

A confrontation was finally taking place, and Gabriel was damned happy about it. He would let each warrior vent his anger, then explain what was going to happen. Those who didn't wish to go along with his decisions could leave.

Unfortunately Johanna looked upset over what was happening. Her face was stark white now, and she was gripping her hands together. Gabriel decided to take the argument outside. He was just about to give that command when his wife stepped forward.

"Calum, Keith didn't call you a coward," she cried out. She turned her gaze to the Maclaurin soldier then. "You don't understand, sir, for you had already left on your errand to speak to Clare MacKay's father," she rushed out. "You see, my husband asked each one of his followers if he had . . . involved himself with Clare, and each man denied any knowledge of the woman."

"But did each man tell the truth?" Keith challenged.

"I'll ask you a question in answer," she countered. "If Laird MacInnes blamed a Maclaurin and every one of you gave your laird your denial, would you expect him to believe you?"

Keith was clever enough to know where she was going with the question. He reluctantly nodded.

"My husband and I both have complete faith

in his followers. If the men say they didn't touch Clare MacKay, then they didn't. I don't understand you, sir. How can you take the word of a mean-hearted MacInnes over one of your own?"

No one had a quick answer to that question. Johanna shook her head again. She was feeling terribly ill now. Her face felt as though it was on fire, yet her arms were covered with goosebumps. She wanted to lean against her husband, but held back, for she didn't want him to know she wasn't feeling well. She didn't want to upset him. She also didn't want to spend the next year in bed; and knowing Gabriel's obsession with rest, she was certain that's what would happen.

Johanna decided to go up to her chamber and wash her face. Surely cold water would help revive her.

"I would appreciate it if everyone of you would consider what I've just explained," she requested. "I can't have bickering in my home. If you'll excuse me now, I'll go up to my chamber."

She turned to leave. Then she stopped and turned around again. "When a lady leaves the room, the men stand."

"Here we go again," a Maclaurin whispered loud enough for her to hear.

"Well?" she demanded.

The men stood. She smiled, satisfied. Then she turned to leave. The room suddenly started spinning. She didn't have anything to hold onto until everything settled back where it was supposed to be.

"You did call me a coward, Keith," Calum muttered.

"If you want to believe I did, then do so, Calum," Keith replied.

"What was the important news m'lady said she just received?"

"Gabriel?" Johanna's voice was weak, but he still heard her.

He turned around. "Yes?"

"Catch me."

Chapter

14

He caught her before she hit the floor. Everyone started shouting at the same time. Father MacKechnie thought he might faint when he saw how ill his mistress looked.

"Clear the table," he shouted. "We'll put her there."

Niall and Lindsay swept their arms across the linen cloth. Trenchers and food went flying. Megan pulled the linen cloth off.

"Someone fetch a healer for God's sake," Niall bellowed. "M'lady needs help."

"She's our healer," Calum snapped.

"What made her swoon?"

"I'm thinking we did," Lindsay decided. "We got her all riled up. It was too much for her."

Gabriel was the only one who didn't seem overly concerned about his wife. Her face did look pale to him, but he didn't think she was really sick.

He'd noticed how upset she became when the men started shouting at each other. She had an aversion to fighting, he knew, and he therefore concluded her faint was just a clever ploy to turn the men's attention away from their argument.

She'd gone a little overboard, of course, and he'd tell her just that when they were alone.

"It's all our fault, all right, making her throw bowls to get our attention," Niall said. "She wants us to have some manners. I can't figure out why, but I'm thinking we'd best be more cooperative."

"Aye," another Maclaurin named Michael agreed. "We can't have her swooning all the time. Laird MacBain might not be close enough to catch her next time."

"Move back, men," Father MacKechnie ordered. "Give the lass some room to breathe."

"She is breathing, isn't she?"

"Aye, Calum, she's breathing," the priest answered. "Your concern for your mistress is praiseworthy."

"She's our mistress today," Lindsay commented. "She's wearing our plaid."

"Today's Saturday," Keith interjected. "She's wearing the wrong plaid."

"She can't seem to get it right, can she?" Calum asked.

"Why are you hesitating, MacBain? Put the lass on the table," Father MacKechnie said. "Men, get out of your laird's way."

The men immediately moved back. As soon as Gabriel placed his wife on the table, they all moved forward again. At least twenty faces loomed over her. Everyone was frowning with concern for Johanna.

Gabriel felt like smiling. The soldiers had their differences, of course, but they were united now in their worry about their mistress. Johanna was neither a Maclaurin nor a MacBain by birth. She was English. If the men could give her their loyalty, they could damned well learn to get along with each other.

"Why won't she open her eyes?" Niall asked.

"She doesn't appear to be finished with her faint just yet," the priest replied.

"Are you going to give her the last rites, Father?"

"I don't believe that's necessary."

"Shouldn't we do something?" Calum asked the question and added a frown in his laird's direction. It was apparent he expected Gabriel to fix whatever was ailing his wife.

Gabriel shook his head. "She'll wake up in a minute or two."

"We shouldn't have upset her," Michael said.

"Why did she suddenly get a bee up her . . . arm?" Lindsay quickly substituted the last word for the one he was going to use when he caught the priest's frown.

"It was our manners that set her off," Bryan reminded the group.

"But why now, I'm wondering," Lindsay blurted out. "M'lady didn't seem to mind what we were doing until tonight."

"Her mother's coming for a visitation."

Their laird gave them the announcement. There was a collective and drawn-out "Ah" over the revelation.

"No wonder she's wanting us to have some manners," Michael said with a nod.

"Poor lass," Keith whispered. "She must be worried we'll shame her in front of her mother."

"Makes sense to me," Calum agreed.

"We'd best get some manners then," Lindsay suggested. He let out a sigh. "She did kill Pet, after all."

"And three more," Keith reminded the soldier.

Gabriel was beginning to wonder how long Johanna was going to drag out her swoon when she suddenly opened her eyes.

She almost let out a scream but stopped herself in time, letting out a loud gasp instead. She stared up at all the soldiers staring down at her while she struggled to get over her startle.

It took her a minute or two to realize she was stretched out on top of the dinner table. She couldn't imagine how she'd gotten there.

"Why am I on the table?"

"It was closer than your bed, m'lady," Calum answered.

"You swooned," Keith added in case she'd forgotten.

"Why didn't you tell us your mother was coming for a visitation?" Niall asked.

Johanna tried to sit up before answering the question. Father MacKechnie put his hand on her shoulder to hold her down. "You'd best stay right where you are, lass. Your husband will be happy to carry you up to bed. Are you feeling better now?"

"Yes, thank you," she answered. "I really fainted? I've never, ever fainted before. I can't imagine why . . ."

Lindsay decided to give her his explanation before she asked for it. "It was our manners that set you off, m'lady."

"It was?"

The soldier nodded. "She should stay in bed a week at least," Keith recommended.

"I can't go to bed," Johanna argued.

No one paid any attention to her protest. "I'm saying she should stay in bed two weeks," Calum announced. "It's the only way to be certain she'll regain her strength. She's puny if you'll remember," he advised.

The men nodded. Johanna was outraged. "I'm not puny," she announced in a near shout. "Father, do let me up. I can't go to bed. I have to take my turn sitting with Clare MacKay."

"I'll be happy to sit with her," Megan offered. "It doesn't seem fair letting only MacBain women tend to her. You don't want the Maclaurin women bickering over the slight, do you now, m'lady?"

"Megan, now isn't the time to bring up that concern," Keith muttered.

"The MacBain women were the only ones who offered to help with Clare," Johanna explained.

"But I'm offering now," Megan insisted.

"Then I thank you and will certainly appreciate your help."

Megan smiled. She was obviously satisfied with her mistress's gratitude.

Johanna put the matter aside and turned her attention to her husband. She'd been deliberately avoiding looking at him, for she knew he'd be frowning and surely getting ready to pounce on her with his I-told-you-you-were-weak reminder. She mentally braced herself and turned her gaze. Gabriel was easy to find in the crowd as he towered over his soldiers. He stood to the left of the table, behind Calum.

Her husband was smiling, which fairly stunned Johanna. She was certain he'd be furious or worried at the very least. She should have been relieved over his obviously cheerful mood, but she wasn't. She had fainted after all, and Gabriel had proven to be quite a worrier about her well-being in the past. Yet he looked . . . happy now. Did he find her faint amusing?

She gave Gabriel a disgruntled look, and he winked back, which confused her.

"When is your mother coming here?" Keith asked her then.

She didn't take her gaze off her husband when she gave the Maclaurin soldier her answer. "In two or three months," she guessed. She smiled up at Father MacKechnie then and gently removed his hand from her shoulder so she could sit up.

Calum tried to lift her into his arms. Keith tried to assist her from the other side of the table. Johanna was suddenly being pulled every which way.

Gabriel finally intervened. He pushed Calum out of his way and took his wife into his arms.

"Rest your head on my shoulder," he commanded.

She wasn't quick enough, so he shoved her head there.

He carried her out of the hall and up the stairs. She protested most of the way. "I'm feeling fine now," she argued. "I can walk, husband. Do put me down."

"I want to carry you," he explained. "It's the least I can do after all the trouble you went to convincing my men."

"The least you can do?"

"Aye," he answered.

She didn't have any idea what he was talking about. His smile was even more confusing to her. "You act as though my faint amused you," she blurted out.

Gabriel opened the door to their bedchamber and carried her inside. " 'Tis the truth you did amuse me," he admitted.

Her eyes widened. "But you're usually overly concerned about me, nagging me to rest all day along. Why this sudden change in your attitude, I'm wondering."

"I don't nag. Old women nag, not warriors."

"You used to nag," she countered. She couldn't help but become a little irritated. Her husband's callous attitude bothered her. A husband should be a little concerned when his wife fainted, shouldn't he?

"Your ploy worked," he said. "My men forgot their argument. That was the reason you pretended to faint, wasn't it?"

He all but tossed her on the bed. She bounced twice before settling.

She felt like laughing now. She was certainly filled with relief. Gabriel wasn't such an unfeeling clout after all. He really believed she'd pretended to swoon.

Johanna didn't want to lie to her husband, but she didn't particularly want to set him straight either. If he realized she hadn't been pretending, he'd probably force her to stay in bed until next spring.

She didn't agree or disagree with her husband. If he decided to take her silence as agreement over his own conclusion, so be it.

He'd turned her attention anyway. He was taking his boots off.

"Aren't you going to boast over your cleverness?" he asked. He tossed his boots to the floor and began to untie the knot in his belt. He kept his gaze on her all the while.

"Old men boast, m'lord," she answered. Her gaze was on his waist. "Not warriors' wives."

Lord, how she pleased him. He liked the way she turned his own words back on him. Johanna was becoming downright sassy. Such behavior was proof enough she'd conquered her fear of him.

She still blushed quite easily. She was blushing now. She obviously guessed what he intended to do. He decided to tell her anyway just to further her embarrassment. She'd get all flustered then, and Lord, how he liked that feminine trait.

356

He stood by the side of the bed and told her in explicit detail exactly what he planned to do to her. The pictures he painted with his erotic words made her face burn, and the way he wanted to make love to her made her think she was going to faint again.

The dark and incredibly arousing look on his face made her think he wasn't jesting with her. Still, she needed to be sure.

"Do men and women really make love in such a way?"

She sounded breathless, but she couldn't help it. Her heart was slamming a wild beat, and she was fighting her own arousal while she tried to decide if such a thing was possible. The thoughts Gabriel had deliberately planted in her mind both appalled and excited her.

He pulled her to her feet and began to take her clothes off her.

"You're jesting with me, aren't you, husband?"

He laughed. "No."

"Then husbands and wives really . . ."

"We're going to," he answered, his voice a rough whisper.

She shivered. " 'Tis the truth I've never heard of such a . . ."

"I'll make you like it," he promised.

"Will you like . . ."

"Oh, yes."

"What will I . . ."

His wife was having difficulty finishing her sentences. She was obviously shaken. So was he, he realized. He was certainly aroused. His movements were damned awkward as he fought the tiny ribbons holding her undergarments together.

He let out a sigh of satisfaction when he finally got rid of the last of her clothes and then roughly pulled her up against him. He lifted her up so his hard arousal could press against the junction of her thighs.

She instinctively moved until she was cuddling him. He grunted with pleasure.

They fell into bed together. Gabriel rolled on top of her. He braced his weight with his elbows on either side of her and leaned down to capture her mouth for a long, drugging kiss. Their tongues dueled and stroked each other; and when he finally moved to kiss a path down the side of her silky neck, he could feel her trembling with pleasure.

She wasn't quite finished plying him with questions. She was a worrier she supposed, and that was surely the reason she wanted a full explanation.

"Gabriel, you really think to use your mouth to kiss me . . . there?"

"Oh, yes," he whispered against her ear. His breath, so sweet and warm against her sensitive skin made her tremble with desire.

"Then I'm going to . . . you know . . . kiss you . . . there."

He went completely still. She began to worry. A scant second later he slowly lifted his head to look at her.

"You don't have to do anything," he told her.

"Do you want me to?"

"Aye."

He'd drawled out the word, and God, he was such a sexy man. She felt as though she'd already pleased him. She reached up to stroke the side of his face. He leaned into her hand.

He liked her to touch him. He needed her to, she realized . . . almost as much as she needed him now to stroke her.

She let out a sigh and put her arms around her husband's neck. She tried to pull him down for a long kiss, but he resisted.

"Johanna, you don't have to . . ."

She smiled up at him. "I'll make you like it," she whispered.

His head dropped to the crook in her shoulder. He leaned up, bit her earlobe, and then said, "I know I'll like it, but I don't know if you'll . . ."

Now he was having trouble finishing his sentences. It was all his wife's fault. She reached down and gently stroked his arousal. He was too busy shuddering to think coherent thoughts.

He'd been worried she wouldn't like tasting him. She started out timid, but she got over being shy soon enough and became damned enthusiastic.

She made him crazy. His heart felt as though it had stopped when she took his arousal into her mouth. She was wild now, completely uninhibited as she stroked him with her mouth, her tongue, and dear God, she made him just as wild to please her.

He couldn't stand the ecstasy for very long. He

came before she did, but once he'd recovered from the spasms that racked his body, and he could think again, he turned his full attention to pleasuring his wife.

Her whimpers soon turned to shouts. The intensity of her own orgasm made her forget to breathe. She demanded he stop his wonderful agony even as she clung to him and pressed herself against him in a contradictory plea for more.

The taste of her made him hard and throbbing in scant minutes. He was suddenly desperate to be inside her. He moved, pinned her to the bed, and knelt between her thighs. His hands cupped her backside and he lifted her up at the same instant he thrust deep inside.

He felt as though he'd died and gone to heaven. She was so damned tight, so incredibly sweet and giving, and he knew he would never be able to get enough of her.

The bed squeaked from their forceful movements. Their breathing was harsh and choppy, and when she found fulfillment again, her scream made his ears ring.

He was thoroughly satisfied. He collapsed on top of his wife and let out a loud groan.

He could hear her heart hammering inside her chest. He was arrogantly pleased and satisfied. He'd made her completely forget herself.

She'd done the same to him. He frowned over the acknowledgment. It had become impossible to distance himself from his wife, he realized. He couldn't simply make love to her and then go back to his duties and put her out of his thoughts. She had become more than simply a woman to mate with during the dark hours of the night. She was his wife, and damn it all, she was even more than that.

She was the love of his life.

"Hell."

He muttered the expletive, then lifted his head to look at her. She was sound asleep. He was relieved, for he wouldn't have to explain the appalled look he was certain he had on his face or the blasphemy he'd just uttered.

He couldn't seem to make himself leave her. He stared down at her for long minutes. She was so beautiful to him. Yet her appearance wasn't the reason he'd lost his mind and fallen in love with her, God help him. Nay, it was her character that wooed him into forgetting his shields. Looks faded with age, but the beauty in Johanna's heart and in her soul seemed to grow more wonderful with each new day.

She'd snared him all right, blindsided him she had, and now it was too late to do anything about protecting himself from her.

There was only one course of action left to him. Johanna was going to have to love him. By God, he wasn't about to let himself become this vulnerable without gaining equal measure.

Gabriel felt better. The plan made sound sense to him. He wasn't certain how he'd get her to fall in love with him, but he was an intelligent man. He'd think of something.

He leaned down, kissed her brow, and then got out of bed. Their lovemaking had worn her out, he supposed, as he reached for his plaid. That possibility made him smile until he yawned. He realized then she'd worn him out, too.

He stared down at her all the while he dressed; and when he was finished, he took time to cover her up. Then, damned if he didn't have to kiss her one last time before he left the chamber. He was becoming appalled again by his own shameful behavior. Loving was a tricky affair, he decided. Perhaps, in time, he'd get the hang of it. He started to forcefully pull the door closed, caught himself in time, and shut it as quietly as possible.

Hell, he was becoming considerate. He had to shake his head over that disgusting trait. He wondered what other surprises were going to come his way now that he'd acknowledged to himself the fact that he did indeed love his wife. The future worried him. If he turned into a doting husband, he swore he'd have to kill someone.

Aye, loving was a tricky affair.

Johanna slept through the night. Gabriel left the chamber before she awakened. She was thankful for her privacy. She felt so sick, she could barely breathe without gagging. She tried to get out of bed twice, but each time the room would begin to spin and her stomach would lurch in protest of the movement. She took deep, gulping breaths to try to calm her nausea. It didn't help. She made it over to the washstand and slapped a wet cloth against her forehead, but that didn't help either. Johanna finally quit fighting the inevitable and ended up kneeling over the chamber pot, wretching until she was certain she was going to faint again.

While she'd been throwing up, she thought she was surely going to die; yet after she was finished, she felt surprisingly fit again. Whatever sickness had claimed her had either ended abruptly or had strange symptoms. Until she knew what was ailing her, she couldn't treat herself.

Johanna wasn't one to pamper herself, yet she couldn't help but be worried. She'd believed her faint the night before was due to an empty stomach mixed with the unpleasant aroma of cooked meat. But she'd almost fainted again this morning and the only aroma in the chamber was the scent of the outdoors coming through the opened window.

She tried not to think about being sick. She'd missed Mass and knew she would have to take Father aside later and explain that she'd been indisposed. The color had come back to her face by the time she dressed. She braided her hair, straightened the chamber, and then went to look in on Clare MacKay.

Hilda opened the door for her. Johanna smiled when she saw Clare was sitting up in bed. Her face was still horribly swollen, of course, and the left side of her face was black and blue from bruises, but her eyes looked clear, not murky, and Johanna surmised the blow to the head hadn't done irreparable damage.

"How are you feeling this morning, Clare?" Johanna asked.

"Better, thank you," the MacKay woman answered in a weak, pitiful voice.

"She barely ate a morsel of the food I carried up," Hilda interjected. "Says her throat pains her too much. I'm going back to the kitchens to mix a tonic for her."

Johanna nodded. She kept her gaze on Clare. "You're going to have to eat in order to regain your strength."

Clare shrugged in answer. Johanna shut the door behind Hilda and went over to sit down on the side of the bed next to her patient.

"You do want to get better, don't you?"

Clare stared at Johanna a long minute before answering. "I suppose I'll have to," she whispered. She deliberately tried to turn the topic then. "It was good of you to take me in, Lady Johanna. I haven't properly thanked you yet. I'm most appreciative."

"You needn't thank me," Johanna protested. "Why did you sound so sad when you said you would probably have to get better?"

The MacKay woman didn't answer her. She was obviously nervous, for she was twisting the end of the blanket into a knot.

"Is my father going to come here?"

"I don't know," Johanna answered. She reached over and placed her hand on top of Clare's. "Will you be happy to see him if he does come to see you?"

"Yes, of course," Clare rushed out.

She didn't sound very sincere. Johanna was determined to gain some answers, but she wasn't going to demand anything from the battered woman. She would use patience and understanding. Eventually Clare would tell her why she was so worried.

She decided to soothe her now. "You needn't be afraid, you know. You're safe here. No one's going to hurt you. After your baby's born and you've regained your strength, my husband and I will help you decide what's to be done. You may stay with us for as long as you wish. You have my word."

Clare's eyes filled with tears. "I'm very weary now. I would like to rest."

Johanna immediately stood up. She tucked the covers around the woman, acting like a concerned mother now. She put her hand to Clare's forehead to make certain she didn't have fever, then went over to check the pitcher to make sure her patient had enough water to drink.

Clare appeared to be sound asleep by the time Johanna left the chamber. Hilda went back inside to take over the watch.

Johanna tried to talk to Clare later in the morning; but as soon as she started asking questions, Clare became weary and fell asleep again.

Megan took a turn sitting with Clare that afternoon so Hilda could supervise the preparations for dinner. Johanna thought to try and question her patient once again, but she was waylaid when her husband came striding into the great hall with his son at his side.

Johanna had just finished removing Calum's stitches. She was trying to make him pay attention to her while she gave him instructions. He was like a fidgety child, anxious to get back outside.

"You aren't leaving until you promise to apply this salve every morning and night for a week's time, Calum."

"I promise," the soldier replied. He jumped to his feet and went hurrying across the room, leaving the jar of salve on the table.

"I'm here!"

Alex bellowed his important announcement and spread his arms wide in a gesture so dramatic his father couldn't help but smile. The boy certainly didn't have a problem with his own self-worth. Of course Gabriel had assured him several times on the way back home that Johanna was anxious to see him.

His wife's reaction was just as amusing to Gabriel. She let out a loud gasp, picked up her skirts, and ran across the hall to greet Alex.

The little boy threw himself into her arms. She hugged him tight. The top of his head only reached her waist. He was such an adorable little boy, and she was so happy to have him home, her eyes filled with tears.

Gabriel left the two of them and went upstairs to try to talk to Clare MacKay once again. He was determined to find out the name of the warrior who had disgraced the woman. He also wanted to give her the news that her father would be arriving tomorrow to take her back home, providing of course that she was strong enough.

Gabriel came back downstairs a few minutes later. Clare was still too ill to answer his questions. Why, she was so exhausted, she fell asleep a scant minute after he'd explained his reason for the audience.

Johanna and Alex were waiting for him at the bottom of the steps.

"Is something wrong, husband?" she asked when she spotted the frown on his face.

"Everytime I try to talk to the MacKay woman, she falls asleep. How long do you think it will be before she's strong enough to answer my questions?"

"I don't know, Gabriel," she answered. "You saw what she looked like the day she came here. It's going to take time for her to mend. Be patient with her," she suggested with a nod. "It's a miracle she's alive."

"I suppose it is," he agreed. "Johanna, her father's coming here tomorrow to take her back home."

She didn't like hearing that news. She shook her head. "Clare's in no condition to go anywhere. Her father's going to have to understand."

Gabriel wasn't in the mood to argue with his wife. The joy he'd seen on her face when Alex had run to her had filled him with such pleasure and contentment. He didn't want to mar the reunion with important talk now. Tonight would

367

be soon enough to discuss Clare's future.

"Why don't you take Alex outside, wife. It's too fine a day to stay inside."

His attention was centered on his son now. Alex was holding Johanna's hand and staring up at her in true wonder. It suddenly occurred to Gabriel that the boy was in desperate need of a mother. Just as revealing was the fact that Johanna needed Alex almost as much.

"Yes, it is a fine day," Johanna said. A look of tenderness had come into Gabriel's eyes. He was being very unguarded now. The love he felt for his son was most apparent.

Lord, she was feeling emotional today. She knew she was about to burst into tears and turned so that her husband wouldn't see her distress. He wouldn't understand of course. Men believed women only wept when they were unhappy or in pain, or so Johanna believed, but her tears were simply an emotional response to the wonderful feeling of happiness and contentment she was feeling. God had blessed her. She was barren, yet now had a son to love. Aye, she would love Alex, for it simply wasn't possible for her to steel her heart against such an innocent child.

"Could we go and see the horses, Mama?"

She burst into tears. Both Gabriel and his son were horrified. "Johanna, what's wrong with you?" Her husband's concern sharpened his voice to a near bellow.

"We don't have to see the horses," Alex blurted out, thinking he might be the cause of her distress.

Johanna tried to regain her control. She dabbed at the corners of her eyes with the hem of her plaid before trying to explain.

"Nothing's wrong," she told her husband. "Alex called me mama. He took me by surprise, you see, and I seem to be very emotional today."

"Papa said I should call you mama," Alex said. "He said you'd like it."

The little boy's face was puckered in a frown. He was obviously fretting. Johanna hurried to soothe him. "Your father was correct. You should call me mama."

"Then why are you crying like a baby?" Alex asked.

She smiled. "Because you make me happy," she answered. "Alex, it's too fine a day to stay inside. Let's go and see the horses."

She tried to leave. Gabriel reached out and grabbed her by her shoulders. "First you'll tell me thank you for bringing your son home," he announced.

He wanted praise, she supposed. "I'll thank you later, m'lord, when I'm ready."

She stretched up on tiptoe and kissed him. She heard Alex make a gagging sound and burst into laughter. Gabriel smiled. He watched his wife and his son go outside. Then he followed them and stood on the top step. He continued to watch his wife and his son until they disappeared down the hill.

"What has you smiling so, Laird?"

Father MacKechnie climbed up the steps and

stopped by his laird's side.

"I was watching my family," Gabriel answered.

Father MacKechnie nodded. "A handsome family you have, son. God's blessed the three of you."

Gabriel didn't consider himself a religious man, yet he found he had to agree with the priest's evaluation. When he was young and foolish, he'd prayed for a family. Now he had Alex and Johanna to call his own. Fair was fair, he decided, and he guessed he'd have to give his Maker his due. He had answered his prayer after all.

Johanna's laughter echoed across the courtyard then, interrupting Gabriel's thoughts. He instinctively smiled. Damn but he liked the sound of her joy.

Johanna didn't have any idea her husband was listening to her. Alex was so filled with enthusiasm and excitement to be outside he couldn't maintain a slow pace. He ran so fast the heels of his feet smacked his backside. She could barely keep up with him.

They spent the afternoon together. They looked over the horses first, then made their way down to the meadow to visit Auggie. The old warrior had just returned from the ridge and looked like he was in a foul mood.

"What has you scowling, Auggie?" Johanna called out.

Alex saw the soldier's glare and immediately edged behind Johanna's skirts.

"It's all right, Alex," she whispered. "Auggie

likes to grumble, but he has a kind heart."

"Like Papa?"

Johanna smiled. "Yes," she answered, thinking what a clever child Alex was. He was perceptive, too.

Auggie waited until the pair reached him before giving an answer for his frown. "I'm ready to give up my game," he announced with a dramatic nod. "It's no use hitting the stones any distance. Most crumble from the force of the whack I give them. They splinter in the air. No point to it then, is there now? Who's that hiding behind you, peeking up at me with such wide blue eyes?"

"This is Alex," Johanna answered. "Do you remember Gabriel's son?"

"Of course I remember the lad," Auggie answered. "But I'm in the middle of a sour mood, Johanna. I'm not fit for company today. Go away and leave me to my pout."

Johanna tried not to laugh. "Couldn't you spare a few minutes to show Alex how to strike the stones into the holes here in the meadow?"

"No, I couldn't spare a few minutes," Auggie muttered even as he motioned the little boy over to his side. "This isn't a child's game. How old are you, boy?"

Alex had a death grip on Johanna's hand. He wasn't about to leave her side. She had to walk with him over to Auggie.

"Alex doesn't know how old he is," Johanna explained. "I'm thinking he's four or five summers."

371

Auggie rubbed his jaw with concentration. "Open your mouth, boy. Let me have a look at your teeth. I can tell you how old you are."

Johanna burst into laughter. "He isn't a horse," she said.

"When it comes to teeth, they could be the same, at least with the young ones."

Alex tilted his head up and opened his mouth. Auggie nodded with approval. "You've been taking good care of your teeth, haven't you now?"

"Papa showed me how to rub them with green hazel and wipe them with a woolen cloth," Alex answered. "I only forget some of the time."

Auggie squinted against the sunlight as he bent down to have a good look.

"He's close to five, I'm guessing. He couldn't be any older. His first teeth are still nice and tight," he explained after he'd reached in and tried to wiggle Alex's two top front teeth. "Too snug for six and two big for three. Aye, he's going on five. I'd wager my game on it."

Alex was finally allowed to close his mouth. He turned his gaze up to Johanna. "I'm five?"

"Almost," she answered. "We'll have to choose a day and give you a proper birthday celebration, Alex. Then you'll officially become five."

Alex had gotten over his fear of the leathery-looking warrior and now begged to play the game. Auggie spent close to two hours supervising the child. Alex didn't understand the word *concentrate* and he talked nonstop all the while. Auggie was extremely patient with the boy, but he did cast several glares in Johanna's direction every now and again. Alex couldn't seem to remember he was to keep quiet when Auggie was about to strike his stone.

Johanna sat on the side of the hill to watch the pair. She listened to Auggie tell stories about the past, and it soon became apparent to her that Alex was in awe of the warrior. He begged to hear more.

The sun was setting and Alex had started yawning when Johanna finally called a halt to the entertainment. She stood up, adjusted the pleats of her plaid, and started to thank Auggie.

She didn't remember what happened next. She opened her eyes and found both Auggie and Alex leaning over her. Alex was crying. Auggie was gently patting the side of her face and trying to soothe the boy at the same time.

It didn't take Johanna any time at all to realize what had happened.

"Oh, Lord, I fainted again, didn't I?"

"Again?" Auggie asked, his brow wrinkled with worry. He helped his mistress sit up. Alex immediately sat down on her lap and leaned against her chest. He obviously needed her assurance, she decided. She put her arm around the child and gave him a quick hug.

"I'm quite all right now, Alex."

"You fainted before?" Auggie persisted.

Johanna nodded. The movement made her head spin. "Last night," she answered. "Gabriel caught me. It happened so quickly that I didn't have any warning."

"It sure as certain was quick," Auggie agreed. He squatted on the ground next to Johanna and continued to brace her back with his arms. "You were standing one minute and flat on the ground looking as dead as a corpse the next."

Auggie was deliberately trying to make light of the topic for the child's sake. He hid his worry as best he could.

"I don't understand what's wrong with me," she whispered.

"You'd best go and see Glynis," Auggie advised. "She knows a few healing tricks."

"She wanted to sew Calum's arm, so she must have some experience," Johanna remarked. "Yes, I'll go and see her tomorrow."

"No," Auggie countered. "You'll go now. I'll take Alex home."

From the stubborn set of his jaw, Johanna knew it would be pointless to argue with the man. "All right then," she agreed. She turned her attention to her son.

"Alex, let's not mention this faint to your father. We don't want to worry him, do we?"

"Shame on you telling the boy not to . . ."

"Auggie, I'm thinking of Gabriel's feelings now," Johanna argued. "I don't want him to worry."

Auggie nodded agreement. He had every intention of telling his laird what had happened, of course; and when his mistress pitched a fit, he'd remind her she hadn't made him give her his promise not to stay a word.

Both he and Alex accompanied Johanna to Glynis's door. They left her there, but only after Auggie pounded on the door and the Maclaurin woman had answered the summons.

"Lady Johanna's got a complaint to give you," Auggie announced. "Come along, boy. It's time for your supper."

"Have I done something to displease you, m'lady?" Glynis asked.

Johanna shook her head. She motioned her over to the rock ledge away from the entrance so that Glynis's husband wouldn't chance to overhear the conversation.

"Please sit down, Glynis," she requested. "A friend of mine is ill and I would like to gain your advice on what's to be done to help her."

Glynis immediately looked relieved. She sat on the ledge, folded her hands in her lap, and waited for Johanna to continue.

"Twice now this woman has fainted for no apparent reason," Johanna blurted out. She stood in front of the Maclaurin woman and waited for her response to that news.

Glynis simply nodded. Johanna didn't know what to make of that reaction.

"Is she dying of some dread disease?"

Johanna was wringing her hands together now and trying not to let Glynis see how upset she was.

"She could be," Glynis replied. "I'm needing more facts before I give you my suggestions for treatment, m'lady. Is your friend young or old?"

"Young."

"Is she married?"

"Yes. "

Glynis nodded. "Does she have any other symptoms to speak of?"

"I . . . that is to say, *she* awakened feeling very sick and did in fact throw up. Her stomach is queasy most of the morning. Yet when she isn't feeling queasy, she's feeling quite fit."

"I'll have to ask a few personal questions before I give you my opinion, m'lady," Glynis told her mistress in a low whisper.

"I'll answer them if I know the answers," Johanna replied.

"Has your friend missed her monthly?"

Johanna nodded. "She's missed two months now but that isn't unusual, for she isn't at all consistent."

Glynis was trying not to smile. "Would you happen to know if her breasts are feeling tender?"

Johanna almost checked to see before she gave her answer. She caught herself in time. "Perhaps just a little, but not overly much."

"Is she newly married?"

Johanna thought that was an odd question to ask. She nodded. "Do you think the strain of the new marriage would cause such symptoms? I don't believe so, Glynis, for the woman was married before."

"Did she have children with the first —"

Johanna didn't let her finish her question. "She's

barren," she interrupted.

"Perhaps by one man she was," Glynis remarked.

Johanna didn't know what to make of that remark. Then Glynis turned her attention with yet another question. "Are you . . . I mean to ask, is she sleeping more than usual?"

"Yes, she is," Johanna cried out. She was amazed by the clever questions Glynis was asking now. "You've heard of this sickness before, haven't you?"

" 'Tis the truth I have," Glynis answered.

"Will she die?"

"Nay, m'lady. She won't die."

"Then what should she do?"

Johanna was close to tears now. Glynis hurried to assure her. Her smile was wide when she gave her answer.

"She should tell her husband she's carrying his child."

Chapter

15

It was a blessing Glynis was such a strong, strapping woman. She proved to be quick on her feet, too. She caught her mistress before she hit her head on the stone wall.

The joyful news had sent Lady Johanna into a dead faint. She awakened a few minutes later in Glynis's bed. The first words out of her mouth were given in a shout.

"I'm barren!"

Glynis patted her hand. "By one man you were, but not by our laird. You've got all the symptoms, m'lady. You're carrying, all right."

Johanna shook her head. Her mind couldn't accept such a possibility. "Women are barren, not men."

Glynis snorted. "So men say," she muttered. "You and I have had our differences, m'lady, but I'd like to think we've come to an understanding. I count you as a friend, especially on the days you're wearing our fine Maclaurin plaid," she added with a grin.

"I'm happy to have you for a friend, Glynis," Johanna replied, wondering why in heaven's name the woman would bring up that topic now.

Glynis was quick to explain her reasons. "Friends hold each other's confidences," she said. "And so I would ask you if your first husband ever took any other woman to his bed. I'm not trying to shame you, m'lady, only sort out the truth."

Johanna sat up before. "Yes, he did take other women to his bed," she admitted. "And not just a few. He seemed determined to bed as many as he could. He liked to flaunt his women in front of me. I didn't mind, though," she added in a rush when she caught Glynis's pitying look. "I didn't like my husband. He was an evil man."

"But what I'm really asking, m'lady, is if you'd be knowing if there were any illegitimate bairns as a result of his dalliances?"

"No, there weren't any babies born," Johanna answered. "Raulf told me the women used a potion to keep from getting pregnant. He thought I used one, too, and would go into a rage each month because he was sure I was deliberately foiling his attempts to have a child."

"There are such potions around," Glynis replied. "You're certainly carrying now, m'lady, so we can conclude you aren't barren after all. I'm going to keep silent about this joyful news. It's up to you to pick your time and tell your husband. Our laird will be very pleased."

Johanna left the cottage a few minutes later.

Glynis followed her to the stone wall. Johanna suddenly turned around.

"My husband won't allow me to work in the fields," she announced.

"No, of course not," Glynis replied. "You're our mistress. You shouldn't be doing common work."

"I can sew," Johanna said. She added a nod. "Each night I sit by the hearth and either work on my tapestry or do a little embroidery. I can fashion flowers on . . . things," she added.

"What are you getting at, m'lady? Just spit it out, why don't you?"

"I noticed you wear saffron-colored blouses under your plaid, and I was wondering if you'd like me to sew a border of flowers around the neckline for you."

Glynis's eyes widened. "Why would you want . . ."

"You tend the fields all day long, Glynis, and I would like to do something to show my appreciation. If you'll bring one of your blouses up to the hall, I'll start work tonight."

She was too embarrassed to wait for an answer. Johanna didn't understand why she was suddenly feeling so shy and unsure of herself. She waved as she ran down the path leading to the courtyard.

She slowed her pace when she reached the hill. The fullness of her condition hit her again. She walked the rest of the distance home in a daze.

Auggie caught up with her in the center of the courtyard. "I'll be coming to supper tonight," he began. "I'm going to tell your husband . . ."

He quit his explanation that he was going to tell his laird Johanna had fainted when he saw the look on her face. "What has you smiling like you just found a pot of gold, lass?"

She shook her head. "I'll tell you tonight," she promised. "It's a grand day, isn't it, Auggie, even though the weather's a bit unusually cold."

"Now, lass, you'd best be knowing something about the weather here."

Auggie wanted to tell her the truth that the weather was actually mild for early fall. Keith had told him their mistress believed the Highlands were as warm as the summer all year long. He didn't want the soldiers laughing behind Johanna's back over her naivete, but his mistress went sailing right on past him, her head apparently lost in the clouds, before he could set her straight on the topic of the Highland weather. He decided he'd wait until later to tell her the truth.

Johanna sat with Alex at the table while he ate his supper. He was too young to wait for his elders. When he was finished, she sent him to the buttery to wash his face and hands.

She went over to sit by the hearth. Dumfries came loping into the hall. She gave him a firm pat of affection, then settled herself in the chair to do some sewing. Dumfries collapsed with a loud thud next to her chair and rested his head on her shoes.

Alex joined her a scant minute later. He was still wearing stew on his face. Johanna fetched a wet cloth and cleaned him properly. He wanted to sit next to her in the same chair. She scooted over to accommodate him.

"Will you want to stay here with your father and me, or will you miss your other relatives, Alex?"

"I want to stay here," he replied. He let out a loud yawn and leaned against Johanna, watching as she threaded her needle.

"I want you to stay, too," Johanna whispered.

"Papa says you missed me."

"He's right. I did miss you."

Alex's chest swelled up with importance. "Did you cry like a baby when you missed me?"

She smiled over his choice of words. "I most certainly did," she lied. "Would you like me to tell you a story before you go to bed?"

Alex nodded. "Where did you learn the story? From Auggie?"

"No," she answered. "My mother told me stories when I was a little girl; and when I grew up, I learned how to read and I . . ."

"Why?"

"Why what?"

"Why did you learn to read?"

Johanna's gaze was fully directed on Alex's up-turned face, and for that reason she didn't notice her husband had walked into the hall. He stood on the top step watching his wife and his son while he waited for one of them to acknowledge his presence.

"I learned because it was forbidden," she an-

382

swered. "I was told I was too ignorant to read, and for a time I believed that nonsense. Then I got my gumption back and decided I was just as clever as anyone else. That is when I learned how to read, Alex; and when you're older, I'll teach you."

Alex was fingering her plaid while he listened to her explanation. He suddenly yawned wide enough for her to see the back of his throat. She instructed him to cover his mouth with his hand and then began a story that used to be her favorite when she was a child.

Alex was sound asleep less than a minute later. His head dropped to the side of her chest. Johanna was so content to have the little one in her arms, she closed her eyes to say a prayer of thanksgiving. She fell asleep almost as quickly as Alex had.

Gabriel didn't know who to carry up to bed first. Calum came to his rescue. He took Alex.

"Where should I put him for the night, MacBain?" he asked in a low whisper so the little one wouldn't wake up.

Gabriel didn't have any idea. Clare was using the second chamber and so he couldn't put his son in there.

He didn't want Alex to sleep with the soldiers either. The boy was too young and needed to be close to his mother and father in the event he became fearful or disoriented during the night.

"Put him in my bed for now," Gabriel instructed. "I'll figure something out before tonight."

He waited until Calum had carried Alex out of the hall before turning his attention back to his wife. He squatted down next to her chair and started to reach for her when she suddenly opened her eyes.

"Gabriel." She said his name with wonder in her voice. He felt as though he'd just been caressed.

"Were you dreaming about me perchance?"

He was trying to tease her, but his voice was gruff with emotion. Damn but he loved this woman. He let out a sigh then and added a frown in a bid to get his thoughts under control.

He wanted to bed her. He knew he'd have to wait, so he decided to growl at her instead. "You should go upstairs, wife. You're clearly exhausted. You're doing too much work. I've told you time and time again to rest, but you blatantly . . ."

She reached over and brushed her fingertips down the side of his face. Needless to say, his concentration was broken. He thought it might be a deliberate ploy.

"I'm not doing too much," she replied. "I wasn't sleeping just now. I was dozing and thinking about something wonderful. I still can't quite believe it, Gabriel. It doesn't seem possible, and when I tell you my important news . . ."

She suddenly stopped and peeked around her husband to make certain they were alone. She didn't want anyone else sharing in this special moment.

Keith and three other Maclaurin soldiers came

384

strutting into the hall just as she realized Alex was missing.

"Do you see, you were sleeping," Gabriel told her. "You didn't even notice Calum took my son upstairs."

"He's our son," she corrected.

He liked the sound of that. Johanna was becoming possessive, and he thought that was a good sign. In time he hoped her possessiveness would extend to him.

"Yes, he is our son," he agreed. "Now tell me your news."

"It will have to wait until later."

"Tell me now."

"Nay."

His eyes widened. He stood up, then hauled her to her feet. "You dare to deny me?"

She smiled. "I dare anything these days, thanks to you, husband."

He didn't know what she was talking about. He decided he'd wait until later to badger her into giving him a proper explanation. Now he was determined to make her tell him her news.

"I wish to know what has you worrying. You will tell me now," he commanded.

He was sounding arrogant again. Heaven help her, she was beginning to appreciate that flaw. "I'm not worrying," she said. "I'll tell you my news when I'm ready, m'lord, and not a moment before. I won't be rushed."

"You going to tell your laird what happened down in the meadow?"

Auggie shouted his question from the entrance. Johanna turned to look at him. The old warrior bounded down the steps and started across the room. Dumfries let out a loud growl. Auggie hushed him with a quick growl back.

"Yes," Johanna called out. "I'm going to tell him after dinner."

"If you don't, I'll be telling on you come morning, lass. Just see if I don't."

"What in thunder . . ."

She deliberately interrupted her husband's mutterings to call out a greeting to the priest. "Good evening, Father." In a low whisper she said to her husband, "Do try to be patient this once. I promise you'll be richly rewarded."

He grunted. She couldn't tell from his expression if he was going to be agreeable or not. "I wish to have some privacy when I tell you my important news."

He finally nodded. Gabriel tried not to smile. He thought he'd finally figured out what it was she wanted to tell him. Lord, he felt good, and all because the daft woman had finally realized she loved her husband.

He would let her have her way, he decided. If she wanted to give him her declaration in the privacy of their bedchamber, he would accommodate her. Damn, but he wished dinner was over. He was anxious to be alone with her. He hadn't realized until this minute how important her love was to him. Wives didn't have to love their husbands, but this one had to love him, he decided.

If he was going to be miserable, then by God so was she.

"Matters of the heart are damned confusing." He'd muttered his opinion in a low voice.

"I beg your pardon?" she asked, not certain she'd heard what he'd said.

"Never mind," he snapped.

"Your moods, m'lord, are like the weather here," she remarked. "You're most unpredictable."

He shrugged. Johanna's attention was turned when the soldiers filed into the hall.

She noticed a serious breach in their manners immediately. "You should bow your heads to your laird and his wife when you enter the room."

She called out her instruction and then waited to see if the soldiers were in the mood to be polite. If they gave her any trouble, she was fully prepared to ask Megan to fetch a few more bowls.

The men bowed their heads. Johanna was satisfied. She left her husband standing by the hearth and went over to the MacBain table. Two of the younger soldiers, allowed the privilege of dining with their laird tonight, had already taken their seats. She asked them to stand up again.

"No one sits down until your laird and his wife have taken their places," she patiently explained.

There was a bit of grumbling over her dictate, but in the end everyone complied with her request.

Johanna didn't want to prod the men too much. For that reason she didn't scold them for shouting every other word during their supper. She was quite pleased with their progress. The men were trying to be polite. She didn't hear a single belch throughout the meal.

Auggie asked his laird what he was going to do with the liquid gold sleeping in the cave. Because he'd stated his question in a low whisper, everyone was alerted something secretive might be going on.

Johanna was astonished. The men had ignored her shouts the night before but now fell silent as soon as Auggie's whisper caught their attention. She put that observation away in the back of her mind for further use.

"What's Auggie talking about?" Keith asked his laird.

Gabriel leaned back in his chair and told the group about the barrels in the cave. There was a considerable amount of hooting and cheering over the news; and when the men had calmed down, Gabriel added the fact that they all had Auggie to thank for the treasure.

"Let's go and get a barrel or two to drink tonight," Bryan enthusiastically suggested.

Johanna didn't give her husband time to agree or disagree with Bryan's request. She stood up and shook her head at the soldiers.

The soldiers immediately stood up. The show of manners was impressive.

"Are you leaving or staying?" Niall asked.

"I'm staying," she answered. "You may sit down, gentlemen."

"But you're still standing," Lindsay pointed out.

"It's a trick, isn't it, m'lady? Once we sit down, you'll start in throwing bowls again."

Johanna held onto her patience. "I'll do no such thing," she promised. "I just wanted to stand to get your attention."

"Why?"

She frowned at the MacBain soldier who asked her the question. "If you'll be patient for just a moment, I'll explain. The barrels aren't for drinking. The brew is too precious. We're going to use it to barter for goods we need."

She expected an argument. She wasn't disappointed. Everyone started shouting at the same time. Only Father MacKechnie and Gabriel remained silent. They were both watching Johanna and smiling while she tried to placate the men.

"Once you ve had time to think about it, you'll realize bartering is the only option open to us."

"But why in God's name would we want to barter it away?" Keith demanded above the noise.

She heard his question and turned to answer him. "It's sinful to steal, you see, and if we use . . ."

She quit trying to explain her reasons when she realized no one was listening to her. She turned to her husband. The look on his face told her he found his men's behavior vastly amusing. She leaned close to him so he could hear her above the shouting going on between the Maclaurins and the MacBains and demanded he explain the reasons why they were going to use the barrels for trade.

He nodded agreement. She thanked him and

then resumed her seat.

"Be silent!" While Gabriel's roar was certainly rude conduct at the dinner table, Johanna thought, it proved to be effective. The men immediately stopped arguing.

He nodded, satisfied, and then turned to her. "You may now explain your position on the distribution of the drink."

"But I wish for you to explain."

He shook his head. "You'll have to try to make them understand," he ordered. "And while you're at it, you'll have to make me understand as well."

She jumped to her feet again. "Do you mean to say you don't agree with me?"

"Nay, I don't agree with you."

He waited for her to finish her gasp, then continued on. "Stealing has proven effective in the past, Johanna. Don't give me that look. I haven't betrayed you."

"Stealing's wrong, isn't it, Father?"

The priest nodded. "She speaks the truth, Laird."

It was difficult to hear the priest over the scraping noise of the stools when the men once again stood up.

"Will you make up your mind, lass," Keith requested.

"Is she leaving this time?" Niall asked in a whisper loud enough for everyone to hear.

"She doesn't appear to be going anywhere," Calum drawled out.

"Oh, do sit down," Johanna muttered.

They wouldn't obey her command until she had once again taken her seat.

She kept her frowning gaze on her husband. "It would please me, and please God, too, I might add, if you quit thieving and used the barrels to trade for what our clan needs."

"Aye, it would please God," Father MacKechnie agreed. "Begging your pardon for interrupting, but I've a suggestion to make."

"What is it, Father?" Gabriel asked.

"Use only a few of the barrels to get what we need and save the rest for the clan."

There was more discussion after the priest gave his suggestion. Most of the Maclaurins were in agreement. The MacBains, however, were stubbornly united in keeping all the treasure for themselves. They were behaving like children who didn't want to share their toys. Gabriel, unfortunately, fell into that group.

Johanna was openly glaring at her husband now. He was trying not to laugh at her. The issue seemed terribly important to his wife, and he finally decided he could give up the amusement of stealing to please her.

"We'll do as our priest suggests," he commanded.

Johanna let out a sigh of relief. Gabriel winked at her. "You aren't always going to get your way," he warned.

"No, of course I won't," she quickly agreed. She was so happy with her husband, she reached across the table and took hold of his hand.

"You're going to be needing a noser."

Auggie made the announcement. Everyone turned to look at him. The younger soldiers didn't know what he was talking about. Lindsay was the first to ask what the others were thinking.

"What in God's name is a noser, Auggie?"

"An expert," he answered with a nod for emphasis. "He'll be able to tell us which barrels to hold back. You wouldn't want to be giving away the best, would you?"

"No, of course we wouldn't," Niall blurted out.

"Won't a noser drink up all the new brew he's testing?" Bryan asked.

"I've got a good taste for the drink," Lindsay boasted. "I'll be happy to be your noser."

Everyone laughed over the soldier's suggestion. When the noise had quieted down, Auggie explained. "A noser doesn't taste the drink," he instructed. "He uses his nose to sniff out the aroma. He can tell just by the smell the good from the sour."

"Then we best get Spencer," Calum suggested. "He's got the biggest nose of any MacBain or Maclaurin."

Auggie smiled. "It isn't the size but the experience, son," he said. "Skill is what matters. Nosing can be taught, but the best are the ones who have a natural talent for the task. There's a noser up near the Isle of Islay we could send for, assuming he's still alive, and I heard tell of another noser living in the south, close enough to the Lowlands to make me think he might be a MacDonnell."

"We can't have an outsider coming here," Calum protested. "As soon as he sees the treasure, he'll go back and tell his laird. The MacDonnells will all come running then."

Johanna wasn't paying much attention to the discussion now. She was busy thinking about her joyful condition. She would tell Gabriel about the baby tonight when they were in bed together. She would make certain the candles were still burning so she could see the look of surprise on his face after she gave him her announcement. Her hand moved to her stomach. Dear God, she was going to have a baby.

"Then it's settled?"

Gabriel asked the question. Everyone was shouting aye when Johanna happened to catch Father MacKechnie's horrified expression. He was staring at her; and as soon as he had her attention, he tilted his head toward her husband.

She guessed whatever had just been decided didn't sit well with the priest.

"What have you just settled?"

"Haven't you been paying attention to the discussion?"

"No."

"MacBain," Calum called out. "We can't just send a messenger to request the noser. His clan will become suspicious."

"Aye, they'd wonder why we wanted a noser and would surely follow him back," Keith interjected.

"We'll have to snatch him," Auggie suggested.

"How will we know which one to take?" Lindsay asked.

"If we go after Nevers, I'll go along and point him out to you."

"Nevers? What kind of name is that?" one of the Maclaurins asked.

"Gabriel, will you please explain what was just settled?" Johanna insisted.

"We settled the question of what to do with the noser," Calum answered for his laird, "after he's selected the best of the brew for us."

"Aye, we did," Keith added.

"Are we all in agreement then?" Auggie asked. "We snatch Nevers?"

Everyone shouted his opinion of Auggie's plan to kidnap the noser while Johanna impatiently drummed her fingertips on the tabletop.

"Please explain . . ." she began again.

"Shouldn't we move the barrels into the hall?" Bryan asked at the same time.

"Where is the cave?" Keith wanted to know.

Johanna wasn't going to wait for an answer any longer. Father MacKechnie still looked worried. She was determined to find out why.

"Just one minute, please," she called out. "Keith, you said you had decided what you were going to do with the noser . . ."

"We all decided," he corrected.

"And?" she prodded.

"And what, m'lady?"

"What are you going to do? The noser will

go home, won't he?"

"Good Lord, no, lass," Auggie said. The very idea made him grimace.

"He can't go home, m'lady."

"And why not?" she demanded.

"He would tell his laird about the barrels," Keith explained.

"We can't have the noser talking," Bryan interjected.

"Sure as certain he would tell," Niall agreed. "I would tell our laird."

Keith tried to turn the topic then. Johanna wouldn't let him. "You still haven't answered my question," she persisted. "Exactly what is it you intend to do with the man?"

"Now, Johanna, this doesn't concern you," Gabriel said. "Why don't you go over to the hearth and sew for a spell."

He was deliberately trying to turn her attention. Her suspicion grew. "I'm not in the mood to sew, m'lord, and I'm not going anywhere until someone answers my question."

Gabriel let out a sigh. "You're a stubborn woman," he remarked.

The soldiers all nodded, for they were obviously in agreement with their laird's evaluation.

The priest decided it was his duty to tell his mistress what had been decided. No one else seemed inclined.

"They're thinking to kill him, lass."

She couldn't believe what she'd just heard. She made the priest repeat himself. Then she let out a gasp, bounded to her feet, and vehemently shook her head.

"Were you in favor of this solution?" she asked her husband.

"He's laird, m'lady," Calum said. "He didn't voice an opimon."

"Our laird waits, you see; and after we've all given our suggestions, he decides for or against."

"He'll veto your sinful idea then," she announced.

"Why would he do that, m'lady? It's a sound plan," Michael argued.

Gabriel had every intention of denying the vote to kill the noser, for he didn't think it would be honorable to gain the man's assistance and then repay him in such a foul way, but he didn't like the idea of his wife instructing him in his duties. He was also trying to come up with a viable alternative to the problem.

"No one is going to kill the noser."

Several soldiers groaned in protest over her dictate. "But, m'lady, it's the truth this is the very first time all the Maclaurins and all the MacBains have ever agreed on anything," Keith remarked.

Johanna was incensed. She kept her gaze on her husband. "Do I understand correctly? You plan to use the noser's skill; and when he's finished helping you, you're going to kill him?"

"It seems we are," Calum answered for his laird.

The MacBain soldier had the gall to smile after admitting his future sin.

"So this is how you men repay a favor?"

No one responded to her question. She scanned her audience, then turned back to her husband. He nodded. He was obviously agreeable to the foul plan.

Johanna decided to try to use reason to sway him. "Gabriel, if stealing is a sin, what do you suppose killing is?"

"Necessary," he replied.

"It isn't."

She was getting all riled up, and he knew he should calm her by telling her he wasn't going to let any harm come to the noser, but Lord, she was such a joy to watch when she was angry. How had he ever thought her timid? He remembered how she had behaved the first day they'd met. She had been timid then, terrified, too. His gentle little bride had come a long way in a very short while. The changes were all for the good, of course, but he liked to believe he was partially responsible. She hadn't felt safe when she first came to the Highlands, but she certainly felt safe now. She trusted him, too. She wouldn't be ranting and raving at him now if she still feared him.

"I cannot believe you're smiling, Gabriel. Have you lost your senses?"

"You make me smile, Johanna. You've certainly changed since you married me. The traits were all there, but you kept them well hidden behind your shields of indifference. God's truth, you make me proud when you stand up to me. Aye, you do."

She couldn't believe he was giving her compliments now when they were in the middle of a heated debate she was determined to win. He was using trickery, she thought to herself. Aye, that was what he was doing. He wanted to turn her attention with a bit of praise.

She wasn't going to accommodate him. "You make me proud, too," she snapped. "But you still aren't going to kill the noser. I'm putting my foot down, husband, so you'd best give in to me. I won't let up until you do."

She looked ready to kill someone, and he thought he might very well be her target. He couldn't resist goading her just a little bit more. "I've decided to be accommodating about bartering just to please you, but I'm going to have to put both feet down on the issue of the noser."

Several loud grunts of approval followed the laird's statement.

"We can't allow the man to go back home. He'll bring back an army to steal the barrels," Keith explained when her frown settled on him.

"Nay, we can't have that," another Maclaurin shouted.

"She's standing again," Bryan blurted out.

"For the love of . . ."

The men muttered as they hurried to stand. Johanna ignored them. "Gabriel, if the noser doesn't know where the cave is, and if he can't see his way there, well then he can't lead anyone to the barrels, now can he? Therefore . . ."

She let her husband draw his own conclusion. He was a barbarian, yes, but he was an intelligent one. He would be able to sort it out in his mind and figure out what she was suggesting.

Calum slapped his hand on the tabletop. "By God, she's got a sound plan, Laird."

"It's a little mean-hearted," Keith remarked. "I think I'd rather be killed; but if our mistress is set on keeping the noser alive, I'd have to agree it's a good alternative."

"She's a clever one all right," Auggie announced. His voice was filled with pride.

Johanna didn't know what the men were talking about now. Her gaze was locked on her husband. He stared at her a long minute, then said, "You aren't going to let me kill him, are you, lass?"

He sounded forlorn to her. She let him see her exasperation. " 'Tis the truth I'm not."

His sigh was long and dramatic. "Hell."

She interpreted his blasphemy to mean she'd won. "Thank you," she whispered. "I knew you could be reasonable."

She was so relieved she collapsed back into her chair. The men all sat down again.

"We'll follow your suggestion," Gabriel announced.

"It's a mean one, but fair." Keith sounded as though he was praising his mistress.

"Mean?" She didn't think Keith was making any sense. The sparkle in Gabriel's eyes didn't make sense either. Was he happy he'd lost the argument?

She glanced over to see how Father MacKechnie was reacting. He should have been smiling over the victory. He wasn't though. He was looking worried again.

Her guard was immediately back up. "Keith, exactly what do you think is mean-hearted?"

"It's a clever plan, m'lady, mean or not," Calum said.

"What plan?"

"The one you just gave us," he answered. "Don't you remember?"

"She does have trouble remembering," Keith remarked. "She can't seem to keep her days straight. Why, even now she's wearing the wrong plaid."

"Will someone please explain my plan to me?"

"We're going to blind him."

Keith gave her the atrocious news. A round of grunts followed.

She jumped to her feet again. The men all immediately joined her.

"I've a plan to tie m'lady to her chair," Auggie muttered. "I'm getting weary of sitting and standing every other minute."

Johanna was getting a pounding headache. Her patience had been all used up. She ordered the men to sit down in a near roar.

She realized she'd shouted, of course, and immediately tried to calm herself. Reason, she thought to herself, aye, she would reason with the savages.

"Men, there is always more than one way into a keep," she began, her voice hoarse with control.

"M'lady," Keith interrupted. "We've been

400

over that before. Don't you have it straight in your head yet? We've got us a back door and a front . . ."

"Do be quiet!" Johanna ordered in another shout. She threaded her fingers through her hair and lowered her voice when she continued. "You make me want to scream! God's truth, you do!"

"You are screaming, m'lady," Lindsay pointed out.

She took a deep breath. By God, she would make them listen to reason or die trying. Surely a few of them realized how sinful their idea was. It was up to her to convince the others. They were members of her clan, after all, and, therefore, her responsibility.

"Heaven help me," she whispered.

"What did she say?" Lindsay asked.

"I cannot believe you would consider blinding the poor man," she cried out.

"You gave us the idea, m'lady."

"Keith, if I had a bowl handy, I swear I would . . ."

"You're getting your mistress riled up," Auggie warned.

She turned to her husband. "No one's going to blind the man. I won't hear of it. When I said there was more than one way into the keep, I was giving the men a lesson and I — dear God, Keith, if you try to instruct me again about the number of entrances I swear I will throw something at you — what I mean to say, husband . . . Oh, Lord, now I've lost my thought."

"You were trying to remember how to get into the keep," Bryan reminded her.

"I was not," she snapped. "I was giving you a lesson, you daft men. There's more than one way to skin a fish, you see; and if you don't want the noser to see the cave, then you simply blindfold him when you take him there."

"We don't skin our fish here," Lindsay said. "We eat them whole."

She wanted to kill the soldier. She glared him into silence instead.

"You're getting her upset," Auggie shouted. "It ain't good, given her illness. Make your apology, boy," he ordered.

"Gabriel, I want your word you won't harm the noser," Johanna demanded.

Her husband was frowning at her. Lindsay was stammering out his apology, Keith thought it necessary to go over the number of entrances to the keep one last time, and Calum was wondering aloud if the English skinned their fish before they ate them. He believed they were ignorant enough to follow such a practice.

"Shouldn't m'lady be wearing our colors today?" Michael, the youngest of the Maclaurin soldiers, had only just noticed the breach.

Keith nodded. He sounded resigned when he said, "She should."

"Auggie, what the hell did you mean when you said my wife was ailing?"

"She fainted this afternoon, Laird," Auggie explained. "Went down like a corpse, she did."

Gabriel's roar echoed throughout the hall. Everyone immediately fell silent.

Two months ago, such behavior would have sent her running. Aye, she would have been terrified. She'd come a long way, she thought to herself, for Gabriel's fury merely irritated her now.

Her ears were ringing from his bellow. She covered them with her hands and glared at her husband. "Must you do that?" she asked.

He ignored her rebuke. "You actually fainted? You weren't pretending this time?"

She didn't answer him. "Why does everyone have to shout all the time? I'm warning you now, men," she added as she scanned her audience. "When my mama comes here, no one's going to speak above a respectable whisper."

The men didn't agree with her dictate fast enough. "Do you understand me?" she asked in a fair bellow of her own.

The soldiers nodded in unison. She let out a very unladylike grunt of satisfaction. Then she caught Father MacKechnie's smile. Her attention was turned, of course, because she couldn't imagine what he found so amusing. She had to think about his odd behavior for a second or two.

Gabriel wasn't going to be ignored. "Answer me, damn it."

He was determined to gain a proper explanation. Her shoulders slumped. She pictured herself in bed for the next five or six months and grimaced in reaction.

She guessed she'd better try to placate him. He

was her husband, after all, and he seemed to be very distressed over her possible illness.

"It isn't at all what it seems to be," she said. "I'm not sick."

"Did you or did you not faint?"

The chair flew backward when Gabriel stood up. He loomed over her like the avenging archangel she'd likened him to in her fantasies, and Lord, he was magnificent. He leaned down until his face was just inches away from hers, obviously intent on intimidating her into answering him.

She reached up and placed her hand on the side of his face. "Promise me you won't harm the noser, then I'll explain what happened."

He caught hold of her hand before replying. "I'm not in the mood to negotiate, wife. What reason would you have to pretend to faint in front of Auggie?"

"It weren't a pretense, Laird. I'd be knowing the difference."

"I'll be happy to discuss this matter in privacy with you," Johanna whispered.

"I took her over to Glynis to gain some advice," Auggie announced.

"Does our laird think she pretended to faint last night?" Bryan asked.

"She's mean enough to try to trick us," Lindsay commented.

Calum was in agreement with the Maclaurin. "Aye, she is mean enough."

Johanna was aghast by the men's insults against her character. She jerked her hand away from her

404

husband's hold and turned to the soldiers.

"How can you say I'm mean?" she cried out.

" 'Cause you are, m'lady," Bryan cheerfully told her.

She turned back to Gabriel. She fully expected him to come to her defense.

He fully expected her to tell him what the hell was the matter with her.

"Gabriel, how can you allow your men to defame me?"

"It's a compliment they're giving you, damn it. You will give me your full attention. When I ask a question, I expect to have it answered."

"Yes, of course you do," she agreed, trying to soothe him. "It's just that now isn't the time . . ." Her mind was still focused on the soldiers' opinion of her. "I cannot believe you think I'm mean!" she cried out.

"You killed our pet and three others," Calum reminded her.

"That was necessary, not mean."

"You came up with the plan to blind the noser," Keith said.

"Blindfold him," she corrected.

"You put an arrow in the MacInnes soldier. That was damned mean, m'lady."

"I'd do it again," she announced. She wasn't about to pretend she was sorry she'd injured the soldier. He had meant to kick Clare MacKay, and she couldn't let that happen.

"Aye, you would do it again," Keith agreed. "And that's the reason we're all thinking you're

405

a mean one, m'lady. It's an honor to have you for our mistress."

Grunts of approval followed Keith's compliment. Johanna became flustered. She brushed her hair back over her shoulders in an attempt to act as though she hadn't been overly affected by Keith's remarks. "I suppose it's all right for you to call me mean, men, but you won't be saying such things in front of my mama. She wouldn't understand."

"Johanna!"

Gabriel shouted her name. She decided he'd run out of patience. He had waited a long while to get her full attention. She turned back to her husband and smiled up at him.

"Did you want something, m'lord?"

His eyelid twitched. He'd used up all his patience all right. Johanna braced herself and then blurted out, "I didn't pretend to faint the first time and I did faint again this afternoon. However," she quickly added before he could start in bellowing again, "I'm really not sick. Glynis explained what was wrong with me."

"You're going to bed."

"I knew you would overreact!" she cried out.

He took hold of her hand and turned to drag her across the hall. She wasn't being very cooperative. She kept trying to pull away. "How long must I stay in bed?"

"Until you've recovered from whatever it is ailing you," he commanded. "Damn it, I knew you weren't strong enough to last a full year."

Her gasp filled the hall. She'd taken grave exception to his remark. The soldiers were all watching, of course, and when they heard their laird's comment and his wife's reaction, they smiled in unison.

"If you believed I was such a weakling, you shouldn't have married me."

He grinned. She jerked her hand away from his and backed up a space before he could catch hold of her again.

"I'm wagering she's about to get mean again," Lindsay said.

Father MacKechnie shook his head. "Not with our laird," he told the soldier. "She's partial to the MacBain."

"She doesn't look partial to him now," Bryan said. "Her scowl's every bit as set as his is."

Johanna wasn't paying any attention to the soldiers' mutterings. Her concentration was centered on her stubborn husband. "You're sorry you married me, aren't you?"

He didn't answer her fast enough. "You only married me to get the land, and after I'm dead and gone, you'll have to remember to marry a big giant of a woman, preferably one who can belch as loud as any of your men."

The look on his face gave her pause.

"You will not die."

He'd whispered his command in a harsh voice filled with anguish. She was stunned. Gabriel sounded terrified.

"I will not lose you."

"No, you will not lose me."

She walked forward and took hold of his hand. Tears filled her eyes as she stared up at the wonderful man trying to glare some sense into her.

He loved her. He hadn't given her the words yet, but the proof was there in his eyes. Johanna felt overwhelmed.

They went up the steps leading to the entrance together. She could feel him shaking. She didn't want him to worry any longer, and so she stopped at the foot of the stairs leading up to the bedchambers and turned to her husband.

The men were all craning their necks to see what was happening, but they were too far away to hear the conversation.

"Gabriel, do you remember my concern before we were married?"

"You had too many concerns for me to keep track of, wife. Don't push my hands away. I'm going to carry you upstairs. Don't you realize you could break your neck if you fainted while trying to climb these steep steps? You may not be worried about your welfare, but I sure as hell am."

He knew he was wearing his heart on his sleeve. He didn't like feeling this vulnerable. "What will your mother say when she arrives and finds her daughter dead?" he muttered.

She smiled. "Mama's going to like you, Gabriel."

Her husband looked exasperated. He lifted her into his arms. She immediately kissed him.

"You're still going to bed," he announced.

"On the night after we were married, I told you I was barren."

"No, you didn't. Nicholas told me."

She nodded. "On our wedding night, I'm certain I mentioned it."

He nodded. "Yes, you did," he said. "Several times in fact."

He started up the steps. She rested her head against his shoulder. Her fingers were fully occupied stroking the back of his neck.

She wondered if their baby would have her husband's coloring. She thought she might like to have a little girl, then decided she would be just as happy with a boy.

"I'm not," she whispered with a sigh.

She waited for him to understand. He didn't say anything until they reached their bedchamber.

"Did you hear what I just said? I'm not," she repeated.

"You're not what?"

"I'm not barren."

He opened the door but hesitated at the threshold. His gaze was fully directed on his wife. He slowly lowered her to the floor. "Do you honestly believe it matters to me? You and Alex are all the family I want. I don't need another child. Damn it, woman, haven't you realized yet how much I . . . you mean more to . . . ."

Hell, he was rambling like an old woman. He motioned for her to go inside. "Warriors do not concern themselves with matters of love," he muttered.

He looked miserable. She didn't smile. She knew he didn't like telling her what he was feeling.

It was a trait they both shared, she realized. "Gabriel . . ."

"I don't ever want you to bring up the fact that you're barren, Johanna. Now quit fretting."

She strolled into their chamber. "You may not need another child, m'lord, but I do declare in six or seven months you're going to be getting one."

He didn't understand. He shook his head. She nodded. "We're going to have a baby."

For the first time in his life, Gabriel MacBain was rendered speechless. His wife believed that was a most appropriate reaction.

They had, after all, just been given a miracle.

Chapter

16

You're certain?"

Gabriel whispered his question so his son wouldn't wake up. Alex was sleeping on a mat across the chamber. Only the top of his head was visible above the mound of covers Johanna felt he needed to stay warm.

She and her husband were in bed. Gabriel held Johanna in his arms. She was so relieved he was finally reacting, she let out a little sigh. She'd given Gabriel her good news over an hour ago, then waited for him to tell her how happy she'd made him. He hadn't said a word until now.

"I have all the symptoms," she whispered back. "I was disbelieving at first, of course, because I thought I was barren for a very long while. Are you happy about the baby, Gabriel?"

"Yes."

She sighed again. It was too dark in the chamber to see his face, but she guessed he was smiling.

"Glynis told me a woman can be barren with

one man and fertile with another. Do you know what that means?"

"What?"

"Men can be barren, too."

He laughed. She hushed him so he wouldn't wake Alex. "Your first husband obviously was," he said.

"Why does that please you?"

"He was a bastard."

She couldn't fault his reasoning. "Why don't men acknowledge that they could be the barren ones in a marriage?"

"Such an admission would wound their pride, I suppose. It's easier to blame the women. It isn't right, just easier."

She let out a loud, lusty yawn. Gabriel was stroking her back. The caress made her sleepy. He asked her something, but she was too tired to answer him. She closed her eyes and was dead to the world a minute later.

Gabriel didn't fall asleep for another hour. He held Johanna close and thought about the baby. He should have wanted a boy as his first choice, for a man couldn't have enough sons to help with the building of an empire, but he really hoped for a baby girl. She would have blue eyes and yellow hair, like her mother, and if God was willing to recreate perfection, his daughter would be every bit as sassy.

He fell asleep with a smile on his face.

Laird MacBain told his clan about the baby the

following morning. Johanna stood next to her husband on the top step outside the doors. Alex stood next to her. Both the Maclaurins and the MacBains cheered the news. Johanna and Gabriel had already told Alex. The little boy didn't seem overly interested about a new brother or sister, and his lack of interest convinced his parents he was feeling secure.

He could barely stand still during the announcement. His father had promised to take him riding, and to a four-year-old, a minute of waiting seemed to feel as long as an hour.

After Gabriel dismissed the well-wishers, Johanna turned to Calum and Keith.

"I've come up with several names I'd like to . . ."

"Good God, lass, you can't tell us the baby's name," Keith blurted out.

The Maclaurin soldier was horrified by her ignorance. Didn't she realize the bairn's name should never, ever be told to another person before the baptism? As soon as he was able to stop sputtering, he asked her just that question. She told him she guessed she didn't realize.

"I was never concerned about the traditions regarding babies," she explained.

"Why is that, m'lady?" Calum asked. "Most married women are careful to follow every tradition."

"I thought I was barren."

"You're not," Keith remarked.

She smiled. "No, I'm not," she agreed.

413

"We'll have to do our best to instruct you, then, on the importance of the name you select."

"A man's name is far more important than just a name," Calum announced.

Before she could ask what in heaven's name he meant by that statement, Keith turned her attention. "If another person has knowledge of the name before the christening, he could use it to work magic on the babe."

Calum nodded agreement.

Johanna could tell from their serious expressions they weren't jesting with her. They really believed their nonsense. "Is this tradition or superstition you're giving me?" she asked.

Glynis stepped forward to join the conversation. She wanted to add a few important reminders of her own.

"If the babe cries during the christening, then it is sufficient proof the devil's been driven out, m'lady. Did you already know that truth?"

Johanna shook her head. She had never heard of anything so preposterous. She didn't want to injure Glynis's feelings, however, and for that reason she didn't smile.

"Then I shall hope the baby cries," she said.

"You might also give the wee one a tiny pinch to ensure he does cry out," Glynis suggested.

"Some mothers probably do," Keith speculated.

"If your baby's born at midnight or at the twilight hour, he'll have the gift of second sight, of course. Heaven help the babe if he comes during the chime hours, for then he'll have the ability to see ghosts and spirits hidden from the rest of us."

"Papa, aren't you ready to leave yet?" Alex asked.

Gabriel nodded. He leaned down, ordered Johanna not to exhaust herself, and then lifted his son on his shoulder and started for the stables.

Leila walked across the courtyard, bowed her head to her laird when she passed him, and then hurried over to Johanna to offer her congratulations.

"It's joyful news," she said.

"Aye, it is," Glynis agreed. "I was just giving m'lady a few suggestions," she told Leila.

"And I shall try to remember every one of them," Johanna promised.

Keith shook his head. "I doubt you'll remember," he said. "You've forgotten what day this is," he added. "You're wearing the wrong plaid again."

"I'm beginning to wonder if she's doing it on purpose," Calum remarked. There was a hint of amusement in his voice. As soon as the MacBain soldier spoke, Leila deliberately turned so that her back was to Calum. She kept her gaze directed on the ground. Johanna noticed the action and was intrigued by it.

"Glynis, Megan told me you had a good hand at cutting hair," Johanna said.

" 'Tis the truth I do have a talent for the task."

"Clare MacKay could use your assistance," Johanna said. "The MacInnes men made a mess out of her hair."

"I know they did," Glynis said. "They meant to make a mess so anyone seeing her would know her shame."

Johanna didn't want to get into a long discussion about Clare now. "Yes," she agreed. "But Clare's father is coming here today, and I was wondering if you could . . ."

"Say no more, m'lady. I'll be happy to fetch my scissors and try to make the lass look a little more presentable."

"Thank you," Johanna said. "Leila, please don't leave just yet," she added when the Maclaurin woman turned to walk with Glynis across the yard.

"Since Lady Johanna's wearing the MacBain colors, I assume she's your responsibility today," Keith told Calum.

"I can take care of myself, gentlemen," Johanna said. "You both waste your time following me around."

The two men ignored her protest. "Aye, she is my responsibility," Calum said.

Johanna decided she would have to talk to Gabriel about the foolishness in his command. The men would continue to trail after her until they were released from the duty by their laird.

Keith bowed to his mistress and left to see his duties completed. Calum was about to go back inside, but Johanna stayed him with her hand on his arm.

"Calum, may I have a minute of your time? I would like to introduce you to Leila."

He gave her a look that suggested she'd lost her

senses. "I've known Leila for some time, m'lady."

He didn't spare the Maclaurin woman a glance when he said her name. Johanna turned to Leila. She was diligently staring at the ground. "Leila, have you met Calum?"

"You know I have," Leila whispered.

"Then tell me please, both of you, why you act as though you've never met before? I'm very curious and probably interfering, but I assure you I have the best of intentions. I thought, from the looks you try not to give each other, well, that you might actually care about each other a great deal."

"He's a MacBain."

"She's a Maclaurin."

"Please excuse me, m'lady," Calum said, his voice clipped and hard. "I have duties that need my attention. I don't have time for such foolish talk."

He didn't even nod in Leila's direction when he left. She kept her gaze turned away. Johanna reached out to touch her arm. "I'm sorry. I didn't mean to make either one of you upset. You do care about Calum, don't you?"

She gave an abrupt nod. "I have tried not to have these feelings, m'lady," she whispered. "I cannot seem to help myself."

"I believe Calum has feelings for you, Leila."

"Nay," she argued. "He would never allow himself to become attracted to a Maclaurin."

"I didn't realize the separation between the clans ran this deep," Johanna remarked.

"How could you not know? The way the men carry on whenever you wear the wrong plaid should be proof enough of the importance they attach to the issue. We're all trying to get along with each other yet stay separate at the same time."

"But why must everyone stay separate?"

Leila confessed she didn't know. "We're all most appreciative of our laird's patience with us," she said. "I heard what you said at the supper table about the land belonging to the MacBains now. Everyone was talking about it, m'lady. What you said made sense to some of us. The Maclaurin soldiers didn't like hearing the truth, however."

"Do you know what I think? We have one too many plaids."

"Aye, we do," Leila agreed. "But neither clan is going to give up its colors, no matter how much you plead."

"I'm not going to plead with anyone," Johanna said. "Will you answer a question please? If Calum was a Maclaurin, would he court you?"

"I would hope he would," she answered. "But he isn't a Maclaurin, and he doesn't have any feelings for me anyway."

Johanna turned the topic then. "Would you like to come back to the hall and help with the tasks every now and again?"

"Oh, yes, m'lady, I would. I could see . . ." She stopped before she gave herself away.

Johanna wasn't fooled. "Yes, you would be able to see Calum more often."

Leila blushed. "Our laird doesn't want me to . . . "

"But of course he does," Johanna said. "Come for dinner tonight, Leila. You'll sit next to me. We'll discuss your duties after we've eaten."

"I would be honored to sit at your table," Leila whispered. Her voice shook with emotion.

"I must go inside now and take my turn sitting with Clare. I'll see you tonight, Leila."

Johanna hurried upstairs and went directly to Clare's chamber. She dismissed Megan from her task of watching over the woman and sat down to talk to her.

"Did you climb the stairs without assistance, m'lady?" Megan demanded to know.

"Of course," Johanna answered, surprised by the censure in Megan's tone.

"You could fall," Megan countered. "You shouldn't be taking such chances."

"Megan, I have enough people fretting over me. 'Tis the truth I'll go daft if I'm followed around day and night. I held onto the railing," she added when Megan looked ready to protest.

"Are you ill, Lady Johanna?" Clare asked.

"She's carrying, like you," Megan blurted out. She nodded, then closed the door behind her.

"Congratulations, m'lady. I hope you give your husband a sound boy."

Clare struggled to sit up in bed. Johanna tucked the covers around the woman before taking her seat again.

"A girl will be just as pleasing," she remarked.

Clare shook her head. "I wouldn't want a girl. Boys have far more advantages, but girls are only used for barter. Isn't that so?"

"Yes," Johanna agreed. She folded her hands in her lap and smiled at the MacKay woman.

Clare was frowning at her. "Then why would you want one? You'll have the worry your husband will give her in marriage to some evil man, and she'll spend the rest of her life . . ."

"Being afraid?"

Clare nodded. "And hurt," she whispered.

"My husband would not deliberately give his daughter to a monster," she said. "Did your father know MacInnes was cruel-hearted?"

Clare shrugged. "He only cared about uniting the two clans."

Johanna was disheartened to hear that news. "Does your father love you?"

"As much as any father would love a daughter," she replied.

"Girls are more clever," Johanna said. "Even Father MacKechnie believes this to be true."

"They can still be beaten and humiliated. You don't realize how fortunate you are, Lady Johanna. Your husband treats you well."

Johanna leaned back in her chair. "I wouldn't stay here if he didn't treat me well."

Clare didn't look like she believed Johanna. "How could you leave?" she asked.

"I would find a way," Johanna explained. "Clare, when I was married before, to an Englishman, I would pray every night I wouldn't conceive.

420

I didn't want to give him a girl because I knew he would mistreat her whenever he felt inclined to vent his anger, and I didn't want to give him a boy because I knew he would be taken away from me and raised in his father's image. I didn't want such foul attitudes about women to be passed down, you see."

"Were you beaten?"

"Yes."

"How did the Englishman die? Did you kill him?"

Johanna was surprised by the question. She shook her head. "There were times I wanted to kill him, and I'll surely burn in hell for admitting such a sin of contemplation, but I didn't give in to my anger. I didn't want to be like him, Clare. I felt trapped, yes, and then I realized I was intelligent enough to find a way to leave."

"How did he die?"

"I was told by King John he fell from a cliff near the city on the waters. I didn't even know he'd left England."

Clare nodded. Johanna decided to turn the topic. "Glynis will be here in a few minutes with her scissors. She'll try to repair your hair."

"When will my father get here?"

"We expect him this afternoon."

"I don't want my hair repaired. It used to be as long as yours until they butchered it. I want my father to see what the MacInnes men did to his daughter."

"What about your mother?"

"She's dead," Clare answered. "Four years now. I'm glad she isn't here now. It would break her heart to see me like this."

"The baby you're carrying . . . will your father . . ."

"I'm very weary now, m'lady. I would like to rest." Johanna stared at Clare a long while. The MacKay woman closed her eyes. She was feigning sleep.

"Clare, you can't keep this up much longer," Johanna said. "You're going to have to talk about what happened."

"I'm in pain, Johanna. Have you no mercy?"

Johanna nodded. "I know you ache."

"Then please . . ."

"Clare," Johanna interrupted. "My husband is most anxious for you to tell him who the MacBain soldier —"

"I will not name the man."

Clare burst into tears. Johanna reached out to take hold of her hand.

"It's going to be all right," she whispered. "You don't have to be afraid."

"You told me you felt trapped, and I felt the same way. I couldn't marry the bastard. I couldn't. I did something I wish now . . ."

"Yes?"

Clare shook her head. "It doesn't matter," she whispered. "I'll be found out soon enough. Please let me rest now. I'm not strong enough to talk about what happened."

Johanna gave in. Glynis pounded on the door

and then walked inside. She carried a brush and her scissors in her hand.

"I'm ready to see what I can do," she announced.

Johanna stood up. "Clare isn't up to having her hair fussed over."

"Do you mean all the trouble I went to searching out these scissors was for nothing, m'lady?"

"Actually no, Glynis. I could do with your services. I've been wanting to cut my hair for quite some time. Come along to my bedroom and you can use your scissors on me."

Glynis perked up. Her errand hadn't been in vain after all. She and Johanna got into an argument about the length to be trimmed, however. Glynis didn't want to cut so much away, but her mistress was emphatic.

Johanna's hair barely reached her shoulders when Glynis was finished.

"I'll admit you look fetching, m'lady."

"I didn't realize it would be so curly."

"The weight kept the curls out," Glynis explained.

"The weight gave me a fair-sized headache every day," Johanna added. "Thank you so much, Glynis." She threaded her fingers through her hair and laughed. "I'm not so certain how it looks, but it feels wonderful."

"Will the MacBain throw a fit when he sees what I've done?"

Johanna could tell from Glynis's smile she was jesting with her question.

"I doubt he'll even notice."

"He'll notice, all right. He notices everything about you. We all smile over the way he stares at you. He holds affection for you, m'lady."

"I pray he'll continue to feel affection for me tonight. He's sure to become irritated when I join him at the dinner table. 'Tis the truth everyone's going to be rattled by the surprise I've decided upon."

Glynis's curiosity was captured, of course. "What do you have planned?"

"I can't tell you," Johanna replied. "You'll have to wait and see."

Glynis nagged her mistress for several more minutes before giving up. "Will you be going downstairs? I'll take hold of your arm and make certain you don't fall on the steps."

"I'm going to stay here," she replied. "Would you mind if I borrowed your scissors? I'll return them to you this evening."

"Keep them here," Glynis said. "When Clare's wanting her hair trimmed, I'll know where to look. Good day to you, m'lady."

Glynis was just reaching for the door latch when Johanna stopped her with a question.

"Do all women have the same symptoms when they're carrying?"

Glynis turned around. "Most do," she answered. "Why do you ask?"

"I was just wondering," Johanna answered. "When does a woman start showing?"

"Depends," Glynis replied. "Some show by the fourth month, others wait another month for their middles to fatten. You should be starting to lose your waist," she added. "Are you?"

"I am," Johanna said.

She thanked Glynis again. As soon as the door closed behind the woman, Johanna began work on her surprise. She spread the MacBain plaid lengthwise over the bed and cut it down the middle. She made the same long cut in the Maclaurin plaid. Then she sat down on the bed with the two halves and sewed them together. When she was finished, it was impossible to tell where the MacBain plaid ended and the Maclaurin plaid began.

Keith would probably have to take to his bed for a week when he saw what she'd done. Johanna knew she was going to cause an uproar. She didn't care. It was high time everyone put his differences aside and joined together to form one clan under Gabriel's leadership.

She probably should tell her husband what she was going to do. Johanna folded the leftover strips and put them under the bed. She hid the new plaid she'd sewn together there, too. She wouldn't put the garment on until dinner.

She was yawning by the time she'd completed her task. She needed a nap. She took off her plaid, draped it over the chair with her belt, and then stretched out on the bed. She would only rest a minute or two.

Johanna fell asleep thinking about Clare MacKay. The woman had started to tell her something she'd done, then changed her mind. She'd looked terribly frightened.

She was certainly a puzzle. What had she meant when she'd said in time she would be found out?

Johanna slept for three hours. She opened her eyes and found Alex sound asleep beside her. Her son was drooling all over her arm. He was obviously a sound sleeper, a trait she hoped his little brother or sister would share.

She slowly sat up so she wouldn't disturb Alex and almost burst into laughter when she spotted Dumfries sound asleep at the foot of the bed.

She couldn't order the dog down without waking Alex. She scooted out of bed, washed, and then got dressed in the MacBain plaid again. Waves of nausea made the simple task seem to take forever. Johanna had to sit down several times to wait until the sickness passed.

Gabriel opened the door just as she was tightening her belt around her waist. He saw that his son was still sleeping and motioned with the crook of his finger for Johanna to join him in the hall.

He was staring at her hair, or so she believed, and frowning with obvious displeasure.

He would eventually get over his irritation, she decided. She hurried across the chamber, a smile on her face, and went out into the corridor. Gabriel pulled the door closed and turned to her.

"You're too damned pale," he muttered.

"And that is why you're frowning, m'lord?"

He nodded. She pinched her cheeks to gain some color. "Have you perchance noticed anything else?"

"Clare's father was spotted coming up the ridge."

She forgot all about trying to gain a compliment over her haircut when Gabriel gave her his news.

"I want you and Alex to stay inside our chamber until Laird MacKay and his men have left."

"How many soldiers ride with the laird?"

He shrugged. "Enough," he answered.

Gabriel was just turning away when she shook her head at him. "I wish to speak to Clare's father," she announced.

"He won't be in the mood to be polite, Johanna. Do as I order."

"The laird's angry with the MacInnes clan, not us," she reminded him.

"Nay," he said. "His fury is fully directed on all the MacBains. He blames us for his daughter's disgrace."

Johanna's complexion underwent a radical change. She wasn't pale now. In the space of a heartbeat, her face had turned red with anger.

She didn't ask her husband how he'd gained his information. If he said the Laird MacKay blamed them, then it must be true. Gabriel wasn't one to jump to conclusions without first gaining all the facts.

"Who is sitting with Clare now?"

"Hilda," he answered. "Go back inside," he ordered. "I don't want any of the MacKay's anger near you."

She didn't agree or disagree with her husband's command. He assumed she was going to be cooperative. She did go back inside her chamber, but only for a minute or two, until she was certain her husband had gone back downstairs to wait for Clare's father. Then she hurried down the hallway to Clare's room. She sent Hilda to sit with Alex.

"Your father's going to be here in just a few minutes, Clare. Do you want to see him alone, or do you want me to stay with you?"

Clare struggled to sit up in bed. She let out a little whimper of distress. Johanna wasn't certain if the movement caused her pain or if the announcement was the reason. The fear on Clare's face was aching to see.

"Please stay," she said.

Johanna straightened the blankets around the bed, more to cover her own nervousness than to make Clare comfortable.

"I don't know what to say to him."

"Just tell him what happened," Johanna advised.

Tears gathered in Clare's eyes. "I can't," she cried out.

The truth hit Johanna all at once. It was a blessing she was standing next to the chair. She was able to sit down before she fell.

"You don't understand, Johanna."

"Oh, Lord, I think I do understand. You made it all up, didn't you? There wasn't any MacBain . . . you aren't carrying . . ."

Clare started crying. She shook her head, trying to deny Johanna's accusation. The fear in her eyes made a mockery of her attempt to cling to her lie, however.

"You're wrong," she protested.

"Am I?" Johanna asked. "Every time one of us tried to ask you questions, you feigned weariness."

Clare didn't give Johanna time to continue. "I was weary," she defended.

Johanna could feel Clare's panic. She wanted to comfort her. She didn't, though. Instead she tried to be heartless to her pain, for she was determined to get to the truth. Only then could she help Clare.

"You gave yourself away, you know."

"I didn't."

"You told me you felt trapped and that you did something you knew would eventually be found out. Pretending to be carrying a baby would eventually be found out, wouldn't it? Didn't you realize people would notice you weren't getting bigger?"

Clare was openly sobbing now. "I didn't think at all," she confessed.

Johanna slowly leaned back in her chair. "What in heaven's name are we going to do about this mess?"

"We? I'm the one who will suffer the consequences when my father finds out I lied."

"Why did you make up such a tale?"

"I was desperate," Clare admitted. "Can't you understand? It was so horrible living there. Each day got worse."

"I do understand," Johanna said. "But . . ."

Clare interrupted. She was anxious to explain her reasons so Johanna wouldn't condemn her.

"Father placed me in the MacInnes household for training. I was supposed to marry the laird's son in six months' time. It didn't take me long to realize how terrible they all were. Did you know the laird has two older daughters? They were born before his precious son," she added in a rush. "One of the servants told me that each time the laird was given the news his wife had delivered him a daughter, he went up to the birthing chamber and beat the poor woman. She died after giving him a son. She probably welcomed death. I know I would have if I were married to such a monster."

"And his son is just like his father, isn't he?" Johanna already knew the answer to her question. She had vivid memories of the laird's son standing over Clare with his hands formed into fists at his sides.

"He's worse than his father," Clare said. Her voice reeked with disgust. "I couldn't abide the thought of being married to him. I tried to talk to my father, but he wouldn't listen to me. I had run back home, you see, but . . ."

Clare couldn't go on for several minutes. Her sobs were wrenching. Johanna found it extremely difficult to maintain her own composure. Not only had Clare been placed in the hands of a monster, she'd also been betrayed by her father. It was unthinkable to Johanna, for her own father would have killed Raulf had the dear older man been alive and known the anguish his daughter suffered.

"Your father took you back to the MacInnes clan, didn't he, Clare?"

"Yes," she whispered. "I don't believe I've ever felt so abandoned . . . or . . . desperate. A few days later, I heard the MacInnes soldiers talking.

They'd spotted warriors wearing the MacBain plaid crossing their border."

"And that is when you came up with the lie?"

Clare shook her head. "The soldiers didn't realize I was listening to them. When they whispered your husband's name, I could hear the fear in their voices. I decided then that I would go searching for these soldiers. I don't know what I thought would happen if I found them. I didn't have a plan, Johanna. I just wanted someone to help me."

"Yes," Johanna agreed, her voice a soothing whisper. She handed Clare a linen cloth to wipe her face, then took hold of her hand. "I would have done the same thing."

"You would?"

"Yes."

The conviction in her voice assured Clare. Johanna felt a strong bond with the woman. They were united now, for their memories of nightmares past joined them together against the atrocities forced on women by a few bullying, frightened men.

"I had already been beaten once for insolence," Clare said. "And I knew it would happen again and again. I never found the MacBain soldiers; and by the time I gave up my search, it was getting dark. I stayed in an abandoned cropper's cottage all night. Dear God, I was afraid. I was terrified of going back to the MacInnes keep and terrified not to," she added. "They found me the next morning." Clare was holding onto Johanna's hand with such a strong grip, she was bruising the skin.

"You felt helpless, didn't you?"

"Oh, yes," Clare answered. "I still hadn't thought up the lie though. Three months went by, and then one morning the laird announced he'd decided to move up the marriage date. Robert and I were to be wed the following Saturday."

Clare's voice was hoarse from strain and weeping. Johanna was going to get up to fetch her a drink of water, but Clare wouldn't let go of her hand.

"My lie wasn't planned ahead of time," she said. "I gathered my courage and stood up to Robert. I told him I would never marry him. He went into a rage. He's a possessive man, and jealous. I knew he wouldn't want me if he believed I had willingly given myself to another man. I remembered the MacBain soldiers who had crossed the border, remembered, too, the MacInnes' soldiers fear of your laird, and that is when I came up with the lie. I knew what I did was wrong and I'm sorry I lied to you. You have been so kind to me, Johanna. Hilda told me what you did to Robert. I wish your arrow had pierced his black heart. Dear God, how I hate him. I hate all men, even my father."

"You have sound reason to despise Robert," Johanna said. "In time you'll get past your hatred. You might even begin to pity the man."

"I'm not so forgiving."

"Clare, I know you aren't in the mood to listen to me, but I still must instruct you not to blame the majority of men for the sins of a few."

"Didn't you hate your first husband?"

432

Johanna sighed. "Yes," she admitted. "But I didn't hate all men. My father, if he'd been alive, would have protected me from Raulf. I would have found sanctuary with him. My brother, Nicholas, came to my rescue once he became aware of what was going on."

"Once he became aware? Didn't you tell him after the first beating?"

"It's difficult to explain, Clare," Johanna replied. "Raulf wasn't like Robert, and I was much, much younger then. The beatings didn't start right after we were wed. He set about destroying my confidence first. I was naïve, and frightened, too, and when you are called ignorant and unworthy over and over again by someone who is supposed to love and protect you, well, in time a part of you will begin to believe some of the nonsense. I didn't tell my brother because I was too ashamed. I kept thinking I would make it better. I never believed I deserved such foul treatment, and eventually I came to realize Raulf was never going to change. That is when I knew I had to find a way to leave. I would have gone to Nicholas, but as it turned out, it wasn't necessary. My husband was killed."

Johanna paused to take a calming breath. "You wouldn't hate Nicholas if you knew him. He's the reason I married Gabriel," she added. "And you cannot hate my husband. 'Tis the truth I can't imagine how anyone could."

"I don't hate him," Clare said. "He has been protecting me, and I am appreciative. He does frighten me though. You obviously do not notice what a giant of a man he is, m'lady, or that his manner is most . . . abrupt."

"He can be overwhelming, but only if you let him," Johanna replied, a smile in her voice now. "Clare, you showed incredible courage standing up to Robert. You must have known what would happen. You almost got yourself killed."

"My game is over, isn't it? I'll tell my father the truth. I promise."

"Will he make you go back to MacInnes?"

"I don't know," Clare said. "He wants the alliance."

Johanna felt sick. The thought of the woman being forced back into Robert's grasp was simply too appalling to think about. Only one thing was certain in her mind. She wasn't going to let that happen.

"Don't tell your father the truth just yet," she said. "I must think about this. I cannot allow you to go back. No, I can't let that happen. We will have to put our heads together and come up with a solution."

"Why do you care, m'lady? You put yourself in jeopardy by keeping me. Your compassion will get you into trouble. My father . . ."

Johanna wouldn't let her finish her protest. "Clare, I believe you've already conquered the most difficult challenge."

"And what was that, Johanna?"

"You were in an untenable position, and you took the most important first step. I wouldn't have chosen your road to freedom, but that doesn't matter now. You got out. Don't you understand? You cannot consider going backward now."

"What happens when my father's soldiers war against the MacBains because of my lie?"

Johanna shook her head. "We will find a way to avert a conflict," she announced.

"How?"

"I don't know . . . not yet, but you and I are clever. We can find a way to straighten out this mess."

"But why would you put your clan in such a position?"

"I don't believe one must be sacrificed for the other," Johanna said. "I do believe that every woman has a responsibility to look out for the other. When one is in bondage or suffering, then aren't all of us?"

Johanna knew she wasn't making any sense. It was difficult for her to put her feelings into a coherent explanation. "Women are looked down upon by some men. There are members of our church who consider us inferior. God doesn't, though. Remember that one important truth, Clare. It took me a long while to understand. Men make the rules, not women. They tell us they are interpreting God's views, and we are supposed to be naive enough to believe them. We are not so inferior." Her voice was filled with conviction now. "As women, we must try to stand together . . . like sisters, and when we see an injustice, we damned well should try to interfere. Together

. . . if there are enough of us united, we can help. Attitudes can be changed."

"And where do we start? With our sons?"

"We start by helping each other now," Johanna explained. "Later, when we have sons and daughters, we teach them to love and honor one another. We are all made in God's image, men and women alike."

The sound of men coming down the hallway stopped the discussion. Clare surprised Johanna, for she didn't look overly afraid. She let go of her hand, straightened her shoulders, and smoothed her covers.

The door was just opening when Clare whispered, "Together."

Johanna nodded and then echoed the promise. "Together."

Chapter
17

Gabriel was the first to enter the chamber. He didn't look happy to see his wife there. He shook his head at her. She pretended she didn't notice.

Father MacKechnie led Laird MacKay into the room. The priest nodded to Johanna before turning his attention to Clare.

"You look a wee bit better today," he announced.

Laird MacKay moved to the side of the priest so he could see his daughter. He started forward, then came to an abrupt stop. "Dear God," he whispered, loud enough for everyone in the chamber to hear.

The sight of his daughter's bruised face made the laird blanch. Johanna had been prepared to dislike the man. He had refused to listen to his daughter's pleas and had forced her to go back to the MacInnes men. Yet his reaction now made Johanna reevaluate her opinion. Perhaps he hadn't realized how horrible Clare's circumstances were.

No, she thought to herself. She wasn't going

to give him the benefit of the doubt. She didn't care if she was being uncharitable or worse. In her mind he was just as responsible for Clare's near death as Robert MacInnes was.

He wasn't a very appealing man in appearance. He was of medium size, judging by the fact that Gabriel towered over him. He was at least twice her husband's age, too, for he had thick strands of gray streaked through his brown hair. He had deep lines around the corners of his eyes and around his mouth. Like his daughter, he had brown eyes. His nose was his most prominent feature, however. It was quite large, and hawklike. It was fortunate Clare hadn't inherited that feature from her father.

Gabriel walked over to stand next to Johanna. The window was directly behind them. The furs had been tied back, and a faint breeze brushed her back.

"Good day, Father."

Laird MacKay finally recovered from his initial surprise. He walked over to the side of the bed, reached down, and took hold of his daughter's hand.

"Clare, what have you done to yourself?"

The caring was there in his voice, but Johanna thought the question obscene. She saw red. She walked over to put herself between father and daughter. The laird let go of Clare's hand and backed up a space. He caught the look of fury on Johanna's face and backed further away.

"What did Clare do, you ask? Do you honestly

believe she inflicted those marks upon herself?"

The laird's eyes widened. He took another step back, obviously trying to get away from Johanna's anger. It washed over him like boiling water.

"Nay, I don't think she did," he replied.

"Robert MacInnes and his father are responsible . . . and you, Laird MacKay," she announced. "Aye, you are also responsible."

Clare's father turned to Gabriel. "Who is this woman?" he shouted.

Gabriel walked over to stand closer to Johanna. "She is my wife," he announced, his voice hard. "And you will not raise your voice in front of her."

"She isn't from around here." Laird MacKay made the comment in a much softer tone of voice.

"She's from England."

"Are English daughters allowed to speak to their elders in such a disrespectful tone of voice, I'm wondering?"

Gabriel turned to Johanna. He thought she was probably dying to answer MacKay's question.

"She will speak for herself," he said.

Johanna kept her gaze on MacKay. "Most English daughters are encouraged to voice their opinions," she said. "Their fathers, you see, love and cherish them. They protect them, too, unlike some lairds who would put alliances before their daughters' safety and happiness."

MacKay's face turned red. Johanna knew she was provoking his temper. She couldn't seem to care. "Do you love your daughter?" she asked.

"Of course," the laird replied. "I cherish the lass, too."

Johanna nodded. "Do you realize, sir, your daughter almost died?"

The laird shook his head. "I didn't realize," he admitted.

Father MacKechnie cleared his throat to gain his audience. "Perhaps I should explain exactly how Clare came to us."

He waited for the laird's nod and then proceeded to describe the circumstances of Clare's arrival. He told how she'd been stripped naked and then wrapped in a burlap bag. The priest didn't leave any details out of the telling and even included the fact that Robert MacInnes had spit on the lass.

"He was set to give her a good kick," Father MacKechnie added. "Lady Johanna's arrow stopped him."

Clare's father stood with his hands clasped behind his back while he listened to the priest recount the chilling tale. His face didn't show any outward reaction to what he was hearing. His eyes, however, told another story. They were watery with unshed tears.

"The MacInnes clan will pay for their sins against my daughter," MacKay announced, his voice shaking with rage. "I speak of war, MacBain, not alliances. I was told by your first-in-command you are also after vengeance. What is your reason?"

"Robert MacInnes dared to take his knife in his hand and would have hurled it at my wife if I hadn't stopped him."

Johanna hadn't realized her husband planned to war against the MacInnes clan. The fury she heard in his voice as he explained his reason for wanting vengeance made her stomach queasy.

"But he didn't touch your wife," Laird MacKay snapped.

"What are you getting at, MacKay?"

"Robert belongs to me," the laird replied. "It's my right to avenge my daughter."

Gabriel was hard-pressed to agree. "I must consider this," he muttered.

Laird MacKay nodded. He turned his attention back to his daughter. Johanna blocked his view. The laird stepped to the side so he could see Clare.

"I believed you exaggerated your circumstances. I knew you didn't want to marry Robert, and I foolishly thought in time you would learn to get along with him. It never entered my mind that the MacInnes men would treat you with such brutality. Their insult is unforgivable . . . and so is mine, lass. I should have listened to you. MacBain's woman is right. I, too, am responsible."

"Oh, Papa," Clare whispered. "I'm sorry. I shamed you with my . . ." Her sobs prevented her from going on. Johanna hurried to hand Clare a linen cloth.

"Stop that now," her father ordered. "I do not wish to see you weep."

"I'm sorry," Clare said again. "I cannot seem to stop."

The laird shook his head. "You should have made me listen to you when you came running home, daughter, instead of disgracing yourself with a MacBain. Getting yourself with child wasn't the answer. Now you'll give me the bastard's name and I'll settle my grievances with him."

"Begging your pardon for interrupting," Johanna said, "but I thought Clare came home to you after the first beating. Isn't that fact?"

"There were no bruises," the laird replied. "I thought she made the tale up to gain my sympathy. I'm a man who admits he's wrong when he is," he added with a nod.

Father MacKechnie was pleased to hear the laird's confession. "It's a fair start," he remarked.

"Give me the name of the man, Clare."

"Father, I'm sorry you're disappointed in me. You mustn't blame the MacBains, for this was fully my sin."

"I'm wanting the name, daughter."

Johanna didn't care for the laird's harsh tone of voice. She moved to put herself between father and daughter.

Gabriel saw the expression on her face and immediately reached out to take hold of her arm. Laird MacKay also realized what Johanna was doing.

"Do you think to protect my daughter from me?" he asked. He sounded astonished.

Johanna didn't answer his question. She tried to turn his attention.

"I have misjudged you, sir, for I now realize you do love your daughter. Clare needs rest now. She took several blows to the head, and she's very weak. Why, even now she's struggling to keep her eyes open."

She prayed Clare would take the hint. She nodded to the laird to emphasize her lie, then moved aside so he could see his daughter.

Clare had caught onto the plan. Her eyes were closed, and she looked as though she'd already fallen asleep. Johanna lowered her voice when she said, "Do you see, Laird? She needs rest if she is ever going to recover. 'Tis the truth she could still die."

"I was wanting to take her back home with me," the laird whispered back.

"She's getting excellent care here, Laird," Father MacKechnie announced. "Your daughter doesn't appear to be strong enough to go anywhere. Best leave her be. She's under Laird MacBain's protection. She can't have better than that."

"She does have better," Gabriel interjected. "She has my wife's protection as well."

Laird MacKay found his first smile. "I can see that she does."

"Perhaps we should go downstairs to discuss this worrisome topic," Father MacKechnie suggested. "The matter of who fathered her child can wait, can't it?"

"The man will wed my daughter. I'm wanting your assurance, MacBain."

Gabriel frowned. "I put the question to each . . ."

Johanna interrupted. "He asked some of his soldiers," she blurted out. "But not all of them, of course. There are . . . so many, and some haven't returned from . . . duties. Isn't that right, husband?"

Gabriel didn't blink an eye over his wife's lie. "That is correct," he announced.

"But I'm wanting to know, Laird, if you stand with me on the marriage issue," MacKay muttered. "Will you demand the soldier responsible for disgracing Clare marry her?"

"I will."

MacKay looked satisfied. The priest hurried over to the entrance and pulled the door open. Laird MacKay gave his daughter an awkward pat on her shoulder and then turned to leave. Gabriel gave Johanna a hard wait-until-I-get-you-alone look before following Clare's father out the doorway.

"You took my daughter in, MacBain, protected her, too, and your wife has shown her compassion. I won't be warring against you if a marriage comes about. We could have us a fair alliance . . ."

Father MacKechnie pulled the door closed, cutting off Laird MacKay's remarks.

Johanna collapsed into the chair and let out a loud sigh. "You may open your eyes now, Clare."

"What are we going to do, Johanna? I have to tell my father the truth."

Johanna nibbled on her lower lip while she thought about the problem.

"At least now we know you won't be sent back to the MacInnes clan. Your father might have been blinded before by the fever of an alliance, but he certainly had his eyes opened just now. When he saw the bruises on your face, he was convinced. He loves you, Clare."

"I love him, too," Clare whispered. "I didn't mean it when I said I hated him. I was . . . angry. Oh, what a mess I've made. I don't know what Father will do when he finds out I'm not carrying."

Long minutes passed in silence. Then Johanna straightened in her chair. "There's only one solution to this problem."

"I know," Clare said, guessing Johanna was going to instruct her to tell the truth. "I have to . . ."

Johanna smiled. "Get married."

"I what?"

"Don't look so stunned, Clare. It's a sound solution."

"Who would have me? I'm supposed to be carrying, remember?"

"We're clever enough to think of a solution," Johanna insisted. "We'll find someone suitable."

"I don't want to get married."

"Are you being stubborn or sincere?"

"Both, I think," she admitted. "The thought of marrying anyone remotely like Robert Mac-Innes makes my stomach turn."

"Of course it does, but if we can find someone who realizes your value and treats you with respect, then wouldn't you be happy to marry him?"

"Such a man does not exist."

"My husband is such a man."

Clare smiled. "He's already married."

"Aye, he is," Johanna agreed. "But there are other men almost as perfect," she added in a whisper.

"You are so fortunate, Johanna."

"Why is that, Clare?"

"You love your husband."

Johanna didn't react to the truth for a long minute. Then she leaned back in her chair and let all her indecision and her insecurities go.

"I do love him."

The wonder in her voice made Clare smile. "Have you only just realized it?"

Johanna shook her head. "I do love him," she repeated. "But I realize now I have loved him for a long time. Isn't it odd I couldn't acknowledge my feelings, even to myself? I have been foolishly trying to protect myself," she added with a nod. "No one likes to feel vulnerable. Good God, I love him with all my heart."

The sound of her laughter filled the chamber. It was filled with such joy, Clare found herself laughing, too.

"I assume you've never told him how you feel," Clare remarked.

"No," Johanna answered.

"Then what do you say when he tells you he loves you?"

"Oh, Gabriel has never told me he loves me," she explained. "He doesn't realize it, you see, at least not yet. Eventually he'll acknowledge he loves me, but I doubt he'll ever tell me."

She paused to laugh again. "My husband is so unlike the barons in England, and I thank God for that blessing. The men I knew there would sing sweet ballads to the ladies they held in esteem. They hired others to write down poetic words of love for them to recite. The men were quite flowery in their pretty speeches. Most of it was nonsense, of course, and certainly insincere, but the barons believed they were chivalrous. They all held courtly love in high regard."

Clare's curiosity had been caught, and she asked Johanna several more questions about the men in England. A good hour passed in conversation before Johanna finally insisted Clare get some rest.

"Now that your father has seen you, do let Glynis trim your hair."

Clare agreed. Johanna stood up to take her leave. "Will you tell your husband the truth about me?" Clare asked.

"Yes," Johanna answered. "Eventually," she hastily added. "I must choose the right moment."

"What will he do?"

Johanna opened the door before replying. "He'll growl something fierce I imagine, and then he'll help me figure out what to do."

Hilda was coming down the hallway with a tray of food for her patient. Johanna backed up so the cook could get past her.

"Laird MacKay left," Hilda announced. "He's going to let you stay here until you're strong enough to go home with him, lass. Lady Johanna, they're waiting on you to start supper. The men are surly with hunger. You'd best get yourself down there."

Hilda placed the tray on Clare's lap. "You, lass, are going to eat every morsel, and I'm going to stand here to see that you do. You need to regain your strength," she added with a nod.

Johanna turned to leave, then suddenly stopped. "If either of you ladies should hear a commotion coming from the hall, please don't be concerned. I've planned a little surprise, you see, and some of the soldiers might become a bit upset."

Hilda and Clare both demanded to know what the surprise was. Johanna shook her head. "You'll find out soon enough," she promised.

Johanna wouldn't let them prod her into explaining. She went down to her chamber and changed into the plaid she'd hidden under the bed. Alex came into the room while she was adjusting her pleats under her belt.

"Hurry and shut the door," she ordered.

"What for?" Alex asked.

He didn't seem to want an explanation. He didn't notice anything different about her plaid either. The little boy ran over to his bed, lifted the mat, and pulled out a long wooden sword.

"Auggie's going to show me how to fence," he announced.

"Have you had your supper?" Johanna asked.

"I ate with Auggie," Alex answered as he ran for the door.

"One minute, please."

He slid to a halt. "Come and kiss me good-bye," she ordered.

"I don't want you to go away."

He fairly shouted his worry. Johanna hurried to assure him. "I'm not going anywhere," she told him.

Alex wasn't convinced. He dropped his wooden sword and ran to her. He threw himself into her arms and held tight.

"I don't want you to go away," he repeated.

Lord, what had she started? "Alex, now that I'm your mother, I wish for you to kiss me every now and again when you leave. Do you understand? You told me you were going with Auggie, and that is why I asked for a kiss before you left."

It took her another ten minutes to convince the child. She stroked his back until he was ready to let go of her.

"I'm not going away," he said then. "I'm just going outside."

"You're still leaving," she replied. "And so I ask you again for a kiss."

She leaned down close to Alex. He stretched up and gave her a wet kiss on her cheek.

Alex picked up his sword and ran for the door. "You're supposed to sit by the fire and sew, Mama. Papa said so."

"Is that right?"

Alex opened the door. "It is so," he answered. "Papa said."

"What else did your father say?"

Alex turned and pointed at her. "You're supposed to stay where he puts you. Don't you re-member?"

She was going to have to have a talk with Gabriel about the outrageous things he was telling their child.

"I do remember," she answered. "Go along now. You don't want to keep Auggie waiting."

Alex forgot to shut the door. Johanna finished adjusting her plaid, took a deep breath, and then went downstairs.

Megan was just starting up the steps to fetch her mistress. She almost toppled over the banister when she noticed what Johanna was wearing.

"You can't be so cold that you need two plaids, m'lady. Why, it's sweltering in here."

"I'm not wearing two plaids," Johanna explained. "I'm only wearing one."

Megan climbed a few more steps so she could get a closer look. "Good God, you made a new plaid. Does our laird know what you've done?"

"Not yet," Johanna answered.

Megan made the sign of the cross. Johanna tried to make her understand. "I'm sure my husband will give me his full support. My opinions and suggestions are important to him. Yes, I'm sure he'll stand behind me on this issue."

Megan made another sign of the cross. She obviously wasn't convinced.

Johanna was exasperated. "It's going to be fine," she promised. "Stop doing that," she added when Megan's hand flew to her forehead again to make yet another sign of the cross.

"No one's seen you yet," Megan blurted out. "There's still time to change into a proper plaid."

"Nonsense," Johanna replied. She tried to maintain her serene expression. In truth, Megan's reaction did make her a bit nervous. She straightened her shoulders and continued on down the steps. Megan lifted her skirts and hurried past her.

"Where are you going?" Johanna asked when Megan started down the corridor leading to the back of the keep.

"I'm going to fetch a few extra bowls, m'lady. I've a feeling you'll be needing at least five before you gain the men's cooperation."

Megan disappeared around the corner before Johanna could tell her she had no intention of throwing anything. Father MacKechnie drew her attention then when he walked inside. She turned to smile at him. He gawked at her.

Johanna stood on the bottom step and waited until the priest recovered from his surprise.

"Well now," he whispered. "Well now."

"Good evening, Father."

He didn't respond to her greeting. He seemed to be in a bit of a stupor. His reaction was making her apprehensive.

"Do you think my husband and his soldiers will be overly upset with me?"

The priest broke into a wide grin. "I'll stand by your side when we find out," he said. "I would be honored to escort you to your husband."

The priest took hold of Johanna's arm. She didn't notice. "I expect them to be a little upset at first," she explained. "But only just a little."

"Yes," he agreed. "Tell me, lass. When was your last confession?"

"Why do you ask?"

"It's preferred to receive absolution before you meet your Maker."

Johanna's smile was forced. "You exaggerate the men's reaction. None would dare harm me."

"I wasn't thinking about the men," he replied. "I was considering your husband's reaction. Come along, lass. I'm anxious to witness the battle you're about to wage."

"They'll all get past their anger."

"Eventually," the priest speculated. "The Highlanders consider their plaids sacred, Johanna."

"Oh, Lord, I shouldn't have . . ."

"Of course you should have," the priest countered. He was in the process of prying her hand away from the railing.

"Father, are you for or against this change in our plaids?"

"I'm for it," the priest answered. He burst into laughter then. "I almost fasted today for penance. Now I'm glad I didn't. I would have missed . . ."

He didn't finish his explanation. She let out a groan. "You're making me terribly nervous," she confessed.

"Forgive me, lass. I don't mean to tease you. You know you're going to have to let go of that railing eventually."

"I'll act as though nothing is out of the ordinary," she blurted out. "What think you of that plan?"

"It's plain ignorant, lass," he told her.

"Yes, that's what I'll do." She let go of the railing and took hold of Father MacKechnie's arm. "I'll plead ignorance. Thank you. You've given me a wonderful suggestion."

"If I were you, I'd plead insanity."

Father MacKechnie was sorry he'd made the jest the minute the words were out of his mouth. He was paying for his rash comment, too, for he was now having to drag his mistress over to the steps.

"I'll stand by your side," he promised. "Don't you worry. It will all wash out."

The soldiers were all standing around the tables. Gabriel stood near the buttery. He was talking to Calum and Keith. He spotted her before anyone else did.

He squinted at her, then closed his eyes and looked again. She smiled as she continued toward her seat at the table.

Keith and Calum both turned at the same time.

"My God, what's she done to our plaid?" Calum bellowed his question.

"Am I seeing what I think I'm seeing?" Keith asked in a shout of his own at the very same time.

Everyone turned to look at Johanna then. A collective gasp filled the air.

Johanna pretended not to notice the horrified expressions on the men's faces.

"I told you it would be all right," she boasted in a whisper to the priest.

Gabriel leaned back against the wall and continued to stare at his wife.

"MacBain, you'd best do something before all hell breaks loose," Calum said.

Gabriel shook his head. "It's too late," he remarked. "And high time one of us did something," he added.

Keith's face had turned bright red. "Lady Johanna, what have you done?"

"I'm trying to please you, Keith," she replied.

He did a double take. "You think to please me by joining the MacBain plaid to mine? How could you think . . . how could you believe I would . . ."

He was actually sputtering. She prayed it was due to his surprise and not indignation. "You know I can't seem to keep my days straight. You have noticed that flaw, haven't you?"

"Flaw?"

"My faulty memory," she explained. "Come and sit beside me, Keith, and I shall give you a proper explanation for my bold action. Calum, you take Keith's place at the other table."

Johanna kept giving her husband wary glances every other second. He hadn't shown any outward reaction to her surprise . . . yet.

"Gabriel, are you ready to sit down?" she called out.

She had a death grip on Father MacKechnie's arm. He patted her hand in a bid to get her to let go of him.

"Where would you like me to sit, lass?"

"On Gabriel's left," she answered, "and across

454

from me. It will be easier for you to give me the last rites if it becomes necessary," she added in a whisper.

"Did you forget which day it was and that was your reason for wearing both plaids?" Lindsay wanted to know.

"It is only one plaid," Johanna explained. "I cut them each down the middle and then sewed one half of each together to form this one. The colors blend together quite nicely."

Johanna reached her chair and turned to Gabriel. He was still leaning against the wall, staring at her.

His silence made her even more nervous. "Gabriel?"

He didn't answer her. She couldn't stand waiting to hear what he thought of her boldness. "Please tell me how you feel about this change," she asked.

He suddenly pulled away from the wall. His voice was hard and angry when he spoke.

"I'm most displeased."

She turned her attention to the table. She tried to hide her hurt and her disappointment. She'd hoped for his support, of course. 'Tis the truth, she'd expected it. His disappointment fairly overwhelmed her.

She heard several loud grunts of approval. She didn't look up to see who the offenders were.

Gabriel walked over to the table. He nudged her chin up, then put his hands on her shoulders.

"I should have thought of this myself, Johanna."

It took her a full minute to realize he was giving her his approval.

"You're far more clever than I am," he said.

She tried to tell him thank you for his compliment but couldn't. She burst into tears.

Everyone started shouting at the same time. Keith blamed Calum's rude reaction to their mistress's clothing as the reason for her distressed state. Calum was just as emphatic in his opinion that Keith's constant browbeating tactics were the true reason Lady Johanna was weeping.

Gabriel seemed to be the only one not affected by his wife's tears. He ordered her to sit down, then moved to stand behind her. He put one hand on her shoulder and turned his full attention to his soldiers.

"Seeing my wife dressed in both plaids has opened my eyes. I have only just realized the great lengths Johanna has gone to in order to accommodate all of you. She has been told which plaid to wear, which chair to sit in, who to walk with, and so on, and she has never been anything but gracious in her bid to please you. From the day she arrived here, she has accepted all of you, Maclaurins and MacBains alike. She has treated Calum and Keith with equal affection. She has given all of you her devotion and her loyalty. Her repayment has been your criticism and your disdain. She has even been called coward by some, yet she didn't come to me with a single complaint. She suffered the humiliation in silence, proving without a doubt she is far more understanding and forgiving than I could ever be."

Silence followed the laird's speech. Gabriel squeezed his wife's shoulder before continuing. "Aye, she's been damned accommodating," he repeated. "And so have I." His voice was hard now and angry. "I've tried to be patient with you, but I find it's one hell of a strain, for I'm really not a patient man at all. I have had enough of this conflict and, obviously, so has my wife. From this moment on, we are united as one clan. You have accepted me as your laird. Now you will accept each other. Those of you who cannot do this have my permission to leave at first light."

Another minute or two of silence followed the laird's command. Then Lindsay took a step forward. "Laird MacBain, which plaid will we wear?"

Gabriel turned his attention to the Maclaurin soldier. "You have given me your loyalty, and I am a MacBain. You will wear my colors."

"But your father was a Maclaurin," Keith reminded his laird. Gabriel turned his frown on his first-in-command. "He neither claimed me nor gave me his name," he replied. "And I do not claim him. I'm a MacBain. If you follow me, you wear my colors."

Keith nodded. "I follow you, Laird."

"I, too, Laird," Lindsay blurted out. "But I'm wondering now what we will do with the Maclaurin plaids."

Gabriel was going to suggest they burn the things, then changed his mind. "The plaid belongs to your past," he announced. "You will hand it down to your children with the tales of your history. The MacBain plaid you put on tomorrow is the beginning of your future. United, we will become invincible."

The tension in the hall was broken by their laird's last remark. A resounding cheer went up.

" 'Tis cause for a celebration," Father Mac-Kechnie announced. "A toast it is," Gabriel agreed.

"Without spilling," Johanna blurted out.

For some reason, her instruction was found to be vastly amusing by the men. She couldn't imagine why they were carrying on so, then thought that perhaps they were simply laughing with relief. There had been a few worrisome minutes during Gabriel's speech. At least she'd been worried.

She dabbed at the corners of her eyes with her linen square, embarrassed now because she couldn't seem to quit crying.

Dear God, she was thankful she'd married Gabriel. Her life had been so bleak and desolate. She'd never known what joy was until he came into her life.

Such thoughts only made her weep all the more. The men didn't pay her any attention now. She heard Keith whisper it was her delicate condition causing the undignified display of emotions. Calum nodded agreement.

Johanna looked up and spotted Leila standing by the entrance. She immediately stood and motioned for the woman to come to her.

Leila seemed hesitant. The men all stood with

their goblets. The jug was being passed down the line so that each soldier would pour his own. Johanna walked around the group and met Leila in the center of the hall.

"Did you hear . . ."

"Oh, yes, m'lady, I heard," Leila interrupted. "Your husband gave a powerful speech."

"Come and sit down next to me, Leila, at the table."

"But I'm a Maclaurin," she whispered. "At least I was until a few minutes ago."

She blushed after making the comment. Johanna smiled. "You are still a Maclaurin, but you are now also a MacBain. Calum won't have any excuse not to court you now," she added in a low whisper.

Leila's blush intensified. Johanna took hold of her hand and pulled her along.

The soldiers had just finished a toast to their laird and their future. They were about to take their places at the tables when Johanna gained their attention.

"I would like to make a few changes in the seating," she began.

"We like where we sit, m'lady," Michael told her.

She ignored the protest. "It is only fitting that both commanders sit with their laird. Keith will sit on his laird's left, and Calum will sit on his right."

Gabriel shook his head at her. "Why not?" she demanded.

"You will sit next to me."

He didn't sound like he was going to bend on the issue. "All right then," she agreed. "Calum, you'll sit next to me. Leila, come along. You may sit next to Calum."

Johanna wasn't quite finished making changes. When she was finished, a Maclaurin sat next to a MacBain at each table.

Father MacKechnie sat at the head of the second table where Keith used to sit. He was thrilled with the honor bestowed upon him. Keith was just as pleased with the new arrangement, if his smile was an indicator, because he now sat next to his laird.

"Why does it matter where the rest of us sit?" Lindsay asked his mistress.

She wasn't about to tell him the truth that she wanted to completely eliminate the division by the clans. She never again wanted to see the Maclaurins all clumped together at one table and the MacBains seated at the other.

The soldier repeated his question when Johanna didn't immediately answer him. She couldn't think of a logical reason to give the inquisitive man. And so she gave him an illogical one. "Because my mama's coming. That is why."

Lindsay nodded, then turned to repeat her explanation to the MacBain soldier seated next to him. "Her mama's coming. M'lady wants everything to be just so."

The MacBain soldier nodded. "Aye, she does," he agreed.

Johanna turned her attention to the table so the men wouldn't see her smile. She wanted to laugh over Lindsay's naïveté but didn't dare.

Dinner was a wonderful success by her measure. Calum and Leila started out as stiff as boards, but by the time the meal was finished they were talking to each other in low whispers. She was straining to hear what they were talking about when Gabriel realized what she was doing and pulled her closer to him.

"There will be a wedding soon," Gabriel remarked with a nod in Calum's direction.

Johanna smiled. "Yes," she whispered.

The mention of marriage turned her thoughts to Clare. The MacKay woman needed a husband, and in Johanna's estimation, there were several fine possiblities sitting at the table.

"Keith? Have you —" Johanna began, thinking to ask him if he'd considered his future.

Keith wouldn't let her finish her question.

"I've been waiting for you to bring that up," he said.

Her eyes widened in surprise. "You have?"

"It was my duty to tell your husband, m'lady. I tried to keep your promise, even felt a bit relieved because I felt responsible for the Maclaurin women and their offense was mine, but I didn't get through the full day without realizing my first loyalty belonged to the MacBain."

"What are you talking about?"

Johanna had never seen a grown man blush until now. Keith was turning red with embarrassment.

"Never mind, m'lady."

She wasn't about to let the matter drop. "Exactly what did you tell my husband?"

Gabriel answered her. "He explained about the names, Johanna, and how Glynis came up with . . ."

She wouldn't let him finish. "She was most contrite, husband. You mustn't take issue with her. Promise me you won't talk to her about this."

Since Gabriel had already had a talk with Glynis, he felt it safe to give his wife his promise.

She nodded, satisfied. "I wondered where you'd heard I was being called a coward," she said then. She turned her frown to Keith. "It never entered my mind, however, that you would tell my husband. I believed someone else had overheard Glynis and then went to his laird with the tale."

"It was his duty to tell me," Gabriel announced. "You will thank him, wife, not sanction him."

"It all came out in the wash," Johanna announced.

"What in thunder does that mean?" Gabriel asked.

"She's giving us another lesson, Laird," Keith explained with a grin.

"I see," Gabriel replied.

"Nay, Laird, you won't see. None of your wife's lessons make any sense."

Johanna would have explained what she'd meant by her remark, but Alex drew her full attention when he came running into the hall. She saw the frightened look on his face and immediately stood up.

Alex circled the table and hurled himself into

her arms. He buried his face in her plaid.

"What happened, Alex?" she asked, her concern apparent in her voice. "Did you have a bad dream?"

"There's something under the bed. I heard it."

Gabriel rolled his eyes in exasperation. He reached over to pull his son away from Johanna. Alex wouldn't let go until his father ordered him to.

"You're sleeping on a mat on the floor, Alex," Gabriel said. "It isn't possible for anything to get underneath."

"No, Papa," Alex argued. "I got in your bed. It's under there. It might get me if I close my eyes."

"Alex . . ." his father began.

"You'd better go up with him and look under the bed, husband. It's the only way he'll be convinced. Besides, there might really be something under there."

"There is," Alex insisted.

Gabriel let out a loud sigh before complying with his family's wishes. He stood up, lifted his son into his arms, and walked out of the hall.

Johanna took her seat again. She smiled at Keith. She was thrilled to have his attention without Gabriel. Her husband would certainly interfere in the discussion.

"Children," Johanna drawled out. "They're such a joy. When you get married and have a family of your own, you'll understand what I'm saying. You are going to get married someday, aren't you, Keith?"

"Aye, m'lady," he answered. "Next summer as a matter of fact. Bridgid MacCoy has agreed to become my wife."

"Oh."

She couldn't quite hide her disappointment. She turned her gaze down the table and settled on Michael as a possibility.

He caught her staring at him. He smiled. She nodded. "Children," she began again. "They're wonderful, aren't they, Michael?"

"If you say so, m'lady."

"Oh, I do say," she replied. "When you get married, you'll understand. You do plan to marry someday, don't you, Michael?"

"Eventually," he answered with a shrug.

"Have you anyone in mind?"

"Are you matchmaking, m'lady?" Keith asked.

"Why would you think that?"

"I'll marry Helen when I'm ready," Michael interjected. "I've told her I will, and she agreed to wait."

Johanna frowned. The possibilities were becoming a bit limited. She turned to Niall.

"Children . . ." she began.

"She is matchmaking," Keith announced.

It was as though he'd just shouted the alarm that they were under siege. The soldiers literally jumped from their stools. They bowed to Johanna and left the room in the space of a single minute. She didn't even have enough time to order them back into their seats.

Only the soldiers already spoken for remained.

And Father MacKechnie, of course, but then he wasn't a viable possibility either, for priests couldn't marry.

Gabriel came back to an almost empty hall. He looked around him in puzzlement, shrugged, and then sat down again to finish his supper.

He smiled at his wife.

"Well?" she demanded.

He looked sheepish. "There was something under the bed."

She laughed, for she believed he was jesting with her. Then he explained, "Dumfries crawled underneath."

Leila and Calum both stood up. Leila bowed to her laird. "Thank you for giving me the honor of dining with you," she said.

Gabriel nodded. Leila blushed. "Thank you, too, m'lady."

"It's dark," Calum announced.

He didn't have anything more to add. Johanna tried not to smile. "Perhaps you should escort Leila home," she suggested, "if it's dark, Calum."

The soldier nodded. "As you wish, m'lady."

Calum motioned for Leila to walk ahead of him. Johanna turned back to her husband. Keith caught her attention then. The look of surprise on his face indicated he'd only just realized a romance was budding between Leila and Calum.

He suddenly grinned. He stood up, bowed to his laird, and then called out, "Wait up, Calum. I'll walk with you."

Johanna could hear the laughter in his voice.

Calum wasn't amused by Keith's offer. "You don't need to . . ."

"Oh, but I want to," he said. He hurried to catch up with the couple. "It's dark outside."

Leila kept walking. Calum tried to shove Keith aside. The soldier wouldn't be shoved, however. They bickered back and forth as they left the hall.

"I wonder if those two will ever learn to get along," Johanna remarked.

Father MacKechnie was feeling lonely. He picked up his goblet and moved to take Keith's place at the other table.

"It's just a bit of good-hearted rivalry between two commanders," the priest remarked. "Laird, that was a fine speech you gave tonight."

"Yes, it was," Johanna agreed. "I would like to ask you something, though," she added. "Why did you wait so long? Why didn't you give your speech a month ago or two months ago? You would have saved me quite a lot of aggravation, husband."

Gabriel leaned back in his chair. "They weren't ready then, Johanna."

"But they were ready tonight," the priest interjected with a nod.

She was still puzzled. "What made them ready tonight?"

"Not what," the priest said, "but who, lass."

She didn't understand. Gabriel nodded. A warm glint had come into his eyes. "You made them ready to accept the change."

"How did I do that?" she demanded.

"She's begging for compliments," Gabriel told the priest.

"It appears she is," Father MacKechine bantered back.

"I'm begging to understand," she countered.

"It was your quiet defiance," Gabriel finally explained.

She still didn't know what he was talking about. The priest seemed to understand, however, for he nodded several times.

"Explain my quiet defiance to me."

Gabriel laughed. "You will never make me believe you couldn't keep track of which plaid to wear on which day," he said. "You forgot on purpose, didn't you?"

"Gabriel, no one forgets on purpose," she argued.

"You put no importance on keeping track," the priest said.

She sighed. "That is true," she admitted. "I thought it was nonsense, but I . . ."

"Quiet defiance," Gabriel repeated. " 'Twas the reason you learned to read," he added. "Isn't that so?"

"Yes, but that was different," she explained.

"No, it isn't."

Johanna let out a sigh. She knew she shouldn't let her husband believe she'd deliberately worn the wrong plaids just to make the men realize how foolish they were behaving in their determination to maintain their separation from each other. It wouldn't be honorable to accept praise for something she hadn't done.

"I'm not so clever," she remarked.

"Aye, you are," her husband said. "You convinced Laird MacKay to wait another couple of weeks before taking his daughter home."

"Clare isn't up to a long journey."

"And you stopped me from telling MacKay none of my men touched his daughter. I know you were deliberately stalling so that Clare could stay here, and I did keep silent," he added. "But when MacKay comes back, I will have to tell him the truth."

"And so will she," Johanna said. "She'll be strong enough by then." And hopefully married, Johanna thought to herself, if she could find a suitable possibility.

Gabriel could prove helpful. "Husband? I find it honorable indeed that you have such faith in your soldiers. To know without a doubt that none of them would ever have touched Clare . . ."

"Where did you get that notion?"

"From you," she replied, puzzled by his question.

"Now, Johanna, you can't believe my men wouldn't take what was offered."

"But you defended them and led me to believe none had touched her," she argued.

He looked exasperated. "We are talking about two different issues," he explained. "I don't believe any of my men would refuse the opportunity to bed a willing woman," he said. "However, I also believe that if he did touch her, he wouldn't leave her there. He would bring her home with him."

"There is also the fact that the soldier would certainly admit he'd bedded the lass. He wouldn't lie to his laird," Father MacKechnie added.

Gabriel nodded. "And that, you see, is the real issue."

She didn't see, but she didn't want to argue with her husband. In her opinion, he was making the issue far more complicated than it needed to be.

Father MacKechnie stood up to take his leave. He once again praised Gabriel for his cunning and forceful speech, then turned to bow to Johanna.

"You do realize, lass, that you saved the Maclaurins from certain exile? You used your wiles to get their cooperation," he explained. "You gained their affection, too."

Johanna was humbled by the priest's opinion. She whispered her thank you for his kind words, even as she thought that tomorrow she would have to straighten out his opinion. Gabriel was the reason the Maclaurins were cooperating. Surely the priest would realize that fact soon enough.

Father MacKechnie left the hall. Johanna and Gabriel continued to sit at the table. They were finally all alone. She was suddenly feeling embarrassed and shy, for the praise she'd received was overwhelming her.

"I will make Father understand the truth tomorrow," she whispered.

"What truth?"

"That you are the reason the Maclaurins are finally cooperating."

Gabriel stood up and pulled Johanna to her feet. "You're going to have to learn to accept a compliment when it's given to you."

"But the truth . . ."

He wouldn't let her finish. He nudged her chin up so she would look at him and then said, "The truth is simple to understand, lass. You became the Maclaurins' saving grace."

She thought that was the most wonderful thing Gabriel had ever said to her. Tears filled her eyes. She didn't think she was going to cry, however. She wasn't so undisciplined.

Then Gabriel made her forget all about being dignified. "And mine, Johanna. You're my saving grace as well."

Chapter

18

Gabriel left the holding the following morning. He was evasive about his mission. Johanna immediately became suspicious and demanded to know if her husband planned to do any stealing. He took exception to her question, of course, and an argument resulted.

"I have given you my word I won't steal," he muttered. "You'd best learn not to insult me with such accusations, woman."

"It is only because I worry about your safety," she countered. "I would be most unhappy if anything happened to you while you were . . . hunting."

"You have just given me another insult," he announced, though his voice had lost its hard edge. "Have you so little faith in me? My men and I are so quiet when we take what we need, no one hears us. We are in and out of their stores before their animals even catch our scent."

She wasn't at all impressed with his boasts. She let out a rather inelegant snort. "I happen to have complete faith in you," she muttered. "I was merely curious to know where you were going. That was all there was to my question. However, if you don't want to tell me, then don't."

He didn't. When she found out he was planning to be away for at least two weeks, perhaps as many as three, she became even more curious.

She didn't nag him, though certainly not because she thought she was above such tactics. Gabriel simply didn't give her time. He told her he was leaving, argued with her for a minute or two, then kissed her soundly and left.

He didn't confide in her because he didn't want her to worry. He and a full contingent of soldiers were joining Laird MacKay in the war against the MacInnes clan, and once they'd finished with those infidels, Gabriel planned to ride to Laird Gillevrey. Yet another request had come from Baron Goode begging an audience with Johanna. The Englishman obviously didn't understand what the word *no* meant. Gabriel planned to personally and forcefully insist the baron give up. He wanted to make sure the ignorant baron comprehended what would happen to him if he dared to pester Johanna again. He prayed the baron hadn't sent a vassal.

His wife was kept busy with Alex, Clare MacKay, and mundane everyday household affairs. Glynis trimmed Clare's hair; and after another two weeks resting in her chamber, the MacKay woman was finally strong enough to join Johanna for supper in the great hall.

Clare was getting prettier with each new day.

Once the bruises faded and her facial features were no longer distorted from swelling, she turned into a strikingly beautiful woman. She had a wonderful sense of humor and an appealing brogue that sounded musical to Johanna. She tried to copy it, much to Clare's amusement.

Johanna tried to keep her concentration on the preparations for her mother's visitation. She was anxious to see her but actually hoped she wouldn't arrive for another month or two. With a bit of prodding, Johanna was certain she could convince her mama to stay until after the baby was born.

Johanna was getting thick through her middle, but she wasn't actually showing yet. She was sleeping quite a lot now. She took an afternoon nap, then still went to bed early each night. She and Alex kept the same hours. It became a ritual for her to take him up to bed. After he'd washed and cleaned his teeth, they would kneel side by side at the foot of the bed and say their nightly prayers together.

She was usually nodding off by the time they were finished. Alex wanted to delay sleep, and for that reason he liked to include everyone he'd ever met in his prayers. Gabriel was always at the top of their list, of course. They prayed for him first, then for Alex's relatives and Johanna's; and after all the acquaintances had been named, Johanna insisted on a prayer for King John's nephew, Arthur. Alex wanted to know why they were praying for him, and Johanna explained that Arthur should have been king, and since that right had been denied, they would pray he'd made it to heaven.

Gabriel came home just a few minutes after Johanna had taken Alex upstairs, but by the time he finished listening to Keith's report and had his supper, his wife and son were sound asleep.

It was as hot as hell inside the chamber. Fall had come to the Highlands and with it a cooling breeze his wife could barely tolerate. The furs covered the window, and his wife was hidden under a mound of plaids. Since Alex wasn't sleeping on his mat, Gabriel assumed he was also hidden somewhere under the covers.

He found his son at the foot of the bed and carried him over to his mat. Alex must have put in an exhausting day, for he didn't even open his eyes while he was being carried from one bed to another.

Gabriel barely made a sound as he got ready for bed. He stripped out of his clothes, washed, and then started discarding covers in his attempt to find his wife.

Johanna was sleeping in the center of the bed. He stretched out next to her and gently pulled her into his arms.

He needed her tonight. Hell, he always needed her, he thought to himself. Not an hour had passed during their separation that he hadn't thought about her. It was a shameful habit he was getting into, for he was behaving like a lovesick husband who only wanted to stay at home with his wife.

The comforts of family life had actually taken the pleasure out of warring.

Johanna was wearing a long white nightgown. He hated the thing. He wanted to feel her smooth body pressed up against him. He eased the garment up over her thighs and began to stroke her while he nuzzled the side of her neck.

She took her time waking up. He wasn't deterred, however, and when she finally realized where she was and what her husband was doing, she was very enthusiastic in her responses.

It proved to be a difficult challenge to keep her from making any of those arousing sounds he liked so much, but he didn't want Alex to wake up, and so he sealed her cries of ecstasy with long hot kisses. When she found fulfillment, she tightened all around him and let out a soft whimper.

When he found his own pleasure, however, he let out a loud shout.

"Papa?"

Johanna went rigid in her husband's arms. Her hand moved to her mouth to keep herself from laughing.

"It's all right, Alex. Go back to sleep."

"Good night, Papa."

"Good night, son."

Gabriel's head dropped to the crook of Johanna's neck. She turned so she could nibble on his earlobe. "Welcome home, husband."

His grunt in reply made her smile. She fell asleep hugging him tight. He fell asleep wishing he had enough strength to make love to her again.

It was a thoroughly satisfying homecoming.

Nicholas arrived late the following afternoon. Gabriel stood on the steps outside, waiting for his brother-in-law to dismount. Calum stood by his laird's side. He spotted the look of displeasure on Gabriel's face.

"You going to kill him this time?" he asked.

Gabriel shook his head. "I can't," he replied in a voice that sounded a bit forlorn. "My wife would be unhappy, but by God, that is the only reason her brother's still breathing."

Calum hid his grin. He knew his laird's anger was all pretense. He turned to watch their guest.

"Something's wrong, MacBain. The baron isn't wearing his usual daft smile."

Johanna's brother was all alone. He was in a hurry to get to MacBain, too, for he swung his leg over his mount and jumped to the ground before the stallion had stopped. The horse's coat was lathered, indicating he'd been pressed hard.

Something was wrong, all right. Nicholas wasn't the sort of man to abuse his mount.

"Take care of his horse," Gabriel ordered Calum. He went down the steps and walked forward to meet his brother-in-law.

Neither warrior was much on proper greetings. Nicholas was the first to speak. "It's bad, Mac-Bain."

Gabriel didn't question Nicholas. He simply waited for him to explain.

"Where's Johanna?"

"She's upstairs, getting Alex ready for bed."

"I could use a drink."

Gabriel tried to contain his impatience. He followed Nicholas inside, dismissed Megan from finishing her task of preparing the tables for supper so that he and Nicholas would have privacy, and then waited by the buttery while his brother-in-law poured himself a drink.

"You'd better sit down to hear this news," Nicholas suggested. "It's a hell of a mess, and Johanna's in the middle of it."

Johanna had just come down the stairs when she heard her brother's voice. She didn't pick up her skirts and run to Nicholas, but came to an abrupt stop instead, for the anger in his tone, added to his worrisome words, made her wait to hear what mess he was talking about before she intruded.

She knew it wasn't polite to eavesdrop, but concern and curiosity overrode manners now, and she knew that if she interrupted, the men would change the topic. Both her husband and her brother were overly protective of her feelings. Aye, they would change the topic all right, and it would take her a good amount of nagging to get any answers out of either one of them. Listening in on the conversation might not be proper, but it was certainly effective. Besides, she'd heard her name and knew the mess somehow involved her. She edged a little closer to the entrance and waited to hear her brother's next remarks.

"Just get it said, Nicholas," Gabriel commanded.

Johanna nodded. She was in full agreement with

her husband's demand and feeling every bit as impatient as he'd sounded.

"Baron Raulf has returned from the dead. He wants his wife back."

Johanna didn't hear her husband's reaction to Nicholas's news. She was too stunned to hear anything more. She felt as though she'd just been struck a powerful blow. A scream gathered in the back of her throat. She backed up until the railing prevented her from going any further. She shook her head in denial. It couldn't be true. Raulf had fallen from a cliff. There was a witness. He was dead.

Demons stayed in hell, didn't they?

And then she ran. She didn't have any clear destination in mind. She simply wanted to find a place where she could be all alone until she gained control over her panic and her fear.

She went down the back corridor, but by the time she reached the door leading outside, she realized what she was doing and why. The fear had been immediate and instinctive. It was a black remnant from her past, she thought to herself, and in the past her fear had always controlled her. She wouldn't allow it to control her now.

Johanna sat down on the bench and leaned back against the wall. She took several deep, calming breaths. After a few minutes, the panic began to ease, and with it the fear.

She was a different woman now, she reminded herself. She'd found courage and strength, and no one, not even a demon, could take those things away from her.

Her hand moved to her stomach in a protective action. Tears came into her eyes, but they were tears of joy, not apprehension, as she thought about the miracle growing inside her.

She said a prayer in thanksgiving for all the blessings God had given her. She thanked Him for giving her Gabriel and Alex and the baby sleeping inside her and thanked Him, too, for giving her a safe haven where she could be free of pain and where she could learn how to love, and last of all she thanked Him because He'd made her strong and clever.

And then she set about using her cleverness to find a way out of the mess.

Johanna sat on the bench in the dark for almost an hour, but when she finally stood up, she had a clear plan in mind. She was feeling peaceful now, actually serene. Most important in her mind, she was in complete control.

Yes, she had come a long way. She smiled over the compliment she'd just given herself, then had to shake her head because she was acting daft. She wasn't crazed. She believed she would be all right. If it came to a battle of wits, Raulf wouldn't stand a chance against her. In her estimation, men who beat women were ignorant. They were also weak-minded and filled with insecurities. Raulf had all of those sorry traits. Yes, she would be victorious if the battle was waged in London's court with threats and accusations. She would use her knowledge of his sins to condemn him.

But if Raulf decided to use his fists and his sword

to get his way, Johanna knew she wasn't physically strong enough to withstand his attack. It didn't matter though. Raulf could summon an army to aid him, but in the end, she would still be victorious. Because of Gabriel. He was her champion, her protector, her saving grace. She had complete faith in his ability to keep his family safe. Raulf was no match against him.

A demon, after all, could easily be crushed by an archangel.

Johanna let out a sigh. She was ready to let her husband comfort her. She picked up her skirts and ran to him.

Nicholas intercepted her in the center of the hall. He lifted her into his arms and swung her off the floor.

"Oh, Nicholas, I'm so happy to see you!" she cried out.

"Put her down, damn it!" Gabriel roared. "And get your hands off her. My wife isn't in any condition to be tossed about like a caber."

Both Johanna and Nicholas ignored Gabriel's commands. She kissed her brother and hugged him tight. He finally put her down and draped his arm around her shoulders.

"My sister may look delicate, MacBain, but surely you've noticed by now she's really as strong as an ox."

"I've noticed you haven't let go of her yet," Gabriel snapped. "Johanna, come here. You should stand by your husband."

He sounded surly, but the sparkle in his eyes

indicated he was pleased to see her happy. She thought he might actually like Nicholas, too, but Gabriel would go to his grave before admitting it. Men, she'd learned, were a complicated lot.

She pulled away from her brother and went to her husband. He immediately put his arm around her shoulders and hauled her close into his side.

"Why didn't you bring Mama with you, Nicholas? She would have been happy for your company, and she is planning to come here for a visitation. Isn't that right, husband?"

Gabriel nodded. "Yes, Nicholas," he said. "Why didn't you bring her?"

"She wasn't ready to leave England just yet," Nicholas countered. "Besides, there developed a bit of a problem, Johanna . . ."

Gabriel wouldn't let him finish. "Your mother will come next month."

"Explain, please, the problem you mentioned," she requested.

Both men looked wary now. She thought they didn't know how to give her the bad news. After several minutes of prodding, however, she came to the realization neither one had any intention of telling her about Raulf.

Gabriel could barely make himself let go of Johanna. When they sat down at the table to share their dinner, he kept reaching over to take hold of her hand.

Nicholas sat across from his sister and adjacent to Gabriel. Keith sat next to him. Clare joined them a few minutes later and took her seat next to Johanna.

Both Nicholas and Gabriel stood up when Clare entered the room. Johanna had to motion the other soldiers to also stand.

Nicholas kept his gaze on the lovely woman walking toward him. Gabriel kept his full attention on his brother-in-law. He waited to see a sign of recognition.

"Do you know this woman, Nicholas?" he demanded.

His brother-in-law took exception to Gabriel's tone of voice. "How the hell could I know her? I haven't met her yet."

Johanna hurried to make the introductions. Clare made a curtsy; but because Nicholas was scowling, she didn't smile.

Gabriel still wasn't willing to admit defeat. He believed he'd thought the matter through and come up with the only logical conclusion possible. The MacBain plaid had been spotted near MacInnes land. Nicholas had worn the plaid on his last return trip to England. Since none of the other soldiers had been near the holding, Nicholas had to be the man responsible for getting Clare MacKay with child.

"Are you telling me you've never met Clare MacKay before?" he asked.

"That's what I'm telling you all right," Nicholas drawled out.

"Hell."

"Gabriel, what is the matter with you?" Johanna

asked. "Clare, come and sit next to me, please."

"I thought your brother was the one responsible for Clare's condition."

"How could you think that?" Johanna cried out. "He would never abandon . . ."

"It was a logical conclusion," Gabriel defended.

"It was a sinful conclusion," Johanna countered.

Nicholas was trying to follow the budding argument. He understood Gabriel was trying to blame him for something or other and that Johanna was valiantly trying to defend him, but he didn't have a clue as to the topic.

"Exactly what is it you think I'm responsible for?" he asked Gabriel.

"Nicholas, this matter needn't concern you," Johanna said.

"How can it not concern him?" Gabriel asked. "If he is the father . . ."

She wouldn't let him finish. "He isn't," she blurted out.

The frown on Gabriel's face was chilling. "I see," he remarked. He sat down, motioned for Nicholas to do the same, and then turned back to his wife.

"Then you know who the man is, don't you, Johanna?"

Johanna nodded. She fully intended to explain the situation to her husband, but she wanted to wait until they were alone.

"We have company," she whispered, hoping her reminder would make Gabriel realize she didn't wish to discuss the delicate topic now.

He refused to take the hint. "You will give me the man's name," he ordered.

She let out a sigh. Clare had been diligently studying the tabletop with her head bowed and her hands fisted in her lap. She looked up when Johanna's husband demanded an answer, took a deep breath, and then said, "There isn't any man, Laird MacBain."

Gabriel wasn't prepared for that answer. He leaned back in his chair and stared at the MacKay woman for a long minute before he turned to his wife.

Johanna immediately nodded. "There isn't any," she said, repeating Clare's statement.

Johanna kept her gaze on her husband as she reached over and took hold of Clare's hand. "You'd best get ready," she whispered.

"Ready for what, m'lady?" Clare whispered back.

"Growling."

Gabriel ignored the banter. He was still reacting to the news he'd just been given. The ramifications were staggering, and try as he did, he couldn't understand why the woman would put herself in such jeopardy over a lie.

He shook his head. Johanna nodded. "It's joyful news, Gabriel," she remarked.

His face turned red. She guessed he didn't think it was joyful at all. Clare was squeezing her hand now in obvious fear. Johanna turned to her.

"You have no reason to be frightened," she announced. "My husband would never hurt you.

He's just been given a surprise, that's all. In a minute or two he'll get over it."

"Will someone tell me what in thunder is going on?" Nicholas demanded.

"No!" Gabriel, Johanna, and Clare all shouted the denial together.

Johanna was the first to realize how impolite they were being to her brother.

"Gabriel, this matter can wait until later for discussion," she announced. "Please?" she added when he looked like he was going to argue with her.

Her husband finally nodded. "We should only have pleasant conversation at the supper table," she said then. "Isn't that right, Clare?"

"Yes," Clare replied. She let go of Johanna's hand and straightened on her stool. "Have you given your brother your good news?"

"My husband has," Johanna replied.

"No, I haven't," Gabriel said.

He still sounded irritated to her, but she wasn't upset. "Why haven't you told him?"

"I thought you would want to," he answered.

She smiled. Nicholas's curiosity was captured of course. "What is this news?"

"I want you to tell him," Johanna insisted.

"Tell me what?" Nicholas asked.

"Your brother's a very impatient man," Clare remarked. "But then, most Englishmen are, aren't they?"

"No, they aren't," Nicholas snapped. "Johanna, tell me your news."

Clare was startled by Nicholas's hard tone of voice. Her shoulders straightened a bit more, and she frowned at the man she now decided was a rude boar.

"She isn't barren." Gabriel made the announcement and actually smiled. His soldiers all immediately nodded their agreement.

" 'Tis the truth, she isn't barren," Keith remarked.

The men all nodded again. Calum and Leila came into the hall then. Leila was holding Calum's hand. She let go of him when they started down the steps. Johanna smiled over the sight of the happy couple before turning her attention back to her brother.

He still didn't look as though he understood. "I'm going to have a baby, Nicholas."

"How is such a thing possible?"

Johanna started blushing. Gabriel laughed, for he found his wife's embarrassment amusing. He was still determined to give her hell because she hadn't told him the truth about Clare MacKay, of course, but he wouldn't raise his voice to her when he was letting her know how displeased he was, given her delicate condition.

"She is married to a Highlander," Gabriel said in answer to Nicholas's ridiculous question. "And that is how it happened."

Nicholas laughed. He pounded Gabriel on the shoulder while he congratulated him, then turned his attention to his sister.

"This is joyful news," he said. His voice shook

486

with emotion. "Mother will be very happy."

Johanna became teary-eyed. She reached for the linen square she kept tucked in the sleeve of her blouse. "Yes, Mama will be very happy," she said while she dabbed at the corner of her eyes with her cloth. "You must be certain to tell her when you return to England, Nicholas. She'll want to begin sewing for the baby."

"Now do you understand why I don't want my wife upset by any unpleasant news?" Gabriel asked.

"I understand," Nicholas replied.

They really weren't going to tell her about Raulf. She didn't have a shred of doubt about that truth. Both men were trying to protect her from worry. She would have to be told eventually, of course, and she wondered how long they thought they would be able to keep the secret.

Their motives were good-hearted, she supposed, but Johanna wasn't going to let them treat her like a child. Besides, the matter needed to be discussed. She had a sound plan in mind to keep Raulf from making any trouble, and she wanted to talk to Gabriel about it.

Her husband became preoccupied. Nicholas also seemed to be caught up in his own thoughts. Both men were frowning now, and neither was eating.

Johanna wasn't about to bring up the topic until the men had finished their supper. She decided to turn the conversation to everyday matters.

"Have you noticed our wall is almost completed, Nicholas? The men have done a fair amount of work since your last visit."

Nicholas nodded.

"Keith, have I mentioned how fit you look wearing the MacBain plaid?" she remarked.

The soldier grinned. "Aye, m'lady, you have mentioned it at least ten times today."

"She told me my shoulders look wider and stronger with the MacBain plaid," Michael interjected.

"She told me I looked taller," Lindsay called out.

"And I meant every one of my compliments," Johanna blurted out. "Every single one of you does look better in the MacBain plaid."

The soldiers laughed. "We have accepted our laird's colors, m'lady. You don't have to fret any longer."

"I haven't been fretting," she defended.

"Then why are you suddenly complimenting us?" Keith asked.

She shrugged. The men found her reaction vastly amusing. She deliberately changed the subject to a less embarrassing one. The soldiers had all ignored Nicholas; when one mentioned the incident with the wolves, they outshouted each other in their bid to tell the tale of their mistress's cunning.

Johanna didn't believe her brother needed to hear the story, but her protest was ignored. Gabriel reached over and took hold of her hand. The men were laughing and shouting now, and in the middle of the chaos, Gabriel leaned close to Johanna.

"You know I'll always protect you, don't you?"

He whispered his question. Johanna leaned to the side of her chair and kissed her husband. "I know."

Nicholas saw the tender moment between Johanna and Gabriel. He nodded, satisfied. He'd done the right thing by insisting she marry the laird.

Calum asked Gabriel a question then. Johanna scooted back on her stool and turned to Clare.

"Are you feeling all right?" she whispered.

"Yes, m'lady," Clare answered.

Johanna wasn't convinced. Clare had barely touched her food and had stayed remarkably silent for most of the meal.

She thought Nicholas might be the reason for Clare's timid behavior. For some reason the two of them had taken an immediate dislike to each other. If Clare wasn't sick, then Nicholas was the only other reason for her odd conduct. They both kept staring at each other; and when one caught the other looking, a quick frown resulted.

Their behavior was bizarre as well as distressing, for Johanna had grown quite fond of Clare and she wanted the young woman to like her family.

She put the matter aside when the men requested permission to leave. "Where is Father MacKechnie this evening?" she asked.

Keith stood up before answering. "Auggie wanted him to sample a drink of his new batch of brew."

"If you run into him, will you please tell him I would like to speak to him?"

"What do you want to speak to him about?" Gabriel asked.

"An important issue."

"You will discuss your important issue with me," he commanded.

"Yes, of course I will," she agreed. "But I would also like to hear Father MacKechnie's opinion, too."

She turned back to Clare before her husband could question her further. "What do you think of my brother? He's handsome, isn't he?"

"Handsome? M'lady, he's English," Clare whispered.

Johanna laughed. She turned to her brother. "Clare doesn't appear to like Englishmen, Nicholas."

"It's unreasonable to dislike an entire country of men," he remarked.

"I'm not an unreasonable woman," Clare defended. "If I were English, I might think your brother was handsome."

It was all she was willing to concede. Nicholas didn't appear to care what her opinion was. Yet Johanna wasn't fooled by her brother's indifferent behavior. He was interested in Clare MacKay all right and trying not to let anyone know.

Clare was acting a little too defensive. Johanna suddenly straightened on her stool. Gabriel noticed the look of surprise on her face. He demanded to know what the hell was the matter with her.

She patted his hand and gently told him she didn't care for his gruff tone of voice. She deliberately didn't answer his question.

"Nicholas?"

"Yes, Johanna?"

"When are you going to get married?"

Her brother hadn't been prepared for her blunt question. He laughed. "I'm putting it off for as long as possible," he admitted.

"Why?"

"I have other more important matters to think about," he said.

"But do you have anyone in mind when you do decide to marry?"

Nicholas shook his head. "I really haven't thought about it. When I'm ready, I'll marry. Now, enough of this talk."

She wasn't finished discussing the topic just yet. "Would a large dowry be important when making your choice?"

He let out a sigh. "No," he answered. "I don't need a large dowry."

She smiled. Then she turned to Clare. "He wouldn't want a large dowry," she repeated.

Clare frowned in puzzlement but only for a second or two. Then she realized what Johanna's plan was.

Her eyes widened, and she vehemently shook her head. "You cannot think I would ever consider an Englishman," she whispered.

Johanna tried to soothe her. "I wasn't asking you to consider anything," she said. It was a blatant lie, of course, but her motives were sincere and she didn't believe she was committing a sin. She'd achieved her goal, too, for all she wanted was to plant the idea in Clare's head.

"My father would die."

"He would recover."

"How does one recover from death?" Gabriel wanted to know.

Johanna ignored his question. "No one's going to force you to do anything you don't want to do," she told Clare.

She turned to her husband. "Isn't that right, Gabriel?"

"Isn't what right? Johanna, I don't have any idea what you're talking about."

Johanna wasn't bothered by her husband's irritation. "When is Clare's father coming back here?"

"Tomorrow or the day after."

Nicholas was staring at Clare now. The look on her face bothered the hell out of him. When she heard her father was coming, her eyes clouded up with tears, and damned if she didn't look frightened. Nicholas didn't understand his own reaction. He barely knew the woman and had already decided he didn't like her much, yet now he felt the urge to try to straighten out her problem for her.

"You do not wish to see your father?" he asked.

"Of course I want to see him," Clare replied.

"Clare won't be ready to go home tomorrow or the day after," Johanna told her husband. "She hasn't completely recovered yet."

"Johanna," Gabriel began in a warning tone of voice.

"She looks fit enough to me," Nicholas remarked, wondering what the hell they were talking about. "Have you been ill?" he asked Clare.

She shook her head. Johanna nodded. Nicholas was thoroughly exasperated.

"Clare's been very ill," Johanna said then. "She needs time to regain her strength."

"So that is why her hair is cut like a boy's," Nicholas remarked. "She had fever, didn't she?"

"She didn't have fever," Johanna said. "Gabriel, I must insist you tell Laird MacKay his daughter isn't up to a journey just yet."

"I don't think I can put him off," Gabriel replied. He turned to glare at Nicholas. "It's a pity you didn't father her child," he muttered. "It would solve all our problems."

Nicholas opened his mouth to say something but was too stunned to think of anything appropriate.

"I still cannot believe you thought my brother would be so dishonorable," Johanna said.

"It was logical, damn it," her husband countered.

"And just how would it have solved our problem?" Johanna demanded.

"He's here," Gabriel countered. "The priest would marry them. You did hear me promise MacKay there would be a marriage, didn't you?"

"I couldn't possibly marry him."

Since Clare was pointing to Nicholas when she made the emphatic statement, he had to assume she was talking about marrying him.

"Damn right, you couldn't," he snapped. "I

might also mention I haven't asked you to marry me."

Clare bounded to her feet. "Please excuse me," she blurted out. "I suddenly feel the need for some fresh air."

Gabriel nodded. Clare immediately left the hall. Nicholas watched her leave, then turned back to his sister. She was frowning at him.

"Will one of you tell me what in thunder is going on?"

"You've upset Clare, Nicholas. You'd better go after her and make your apology."

"How did I upset her?"

"You refused to marry her," Johanna explained. "Didn't he, Gabriel?"

Her husband was thoroughly enjoying Nicholas's confusion. "Aye, he did refuse," he agreed, just to goad his brother-in-law's temper.

"Start explaining," Nicholas demanded.

"It would be wrong of us to talk about Clare's problem," Johanna said. "She'll tell you when she's ready. Nicholas, why did you come here?"

The switch in topics took him by surprise. He couldn't come up with a quick excuse. He turned to Gabriel for assistance.

Father MacKechnie inadvertently came to Gabriel's and Nicholas's rescue. He came rushing into the hall.

"Keith told me you wished to speak to me, m'lady," he called out. "Is it convenient now, or would you like me to come back later?"

Gabriel and Nicholas literally jumped at the opportunity to turn Johanna's attention.

"Come and join us, Father!" Gabriel shouted.

"It's good to see you again," Nicholas called out at the same time.

If the priest was surprised by the warriors' enthusiastic greetings, he didn't let it show.

"I heard you were back, Nicholas," Father MacKechnie said. "Were you checking up on your sister? You can see she's happy," he added with a nod.

"Is that why you came all this way?" Johanna asked.

It was sinful to admit, but she was really enjoying her brother's discomfort. Lying to her was difficult for him, she decided, if the look on his face was any indication. His frown was quite telling, considering the innocence behind the question.

Gabriel rescued him. "Have you had your dinner, Father? Johanna, where are your manners? You should ask the servants to feed the man."

"I've already eaten," the priest announced. He sat down next to Johanna, declined the offer of a drink, and then went into detail about Auggie's latest batch of brew.

"It's got a kick to it all right," he announced. "One drink and a body could fly across the courtyard."

Johanna laughed over the priest's exaggeration. "It will warm us come the long . . ." The priest was about to say the brew would warm their stomachs on the cold winter nights ahead but hastily changed his remark. "If there's any left."

495

"Long what?" Johanna asked.

"Long warm winter nights," the priest mumbled with a glare in Nicholas's direction. He obviously still blamed Johanna's brother because of the lie he'd told about the warm climate in the Highlands.

Nicholas was surprised everyone was still keeping the truth from his sister. He almost laughed but caught himself in time.

"Nicholas, do you know that since I came here, the weather has turned most unpredictable. Why some nights it's actually cold."

"Nay, lass, it's never cold," Gabriel argued.

"Now Johanna . . ." Nicholas began.

"Are you going to tell me why you came here? There is obviously a problem of some sort, or you would have waited to accompany Mother, Nicholas."

"Why are you here, son?" the priest also wanted to know.

Nicholas was hard-pressed to come up with an answer. "The weather," he announced after a moment's pause. "I couldn't live with the lie any longer, Johanna. I came here to tell you the truth."

Johanna's burst of laughter told him she didn't believe him. Yet once he'd started the fabrication, he was damned if he was going to stop.

"I lied to you. There, I've said what I came here to say."

"Do you mean you lied to me about the weather?"

Nicholas grinned. Her laughter was contagious and so was her cunning. It suddenly dawned on him that she'd always known he was lying.

He leaned forward and pointed his finger at her. "You knew . . . all the while, didn't you?"

She nodded. "I'm wearing a woolen plaid, Nicholas. Of course I knew."

"Then each time one of us lied and told you the weather was unusually cold, you knew the truth, lass?"

The priest sounded appalled. Johanna nodded. "It was kind of you to hold my brother's lie, for you only had my happiness in mind, Father."

"You've got a bent sense of humor, wife," Gabriel announced.

"It's as warped as a shield left out in the rain too long," Nicholas agreed.

She laughed. The men assumed she wasn't bothered by their insults.

Johanna yawned and immediately apologized. Gabriel demanded she go upstairs to bed.

"First I would like to discuss something with all of you," she said. "Then I'll go to bed."

"What is it you want to talk about?" Nicholas asked.

"I'll help if I can," the priest promised.

"I have a problem," Johanna began.

"Tell us what it is, lass," Father MacKechnie insisted.

Johanna stared at Gabriel when she gave her answer. "It seems I have two husbands."

Chapter
19

You have only one husband, Johanna."

Gabriel's tone of voice didn't suggest she argue with him. She took hold of his hand and nodded.

"You listened while I was telling your husband about Raulf, didn't you, Johanna?" Nicholas asked.

"I did," she admitted.

"That wasn't proper conduct, lass," her husband decreed.

She shook her head. "It wasn't proper conduct for you to think you could keep this important news from me."

"I'm trying to get this straight in my head," the priest interjected. "Are you telling me Baron Raulf's alive?"

"We are," Nicholas answered.

"Good Lord above," the priest muttered. "Where's he been all this while?"

"Locked away in a dungeon an ocean away," Nicholas answered. "He was sent halfway across the world to act as King John's representative to negotiate a trade agreement. Raulf left England before John started feuding with the Church. The king doesn't give a damn about placating the pope now."

After finishing his explanation, he turned to his sister. "How much did you overhear?"

"All of it," she lied.

"Damn."

She ignored the blasphemy. "Please explain the mess I'm in the middle of to Father."

Nicholas picked up his goblet and drained the contents in one long swallow. Johanna suddenly felt the need to get closer to Gabriel. She stood up and moved to stand next to him. He put his arm around her waist and pulled her close to his side. She put her arm around his neck and leaned against him.

"Baron Raulf fell from a cliff and everyone believed he died."

"I was in England when word came," the priest reminded Nicholas.

"Yes, well, he didn't die," he muttered. "He's back in England and mad as a hornet because his wife and his lands have all been given away. The king wants to appease the bastard, though only God knows why. John has ordered Johanna to return to Raulf, and in an attempt to pacify MacBain and avert war, he has agreed to let him keep this holding."

Father MacKechnie muttered something under his breath. "It makes no difference what your king wants, son. Johanna's marriage was annulled and that's a fact. The pope himself signed the decree. Isn't that what you told me, lass?"

Johanna nodded. "It is so," she said. "I didn't realize I would really need an annulment. I requested it only to stall the king from making me marry again."

"John has decided to make himself pope. Since he started fighting with the Church, practically all ties with the Holy Father have been severed. Priests have already fled to the Lowlands in anticipation of the interdict. John's sure to be excommunicated."

"So your king believes he can switch husbands as easily as snapping his fingers?" Gabriel asked his brother-in-law.

"He does," Nicholas replied. "He won't listen to reason. I tried to talk to him, but he remains stubbornly determined to keep Raulf happy. I wish to God I knew why."

"What happens when our laird refuses to give up Johanna?" the priest asked.

"John will assign troops to Raulf."

"For what purpose?" the priest asked.

"War."

Nicholas and Gabriel said the word together.

"I can't let that happen," Johanna whispered. "We have only just rebuilt, Gabriel. I will not have it all destroyed."

"I don't think there's anything you can do about it, Johanna," her brother said.

"Have you seen Raulf?" Johanna asked.

"If I had seen him, I would have killed him

because of what he did to you. No, I haven't seen him."

Johanna shook her head. "You cannot kill him. The king would turn his anger on you."

"Listen to her, son," the priest advised. He let out a weary sigh. "We've got quite a problem on our hands."

"How long does Gabriel have before he must give his decision?"

"Johanna, you cannot believe I would consider giving you up," her husband muttered.

"Two messengers and four soldiers riding escort will be here tomorrow or the day after to give your husband King John's demands."

"And where is Raulf?" Johanna asked.

"I gained my king's promise Raulf would be kept in court with him until this is settled."

Johanna sagged against her husband. Gabriel immediately moved his chair back so he could lift her onto his lap.

"That doesn't give us much time to form a plan of action," the priest said.

"Yes, it does," Gabriel argued. "The messengers will have to return to England with the report we've denied the demand. That will give us enough time."

"Time to do what?" Johanna asked.

"Prepare," Nicholas answered.

Johanna changed the subject then. "What have you heard about Arthur? We were told the king's nephew was murdered. Have you heard anything more?"

Nicholas frowned over the switch in subjects. Johanna looked exhausted, however, and he decided she was trying to turn the conversation to a less distressing one.

"There have been several conflicting reports," Nicholas replied. "Baron Goode has vowed to find out what happened to Arthur. He's turning over every rock in his search. More and more believe Arthur was murdered. He was a contender for the throne," he explained for Father MacKechnie's benefit, "and a true threat to John's position. Goode wasn't the only one backing the nephew. Arthur had quite an army supporting his bid."

"What does your king say about this mystery?" Johanna asked.

"He vows he has no knowledge of how his nephew died," Nicholas answered. "The most common belief is that overzealous supporters of King John captured Arthur and threatened to castrate him, and he died of fright."

"That would do it," Gabriel muttered.

"Speculation is still running high," Nicholas said. "I'll tell you this. If any of the barons had proof John was involved in his nephew's death, England would be thrown into rebellion. The barons would hang John by his . . ." Nicholas caught himself before he said something Johanna was certain to take offense to and quickly substituted another more appropriate word, ". . . feet."

Johanna let out another loud yawn. She begged the men's pardon and then said, "And that, you see, is why King John wants to keep Raulf happy."

Gabriel guessed what Johanna was about to say before she spoke another word. It all snapped into place now. Johanna not only knew Arthur had been murdered; she also knew who had killed him.

"Johanna, explain what you just meant," Nicholas asked. "Do you know why John wants to appease Raulf?"

She was about to answer her brother's question when Gabriel gave her a gentle squeeze.

"He's one of his most favored barons," she said.

Gabriel loosened his hold. She guessed her answer pleased him. She would wait until they were alone to ask him why he didn't want her to tell Nicholas anything more.

"John doesn't want to keep Raulf happy," Gabriel said then. "He wants to get him killed. And that, you see, is why he'll eventually send him to me."

The discussion heated up, but Johanna was too exhausted to stay downstairs and listen to her husband and her brother argue about what was to be done.

Father MacKechnie requested the honor of accompanying his mistress up to her chamber. His real goal was to get her alone, and as soon as they had left the hall, he clasped her hand in his and asked her if she was going to fret about this nasty bit of news or if she was going to place the matter in God's hands and get a good night's rest like any intelligent lass would.

Gabriel was also concerned his wife would worry until she made herself ill. He was fully prepared to try to soothe her fears but found it wasn't necessary. He couldn't even get her to wake up long enough to kiss her good night. She was dead to the world and sleeping like an innocent without a care to concern her.

Johanna awakened in the middle of the night. A weight rolled onto her feet, startling her. As soon as she moved, Gabriel sat up. He spotted his son at the foot of the bed and immediately ordered him to go back to his own bed.

"Don't wake him," Johanna whispered. "He's been in our bed for over an hour. Just scoot him off my leg, please."

Her husband let out a sigh loud enough to wake the dead. Alex didn't stir, though. He slept through the transfer from one bed to the other.

"Does he have enough covers?" Johanna whispered. "It's cold in here," she added with a nod.

Gabriel got back into bed and hauled his wife into his arms. "He's my son," he said. "The cold doesn't affect him."

She thought her husband's remark was most illogical. She was going to tell him so, but he turned her attention with his gruff command to kiss him.

He thought only to give her a quick kiss, but she tasted so good to him and she was so wonderfully responsive, he decided he wanted a little more. He kissed her again, long and hard. And then he decided he wanted it all.

It was agony making love without making any noise, and Gabriel's last coherent thought before his wife drove him beyond the limits of his control was that he was going to be damned happy when his son moved into the other chamber.

He liked the way his wife snuggled up against him afterward. Hell, he liked everything about her, he thought with a smile.

"Gabriel?"

"What is it?"

"I would like to tell you something," she whispered in the darkness. "I know why King John wants to be rid of Raulf."

"Rest now, Johanna. We'll talk about it tomorrow."

"I want to talk about it now."

He gave in. "All right," he agreed. "But if you begin to get upset, you will put the worry aside until tomorrow."

She ignored his qualification. "I wanted to tell you earlier," she began.

"You were going to tell Nicholas, too, weren't you?"

"Yes," she replied. "Why did you stop me?"

"Because Nicholas isn't just your brother, he's also an English baron. If he were to hear unsettling news regarding his overlord's behavior, he might be forced to act upon it. No one's going to unseat John now; and if Nicholas tries, he'll get himself killed."

She hadn't considered the possibility that Nicholas might feel compelled to challenge the king. She was thankful now Gabriel had stopped her from telling what she knew.

"How did you come to guess —"

He didn't let her finish. "I have but one question to ask you, Johanna. Your answer won't leave this chamber."

"I'll tell you anything you want to know."

"Did the king kill Arthur or did Raulf?"

She didn't hesitate in giving him her answer. "I believe Raulf killed him, but the order came from King John."

"You're certain?"

"Oh, yes," she whispered. "I'm certain."

She was so relieved to finally share the burden she'd been carrying around, tears came into her eyes.

"How did you come by this knowledge?"

"I heard the king's messenger reading the order," she explained. "Raulf didn't know I was listening, but the messenger spotted me in the doorway. I don't know if he told my husband or not. I'm certain he told the king. Raulf left shortly before Easter. He didn't come home until the middle of the summer. A scant month later I heard the rumor that Arthur had disappeared. Years later, after I'd been told of Raulf's death, I was ordered to London and kept under lock and key. The king came to see me several times, and during each audience, he would deliberately bring up Arthur."

"He was fishing to find out what you knew," Gabriel speculated.

Johanna nodded. "I pretended ignorance, of course."

"Who was this messenger the king sent to Raulf

with the order to kill Arthur?"

"Baron Williams," Johanna answered. "John certainly wouldn't have trusted a court messenger. Williams and Raulf were the king's closest confidants. Yet the two barons didn't trust each other."

"You were damned fortunate the king didn't kill you. He took a chance letting you live with the knowledge."

"He wasn't certain I knew anything," she argued. "Besides, he knew I couldn't give testimony against him. Women aren't allowed to make any accusations in court against anyone but their own husbands and then for only a very few offenses."

"Baron Goode believes you know something, doesn't he? That is why he tried to talk to you."

"Yes," she answered. "All the barons were aware of the relationship between John and his two favorites, Raulf and Williams. As we now know, Raulf left England just before Arthur disappeared. Goode is guessing there might be a tie between the two. He probably wants to question me about the dates involved. He couldn't know I overheard anything."

"I want you to listen carefully," Gabriel commanded. "You will not tell anyone what you overheard, not even your brother. Give me your promise, Johanna."

"But there is one person I really must speak to," she whispered.

"Who?"

"King John."

He caught himself before he shouted, "It's out of the question."

"I believe I can make him listen to reason. It's the only way, husband. I don't want a war."

Gabriel decided to use logic to make her understand her jeopardy. "You've just told me you can't testify against the king. If you think you can threaten him with the promise you'll tell the barons what you know and ignite a rebellion against the crown, John will simply silence you before you can carry through your plan."

A long minute passed in silence. Gabriel believed Johanna was finally realizing the foolishness in her wish to speak to the king.

"I hadn't considered that plan of action," she whispered.

"Then what in God's name was your plan? Did you think you could gain John's sympathy?"

She shook her head. "No," she said. "I just thought I would mention the message he sent Raulf."

"And how would your reminder help?"

"He sent a written message, Gabriel, in his own hand. Raulf believes he burned it."

Gabriel went tense in anticipation. "Didn't he?"

"After Williams read the order to Raulf, he placed it on the table and took his leave. That is when he spotted me. I nodded to him and continued on across the entrance and then went down the back corridor. I wanted Williams to believe I had only just gotten there, you see."

"And then?" Gabriel prodded, impatient to hear the rest of the tale.

"Raulf accompanied Williams outside. When he returned to the hall, he picked up the scroll and tossed it into the fire. He stood there and watched until it had been completely destroyed."

A hint of a smile changed Gabriel's expression. God, he was married to a clever woman.

"What did he burn?"

"One of Bishop Hallwick's important sermons on the inferiority of women."

"Raulf didn't know you could read, did he?"

"Oh, no, he didn't," she rushed out. "He would have beaten me if he'd known I'd deliberately proven him wrong, for he told me again and again I was too ignorant to learn how. Of course, he beat me because I was ignorant, too, so I don't suppose . . ."

It was the very first time she'd spoken so openly about the beatings, and although he'd known the truth for a long time now, it still shook him to hear her say the words.

"Don't suppose what?" he asked, his voice gruff with emotion.

She squeezed herself closer to him before she answered. "I don't suppose he ever needed a reason to beat me," she whispered.

"He'll never touch you again," Gabriel promised.

The fury in his voice was chilling. "I know you will keep me safe," she said.

"Damned right I will," he countered.

She wasn't upset by his harsh reaction but comforted. He was outraged on her behalf.

"You took a terrible risk when you switched the scrolls," he said then. "What if Raulf had decided to reread his king's command?"

"I believed the risk was worth it," she replied. "It was an important paper to save. John's signature appears at the bottom, and his seal is affixed."

"He was a fool to put his name . . ."

"He believes he's invincible," she said. "And I think he knew Raulf wouldn't believe Williams without a written order. Time was important, though I'm not certain why, and surely that was the reason King John didn't summon Raulf to London and tell him what he wanted done."

"Where is the scroll?"

"I wrapped it in soft cotton cloths and hid it inside the altar of the chapel Raulf had just had built for the bishop. It's wedged between two marble squares."

Gabriel felt her shiver and tightened his hold on her.

"Do you know I almost destroyed it just before I was told Raulf was dead. Then I changed my mind."

"Why?"

"I wanted someone in future to find it and know the truth."

"I'm more interested in keeping you safe, Johanna. I will not allow you to talk to King John."

"I don't want war," she whispered.

She sounded close to tears. He kissed her forehead and demanded she quit worrying.

"I'll convince England's king to leave us alone."

She tried to argue with him. "You can't think to go to England?"

He didn't answer her. "It's late, Johanna, and time you went to sleep."

Exhaustion won. She decided she would have to wait until tomorrow to talk some sense into her husband. Of only one thing was she certain. She wasn't about to let him confront King John or Raulf without a foolproof plan in mind. She would demand he take at least a league of Highlanders with him.

Morning proved to be too late to demand her husband be reasonable. When Johanna dressed and went downstairs to find Gabriel, Nicholas gave her the news that he'd already left the holding.

She didn't become hysterical, but it took every bit of strength she possessed to control herself. She spent the day pacing and worrying. By dinnertime, her nerves were flayed.

Father MacKechnie sat at the head of the table at Johanna's insistence. She sat on the priest's right, next to Clare, and Nicholas took his seat across from her.

The thought of food turned Johanna's stomach. She could barely stand to watch anyone else eat. She didn't say a word until the trenchers had been cleared from the table.

"Nicholas, why did you let him go?" she cried out.

"Let him? Johanna, I made a sound argument, but your stubborn husband wouldn't listen."

She tried to calm down. "Then you, too, realize the jeopardy."

Nicholas shook his head. "I didn't argue against his going. I tried to talk him into letting me go with him."

"He didn't take enough soldiers with him."

"He knows what he's doing," Nicholas defended.

"He hasn't had enough time to think of a plan. He can't go barging into John's court and demand a hearing."

Nicholas grinned. "Aye, he can," he replied. "Your husband can be very persuasive when he wants to. He'll get his audience all right."

"You should have gone, Nicholas," Clare blurted out. "You're a baron. Your king would have listened to you."

Nicholas turned his attention to the beautiful woman frowning at him with such obvious indignation.

"That was my argument," he told her.

Johanna shook her head. "Only Gabriel can make the king listen to reason," she said.

Nicholas leaned back on his stool. "Why is that, Johanna?"

She was immediately sorry she'd made the remark. "Because he's my husband," she replied. "Besides, last night you said you had already tried to talk to John and he wouldn't listen to you."

"I still should have gone with him," her brother said.

"Why didn't you?" Clare asked.

"He asked me to stay here," he answered. "Gabriel made me responsible for you, Johanna, and he's going to be damned unhappy when he comes back and finds you've made yourself ill with your worry."

"If he comes back," Johanna whispered.

"You shame Gabriel by making such comments," Nicholas said. "You should have confidence in his ability."

Johanna burst into tears. Father MacKechnie dropped the piece of bread he'd been nibbling on and reached over to pat Johanna's shoulder.

"There, there, lass. It's going to be all right."

While the priest tried to comfort his mistress, Clare attacked Nicholas with a defense of Johanna's conduct.

"She loves her husband," she cried out. "How dare you criticize her? She's worried about his safety, and she certainly doesn't need you to make her feel guilty or ashamed!"

Clare was shouting by the time she finished her speech. She'd bounded to her feet and folded her arms across her chest while she glared at Nicholas.

He showed no reaction to her behavior or her words. In truth, he wasn't offended. Nay, he found Clare's defense of Johanna admirable.

"How did you become so loyal to my sister in such a short time?" His voice was kind and soothing. The bluster seemed to leave her all at once.

She collapsed back onto her stool, straightened her plaid across her shoulder, brushed a strand of hair out of her eyes, and then looked at Nicholas again.

He was smiling at her. He was a handsome man, she thought to herself, and the look of tenderness in his eyes made her feel warm inside. She shook her head against such thoughts and tried to remember his question.

"Your sister saved my life."

Johanna mopped at her eyes, thanked the priest for his concern, and then turned to Clare.

"You saved yourself, Clare."

"You had a hand in it," Father MacKechnie announced.

Alex appeared at the entrance. He was hopping from one foot to the other while he waited to get some attention.

Johanna spotted her son and immediately excused herself from the table. "I must tuck him in," she explained.

"Will you come back down?" Clare asked.

"I'm very weary tonight," Johanna answered. "I believe I'll go to bed."

"I'll go up with you," Clare announced. She stood up, bowed to the priest, and then turned to Nicholas. "I didn't mean to shout at you."

Nicholas had stood up when his sister did. Clare walked around the end of the table to leave the hall but stopped when she reached his side.

He towered over her. She tilted her head back so she could look into his eyes. They were beautiful, she thought to herself . . . for an Englishman.

"I have apologized, Baron. Have you nothing to say in return?"

"And catch hell again? You seem to take exception to everything I say, Clare MacKay."

"I haven't," she defended.

He grinned. Father MacKechnie snorted with his laughter. "He's got you now, lass. You just proved him right."

Clare didn't know if Nicholas was jesting with her or not. She could feel herself blushing and didn't understand why. She certainly hadn't done anything to feel embarrassed about.

She decided she'd wasted enough time trying to understand the strange Englishman. She turned to the priest, bid him good night, and then muttered the same to Nicholas.

"Sleep well, Clare."

The caress in his voice shook her. She glanced up to look at him.

He winked at her.

She didn't run out of the hall. She walked at a ladylike pace. She didn't smile until she reached the entrance. Then she smiled all the way up the stairs. She did a lot of sighing, too. Baron Nicholas was a thoroughly unacceptable man, and heaven help her, she was beginning to like him.

Nicholas watched her leave the hall. Father MacKechnie asked him to sit back down. "Don't leave just yet. Share some brew with me. None of us is going to get much sleep tonight, worrying as we are."

Nicholas reached for the jug and poured a drink into the priest's goblet.

"Clare intrigues me," he remarked.

"Of course she does," Father MacKechnie agreed. "She's a bonny lass, isn't she now?"

Nicholas nodded. "Were you here when she arrived?"

"I was," Father MacKechnie said.

Nicholas waited for the priest to tell him more. Father MacKechnie didn't seem inclined.

"As long as Clare is here, I'm responsible for her safety, too, Father," he said.

"Aye, you are."

"MacBain told me her father will be coming to collect her tomorrow or the day after."

"I hadn't heard that," the priest replied. "What are you going to do? Will you let her leave?"

"You're going to have to tell me what happened to the woman. I can't make any kind of decision until I know her history. Clare seemed upset over the news."

"Do you mean upset because her father's coming to get her?"

Nicholas nodded. The priest let out a loud sigh. "You'd best hear what happened to the poor lass. Clare MacKay arrived here so bloody and torn apart it looked as though the wolves had gotten to her. It's a miracle her face wasn't scarred. It's a miracle she even lived. I gave her the last rites," he added so Nicholas would understand he wasn't exaggerating.

He took a long swallow of his drink and then

516

told Nicholas the full story. He was pleased with the baron's reaction. Nicholas was properly outraged.

"So she's carrying a MacBain?" Nicholas asked when the priest finished his explanation.

"Nay, son, she isn't carrying. She made it up, you see, and confessed the full truth to our laird only last night. Clare told me this morning, though not in confidence or in confession, so I am at liberty to talk about it," he hastily explained. "She said she was feeling relieved. She's a proud woman. She doesn't like to lie."

"Then why did she?"

"It was the only way she could think of to get away from the MacInnes men. She went to an extreme. She could have gotten herself killed."

"From what you've told me about her injuries, she damned near did get herself killed," Nicholas remarked.

The priest agreed with a nod. "Clare's father is the only one who doesn't know the truth yet. He's expecting to meet the father of Clare's babe and set a marriage date."

The bizarre conversation of the night before was suddenly making sense to Nicholas. "The MacBain kept asking me if I recognized Clare. He thought I was the man responsible."

"No one's accusing you now, son. It would have been convenient if you had been the one, at least I imagine our laird thought it would have been convenient."

Nicholas shook his head. "Son of a . . . ."

He stopped himself from saying the blasphemy just in time. "What will Clare's father do when he finds out she lied?"

"No telling," the priest replied. "I will of course try to intercede if he loses his temper. 'Tis the truth I'm afraid for her. Laird MacKay's a hard man. He loves his daughter, but when he finds out she lied, he might marry her off to the first unattached clansman he spots. She's got a hard future in front of her."

Nicholas thought about what the priest had told him for several minutes.

"I wasn't able to save Johanna."

Nicholas's voice was whisper soft, as though he was in confession. The priest put his goblet down and turned to the baron. "You cannot blame yourself for what happened to Johanna. She told me she kept the truth from you because she was ashamed."

"I should have known what was happening," Nicholas muttered. "Raulf kept her hidden away, and I should have been clever enough to realize his reasons. He didn't want me to see her bruises, of course. Dear God, how I want to be the one who kills him."

The priest decided to turn the baron's thoughts. "You'd best be deciding what to do when Laird MacKay gets here. Johanna doesn't want Clare to leave. I'm warning you now, son. You're going to have to contend with your sister as well as Clare's father. You've also got the king's messengers coming here with their demand to take Johanna back to England."

"John assured me he would send only the messengers and four escorts," Nicholas said. "It will only take a few minutes to give them Gabriel's answer and send them home."

"My laird believes he's going to be able to change your king's mind, doesn't he?"

"He does."

"I wonder how he thinks to accomplish his goal," Father MacKechnie said.

Nicholas shook his head. "He was damned confident he would get the king to withdraw his support from Baron Raulf, but Gabriel wouldn't tell me what he planned to say."

"You're caught in the middle, aren't you? You can't call up your own vassals to fight by your side, for you're in the Highlands now and the battle might very well be waged against your own king."

"We're living in difficult times," Nicholas said. "It is unthinkable for a vassal to lose his faith and trust in his overlord. Most of the barons in England have had their fill of John's antics. There's constant talk of rebellion."

"I can understand why," the priest remarked. "Your king's made more enemies than allies."

"That is true," Nicholas agreed. "He has even turned the holy pope against him. Change is in the air, Father, and if John doesn't mend his ways, he'll eventually be forced to hand over his power just to remain king."

"A king without power? How is that possible?"

"John will be forced to give over specific rights to the barons," Nicholas explained.

The priest had never heard of such a thing. Yet in all of his considerable years he'd never seen such an inept leader as John. The stories he'd heard over time regarding King John's behavior couldn't all be exaggerations; and if only a few of them were true, then England's leader would certainly have quite a bit of explaining to do when he stood before his Maker.

"Do you trust your king?"

"I will continue to serve my overlord until he breaks the bond. I am his vassal."

"But do you trust him?"

Nicholas didn't say another word. He pushed his chair back, bid Father MacKechnie good night, and then left the hall.

His silence was his answer.

Chapter

20

All hell broke loose the following day.

The weather was a prelude to disaster. A violent thunderstorm erupted shortly before dawn. Lightning felled two giant pines. One crashed down on top of the tanner's cottage, and the other fairly destroyed the kitchen's roof. Thunder shook the castle walls. The storm seemed relentless.

Alex attached himself to Johanna. The noise frightened the child; and every time another clap of thunder sounded, he tried to bury himself underneath her.

By the time the storm had worn itself out, Johanna and Alex were exhausted. They slept until late in the morning.

Clare shook Johanna awake.

"Please wake up, Johanna. I must talk to you. Father's riding up the last hill. What am I going to tell him? He's going to be furious. I can't think what to do. Oh, Alex, please don't cry. I didn't mean to frighten you."

Johanna sat up in bed just in time to catch her

son as he hurled himself into her arms.

She soothed the little boy first; and when she finally made him realize neither he nor his mother was in any danger, he quit crying. Alex had been fretful since his father's departure, and Johanna thought she might very well be responsible. The little one had latched onto her fear. She decided she was going to have to be more vigilant in hiding her worries.

"Clare, help Alex get dressed please. I must hurry if I'm going to talk to Nicholas before your father gets here. What did I do with my plaid?"

Johanna raced to get dressed. She was thankful the morning sickness had passed. She didn't have time to deal with a bout of nausea now. She washed her face with cold water, cleaned her teeth, but didn't take the time to brush her hair. On her way down the hallway she threaded her fingers through the mess to try to get the tangles out.

"Mama, wait for me," Alex shouted.

Johanna stopped at the top of the steps. Alex ran down the hallway and took hold of her hand.

"How would you like to visit Auggie this morning? Lindsay will take you over to his cottage. He'll be pleased for your company."

Alex was thrilled. Auggie had become one of his favorite companions. He eagerly nodded, let go of Johanna's hand, and ran downstairs shouting Lindsay's name.

Nicholas wasn't in the great hall. Clare called out to Johanna and motioned for her to come to the door, which she had partially opened.

"Father's here," she whispered. "Nicholas is waiting for him."

"Stay inside, Clare," Johanna ordered. "I'll try to get my brother . . ."

"I'm going with you," Clare announced.

Johanna didn't argue. Clare pulled the door wide and then followed Johanna outside.

It was cold and damp. The clouds were gray, and a fine mist was falling.

Laird MacKay spotted his daughter immediately and gave her a quick nod in greeting. He was still mounted on his steed, and there were at least twenty clansmen with him.

"Where's MacBain?" the laird shouted.

Nicholas waited until Clare's father had dismounted before he answered him.

"He had an important matter to take care of and left yesterday morning. I suggest you come back in two or three weeks. He should be back by then."

Laird MacKay frowned with anger. "Clare MacKay," he shouted.

"Yes, Father?"

"You married yet?"

Clare walked down the steps and started across the courtyard. Her voice held a note of fear in it when she gave her answer.

"No, Father."

"Then war it is," Laird MacKay bellowed.

The veins in the side of his neck stood out. Nicholas shook his head. "MacBain doesn't have time to war against you," he announced. "He's got another, more important battle on his hands."

MacKay didn't know if he should be insulted or not. "Who is he warring against?" he demanded to know. "The Gillevreys? Or is it the O'Donnells? They're a sneaky lot. Makes no difference which clan it is, for they're both poorly trained and can be defeated in a day's time."

"Laird MacBain went to war against England, Papa." Clare blurted out the lie.

Her announcement gained her father's full attention. "Well now, that's all right," he decided.

"Laird MacKay, you look soaked through. Won't you come inside and warm yourself by our fire?" Johanna tried to play the gracious hostess now in hopes of soothing the old man's temper. "You must be hungry after your long journey," she added as she walked down the steps.

"I ain't hungry and I can't imagine why I'd be needing to warm myself. It's hot as ever today."

"Father, please come inside."

Laird MacKay shook his head. "I won't be moving a foot until I hear the name of the man who disgraced you, Clare. I'm wanting to know who my son-in-law is, and I'm wanting to know now. Which MacBain shamed you, girl?"

"There wasn't any MacBain."

Clare's voice shook when she gave her father her answer. Johanna tried to hush her before she could say anymore.

Clare shook her head. "He'll have to know," she whispered.

"What did you just say? It wasn't a MacBain?" her father demanded.

"Father, will you please listen to me," Clare implored. "I have to explain what happened."

"The only thing I'm wanting to listen to is the name of the man you're going to wed."

Nicholas hadn't said a word during the debate between father and daughter. He seemed completely unconcerned. Yet when Clare tried to walk past him to get closer to her father, he reached out and grabbed hold of her arm to keep her from going any further.

"Nicholas?" Johanna whispered.

"Hell," Nicholas muttered.

Clare was thoroughly confused by Nicholas's action. "Please let go of me," she said. "This matter doesn't involve you."

"Oh, but it does," he countered.

She shook her head. He nodded. "I'm responsible for you, Clare MacKay, and you are accountable to me. I haven't given you permission to go anywhere. Get behind me and stay there." The last of his command was given in a hard, downright mean, tone of voice.

Clare was simply too astonished to argue. She turned to Johanna for guidance. Nicholas's sister lifted her shoulders in a shrug. She looked as confused as Clare was by Nicholas's behavior.

"Do it now."

Clare obeyed the command before she had time to think about it. She moved to stand behind Nicholas, then leaned up on tiptoe so he could hear her whispered protest. "I am not accountable to you."

Nicholas didn't bother to whisper his reply. "You will be."

Clare still didn't understand what Nicholas was telling her. Johanna understood, though. She walked over to her brother. Keith appeared out of nowhere and blocked her path. He obviously didn't want her to get too close to Laird MacKay.

She tried to ignore the soldier's interference. "Nicholas? Are you certain you want to do this?"

Her brother didn't answer her. Laird MacKay strutted forward. He wanted to snatch his daughter back.

"MacBain promised me a wedding," he announced. "He's not a man to go back on his word."

"No, he isn't," Nicholas agreed. "There will be a wedding."

The laird looked appeased. He grunted low in his throat and gave a brisk nod.

"Papa, there isn't . . ."

"Be silent, lass, while I get my particulars," her father ordered. He kept his gaze centered on Nicholas. "And who is my future son-in-law?"

"I am."

Laird MacKay's mouth dropped open. His eyes looked as though they were going to bulge right out of his face. He shook his head in denial and took a step back in an attempt to distance himself from the Englishman.

"No!" he bellowed.

Nicholas wouldn't let the laird retreat. "Yes,"

he answered, his voice emphatic.

Clare grabbed hold of Nicholas's tunic and tried to pull him back. "Are you crazed?" she asked.

Johanna nudged Keith out of her way and hurried over to Clare's side. "Let go of him," she ordered.

Clare started to protest the outrageous pledge Nicholas had just given her father, but Johanna stopped her by grabbing hold of her hand and demanding in a whisper that she wait until later to argue.

"Is it a trick then?" Clare asked, thinking Nicholas might be giving the rash promise in order to stall for time.

"It could be," Johanna allowed, knowing full well her brother never said anything he didn't mean. He was going to marry Clare MacKay all right, and from the set look on his face, no one was going to stop him, not even a reluctant bride.

"You're English," the laird shouted. "It's unthinkable."

Nicholas didn't seem to be at all affected by the old man's fury. He actually smiled when he said, "I won't require a substantial dowry."

"Clare MacKay, you might as well have taken a dagger and plunged it into your father's very own heart," the laird wailed.

"But, Father . . ."

"Be silent."

Nicholas snapped the command. He didn't take his gaze off Clare's father when he gave his order. He waited for the angry old warrior to either

527

pounce on him or gain control of himself.

Johanna tried to soothe Clare, but it was difficult for her to pay attention to what she was doing and keep her attention on the laird at the same time. She was mesmerized by the man's behavior. Lairds didn't weep, but this one looked like he was going to break down and cry at any moment. He was certainly having difficulty accepting Nicholas's announcement.

"An English baron wed to my daughter? I'll die first, I will."

Johanna quit rubbing Clare's shoulder and stepped forward.

"A very rich baron," she blurted out.

The laird frowned at Johanna with what she thought was indignation. "Wealth is not an issue here," he muttered. "How rich?"

They were married an hour later.

There wasn't time for a celebration. Father MacKechnie had only just blessed the union when Michael came running into the great hall. He was looking for Keith or Nicholas to give his news.

He spotted the baron first. "One of our soldiers doing border patrol has just arrived with the news," he said. "English soldiers were spotted coming onto our land. It's an army, Baron, and only an hour away from the keep."

"How many were sighted?" Keith demanded.

"Too many to ever count," Michael told him.

Nicholas let out a roar so forceful and so filled with fury, the sound surely reached the Lowlands.

He had been betrayed by his king. The bond between vassal and overlord was destroyed. John had lied to his baron, for he hadn't sent a messenger and escort. He'd sent an army.

The keep would be under siege in less than an hour's time. Keith immediately took charge of readying the area for attack by posting guards all along the walls, and Nicholas took on the responsibility of leading a contingent of men down the ridge to meet the English soldiers in a flanking attack.

Laird MacKay was told to go home before the fight began. He refused the order and mounted his horse to ride by his son-in-law's side. He told one of his men to ride like lightning back to his own holding and gather his considerable troops. Nicholas was damned thankful for the old man's interference. He knew they were going to need every fighting man available.

Clare couldn't seem to make up her mind if she wanted to get hysterical because she was now married to an Englishman or if she wanted to be helpful in the battle against the intruders. Then Nicholas turned to leave, and Clare picked up her skirts and ran after him.

"Don't you dare make me a widow, Baron," she demanded. "I'm wanting an annulment, not a funeral."

Nicholas reached his stallion, grabbed the reins in one hand, and then turned to his bride. "You won't be getting either," he announced.

She didn't know what to say to him next. Nicholas stared at her for a long minute, then decided he'd wasted enough time on his new bride. He started to turn away.

"Wait."

"Yes?"

Words still eluded her. And so she simply threw herself into his arms. Nicholas knew what to do next. He let go of the reins, wrapped his arms around his trembling bride, and gave her a kiss filled with promise, commitment, and a fair amount of lust.

"You look like a boy with your hair cut so short, but you sure as hell kiss like a woman, Clare MacKay."

She forgot how to breathe. She couldn't seem to gather her wits about her until her husband was riding away.

"Take care of him, Papa!" she shouted.

"I will, lass. Get yourself inside and stay there."

Clare turned to do just that when she spotted Johanna running across the yard. "Johanna, where are you going? It isn't safe for you to stay out here."

Johanna wasn't listening. She ran all the way to Auggie's cottage. She was crying by the time she got there.

Alex took one look at his mother and started wailing. She picked the child up and hugged him tight.

"Auggie, take Alex up to my chamber. I'm making you responsible for him. Don't let any harm come to him. Promise me."

"I promise you," he said. "And where will you be while I'm looking out for the boy?"

"There isn't time for me to explain," she answered. "King John has sent an army four times the size of our own."

"We've survived before, lass. We'll survive again."

The price was too dear to pay for Johanna to be reasonable. She didn't want a single man to die because of her fight with England's king. She believed she was the only one who could avert a massacre.

"The king betrayed my brother," she said. "He used trickery, Auggie, and so I will use the truth to stop this before it's too late."

Johanna kissed Alex and handed him to Auggie. "Go," she whispered. "I must know both of you will be safe."

"If it gets too threatening, I'll take the boy and hide. I'll bring him back when it's finished."

"How will you get outside the walls?"

"I have my ways,' Auggie boasted. "Quit your crying, boy. We're on an adventure now. Let's fetch your wooden sword and have our own battle."

Johanna stayed inside Auggie's cottage for several minutes. She knelt down and said a prayer for courage.

She finished her petitions, made the sign of the cross, and then stood up. Clare and Keith were both standing in the doorway, watching her.

"They're swarming up the hills, m'lady," Keith

announced. "We're going to have to find a way to get you out of here. We can't defend ourselves against such numbers."

Clare was trying not to cry. "Papa and Nicholas are both going to get killed. I've never seen so many soldiers, Johanna. I don't know what we will do."

"I have a plan," Johanna announced. "They're here to fetch me, aren't they? Keith, you will simply give me to them."

He shook his head. "I cannot, m'lady."

"You don't have a choice in the matter," she countered. "Listen carefully. We were taken by surprise, isn't that so?"

She waited for his nod before continuing. "If we'd had time to prepare, what would you have done?"

"Called up our allies," Keith replied. "And when they arrived, we would outnumber the enemy. Even now the word is being passed through the Highlands, for the sight of such a vast army would be spread like wildfire. Most of our allies are to the north, however, and they are probably only just now hearing the news. They'll come."

"But it will be too late, won't it?"

"There is always hope, m'lady."

"There is also a better plan," she replied. "If I willingly go to the English soldiers, they will retreat."

"They'll take you back to England!" Clare cried out.

"They will if Keith cannot mount an attack in

time. How long before you can gather enough men?"

"A single full day," he answered.

"Gabriel hasn't reached England yet. He will have heard. Add him to your numbers."

Johanna continued to try to make the commander listen to reason. Keith wouldn't agree with her plan, however, and kept insisting he would give up his life to keep her safe.

And so she resorted to trickery to get her way. She pretended to give in. Keith asked her to go back to the great hall and wait there with Clare until he sent men to sneak the two of them out of the keep.

Johanna nodded agreement. She started up the hill with Clare at her side, but just as soon as Keith had regained his mount and ridden away, she turned to her friend.

"You've going to have to help me," she announced. "You know it's the only way, Clare. I won't be harmed."

"You can't know that, Johanna," Clare whispered with fear. "What about your baby?"

"We'll be all right. Raulf doesn't know I'm carrying, and the pleats in my plaid hide my condition." She nodded again. "We'll be all right."

"And if Baron Raulf is leading the army? How will you keep him from hurting you?"

"I have not forgotten how to cower," Johanna replied. Her voice was filled with sadness. "And I will try not to incite his anger. Clare, I love my brother and all these good men here. I cannot let them die because of me."

"Dear God, I don't know what to do."

"Please help me."

Clare was finally swayed. She gave a quick nod. "Aren't you frightened, Johanna?"

"Oh, yes," Johanna answered. "But I'm not overwhelmed with it. In my heart, I know it's a sound plan. Gabriel will find me."

Tears streamed down Clare's face. She forced a smile to hide her terror. "I wish I had someone like Gabriel who I could love and trust."

"Oh, Clare, you do. Nicholas is every bit as gentle and good as my husband."

Her friend's smile became genuine then. "Dear Lord, I forgot I was married," she blurted out. "Come now. We must get you out of here before I also forget I have courage."

The two women turned direction and ran toward the back entrance to the stables. Twenty minutes later, and after considerable subterfuge and plain sneakery, Johanna rode out of the keep and down the steep hill.

She was going back to hell again. Yet when she spotted Raulf riding toward her, her heart didn't stop beating and her stomach didn't twist in agony.

Johanna wasn't terrified now; she was determined. She had a sound plan.

She had Gabriel.

Chapter
21

They took her to the Gillevrey keep. Raulf and his army had crossed the clan's border and immediately found themselves under attack. The Highlander soldiers were courageous in battle, but Laird MacKay's evaluation was proven true. They were a poorly trained group of men, and it had only taken the English infidels one day to conquer the land and the castle.

Laird Gillevrey and thirty of his men were locked away in the cellars below the great hall. The other clansmen were being held in the soldiers' quarters in the lower bailey.

Johanna's surrender had been swift. She rode down the hill and into the jaws of the enemy. They enveloped and surrounded her.

Although she was just a scant foot or two away from Raulf, she didn't speak to him. She simply sat atop her mount with her hands folded together and waited to see what he would do.

Raulf was dressed in full knight's battlewear, but his head was covered with the old-fashioned open conical helmet. He preferred it over the modern fully enclosed gear. He'd told her his vision was improved. She believed vanity was the true reason.

It was difficult for her to look at him. His appearance hadn't changed much. His eyes were just as green, his complexion was still unscarred, and there were only a few added age lines creasing his narrow cheeks now. Then he took his helmet off, and she realized there had been a dramatic change after all. His hair had been the color of wheat when she'd last seen him. It was white now.

"We will go home now, Johanna, and all this will be put behind us."

"Yes," she immediately agreed.

Her answer pleased him. He nudged his mount close to her side and reached over to touch her face.

"You have grown more beautiful," he remarked. "I've missed you, my love."

Johanna couldn't look at him now, for she was certain he would see the disgust in her eyes. She bowed her head in what she prayed looked like submission.

Raulf was apparently satisfied. He put his helmet back on, turned his mount, and then gave the order to ride.

They didn't stop for water or rest and reached the Gillevrey holding late that afternoon.

Johanna immediately pleaded exhaustion. Raulf escorted her inside. The entrance was narrow. Steps leading upstairs were directly in front of her.

To the right was the hall. It was a large room, square in dimensions, and the balcony above surrounded it on all sides. Johanna was disheartened by that notice, for she knew if she was kept upstairs, she couldn't sneak out the door without being spotted by the guards in the hall.

She was given the third chamber. The door was in the center of the balcony. Raulf opened the door for her. She kept her head bowed and tried to hurry past him. He grabbed hold of her arm and tried to kiss her. She wouldn't let him. She turned her head away.

He roughly pulled her into his arms and hugged her. His hands toyed with her hair.

"Did they make you cut your hair?"

She didn't answer him. "Of course they did," he decided. "You never would have willingly cut your hair, for you surely remember how much I liked it."

"I did remember," she whispered.

He let out a sigh. "It will grow again."

"Yes."

Raulf suddenly tightened his hold on her. "Why did you get our marriage annulled?"

The pain he was inflicting upon her made her flinch. "The king wanted me to marry Baron Williams. I demanded an annulment to stall for time. I didn't believe you were dead."

Her answer satisfied Raulf. "John didn't tell me Williams wanted you for wife. The bastard did lust after you, didn't he? And you never did like him much."

"I'm very sleepy," she blurted out. "I don't feel at all well."

Raulf finally let go of her. "The excitement has been too much for you. You were always weak, Johanna, and only I know how to take care of you. Go to bed now. I won't bother you tonight. I put one of your gowns on the bed. You will wear it tomorrow. When you join me downstairs, I will have a surprise for you."

He finally left her alone. The door had a lock, but the key had been removed. She would have to find something to block the entrance, she decided. She didn't trust Raulf to leave her alone; and if he did sneak into the chamber during the night, she would be prepared. If he tried to touch her, she would kill him . . . or die trying.

Johanna had been in complete control of her emotions until now; and although she was exhausted from the strain, she was still feeling proud of herself because she hadn't allowed her anger or her fear to gain the upper hand. It was her sole duty to protect her baby from harm until Gabriel came to fetch her. Yes, that was her only duty.

Messengers had left to chase down Gabriel as soon as the English army had been spotted. Johanna prayed the clansmen wouldn't have to go all the way to London to catch up with their laird.

The MacBain allies were surely preparing to ride now, too, she decided. Why, by tomorrow night or the night after, she would certainly be rescued.

Johanna set about defending her little chamber

from attack. She pushed an empty chest over to the door to block it. She knew it wouldn't keep anyone from breaking in, but she hoped the sound when the chest was moved would wake her up if she accidentally fell asleep.

She hurried over to the window, pulled the fur covering back, and looked down. Then she muttered an expletive. There wouldn't be any escape possible through the opening. It was a straight drop two stories down, and the rock wall was too smooth to find handholds to climb down.

The room was cold and damp. She was suddenly so weary she needed to sit down. She removed her belt and wrapped herself in her plaid. Then she went over to the bed.

She spotted the gown spread out upon the covers. Recognition was swift. Her weariness vanished, and fury such as she'd never known before flooded her. She was consumed by it, and all she wanted to do was scream as loud as a warrior would when he rode into battle.

It was her wedding gown. The shoes she'd worn were there too, she noticed, and the ribbons, dear God, the ribbons she'd entwined in her hair were spread out on the covers as well.

"He's demented," she whispered.

And determined, she silently added. He'd told her he had a surprise for her in the morning, and now she fully understood what he planned. The fool actually believed he was going to marry her again.

Johanna was literally shaking with rage when

she reached for the gown. She hurled it across the chamber. The ribbons and shoes went flying next.

Her anger quickly drained the rest of her strength. Johanna stretched out on the bed, pulled her plaid up over her head, took her dagger out of the sheath she'd tied with string around her thigh, and held the weapon in both hands.

She fell asleep minutes later.

The scraping noise the chest made when it was moved across the stone floor woke her up. Sunlight streamed into the chamber from the sides of the fur covering the window. Johanna had dropped her dagger sometime during the night. She found it in a fold of the plaid and was ready to strike when she sat up.

"May I enter, m'lady?"

The whispered request came from an elderly woman. She held a tray in her hands but hesitated in the doorway until she was given permission.

"You may," Johanna called out.

The woman hurried inside. She used the back of her foot to push the door closed.

"Baron Raulf ordered me to serve you," she said as she walked closer.

"You're a Gillevrey," Johanna guessed when she spotted the colorful plaid.

"I am," the woman replied. "And you're Laird MacBain's wife, aren't you?"

"Yes," Johanna answered. Her voice was sharp, for she was in a hurry now to gain some answers the Gillevrey woman might be able to give her.

"Are there guards posted outside this door?"

"There is one," the servant answered.

"How many in the hall below?"

"Too many to count," the woman answered. She put the tray on the foot of the bed. "My laird's locked in the cellar, m'lady. They're treating him like a common thief. He sends you an important message. I was allowed to carry food to him early this morning, and he whispered the words he wanted me to repeat to you."

"What is his message?"

"The MacBain will avenge this atrocity."

Johanna smiled. The servant looked expectant. "Does your laird require an answer?"

"He does."

"Then tell him, yes, the MacBain will certainly avenge this atrocity."

The woman gave a brisk nod. "And so it will be done," she whispered.

She sounded as though she was in prayer. "What is your name?" Johanna asked.

"Lucy," the woman answered.

Johanna scooted off the bed. She held onto her plaid with one hand and offered her other hand to the woman.

"You are a good and courageous woman, Lucy," she whispered. "And now I have a favor to ask of you."

"I will do anything I can to help, m'lady. I'm old and surely feeble, but I will diligently try to serve you."

"I must find a way to stay inside this chamber for as long as possible. Are you good at lying?"

"When it's called for," Lucy answered.

"Then report to the baron that I am still sleeping soundly. Tell him you put the tray down but didn't disturb me."

"I'll do it," Lucy promised. "The baron doesn't seem to be in a hurry to get you downstairs, m'lady. He's pacing with impatience, but only because the man he sent for has still not arrived."

"What man?"

"I didn't catch the name," Lucy said. "But I heard what he was. He's a bishop, and he's living somewhere near the Lowlands."

"Bishop Hallwick?"

"M'lady, please lower your voice. The guard will hear you. I didn't catch the bishop's name."

Johanna's heartbeat quickened. "Of course it's Hallwick," she muttered.

"Will the bishop help you, m'lady?"

"No," Johanna answered. "He's an evil man, Lucy. He would aid Lucifer if there was gold involved. Tell me this, please. How did you know Baron Raulf sent for anyone?"

"No one pays me any attention because I'm old. I can act dotty when I set my mind to it. I was standing near the corner of the hall when the soldiers came inside to take over our laird's home. The baron didn't waste a minute giving his instructions. He sent six men to ride to the Lowlands. They were to escort the bishop back."

Johanna rubbed her arms to ward off the chill she felt. Raulf had been quite methodical in his plans. She wondered what other surprises were in store for her.

"I'd best get downstairs before the baron notices I've been in here so long, and you'd best get back under the covers so the guard will see you're sleeping when I open the door."

Johanna thanked the servant and then hurried to do as she suggested. She stayed in bed a long while, waiting for the summons to come.

Raulf left her alone. The blessed reprieve lasted until the following afternoon. Johanna spent a good deal of her time staring out the window. The hills below were covered with English soldiers. She thought they probably surrounded the keep on all sides.

How was Gabriel going to get to her?

She straightened her shoulders. That was his problem to worry about, not hers, she decided. But Lord, how she wished he would hurry up.

Lucy came back into the chamber late that afternoon. She carried another tray of food.

"They've been coming and going all day long, m'lady. Now men are fetching pails of hot water and bringing up a wooden tub. The baron has ordered a bath for you. Why in heavens he'd think about your comforts now is beyond me."

"He thinks I'm going to marry him," Johanna explained. "The bishop's here, isn't he?"

"He is," Lucy answered. "There's another baron down below as well. I heard his name. He's called Williams. He's an ugly one all right with his frizzled dirt-colored hair and black eyes. He and Baron Raulf have been arguing most of the afternoon. It's a heated fight all right, and wouldn't it be a blessing if they killed each other and saved your husband the bother?"

Johanna smiled. "It would be a blessing. Lucy, please stay and lean against the door while I bathe."

"Then you're going to accommodate the foul man?"

"I want to look as pretty as possible for my husband," Johanna explained. "He will be here any time now."

"Will you put on the English gown?" Lucy asked. She pointed to the corner where Johanna had thrown the garment.

"I will wear my plaid."

Lucy nodded. "I'm going to fetch you clean underclothes when I go get the soap and drying cloths," she said.

Johanna carried through with her determination to wear her plaid. She knew Raulf would be furious, but she was also certain he wouldn't strike her in front of witnesses. She would have to make certain she was never left alone with him. She wasn't at all certain how she would achieve that miracle, and damn it all, where was Gabriel?

She absolutely refused to consider the possibility her husband might not be able to get to her in time, and whenever a worrisome thought popped into her mind, she pushed it away.

She took her time bathing. She even washed her hair. Then she sat on the side of the bed to dry it with the cloths Lucy gave her. The servant insisted upon brushing her hair for her, and when she was finished and the curls fell just so about her shoulders, Lucy declared she looked as beautiful as a princess.

The summons came an hour later. Lucy was wringing her hands when she repeated the order. Johanna was extremely calm. She knew she couldn't put off the confrontation any longer.

She put in yet another request to her Maker to help Gabriel get to her in time, tucked her dagger in her belt and covered it with a fold from her plaid, and then went downstairs.

They made her wait at the entrance for almost ten minutes before bidding her to come into the hall. Raulf and Williams were standing at a round table on the opposite side of the room, arguing about a paper Williams waved in his hand.

The two barons were opposite in appearance yet quite similar in temperament. They snapped at each other like mad dogs, one with his shock of white hair and the other with his brown-colored locks and black soul. They were both hideous to her.

Bishop Hallwick was also in the hall. He sat in a tall-backed chair in the center of the room. He held a scroll in his hands and appeared to be reading the thing over and over again. Every other minute or so he would shake his head as though in confusion.

The bishop had aged considerably in the past few years. He looked sickly, too, for his complexion had a yellow cast to it now. Lucifer must be dancing with anticipation, Johanna thought to herself. Hallwick was old and worn out, and it wouldn't be long before he was welcomed home by the devil himself.

Johanna noticed a movement above. She looked up and spotted Lucy making her way along the balcony. The servant was pausing at each chamber and pushing the door open before moving on. Johanna assumed she'd been told to air out the chambers.

"But I will take the stand that this marriage is only a formality, a renewal of our vows if you will," Raulf announced in such a loud, angry tone of voice that Johanna heard him.

Williams nodded. "Yes," he agreed. "A renewal. When the pope and our king settle their differences, we'll send these explanations to Rome. I doubt Innocent will involve himself in the matter anyway."

Raulf turned then and spotted Johanna standing in the entrance. He frowned when he saw what she was wearing.

Williams ordered her to come forward. Johanna did as she was commanded. She didn't cross the room however, but stopped when she was several feet in front of Bishop Hallwick.

He nodded to her. She ignored him. Williams noticed her slight.

"Have you forgotten to kneel in the presence of a man of God, Lady Johanna?"

The sneer in his voice disgusted her. "I do not see a man of God in this room," she answered.

"I see only a pathetic mockery dressed in priest's black garb."

Both barons looked quite stunned by her opinion. Williams was the first to recover. He took a step forward. "How dare you speak to Bishop Hallwick with such disrespect."

Raulf nodded. The look of fury in his eyes was chilling. "When the holy bishop hears your confession and gives me your penance, Johanna, you will regret your rash outburst."

She saw Hallwick nod out of the corner of her eye. She still refused to look directly at the old man, however, and kept her attention on Raulf.

"Hallwick isn't holy," she announced. "And I will never kneel before him and give him my confession. He has no hold over me now, Raulf. He teaches blasphemy against women. He is, in fact, a despot and an evildoer. Nay, I will never kneel before him."

"You'll pay for your sins, woman."

The bishop's scratchy voice was filled with malice. She finally turned her gaze to him. "And you will pay for the terrible punishments you've inflicted upon all those honorable women who turned to you for counsel whose only fault was in believing you were God's representative. They didn't realize as I do what a monster you are. I wonder, Hallwick, if you fear going to sleep at night. You should, you know. You're old and sick. You're going to die soon, and then, by all that is truly holy, you will be made accountable for your tortures."

The bishop staggered to his feet. "You speak heresy," he shouted.

"I speak the truth," she countered.

"Tonight you will learn your opinions should best be kept to yourself," Raulf announced. He nodded to Williams and then took several steps toward her.

She didn't back away from him. "You are a fool, Raulf. I won't go through any pretense of remarrying you. I already have a husband. You seem to have conveniently forgotten that important fact."

"She cannot want to stay with the barbarian," Williams said. "Her mind has been broken, Raulf. That's why the demons speak through her."

Raulf stopped. "Have you been possessed by an evil spirit?"

The bishop latched onto the possibility at once and vehemently nodded. He turned to walk toward the side doorway which Baron Williams now blocked. "She'll have to be purified before she can speak her renewal vows," he declared. "I'll get the holy water and the stick, Baron. You'll have to beat the demons out of her. I don't have enough strength."

The bishop was out of breath by the time he finished explaining his errand. He wheezed his way across the chamber. Johanna didn't show any outward reaction to the threat just given. She tried to keep her expression as serene as possible.

Raulf was watching her closely. "You do not

seem to be afraid of what is going to happen to you," he remarked.

She turned her attention back to him. He looked both angry and confused. She laughed. "It's you, Raulf, who has become possessed if you believe I would ever prefer you to my laird."

"You cannot possibly love the savage," Williams blurted out.

She kept her gaze directed on Raulf when she gave her answer. "Oh, but I do love him," she replied, her voice strong with conviction.

"You're going to be punished for such treasonous and disloyal remarks against me," Raulf threatened.

She was neither impressed nor frightened. She tilted her head while she considered the man who had so terrified her in the past. Raulf looked pitiful to her, and she was suddenly so filled with loathing, she could barely stomach the sight of him.

He could never destroy her. Never.

"Do you honestly believe you and Williams and Hallwick are superior to one Highlander? You really are fools," she added with a shake of her head.

"We are King John's closest advisers." Williams shouted the boast.

"Ah, yes, King John," she scoffed. "The three of you are worthy company for each other."

The derision in her voice was a slap to Raulf's pride. He was visibly shaking with his anger now. "What has happened to you?" he demanded in a harsh whisper. "You never would have spoken to me with such blatant disrespect in the past. Do you feel safe because you are in Scotland? Is that it, Johanna? Or do you believe I'm so overcome with joy to have you back I will overlook your slander against my character? You would do well to remember the pain you suffered in the past because of the necessary punishments you forced me to measure out. Aye, you would do well to remember."

She wasn't cowering away from him. Raulf was confused by her behavior. He didn't see fear in her eyes. He saw defiance.

"Tonight I will show you what happens to a wife who has forgotten her place," he threatened.

He thought to terrify her and knew he'd failed when she simply shook her head at him.

"What has happened to you?" he asked again.

"You are too ignorant to ever understand what happened to me," she replied.

"The Highlanders have done this to her!" Williams shouted.

Raulf nodded. "There's no similarity between us and Scotland's waste," Raulf muttered.

She nodded. Her quick agreement gave Raulf pause. Then she clarified her position. "You have spoken your first truth," she said. "There are no similarities between you and my Gabriel, and I thank God for that. You have vowed your love for me a thousand times in the past and then used your fists to show me how very much you love me. Gabriel has never told me he loves me, yet I know he does. He would never ever raise a hand against me or any other woman. He's honorable

550

and courageous and has a heart and a soul as pure as an archangel's. Oh, no, you two are nothing alike."

"How dare you speak such blasphemy!" The veins in the sides of Raulf's neck stood out from the force of his scream.

She knew she was provoking his rage, but she couldn't stop the words from pouring out. It so offended her that he dared consider himself superior to any Highlander. His opinion of himself was perverse, and she was determined to set him straight.

"Show me the companions you keep and I'll tell you who you are. My mother taught me that valuable lesson, but I doubt either one of you will understand the meaning behind it. I happen to keep very good companions. My clan's my family, and each one of us would die to keep the others safe. They're all proud and honorable men and women."

She shook her head at the two barons. Disgust echoed in her voice when she continued. "Nay, you can't understand. How could you? You don't know what honor is. Look at your companions. You cannot turn your back on each other for fear of getting a knife between your shoulders. You would both kill your own fathers if it meant you would gain more power. You, Raulf, have broken every commandment, and so has your overlord. You and Williams both conspired with your king to commit one heinous crime after another. You will pay for your sins one day in the future, and very soon now you will pay for forcing me to leave my sanctuary. You're demented if you believe you can get away with this atrocity. If my husband has any faults at all, it is that he is a terribly possessive man. Oh, Gabriel will come after me all right. You have dared to take away the woman he loves. He won't show you any mercy; and when you're dead, I doubt God will show you much mercy either. You are a demon, Raulf, and Gabriel is my very own archangel. He will crush you."

Raulf's fury became uncontrollable. His roar echoed throughout the hall. Johanna braced herself for his attack and reached for her dagger.

Raulf ran toward her. He was just a few feet away when he raised his fist in preparation for the first blow he would deliver.

An arrow stopped his advance. It went completely through his closed fist. Raulf's bellow of rage turned into a scream of agony. He staggered backward and looked up to find the man who had attacked him.

They were everywhere.

The balcony was filled with warriors wearing the MacBain plaid. They surrounded the great hall on all sides. All but one soldier had arrows nocked to their bows. Baron Raulf was in their sights.

There was but a second or two of awareness in Raulf's eyes before he died, recognition, too, perhaps, as he stared at the giant warrior standing directly above Johanna. Gabriel's gaze was locked on the baron. He slowly reached back to take a second arrow from his carrier.

Death captured Raulf's expression of terror. The next arrow ended his life. It penetrated the center of his forehead. And then another arrow and another and another sliced through the stillness to cut into the target. The force of so many arrows striking at the same time propelled Raulf backward and upward; and when he finally collapsed to the floor, there were over fifty arrows lodged in his body.

Lucifer had his soul.

Johanna turned around and looked up. Gabriel stood above her. Nicholas was at his side. Both warriors handed their bows and carriers to the soldiers standing behind them, then turned to come downstairs. All of the other clansmen had fresh arrows nocked in preparation. Their target was Baron Williams who was now cowering in the corner of the hall.

She didn't wait for Gabriel to come to her. As soon as he reached the entrance of the hall, she dropped her dagger and ran to him.

He wouldn't let her hug him. He wouldn't even look at her. His gaze was fully directed on Baron Williams. "This isn't finished yet," he announced in a gruff tone of voice. He gently pushed her behind his back. "You may show me your affection later, wife."

Her next remark surely saved Williams's life. Gabriel started forward but stopped when he caught her whispered reply. "And you may explain your reason for being so tardy, m'lord."

A slow smile eased his frown. He continued on

553

across the hall; grabbed Williams by his shoulders, forcing him to stand up; and then slammed his fist into his face.

"You're going to live for one purpose only," Gabriel announced. "You're going to take a message to your king and save me the journey. I've been separated from my wife long enough, and I cannot stomach the notion of having to look upon King John."

Blood was pouring down from Baron Williams's broken nose. "Yes, yes," he stammered out. "I'll take any message you wish to give me."

Gabriel dragged the baron over to the table and shoved him into a chair.

Her husband's voice was too low for Johanna to hear what he was saying to Williams. She tried to walk closer but suddenly found herself surrounded by soldiers who deliberately blocked her path.

Nicholas also wanted to find out what Gabriel was telling the baron. The soldiers wouldn't let him get any closer. He turned to his sister, noticed she was staring at Raulf, and immediately walked over to put himself in front of her.

"Do not look at him," Nicholas ordered. "He can't hurt you anymore. He's dead."

It was a ridiculous thing to say, given the fact that arrows covered Raulf's body from head to feet. She was about to point out that fact to her brother when he spoke again. He gave her his boast, not his confession.

"I killed him."

Keith stepped forward. "Nay, Nicholas. I killed him," he announced in a near shout.

Calum came forward next. "Nicholas, you didn't even have your arrow at the ready when I killed him."

Suddenly every soldier in the hall was shouting his boast that he'd been the one to end Baron Raulf's life. Johanna didn't understand what was happening or why it seemed so important for each man to claim he'd been the one responsible for killing the baron.

Then Nicholas smiled. He noticed her confusion and hastened to explain. "Your husband is protecting me from my own king, Johanna. Gabriel won't ever admit it, of course, but he's making damned certain I can't be blamed for killing another baron. Each one of his men will continue to boast the kill. However," he added when Keith nodded, "it is a fact that I really did kill him."

"Nay, boy, I killed him," Laird MacKay shouted from the balcony.

And then it started all over again. The hall was echoing with shouts when Gabriel finished with Baron Williams. He hauled him to his feet, looked around him, and nodded with satisfaction. He waited until the shouting had died down, then said to Williams, "You will tell your king at least sixty men took credit for killing his favored baron."

"Yes," Williams said. "I'll tell him."

"And after you've given him my other important message, I suggest you do one last thing to please me."

"Anything," Williams promised. "I'll do anything."

Gabriel stared at the man a long minute before giving him his final instruction.

"Hide."

He didn't need to say more. Williams fully understood his message. He nodded and ran out of the hall.

Gabriel watched him leave and then turned around. He ordered two soldiers to remove the dead body from the hall. Lindsay and Michael hurried forward to take care of the chore.

Nicholas and Johanna stood side by side across the room with Keith and Calum.

"It's finished, little sister," Nicholas whispered. He put his arm around Johanna's shoulders and pulled her up against him. "He can't ever hurt you again."

"Yes," she replied. "It's finished, and now you will let go of your guilt. You were never responsible for what happened to me in the past. I was in charge of my own destiny, even in those most difficult times."

Her brother shook his head. "I should have known," he said. "I should have protected you."

She tilted her head to look up at him. "That's why you married Clare, isn't it? You were protecting her."

"Someone had to," he admitted.

Johanna smiled. She decided the reasons why her brother married Clare weren't important. What mattered was their future together. Clare,

Johanna believed, would eventually fall in love with Nicholas. He was such a good, kind-hearted man. Clare would realize her good fortune in time. And Nicholas would also grow to love her. Clare was a sweet woman. Aye, Johanna decided. It was going to be a sound marriage.

Gabriel was staring at her. Laird MacKay was standing by his side and waving his hands in agitation as he talked to Johanna's husband. Every now and then Gabriel would shake his head.

"I wonder what has Laird MacKay upset," Johanna remarked.

"He's probably wanting to raid the castle before they let the Gillevrey laird out of the cellar," Nicholas replied.

Johanna couldn't take her gaze off her husband. He was taking forever to come to her. Didn't he realize how much she needed his comfort?

"Why is Gabriel ignoring me?" she asked her brother.

"I can't read his thoughts," Nicholas replied. "I would guess he's trying to calm down before he talks to you. You gave him one hell of a scare. You'd best get a good apology ready. I'd try to look humble," he advised.

"I can't imagine why he would want an apology."

Keith stepped forward to answer. "You didn't stay where you were put, m'lady."

Nicholas tried not to laugh. He could tell from his sister's expression she didn't like hearing his explanation. If looks could do injury, Keith would now be writhing on the floor in acute pain.

Johanna straightened away from her brother. "I did what was necessary," she told Keith.

"What you thought was necessary," Nicholas corrected.

From across the room Gabriel nodded. Johanna knew then he was listening to their discussion.

In a much louder tone of voice she said, "I was protecting my clan by leaving."

"Each one of us would die to protect the others."

Calum interjected the remark. He was smiling at Johanna while he repeated her very words back to her. He had obviously been hiding in one of the opened doorways on the balcony during her confrontation with Raulf.

"How much did you hear?" she asked.

"All of it," Calum answered.

Keith nodded. "We keep good companions," he said. "We all understood your lesson, m'lady."

Johanna started blushing. Nicholas thought the soldiers' obvious adoration for their mistress might be the cause of her embarrassment. Both Keith and Calum looked as though they might kneel down in front of her at any moment to pay her homage.

"You made us very proud, m'lady," Calum whispered in a voice that shook with emotion.

Her blush intensified. If they continued with their praise, she knew she would start weeping, and then they would surely become embarrassed. She couldn't let that happen. She hurried to change the topic. She glanced up at the balcony, then turned to Keith. "It's a straight drop from the windows to the ground," she began. "How in heaven's name did you ever get inside?"

Keith laughed. "I cannot believe you're asking me that question," he said.

"I am asking you," she countered, wondering what he found so amusing. "Please explain. How did you get inside?"

"Lady Johanna, there is always more than one way into a keep."

She burst into laughter. The sound was filled with such joy, Gabriel's entire body reacted. His throat tightened up, his heart started slamming a furious beat, and he found it damned difficult to take a deep breath. He knew that if he didn't take her into his arms soon, he would surely go out of his mind. He wanted privacy, because once he started touching her, he wasn't going to be able to stop.

Dear God, how he loved her.

He started to go to her and then forced himself to stop. By God, she would realize the hell she had put him through first, he thought to himself. Why, she had taken a good twenty years off his life. When his men had chased him down and told him she was in the hands of Baron Raulf, terror such as Gabriel had never known before filled his mind, his heart, and his soul. He was certain he'd died a thousand deaths on his way to the Gillevrey holding. Another scare like that would put him in his grave. Only after he had gained her promise never to take such chances again would he let her comfort him.

Gabriel asked MacKay to go downstairs and let the laird out of his prison and then turned to Johanna.

"MacBain's wanting your attention, Johanna," Nicholas whispered.

She looked at her husband. He nodded to her and then ordered her to come to him by crooking his finger at her.

The look on his face told her she was about to catch hell. She didn't want to waste time listening to him rant and rave about the danger she'd placed herself in. It was finished now and she was safe. That was all that mattered. Besides, she wanted to be comforted, and she'd waited long enough. She was out of patience and in desperate need of her husband's touch.

The only way she was going to get what she wanted was to catch her husband off guard and nudge him into forgetting his bluster.

She took a step toward Gabriel and then stopped. She forced a frown while she folded her arms in front of her chest.

She hoped she looked displeased.

Gabriel was astonished by her behavior. "Johanna?"

The uncertainty in his voice made her want to smile. She didn't dare, of course, because she wanted to soothe his temper, not prod it.

"Yes, Gabriel?"

"Come here."

"In a moment, m'lord," she answered in a voice

as serene as a sweet summer breeze. "First I would like to ask you a question."

"What is it?"

"Does the expression 'in the nick of time' mean anything to you?"

He wanted to smile but glared instead. He knew what she was doing. She thought to make him feel guilty because he hadn't gotten to her sooner.

He wasn't going to let her turn the tables on him. If anyone was going to apologize, by God, it would be his stubborn, ill-disciplined wife.

He shook his head at her, took another step forward, and then announced, "It's going to take you a lifetime to soothe my temper."

She didn't want to contradict her husband, but she was certain it would only take her a minute or two. She walked forward to stand directly in front of him.

She clasped her hands together and smiled. She stared up at him with those beautiful, bewitching blue eyes, and Gabriel knew then there wouldn't be any talk about safety tonight.

"Will it take you a lifetime to get around to telling your wife you love her?"

She reached up and gently stroked the side of his face. Her voice was filled with tenderness when she said, "I love you, Gabriel MacBain."

His voice shook when he answered with his own pledge. "Not nearly as much as I love you, Johanna MacBain."

And then she was in his arms and he was kissing her and hugging her and telling her in broken whispers how much he loved her and how he knew he was damned unworthy of her but it didn't matter because he would never let her go and how she had become the center of his life.

He was rambling, but he didn't care. Some of what he said made sense, most didn't. It didn't matter to her. She was crying and also rambling with all the loving words she'd kept protected inside her.

Their kisses became passionate, and when he finally pulled away, she was trembling. He let go of her, but only for a second, then caught hold of her hand and walked out of the hall. She was blushing and kept her head bowed when they passed her brother and her clansmen. Gabriel slowed his pace when he led the way up the steps so Johanna could keep up with him, then threaded his way through the throng of men standing on the balcony until he reached the first chamber. He pulled his wife inside, shut the door, and then reached for her again.

Clothing became an obstacle. Gabriel didn't want to quit kissing her long enough to get undressed, and so he tried to do both at the same time.

They made it to the bed, though just barely, and made love with an intensity that left them both shaken. He was gentle; she was demanding, and each was eventually thoroughly satisfied.

He stayed inside her a long while afterward. He covered her from head to feet and braced himself on his elbows to keep from crushing her. He kissed her brow, the bridge of her nose, and finally her chin.

She let out a loud, lusty yawn. Gabriel rolled to his side. He covered her with his plaid and pulled her into his arms.

"You should sleep now," he whispered.

"I'm not weak, Gabriel."

He smiled in the darkness. "No, you're not weak," he agreed. "You're strong and courageous and honorable." He leaned down to kiss the top of her head before adding, "But you're carrying, my love. You must rest for the baby's sake. Alex and I would be lost without you. You're the center of our family, Johanna. I've known that truth for a long while. I think that is why I was a bit overprotective. I wanted to keep you under lock and key so nothing would happen to you."

There was a hint of laughter in her voice when she responded. "You let me sew."

"Tell me again you love me. I like hearing your pledge."

She cuddled up against her husband. "I love you," she whispered. "Almost from the very beginning. My heart softened toward you the day we met."

"Nay, it didn't," he countered. "You were afraid of me."

"Until you gave me your promise," she corrected.

"What promise did I give?"

"You wouldn't bite."

"You were still frightened."

"Perhaps, just a little," she agreed. "But then God gave me a sign and I knew everything was going to be all right."

He was intrigued. "Explain this sign," he commanded.

"You'll laugh."

"I won't."

"It was your name," she whispered. "I hadn't heard it before the wedding ceremony. Nicholas called you MacBain, and so did your men. But you had to give your true name to the priest, and that is when I knew I was going to be safe."

He broke his promise and laughed. She didn't mind. She waited until he'd finished and then said, "You were named after the highest of angels," she explained. "Mama taught me to pray to the archangel Gabriel," she added. "And do you know why?"

"Nay, love. I don't know why."

"Because he's the protector of the innocent, the avenger of evil. He watches over women and children and is our own special guardian."

"If that is truth and not fanciful thinking, then he didn't do a very good job of looking out for you," Gabriel said. He thought about the years she'd endured hardship under Raulf's control and immediately started to get angry again.

"Oh, but my archangel did protect me," she said.

"How?" Gabriel demanded.

"He gave me you."

She stretched up and kissed his chin. "It doesn't

matter if you understand or if you think I'm crazed, Gabriel. Just love me."

"I do, lass. I do. Have you any idea how proud I was when I heard the praise you gave me tonight?"

"Do you mean when you were on the balcony?"

"Yes."

"Raulf needed to know the truth," she said. "He had no understanding of what true love is," she added. She leaned up again to smile at her husband. "I know when you realized you loved me," she boasted. "It was when you found me in the tree and saw the wolves."

He shook his head. "No," he said. "It was long before that god-awful incident."

She badgered him to explain. "It was your immediate acceptance of Alex. When he asked you if I had given you a wedding gift, do you remember what you said? I remember every word," he added before she even had time to nod. "You said, 'He gave me a son.' And that is when my heart softened toward you. It just took me a little while to realize it."

The mention of their son made her frown. "Alex is certainly fretting. I want to go home . . . with you. I don't want you to go to England."

"I won't have to," he said. "Williams will give King John my message."

"What will he tell him?"

"To leave us alone."

"Did you tell Williams about the scroll I hid in the chapel?"

"No."

His denial surprised her. "But I thought . . ."

"Raulf's dead," Gabriel explained. "The king doesn't have any reason to bother us now. If he should decide to send additional troops here for whatever reason, then we'll mention the damning evidence."

Johanna thought about her husband's explanation a long while before finally coming to the conclusion he was right. The king didn't need to know she had kept the scroll. "You want him to think it's over."

"I do."

"Will anyone ever know the truth about Arthur?"

"Most of the barons already believe the king was behind the murder," Gabriel said. "Even Nicholas has his own suspicions. He has another reason for turning against his overlord."

"What other reason?"

"John betrayed his trust. He gave Nicholas his word he was only sending a messenger and escort, and he assured your brother Raulf would be kept in London."

"He lied."

"Yes."

"What will Nicholas do?"

"He'll join Baron Goode and the others."

"Rebellion?"

He could hear the worry in her voice. "No," he answered. "But a king without loyal vassals and an army has little power. Nicholas told me the barons plan to force John to make necessary concessions. Do you know why Nicholas gave you to me?"

She smiled over his choice of words. "He didn't give me to you," she whispered. "He was merely matchmaking."

"He was in love with you."

She didn't understand what he was telling her. "He's my brother. Of course he loves me."

"He was there when you were born and saw you raised, but he told me he left to do the king's fighting when you were only nine or ten years old. He returned several years later."

"Yes," she said. "He came back home just a few months before I was wed to Raulf."

"You had become a very beautiful woman," Gabriel said. "And Nicholas was suddenly having unbrotherly thoughts about you."

She bolted up in the bed. "Is that what the argument was about on our wedding day? You became angry and dragged Nicholas away," she reminded him.

He nodded. "When I heard his full name, I knew he wasn't related . . . by blood, and I had already noticed he seemed a bit overly protective for a brother."

She shook her head. "You're mistaken."

"He rarely came to see you when you were married to Raulf. He feels tremendous guilt over that slight, for if he hadn't been so determined to hide his feelings, he would have seen how you were being treated by the bastard."

She shook her head again. He wasn't going to

argue with her. He pulled her down on top of him and wrapped his arms around her. "He seems to have gotten over the affliction."

"He was never afflicted," she countered. "Besides, he's a married man now."

"Nicholas?"

Johanna smiled. Gabriel sounded quite astonished. "Yes, Nicholas," she said. "He married Clare MacKay. Do quit laughing so I can explain," she added. "They'll be happy together once Clare gets past the fact she's married to an Englishman."

Gabriel's laughter echoed around the room. The rumbling in his chest nearly knocked her head off his shoulder.

"I wondered why Laird MacKay joined our fight," he said.

"He didn't tell you?"

"He only said he was protecting his interests. He never mentioned the marriage. I probably wouldn't have paid any attention if he had tried to explain. I was fully occupied trying to get to you."

"It took you a long while."

"It didn't take me much time at all," he countered. "I had already turned around and was on my way back home when my men reached me with the news you'd been taken."

"You had already turned around? Then you heard about the army, didn't you?"

"Yes," he said. "One of the MacDonald soldiers told me."

"I never heard you or saw you on the balcony,

Gabriel. You and your men were as sneaky as thieves," she praised.

"We are thieves," he reminded her.

"You were," she corrected. "You aren't any longer. The father of my children doesn't steal. He barters for what he needs."

"I have everything I could ever want," he whispered. "Johanna . . . those things you said about me . . . to hear you say . . . to know you believed . . ."

"Yes?"

"I'm not any good at putting into words how I feel," he muttered.

"Yes, you are," she whispered. "You told me you loved me. I don't need or want anything more. You please me just the way you are."

Johanna closed her eyes and let out a loud sigh of contentment.

"You aren't ever going to take needless chances in future," he told her. "Do you have any idea of the worry you caused me?"

Gabriel guessed she didn't. He waited a full minute for her to answer his question before he realized she had fallen asleep.

He left the chamber a few minutes later to give his appreciation to Laird Gillevrey for his hospitality. The English army had scattered like mice down the hills under the watchful eyes of Gabriel's allies from the north. The Highlanders outnumbered the enemy by three to one now and made their presence felt. Baron Williams would have been a fool to consider attacking; and although Gabriel was certain he would run back to John, he still wasn't taking any chances. He doubled the number of guards needed along the perimeter of the holding and insisted his allies stay for as long as Johanna was inside the keep.

Johanna slept for twelve straight hours. She was fully recovered from her ordeal the following morning and was anxious to go home. Yet just as they were about to take their leave, she insisted upon returning to the great hall. Gabriel wasn't about to let her out of his sight. He followed her back inside and stood guard at the entrance.

His wife took hold of one of the servants and tugged her along to stand in front of the laird.

"I cannot leave before telling you what a fine, courageous woman Lucy is," Johanna began. "You have none more loyal than this woman, Laird Gillevrey," she added.

She spent a good five minutes praising the servant, and when she was finished, the laird stood up and smiled at Lucy. "You will be richly rewarded," he announced.

Johanna was satisfied she had done her duty. She bowed to the laird, thanked Lucy once again for her help and her comfort, and then turned to leave. She stopped just as suddenly.

Bishop Hallwick captured her full attention. He stood in the center of the doorway on the other side of the hall. He was staring at her. She looked at his face for no more than a second or two, but that was long enough for her to see his expression. It was filled with loathing and disdain.

He was wearing cardinal red robes. Johanna wondered if he decided to increase his status overnight. His satchels were near his feet. Two Gillevrey soldiers stood behind him. Johanna assumed they were going to escort the bishop home.

The sight of him made her skin crawl. She would have left the hall without acknowledging the unholy man; but as she turned, she noticed the long narrow rod protruding from one of his satchels and she knew she couldn't leave without taking care of one last important duty.

She slowly walked over to the bishop. Her gaze was directed on the object of her anger. Before Hallwick could think to stop her, Johanna snatched the punishment stick and moved back until she was standing directly in front of him.

Hallwick took a step back. He tried to leave, but the Gillevrey soldiers blocked his exit.

Johanna slowly lifted the stick up in front of Hallwick's eyes. The hatred in his expression turned to fear.

She stood there a full minute without saying a word. She stared at the stick she held up. Hallwick stared at her. The hall became silent with expectation. Some might have thought she was about to strike the bishop. Gabriel knew better. He had followed her over to the old man and now stood just a foot or two behind her.

Johanna suddenly changed her hold on the stick. She grasped one end with her left hand and took hold of the other end with her right hand. And then she held the weapon up in front of the bishop again. Her grip was as fierce as her determination. Her hands ached from the strain of trying to break the stick in half.

The wood was too thick, too new. Johanna wouldn't give up. If it took her all day to destroy the rod, so be it. Her arms shook as she applied every bit of strength she possessed.

And then she suddenly had the strength of twenty. Gabriel reached over her shoulders and placed his hands on top of hers. He waited for permission. She nodded.

The punishment rod snapped in half. The crack was like an explosion of thunder in the silent hall. Gabriel let go and moved back. Johanna continued to hold the broken weapon for another few seconds, then threw the two ends at the bishop's feet. She turned around, took hold of her husband's hand, and walked by his side out of the hall.

She didn't look back.

Evening was Gabriel's favorite time of day. He liked to linger at the table to discuss the day's events and to plan tomorrow's duties with his soldiers. He never really listened to the men's suggestions or remarks, however. He pretended to, of course, but all the while he watched Johanna.

Nicholas and Clare had left for England over three months ago. Clare hadn't wanted to leave the Highlands, and it took Nicholas time and patience to coax her into going.

One relative had left, but another was on her way. Johanna's mother was expected to arrive tomorrow or the day after. As soon as word arrived she was on her way, Gabriel had sent an escort to wait at the border of his land for her.

In two weeks' time he would leave to attend his first council meeting with the other lairds. He wouldn't be gone long, because Johanna was expected to deliver their babe in about a month's time.

Auggie and Keith had stolen the noser from the Kirkcaldy clan. Laird Gillevrey had mentioned the man and had made the comment he was the best noser in all of the Highlands. Auggie kept the noser locked up for a good long while once he'd selected the finest of the brew for them. The noser was named Giddy, and he was harmless enough. After a month or two of boredom, Auggie took mercy on him and let him try his hand at the game of striking the stones. Within a week, Giddy caught the fever. Now there were two fanatics digging holes all over the courtyard, the meadow, and the valley below, and Gabriel had the suspicion that, once the barrels had been traded and Giddy could go home, he probably wouldn't leave. He and Auggie had become fast friends; and when they weren't striking stones, they were dragging copper kettles to Auggie's cottage to convert into a more effective brewing apparatus.

Johanna sat by the fire every night and worked on her tapestry. Dumfries waited until she was settled in her chair and then draped himself across her feet. It became a ritual for Alex to squeeze himself up next to her and fall asleep during her stories about fierce warriors and fair maidens. Johanna's tales all had a unique twist, for none of the heroines she told stories about ever needed to be rescued by their knights in shining armor. More often than not, the fair maidens rescued their knights.

Gabriel couldn't take issue with his wife. She was telling Alex the truth. It was a fact that maidens could rescue mighty, arrogant warriors. Johanna had certainly rescued him from a bleak, cold existence. She'd given him a family and a home. She was his love, his joy, his companion.

She was his saving grace.

Epilogue

England, 1210

The chamber was stale and musty with the scent of dying flesh. The room was filled with priests and students who surrounded the bed on all sides. They held candles up and chanted prayers over their esteemed bishop.

Hallwick was dying. His breath was shallow and uneven. He didn't have enough strength to open his eyes. Across the room was a round table covered with coins the priests had collected from the congregation to pay for indulgences for their bishop. They thought to buy his way into heaven, and the gold would be given to the church as assurance that any past sins the holy man might have inadvertently committed would be forgiven.

Hallwick had never tried to hide his hatred and his disgust for women. Yet the priests he'd trained didn't believe those views were sinful. They accepted as fact each and every dictate the bishop gave them and were determined to preach his beliefs to their own subjects so that Bishop Hallwick's good word would be carried down through the generations.

Yet in death the bishop contradicted himself. He died crying his mother's name.